$24.00

McLeay, Alison
The summer house

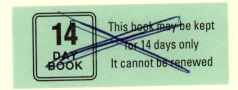

14 DAY BOOK

This book may be kept for 14 days only
It cannot be renewed

Also by Alison McLeay

Passage Home
After Shanghai

Alison McLeay

The
Summer House

St. Martin's Press ⚏ New York

Library of Congress Cataloging-in-Publication Data

McLeay, Alison.
    The summer house / Alison McLeay.
      p.   cm.
    ISBN 0-312-15666-9
    I. Title.
    PR6063.C55S8   1997
    823'.914—dc21   97-7198
                                            CIP

First published in Great Britain by Macmillan, an imprint of Macmillan Publishers Ltd

First U.S. Edition: June 1997

10 9 8 7 6 5 4 3 2 1

The
Summer House

Chapter One

'THE ROGUE! The robber! The *rapscallion*!'

They were the harshest words my father could think of, accompanied by the thump of a slight, blue-veined fist. The General's bemused little widow hadn't wanted to stay on in the house by the lake after her husband's death; but that didn't mean she should have been cheated out of half its value by some swaggering businessman from Manchester.

My father's weekly visits to the house had been dear to his heart. Beyond the tall Georgian windows Lake Windermere lay like a splinter of light, cut off from its parent sky by the dark blue-green fells of the opposite shore. The General had talked about soldiering, my father about pictures, and though neither of them ever listened to a single word from the other (or because of it perhaps) they'd enjoyed a perfect companionship.

And now the General was dead and his widow had gone and the house was the property of Alfred Dunstan of the city of Manchester, maker of the Dunstan Patent Coil Spring. To make matters worse, in March 1912, with the ink hardly dry on his contract, the springmaker pulled the General's house down.

I was fifteen years old then, without much to fill my time. I clearly remember my parents' fussy, academic outrage when they realized all 'that man Dunstan' had ever wanted was the site at Waterside – that gentle slope of ancient lawn and garden – to build a monstrous country dwelling of his own.

Yet it was amazing how quickly the General's widow, now

living with her sister in Durham, slipped from our memories behind the carts of stone and brick that began to roll in a continuous procession along the lakeside road. The railway station in Windermere village became a timber yard and a store for nails, pipes and guttering. Workmen in canvas trousers and pea-jackets poured out of third-class carriages with the tools of their trades on their broad shoulders, enquiring for the hut encampment at Waterside in accents quite foreign to the English Lakes.

We began to speculate about the Dunstans. Clearly, they were nothing like my own family, the Aschams, who by temperament and training were observers of the world about us; we measured, compared and recorded. The Dunstans were people who *did* things, people who'd set about changing our landscape with the same unthinking, imperious vigour with which they stamped out springs for the Empire. To my parents, a desire to alter things seemed the grossest of ambitions. Yet the Dunstans did it and appeared to thrive.

As the end of 1912 approached without any sign of the new owners, we manufactured Dunstans for ourselves and invested them with our own individual hopes and preferences. Hosanna Greendew, who typed up my father's lectures and gave me my lessons, decided they must be cultivated people who'd take an interest in her poetry and buy her brother's paintings. Dr Cole, on the lookout for wealthy patients, hoped for one chronic invalid at least; the Rector looked at his church roof and rubbed his hands; the butcher dreamed of sides of beef; the provisions merchant of chests of tea, for the servants' hall, at least, if the gentleman had his own first-flush souchong sent up directly from Manchester. My brother Noël, five years older than me and studying Humanities at Oxford, hoped they might have a large library and no meanness about lending books; while I hoped . . . I hoped they might be *different* from all the people I'd encountered so far – different, and exciting.

It wasn't until the late summer of the following year that the Dunstans themselves appeared in Windermere. As it happened, I

2

was among the first people to meet one – not, I'm afraid, in the happiest of circumstances, but that was hardly my fault.

Let's be quite clear: I didn't steal their dog. If your father is the country's leading authority on Renaissance art (following the death of Mr Ruskin), you don't go around stealing people's dogs. And anyway, if I had been going to take someone's dog it would have been a proper, bounding, country animal, like a sheepdog from a fell farm or one of the lean, shifty poacher's curs that skulked down the evening lanes in their masters' shadows. I'd never, ever, have chosen a short-legged, curly-haired, treacle-coloured creature that looked as if it had never smelled a rabbit before in its entire life. The truth – no matter what Beatrice Dunstan may have thought at the time – was that the blessed thing simply wouldn't leave me alone.

I was sitting on the lowest branch of the big beech tree at the bottom of our grounds, the branch which overhung the lane. I often sat there while Noël, my principal confidant, was away at university. He was an indulgent older brother; perhaps if there'd been fewer than five years between us there might have been more rivalry, but Noël, with his disproportionately large head stuffed with odd and amazing facts, was so like a younger, less stooping version of our father that I'd always held him in much the same kind of awe. In return, he treated me with benevolent affection and I missed him badly when he wasn't there. My beech tree was a refuge and an uncritical listener when I'd no one else to share my thoughts with. I'd chosen the beech particularly; there's something flightly about a sycamore, as if it can't keep its attention from wandering, and oaks have such an air of ancient grimness; oaks, I suspect, are a little short of compassion. But a good green beech, with its craggy face and its big-hearted embrace, is a tree to pour out your troubles to.

At any rate, that's where I was, deep in my own thoughts, when the curly-haired dog appeared. No doubt it assumed I was just another part of its joyful discovery, all bound up with the delicious reek of ancient leaf-mould and the satisfying wrenching of undergrowth round its questing nose. It promptly pressed its whiskery nostrils against my naked toes where they dangled under the branch and tickled between them with its busy breath. I tried to kick it away, but the beast rolled over, grinning, and coiled and uncoiled itself exactly like one of the furry black Garden Tiger caterpillars I used to find among the ragwort near our gates.

'Topsy! Oh, Topsykins! Where have you got to, you bad girl?'

A hundred yards away, a broad straw hat bobbed into sight beyond the nettle-beds, in the shadows where the trees met above the lane. Its crown was encircled by white ostrich feathers which wagged up and down as the hat's owner searched diligently along the verges.

'Topseeee!'

The voice held a hint of petulance. At the first sound, the dog plunged into a thicket of foxgloves, where its route was marked by the towers of pinkish bells set shivering and swaying above its head.

A surprisingly youthful figure came marching round the nettles, a smart, citified figure whose face, under the hat, was round and red and instantly suspicious.

'What have you done with my dog?' She strode forward, 'her bosom at battle stations' as Par used to say. 'I know she came down here. I heard her bark. I know you people steal dogs, so you needn't pretend.' She stuck out her chin. 'Well? What have you done with her?'

She thinks I'm a gypsy. From the distance of a yard I examined the hat with the ostrich feathers and the elegant, embroidered pink linen frock that went with it. Two rows of dainty buttons led down to the pink hem, pale silk stockings, and a pair of unsuitable ivory kid slippers with the Eiffel heels that were so fashionable at the time. I knew they were Eiffel heels because I'd glimpsed them in one of the magazines which Annie, our parlourmaid, kept under the cushion of the kitchen chair. They ruined your feet, my mother said, which was why, at sixteen years of age, all I had were patent pumps with a schoolgirl strap, which in turn, was why I went barefoot all summer. I'd have liked to try shoes that ruined your feet – just for once.

The girl with the straw hat was staring at me. I slipped down from my branch and saw her eyes travel slowly over my plain green cotton blouse and skirt, from the beaten-copper hair that flew loose round my shoulders to my bare brown toes curling among the weeds. ('Just like Janey Morris!' Hosanna used to say. She'd known the painter Rossetti's soulful model and muse in her later years.) The strange girl was clearly no admirer of Pre-Raphaelite art. Her eyes moved back to my face and narrowed.

'Where's my dog?'

I drew myself up as tall as I could, but the heels still gave her an inch.

'Your dog is in there.' I pointed to the clump of wavering foxgloves. 'Can't you hear it?'

'Oh.' She eyed the thicket and then gazed in dismay at her elegant shoes.

'Oh, for heaven's sake—' In frustration, I swooped down among the foxgloves. Fortunately, the wretched Topsy was wearing a little stitched-leather collar and after a few squirming seconds my fingers found the loop under its fur.

'Here.' I pushed the creature into its owner's arms.

The dog grinned impudently into the girl's face while she fumbled in a gold-clasped bag dangling from a gilt chain at her waist. After a moment she stretched out her hand.

'This is for you. For catching my dog.'

Her manner was so crisp that I'd already reached out, and, to my astonishment, before I could withdraw my hand, I found a sixpence in my palm.

'I don't want your money!' I tried to hand it back, but her hands were buried again in the dog's glossy coat.

Less confidently now, perhaps suspecting her *faux pas*, the girl peered at me from under the brim of her hat. Her eyes must have been round at the best of times, but now they'd begun to bulge apprehensively under their prominent dark lashes. She was younger than I'd guessed from her citified headgear, young enough for her round, full cheeks to warm with a glow of embarrassment above her white ribbon bow. Yet my bare feet obviously puzzled her. Bare feet, in the city, meant poverty. For several seconds she stared at my toes, her well-defined brows almost meeting in perplexity. At last she raised her eyes for a conclusive test of my social status.

'I have forty-three pairs of shoes in my dressing room at home. How many have you?'

No doubt to a city girl like Beatrice Dunstan the mere fact that we lived in the region known as the English Lakes was enough to make us country folk. Yet we didn't keep hens, or raise wild little Herdwick sheep, or build drystone walls or make baskets. We lived in the English Lakes simply because my parents, Benedict and Sybil Ascham, loved the peace of the place and had no desire to live amid the clamour of a city. While Par wrote his lectures and gave judgements on the influence of the *maniera greca*, my botanist mother drew, dissected and considered the effect of the Ice Ages on the local flora.

My brother Noël and I always considered it pretty remarkable that Mar and Par had got together at all in something so mundane as a conventional marriage. (They even had a horror of 'Mama' and 'Papa'. The names *Mar* and *Par* had come from Noël's first letter home from prep school and had been deemed more acceptable.) I dare say if they hadn't quite literally bumped into one another on the stairs of the Bodleian Library in Oxford – the bluestocking daughter of a don colliding with an earnest young Fellow of Balliol, both with their heads buried in books – well, I shouldn't have been here to tell you about it, for one thing. It's a measure of my solitary childhood that until my meeting with Beatrice in the lane, it never seemed at all unusual to have the author of *Giovanni Bellini and the Venetian High Renaissance* for a father, or a lecture over dinner on the significance of the peacock as an expression of eternity in art.

The Dunstans had taken the house next door to our own for their six-week stay and I remember wondering what my mother would make of that winsome straw hat when she saw it – or the rows of pink buttons and the Eiffel heels. My summer wardrobe was almost entirely a kind of verdigris-green, because Mar believed that particular shade kept off insects and should always be worn by the young. She was bound to see the hat quite soon, and the thought created a great, wobbling bubble of excitement inside me. Clearly, Beatrice and her jaunty expensive ostrich-feather top-knot had simply been the vanguard of the Dunstan family, sailing momentously into our lives.

At our first meeting, Beatrice and I had done no more than exchange names, awkwardly, after our little misunderstanding.

'Christabel,' I volunteered. 'Christabel Ascham. After Coleridge's poem. You know, "What makes her in the wood so late, a furlong from the castle gate?"' I waved a hand towards the head of the lake. 'The three ghostly sextons were supposed to be shut up in Dungeon Ghyll, beyond the end of Windermere there.'

Beatrice continued to look baffled. Then all at once her face cleared, as if doubt could only last so long.

'I've a brother called Jack, he's almost eighteen, but he's stopping in Manchester for a bit, and a little sister called Ida. She's nine.' Beatrice's curled lip indicated what she thought of her sister. She heaved the dog higher against her buttoned bosom. 'I told Ida to come and help me find Topsy, but she wouldn't. She was scared of getting her frock dirty.'

The animal was evidently growing heavy in her arms, so I dragged up some foxglove stems and wound them together to make a temporary leash so that she could lead the dog home. My mind was full of things I wanted to know, but none of them lent themselves to simple questions – such as why there should be such a rosy roundness to Beatrice Dunstan, not fatness, but a triumphant abundance as if every inch of her skin were packed with a healthy, glowing self-belief not a bit diminished by never having heard the name of Samuel Taylor Coleridge before.

And it seemed there was a whole tribe of these Dunstans, these Eiffel-heeled vandals – these *rapscallions*, to use Par's word. I imagined Ida as a mincing miniature of her sister, even down to the hat. I pictured the boy, Jack, in knickerbockers and a striped cap, with his thumbs hooked into the pockets of his waistcoat, a springmaker in perfect embryo. As for Alfred Dunstan himself, here my imagination ran out.

And yet . . . there was an undeniable glamour in making springs for the locomotives of Turkestan and the water-pumps of Patagonia.

It was at the new Waterside – or what there was of it after eighteen months' work – that I first set eyes on the springmaker. I'd known the General's grounds as well as our own garden. Noël and I had always considered them part of our own territory and it seemed a pity to have to stay away, especially when such exciting things were happening there. I compromised by restricting my rambles to the trees that fringed the grounds on three sides, leaving the fourth open to sloping lawns and the shore of the lake.

It had been strange, at first, to see an empty space at the top of the rise where the General's house had stood. Yet that great area of bare earth had been filled almost at once with criss-crossing trenches, piles of sawn timber and heaps of brick and stone. And before long, foundations had begun to rise out of the trenches, foundations that seemed big enough for a whole town, or at least for a much grander dwelling than our broad-gabled old house at Fellwood, every bit the sort of place where ostrich-feather hats would feel at home.

One day, shortly after my encounter with Beatrice Dunstan

in the lane, I pushed my way through the undergrowth at Waterside to find an enormously long shiny motor car drawn up at one side of the new building, with a grey-uniformed chauffeur leaning against its bonnet. Nearby, two men were staring at a sheet of plans. The page was wide and flapped like a papery wing, so that the bowler-hatted man struggled to hold it out. His companion, in a motoring cap and pepper-and-salt tweed, simply stood back and let him claw at it, offering him no help at all. For several minutes I watched this little pantomime, trying to puzzle out the reason for the bowler-hatted man's anxious flailing at his plans and his companion's lordly disinterest.

'Always look for a rational explanation,' my mother had taught me since I was little, '*Never* descend to instinct.'

It had become a habit with me, to watch people and try to make sense of them, to work out the pattern of their lives, like the wheel-trains of our grandfather clock behind its little glass window. Noël always used to say I thought too much and made a muddle of simple things. And yet the only trouble with thinking, it seemed to me in those days, was that sometimes you could be so busy at it, you got knocked all of a heap by some artful instinct sneaking up from behind.

The pepper-and-salt man was staring round now, his chin stuck out and his hands clasped behind his back, rocking on his heels and nodding a little. Something about that out-thrust chin reminded me of the girl in the ostrich-feather hat. This, I guessed – no, I *deduced* – could only be her father, Alfred Dunstan himself, the owner of the enormous motor car, the eater-up of the General's house and the defrauder of helpless widows.

I crept closer through the trees. Alfred Dunstan, I decided, was almost completely rectangular, with the short side uppermost, all except for his head, which was fixed straight on to his shoulders like the stopper of a pocket-flask. When he went back to his motor he tramped rather than walked, planting each foot in front of him as if taking possession of the ground under its sole. He didn't swing his arms like a countryman either, but held his pink little hands hollow by his sides, like grocer's scoops, so that the ends of his fingers made a straight, blunt line.

I remembered what Beatrice had told me about her father, what she'd made a point of telling me, as if it was something missing from my education: that Alfred Dunstan was the sole supplier of the Dunstan Patent Coil Spring, which comprised, in fact, a whole family of springs, from a baby of half an inch to a great-grandfather more than two feet tall. Many other factories made springs, but by some secret of its manufacture the Dunstan Spring was so sturdy and yet so tensile, so resilient and yet so instantly responsive, that there wasn't a bed or a sewing machine, a propelling pencil or a motor car made in any enlightened part of the world that could function properly without Dunstan springs.

Sixteen years old, I gazed at the bearer of such awesome responsibility. Alfred Dunstan and his daughter, I decided, had the sleek, smooth roundness of well-fed cannibals, their skins filled to bursting. With such people, surely anything was possible.

Hidden among the trees, I was suddenly conscious of being overcome by an odd feeling of apprehension that didn't seem to have any rational source. It was like knowing for certain that *something* was going to happen – had already happened, perhaps – without having any idea what that something might be. I'd known it before in the instant of dropping off to sleep, that sensation of tumbling through the air without bearings or direction, thrilled and frightened, both at the same time.

Yet this was broad daylight. It had only happened once before with my eyes wide open.

Four years earlier, when I was eleven years old, I'd fallen deeply in love with my Uncle Hereward's coachman, which was still just possible in those closing days of horse transport. Uncle Hereward – Par's brother – was the Marquess of Hornby and very traditional. His coachman was tall and brown with supple hands and a body as spare and string-tight as one of his own carriage whips. There was something in his face that convinced me he'd have wild and impassioned things to say if he ever spoke – which he almost never did. I haunted the stable yard, just watching.

'Chrissie loves horses,' Mar told everyone.

I was all churned up inside, but I didn't even know what I wanted from my hero. I used to perch on a mounting block, silently adoring his white buckskin breeches and learning the name of every particle of the coach-harness that had felt the blessing of his touch. It was almost a prayer; all the hames and hip-straps and c-springs and swingletrees. It became an article of my faith to be able to chant the whole list, from the nose of the lead horse to the cords at the rear of the coach where the footmen clung on. One mistake and I had to go right back to the beginning. 'Dear God, please make Archer the coachman notice me—'

We stayed at Wickham for six whole weeks and when we came home to Windermere I was sure I'd be dead within a very few days. To my surprise, I didn't die after all. But from that summer on, like the scars of a disease, I knew I'd been left with a weakness for tall brown men with lean bodies and supple hands whose silence seemed to guard something deep and complex inside them. Summer and brown, bedevilled men.

I never told a soul about the coachman at Wickham. I had no one to tell, except the big beech tree at the bottom of our garden overlooking the lane, where I never felt quite so alone. Now, watching Alfred Dunstan packing his sturdy self into his enormous motor, I knew that the odd, unsettled feeling inside me was something of the same thing again. Not that I admired the springmaker – far from it, he seemed positively horrid in every way – but I knew *instinctively* from that moment that there was a raw energy about the Dunstans, a vigour, an uncontainable force which could cause explosive change in everything that touched them.

★

Already the village was alive with all that one might care to know about our new residents. Hosanna Greendew, who had the interesting facility of typing and talking about two quite different subjects at the same time, poured out the story as she sat pressing the keys of Par's Underwood No. 5, swinging between gossip and a commentary on *contraposto* in portraiture like an organist giving directions over her shoulder to the choir.

Alfred Dunstan, she'd discovered, had started out as a manufacturer in quite a small way, learning the metal-working trade from his father, a Manchester blacksmith. He became famous for working all hours and selling his stock for whatever price he could get, ruthlessly selling at a loss if he had to, and paying his workers little or nothing. One by one, his stunned competitors were driven out of business, until at last the triumph of the Dunstan Patent Coil Spring set the seal on his success.

When his kingdom of springs was half-grown Alfred Dunstan gave himself a morning off to marry eighteen-year-old Letty Clement, the only child of a small steel-roller whose business fitted as perfectly into Dunstan's enterprise as a bolt into a wing-nut. After an hour-and-a-half at his wedding breakfast, the bridegroom left for his Bolton works, where the foreman had reported a problem with a worming-machine.

And now, nineteen years and three children later, the spring-maker had suddenly announced his intention of living the life of a semi-retired gentleman on a country estate. My father, who hated change of any kind, called it 'The Englishman's Folly.'

'Does a New York stockbroker dream of setting himself up with a cattle ranch? Does the President of France dream of raising goats? Of course he doesn't! It's only the English who suffer from this compulsion to run off to the country and play the squire. You'd think their ancestors had held their acres since the Conquest, instead of having a dozen generations of iron filings under their fingernails.'

'Perhaps it's something to do with being out in the fresh air.' I remembered Alfred Dunstan in his country tweeds, staring about with such satisfaction. 'It can't be much fun, making springs all day.'

'Nonsense! Fresh air has nothing to do with it.' My father pointed to the paper rising vertically out of the Underwood. '*Analogy*, Miss Greendew, not *anthology*. No, no, if it was simply a desire to be out of doors in the country, why this compulsion to build on it? Give a factory owner a pound or two and all he can think of is putting up a row of Corinthian columns on a perfectly good bit of meadow. There has to be more to it than a need for fresh air.'

I am now going to try to explain something without sounding a terrible snob; why, exactly, I didn't have lots of friends of my own age living in the village or in the farms round about. It's one of those delicate matters — a bit like Noël having to learn whom to address as 'sir' and whom not to — that in England in 1913 were considered vitally important.

Par and Mar were gentlefolk, you see, especially in the light of Par's connection with Uncle Hereward and 'Aunt Marchioness', as Noël and I called Aunt Maud. Uncle Hereward was *sir*, of course, the Rector was *sir* and Dr Cole, too, who played bridge with my parents and whose wife always repeated the last thing anyone said to her — '. . . said to her' — until Noël and I had to stuff our fingers into our mouths to stop ourselves giggling. Mr Childewood of Holt Hall, who owned five farms and had tenants, was *sir*, but not Ernest Otley, who worked his own fields and hill land and whom Noël was taught to address simply as *Mr Otley*.

Mar used to press flowers in aid of Unfortunate Gentlewomen.

'If they're all so unfortunate,' I asked her once, 'how do you know which ones are the gentlewomen?'

She smiled an unfathomable smile, and meticulously laid out a Welsh poppy, 'One simply knows, dear. That's all. One simply *knows*.'

13

If the Rector had had children, I might have played with them as a child, but he didn't. Holt Hall was too far away for regular comings and goings and as far as Dr Cole's offspring were concerned, Christopher was eight years older than me and almost a doctor himself and his sister Irene, who was seventeen, could talk about nothing but the new curate, which in my opinion made her useless as a friend. Once upon a time I'd hoped that the new family, the Dunstans, might have had a girl of my own age who'd be happy to climb through the woods to look over to the Old Man of Coniston, or hike up to Brant Fell by way of Biskey Howe, or cycle right round the lake with the wind in her hair, as I used to do with Noël. But now that I'd seen Beatrice, all that seemed rather unlikely.

My mother put aside her flower press and her tin collecting box, and went to call on Letty Dunstan.

'Poor creature,' she reported at dinner. 'Nothing but Alfred-this and Alfred-that and how everything must be done to please Alfred, even though she obviously hates this whole business of moving to the country. She only knows Manchester: born there, brought up there, spent all her married life in the city. They're going back to it at the end of September and she can't wait to see a factory chimney again. Positively dreads the day the new house is finished.'

Mar shook her head, shivering her earrings. 'Can you imagine, the younger girl – Ida – ran screaming from a dragonfly? They have no idea of the country at all. I really must help Letty Dunstan settle in.'

Mrs Dunstan called on us, with Beatrice and Ida; dark foils to her gold-tinted fairness. I discovered later that all three of her children took their dark colouring from their father, as if gentle, hesitant

Letty had been no more than the means of bringing her husband's lusty, ferocious offspring into the world.

She exclaimed over our herbaceous borders. Alfred was planning a terrace to run along the front of their new house, which would no doubt have tub-plants of some kind; he'd already put men to work on the General's lawn and rose beds. She gazed vaguely out over our garden as if it ought to contain a message, obvious to everyone but her. Alfred would decide. Such a blessing. Alfred always knew what was what.

'Jack's arriving next week,' Beatrice informed me as we followed our mothers round the paths. 'Then there'll be trouble.'

'Why will there be trouble?'

'Because Jack hates Father,' Ida put in, skipping energetically over the paving, just within earshot. 'They always fight, whenever Jack's home from school. That's why Jack hasn't come here yet, because Father's here and that's enough to keep Jack away.'

'Get along, Ida. Go and look at the stream or something.' Beatrice gave her sister a vigorous poke between her shoulder blades. 'Though it's true enough, what she says. Father expects everything to be done his way and he gets furious if anyone argues.'

Ida bobbed up again between us like a dark, glossy ball. 'Father used to hit Jack with his fists until Jack got too fast for him.'

'Ida!' This time, Beatrice's push was quite violent. 'Don't say such things.' She smiled apologetically. 'You know what fathers can be like. I expect yours is the same.'

My gentle, bookish father would never have dreamed of raising a hand to either of his children, but it seemed unfriendly to say so.

Ida had skipped a few steps away, but hurtled back with the persistence of a rubber band. 'Father used to lock us in a cupboard when he reckoned we'd been really bad. He shut us in the dark with the water tank, and told us to think of all the nice things

15

he'd done for us and how we ought to be grateful. But when he wasn't looking, Mother would bring us cake and a candle.'

Some instinct inspired Letty Dunstan to turn round just then, with that soft, wondering gaze of hers.

'Isn't it lovely, this garden?' She smiled, and the faint down on her cheeks glittered like gold dust where the sunlight eluded the brim of her hat. 'Perhaps your father will have one made for us, just the same. What do you think?' She spread her arms and spun round, suddenly girlish – younger than Beatrice, more innocent than Ida. She had hazel eyes, I noticed, flecked with that same gold; her daughters' eyes were the hard blue of speedwell and unchanging, while their mother's were alive with hope in the shadow of her hat brim.

Beatrice had no interest in climbing hills. As for cycling, she fancied her brother might own a machine, but she wasn't sure. What she really liked to do was shop; twice a year, her father took them all to London for a tour of the big department stores, where everything could be charged to his account. She'd exhausted Windermere in five minutes on her very first outing.

Letty Dunstan invited Mar and me to a picnic on the lawn at Waterside, where the walls of the new house were now more than one storey high.

'"Spare nothing",' Beatrice told me, 'that's what Father always says. "Let's do it in style." When the mayor of Munich came to visit, he took Father's new Bolton screw works for the town hall.'

'Your new house is going to be awfully large.'

'Oh, yes.' Beatrice smiled and smoothed her flounced crêpe skirt. 'I can't tell you how many rooms. We're having marble pillars in the drawing room, and an organ, and turrets on the roof like Hampton Court. And we're going to have a "living hall", Father says, because no one elegant sits in a drawing room any more after dinner. He saw one in *Country Life*, all panelled in oak, and just called in the architect and said "Give me a living hall."

Father's like that,' she added complacently. 'Once he's made up his mind, there's no shifting him.'

The enormous motor car arrived while we were taking tea. Letty poured an extra cup at once and Beatrice carried it across the grass, together with an especially large piece of cake.

'Alfred won't join us. I hope you don't mind.' Letty Dunstan's hand fluttered an insect away from the strawberry preserve and she gave a nervous little laugh. 'He says he leaves all the socializing to me. Never enough hours in the day – he's so busy.' She folded her slender fingers in her lap and studied them for a moment. Then she raised her eyes to follow the squat figure of her husband as he tramped along his half-built terrace, teacup in hand. An ineffable sadness had come into her face, as if the rising walls of her future home only filled her with despair.

'Look at Father,' muttered Beatrice, frowning. 'Ten to one he's lost the saucer.'

The springmaker was wearing a lounge suit in checked tweed which emphasized his rectangularity. I watched him exchange a word or two with the labourers, too far off to be audible, though I could guess the tone of his remarks by the way the men stared after him when he moved on.

Soon my eye was drawn to a tall, dark-headed, sun-burned young man, standing by the nearest corner of the brickwork, apparently lost in thought. His coat was off and his shirt was open at the neck, but his hands were in his pockets and he showed no sign of doing any work. As luck would have it, he was directly in Alfred Dunstan's path and my heart lurched for him as the springmaker's checked figure strutted nearer. I couldn't hear anything of the argument, but most of it seemed to involve the springmaker's finger stabbing unpleasantly at the young man's chest. Yet the young labourer stood straight and tall and I could have cheered at the way he stared his employer down, without fawning or cringing or trying to excuse himself, so that eventually Alfred Dunstan had to step on to a crate to shout into his face. He was still shouting when the young man turned his back and strolled away, leaving him stranded on the crate like Robinson Crusoe on his island. I glanced at Beatrice to see if she'd noticed; her cheeks were pink, but her eyes were on Topsy, rolling on the lawn, and she didn't say a word.

There was an ancient boathouse at the bottom of the property, half-hidden among the alders, and a wooden jetty big enough for one of the small steam launches which had plied the lake in Victorian times. Alfred Dunstan's destructive zeal didn't seem to have reached them, I was delighted to see, or perhaps it was simply that he hadn't noticed what lay at the bottom of his lawn. After Noël went to Oxford I'd come to consider the jetty and boathouse my own secret preserve, since no one else ever came there, and I'd spent many contented hours dangling my toes over the water and watching the trout, or in May and June the gold-spotted char, drifting like ghosts below.

Now the wretched Topsy went pattering out along the jetty as if she owned the place. Beatrice rose in a flutter of flounced crêpe, bleating a warning. Kicking off my shoes, I set off down to the shore. The last thing I wanted was for that stupid dog to drown herself in my favourite spot.

A small dinghy was working its way towards us along the edge of the lake, moving quite swiftly through the water for an ungainly craft. All I could see was the white back of someone rowing like a dervish, plunging forward as if each haul on the oars mined some terrible anger which had to be exhausted. For all its passion, it was expert rowing and while Beatrice scrambled for her dog, I watched the dinghy draw nearer. To my surprise, the rower was the tall young labourer I'd seen turn on his heel and leave Alfred Dunstan marooned, still shouting, on his crate. A skilful pull on one oar brought the dinghy gliding against the timbers of the little pier. As the young man reached out towards the planking, Beatrice arrived at my side.

'Hello, Jack,' she greeted him. 'I see you fell out with Father again.'

Chapter Two

IT WASN'T, perhaps, the best moment to meet Jack Dunstan. He'd had a long hard row in a heavy boat, trying – almost embarrassingly – to bury in sheer physical exhaustion the memory of that clash with his father. His chest rose and fell under the clinging dampness of his shirt. A flush of blood tinted the sun-browned skin along his cheek-bones and his dark hair clung wetly to his forehead, yet his eyes conceded nothing; they were as hard as flakes of blue lapis. From the look on his face, he'd have rowed to hell at the same grinding pace.

As his fingers gripped the jetty I stepped back; I'd never in my life sensed so much uncontained savage energy in one human being. Until that moment, the only young man I'd known at all well was my brother Noël, with his donnish stoop and his air of dreamy preoccupation. This Jack Dunstan, who could row like a fiend and wordlessly stare his father down, was an animal of a very different kind.

'Well?' Beatrice hugged her dog, waiting for an explanation. 'What was it this time? Money, as usual? Or has someone told him you've been going down to the factory again?'

For a second, Jack seemed about to snap out an answer. Then he thought better of it, climbed up on to the jetty and proceeded to tie up his dinghy in silence.

'Jack isn't supposed to have anything to do with springs, you see.' Beatrice raised her voice for her brother's benefit. 'Latin and Greek, that's what young gentlemen are supposed to know about, or running after a pack of beagles. But not getting their hands dirty in a factory, that's what Father says. The trouble is, Jack doesn't want to be a young gentleman – do you, Jack?' She tossed the question at her brother's back. 'Jack wants to be an engineer and make things. He likes tinkering with machinery, does Jack – and it drives Father wild.' Out went her chin again, in a startlingly good imitation of Alfred Dunstan himself. '"Why d'you think I've spent my whole life in smoke and grime, if not so's you can hold your head up alongside the best in the land?"'

'Leave it, Bea.' Jack's voice was so quiet it made me jump. 'I've had enough of that from him.'

'And there'll be more to come, if I know Father. By the way . . .' The irrepressible Beatrice jiggled one of Topsy's front paws in my direction. 'This is Christabel.'

'Chrissie,' I corrected her. 'Please.'

Her brother barely gave me a glance before staring up the slope towards the half-built house. 'Hello, Chrissie.'

'Chrissie's people live at Fellwood. You know, the house with the big gables you can just see from the road.'

'I remember.' But Jack's attention was elsewhere and his eyes searched intently among the distant piles of bricks.

I assumed he was looking for the chequered shape of his father and wondered if he was tempted to go and begin the argument all over again. His face was rigidly set and every sinew of his body signalled battle-readiness. Standing so near him on the jetty, I sensed even more strongly the anger that had fuelled his rowing. Whatever had passed between father and son had been no mere squabble. This was a violent, deep-rooted war, with no quarter given and no mercy shown to the vanquished.

'I think I saw your father's motor drive off, if that's what you're looking for.'

He swung round to regard me. I remember thinking he'd have been quite good-looking without the suspicion that had leapt into his face. He'd inherited the same dark hair and sharply-defined brows as his sisters, but there was a spareness about him where Beatrice and Ida were smoothly covered, as if the war with his father had eaten up every reserve but the fierce spirit within. And yet, oddly, that very spareness gave him a look of his gentle mother; as I came to know him better, I noticed that sometimes, in rare unguarded moments, his face wore a copy of Letty's unworldly gaze, alive with hope under the brim of her hat.

'Come on, Chrissie.' Beatrice tucked her dog under one arm and reached out for my elbow. 'Let's go back to the picnic. We shan't bother with Jack. He's in one of his moods.'

I glanced back as we reached the picnic spot. Jack Dunstan had already discovered my old place on the edge of the jetty. He was sitting there with one foot drawn up and the other dangling, contemplating the grey expanse of the lake. Once again, he'd turned his back on us.

In Manchester, Mrs Dunstan explained to my mother, Beatrice and Ida had been taught deportment and the three 'Rs' by a Mrs Whitney who called every weekday morning. Beatrice, at sixteen, was now as educated as her father considered necessary ('Indeed?' said my mother), but Ida had hardly opened a book since coming to the Lakes and if Mar could suggest a respectable lady to continue her lessons . . .

'But of course – you must share Miss Greendew!' Mar clasped her hands, delighted to be the maker of such a perfect match. 'Hosanna Greendew – the most erudite person! In the mornings she helps Chrissie with Latin and mathematics, since unlike Mr Dunstan, I don't consider any girl educated at sixteen, and in the afternoons she types out articles and lecture notes for my husband. She'd be perfect for Ida. Oh, yes, certainly she would.'

Perhaps *perfect* was putting it a little strongly. In 1913 Hosanna Greendew was thirty-three years of age, a poet in her own right and a woman of decided views, one of which was a preference for dressing in the 'aesthetic' style, in faded greens and russets falling fluidly from a waistband high up under her bosom. Since she wasn't an inch under six feet tall, this had made her a well-known figure in the village, with her light brown hair bobbed like a medieval page-boy's and a cape or a fringed plaid thrown over her gown.

Her brother Jeremy was quite well known as a Vorticist painter and a member of the Pimlico Group in London. At home in the Lakes, he stayed with Hosanna in a small cottage surrounded by roses and hollyhocks and filled with dried lavender and blue-and-white spongeware china.

My parents had taken Hosanna under their wing at Oxford, just after the collapse of her engagement to a fellow poet. The pain of her loss produced the slim volume of verses entitled *Drown'd In The Sun* which had made Hosanna's name in various intellectual circles but hadn't, unfortunately, brought in any money. Not long after Mar and Par moved to Windermere, Hosanna followed. Devoted to her brother and, by extension, to my father, she'd become a handmaiden to art.

'I could never,' she always assured me, 'love a man with no passion for paint.'

From the start, her intellect was fierce and untiring. Even her poetry was relentlessly analytical, with every emotion dissected and every soft impulse of the heart hunted down and anatomized. 'Allow *untidy thinking* to creep in,' she'd warn, 'and before you know it, you're acting on a *whim*.' She'd give a shiver of distaste and add, 'I could never love a man who could not explain his preference for me.'

After a while, I began to think Hosanna had set her standard of love too high; her list of conditions seemed to get longer by the day, until I couldn't imagine any mortal man meeting half of them. For a while, one or two tried, only to reel away, scorched by the white heat of Hosanna's principles.

'Gone?' my mother would ask gently. 'No hope?'

'Gone!' Hosanna's hawk-like head would toss in contempt. 'Gone – and not a moment too soon. When I compared him to Jeremy or dear Dr Ascham! Not *possible*!'

It was fascinating, her trick of putting certain words into italic type as she spoke. Goodness knows how she did it – by a sudden hollowness of the voice, perhaps, or a way of leaning on the syllables to squash them out and give them extra importance. When Miss Greendew declared that *cultivation* was like chickenpox and could be caught from the presence of *great art*, the favoured words seemed to hover in the air on cushions of grandeur.

She must have said something of that sort to Letty Dunstan, since the result was Beatrice being sent, sullen and resentful, to share my morning study sessions for the few weeks that remained of their stay. That was when Hosanna found out I'd told Beatrice there were whales in Lake Windermere and wild boars in the hills and loathsome creatures called *zools* that crawled out of the water after dark to bite the ankles of anyone walking on the shore. (The zools, in fact, had been one of Noël's inventions. What else do zoologists study, if not zools?) Fortunately, Beatrice didn't appear to have passed on what I'd said about wood-zools that lived in burrows like rabbits and honey-zools that took over the nests of wild bees.

'You should take pity on ignorance, Chrissie, and not make a sport of it. To be ignorant is a tragedy. It isn't funny in the least.'

There – for once – I think Hosanna Greendew was wrong. I've come to believe there's a kind of holy ignorance which protects the innocent from danger and which we shatter at our peril. It's like the shining, blissful trust of childhood, a shield against pain. Those who sleep as a child sleeps should be left to their dreams; their ignorance is no tragedy, but a priceless, enviable gift. Hosanna never understood this. Her mission in life was to trample on ignorance wherever she found it – to awaken the dreamers – to force the truth on us all with reckless evangelism. Letty Dunstan was an innocent; in my own way, so was I, not a quarter as wise as I imagined. But before any of us had guessed what the outcome might be, Hosanna had set herself up as a fateful missionary to the Dunstans at Waterside.

★

23

The Dunstans went back to Manchester at the end of September and immediately I felt a vague and rather puzzling sense of loss, as if a whole new dimension had gone from my life. My family, you see, were all mind-people, if I can put it that way. They *were* what they *thought*; they only existed, you might say, from the neck up. The Dunstans were what they felt; they made and built up and tore down. When they were hungry, they ate; they didn't agonize over the benefits of regular mealtimes. When they were cross, they quarrelled. When Beatrice was in a temper, she threw things – anything – with strength and accuracy. And Jack . . . even though I'd seen very little of him in the short time he'd been in the Lakes, I'd noticed that Jack Dunstan seemed almost to burn with the same raw energy that drove his entire family, always excepting his mother.

Jack never said much, but even his silence was charged with barely contained force. In his father's presence that brooding silence became wordless mutiny. I suspected he knew to a fault how much it irritated Alfred, but what was the point of delaying the storm which sooner or later was bound to burst over his head? The very air was alive with tension when father and son were together. They were like two tigers in the same patch of jungle. The mere sight of his son seemed to drive Alfred Dunstan to crush and humiliate, to make himself recognized by everyone as Jack's master.

My mother and I were leaving the Dunstans' rented house one afternoon, accompanied to the gate by Letty, when Jack appeared in the lane beyond. He hurried forward to lift the latch for us, but just as he took it in his hand, I heard his father's footsteps on the path behind us and his voice rasping 'Open the gate, boy, blast your insolence! Don't they teach you any manners at that school of yours? I pay enough for it, I'm sure.'

I saw Jack stiffen and then silently go through the motions of lifting the latch and swinging the gate wide, as he'd intended to all along.

'Thank you,' said my mother sweetly and laid a hand on Jack's sleeve, but his eyes were fastened on his father with an expression which, if I'd been Alfred Dunstan at that moment, would have made me tremble.

I remember once telling Jack and Beatrice about a fox that had got into a neighbouring farmer's hen-run and killed far more birds than it could ever eat, simply out of blood-lust.

'I can understand that.' Jack began nodding, long before I'd finished. 'It's like a drug to the fox, to feel the hens' hearts almost burst with fear and know he's so much stronger.'

I was shocked into silence. Jack must have thought I didn't believe him, since he glanced round and added 'My father's just the same.'

As autumn slid into winter, I found myself missing Jack and the rest of the Dunstans as well. Our corner of the lake had begun to seem amazingly dull as soon as they'd returned to Manchester. Only their new house, now almost at roof level, showed they'd been among us at all and would return in the spring. That was reason enough to keep going back to look at it.

In the village the new Waterside was already becoming known as 'Dunstan's Palace'. The springmaker had followed his own rule to 'spare nothing' and, as soon as the roof was on, an army of plasterers, cabinet-makers, plumbers and electrical engineers began to fill the local guest houses until it seemed as if every craftsman in the country had been drafted in to finish Alfred Dunstan's house as quickly as possible.

Beatrice always claimed the stone terrace and the curving flights of steps to the front door were in the Italianate style, although the main facade of the house (in my father's opinion) fell somewhere between Queen Anne and Victorian Gothic ('and, I'm greatly afraid, goes on falling.'). It was certainly hard to see an overall plan. Patterned Tudor brick rubbed up against stone columns and arches; the roof was crowded with tall chimneys clumped together like fork-prongs, linked here and there by strips

25

of classical balustrade. Inside, Beatrice had told me, all the radiators would be hidden behind Louis XIV grilles, the chateau-style clock tower was really a luggage lift, and the towering marble fireplace in the living hall had been inspired by a photograph of a building in the ancient city of Petra. The most important thing, her father had insisted, was that it must be six inches bigger all round than Lord Armstrong's famous fireplace at Cragside.

'Father's been reading *Country Life* for years,' she'd confided, 'deciding what he wanted. He used to buy it from a bookstall near the station, without telling a soul — wasn't that dear of him?'

I imagined the springmaker smoothing the pages of *Country Life* with those round paws of his, studying the illustrations intently, drawing bold rings round a doorway from one house, a staircase from another and a piece of plasterwork from somewhere else. Why shouldn't he have what he wanted, after all? If a particular wood or exotic stone had to be shipped from the other side of the world, then why not? Alfred Dunstan could afford it, and more.

The staff wing of the house was almost as lavish as the main building, built round its own courtyard at the rear. The nearby garages had a specially drained floor for washing the springmaker's enormous motor cars, while the powerhouse and its coal store had been designed as a rustic cottage, complete with ivy round the door. With the outside of the house complete, as soon as winter slackened its grip, every unemployed man in the area was drafted in, supplied with a spade and a fork, and set to planting, tying up and generally restoring the glory of the General's gardens.

'Fifteen bathrooms!' The Dunstans returned in March to their rented house, but the end of the building work was in sight and Beatrice's greeting was short and to the point. 'Imagine it, Chrissie, fifteen bathrooms and so many bedrooms and dressing rooms and lobbies you can't begin to count.'

For the first time I felt a pang of jealousy. 'I suppose you'll have hordes of cousins to stay.'

Beatrice stopped bouncing and frowned. She didn't seem to have considered who might sleep in all the new rooms.

'Cousins? I must have some, I suppose.' She scratched her nose, screwing up her face with the effort of memory. 'There's a brother of Father's, I think, who works on a canal boat, but I don't know whether he's got any children. Father doesn't even talk about him. Mother keeps up with some of her relatives, but they don't call if Father's at home. Not quite *Country Life*, you know. Inclined to take off their shoes and put their feet up on the fender.' She laughed with a deep and rather brutal relish. 'I doubt if they'll be invited here.'

I was curious to see who would be invited once the Dunstans had moved into their new home. Try as I might, I couldn't imagine the springmaker fitting easily into any social milieu. Away from his factories and his worming-machines, he was like a fish out of water, or a toad, perhaps, a resemblance he sometimes encouraged by squaring his bulky shoulders and putting his fists on his hips, while his chin jutted out, amphibian-style.

Yet under all the bluster, I sometimes sensed an uncertainty, a discomfort with people he could neither pay nor bully. For instance, my parents clearly baffled him. He'd no idea what to make of a couple so fascinated by facts and so obviously uninterested in luggage lifts and carriage houses. With my father he was as nearly deferential as I ever saw him. There can't have been more than five years between them in age, but the springmaker treated my father like an elderly and rather miraculous relative from whom he expected an enormous legacy. He'd hover round him, nodding earnestly at references to the late Quattrocento and oil-mixed-with-tempera as if he'd only that second had the same thought himself. Yet when my father paused to listen to someone else – which wasn't often – I sometimes caught the springmaker studying him out of the corner of his eye with the same mystified gaze he'd have turned on an anteater or an elephant seal. My mother, who combined comfortable femininity with learning, seemed to defeat him altogether. Alfred Dunstan never went nearer to her than a good six feet if he could avoid it.

As far as sending Beatrice to share my morning lessons was concerned, I think he hoped she'd catch some *cultivation*, as Hosanna had suggested, some infection with great ideas. I often wondered what startling notions Hosanna was putting into the mind of ten-year-old Ida, who had her lessons alone in the afternoon. For instance, I could imagine Alfred Dunstan taking a poor view of votes for women, one of Hosanna's (and my mother's) most cherished causes, and I doubted if he'd like her interpretation of some of the classics.

'Not the Bos*phorous*, please note, but *Bos Porus*, the Passage of the Cow, from the Greek legend of Io who swam the straits, transformed by her lover, Zeus, into a white heifer to save her from the anger of his wife. You will notice, I dare say, that Io, poor girl, was the one to suffer, although it was Zeus, the married man, who desired her.' Hosanna's great, lugubrious eyes would roll up towards the ceiling. 'Why women should be punished while men get off scot-free is quite beyond my comprehension.'

I suppose my mother would have been called 'progressive' in those days. Noël and I had grown up with dogs and trains, not bow-wows and choo-choos and, as soon as we were tall enough to look over the drystone walls, Mar had explained why the sheep were giving pick-a-back rides to the ram. Perhaps it had something to do with spending her life amid the busy trembling of pistils and stamens. There was no suggestion, of course, that extra-marital carrying-on could happen anywhere but on Mount Olympus – but Beatrice Dunstan's mouth hung open, all the same.

And yet, when it came to getting an idea fixed in her head, Beatrice could be every bit as tenacious as her father.

'Miss Greendew says she could never love a man who didn't love Venice.' Beatrice paused in the middle of collecting our pencils and put her head on one side.

I hadn't attached much importance to the remark. 'Hosanna often says things like that.'

'She says *To love Venice is to understand civilization.* Do you think that's true?'

'Probably. If Hosanna says so.'

'She says Venice is beyond description, which doesn't help very much.'

'It has lots of canals, I know that. And a cathedral – and lots of pictures. You could ask my father about them, I should think he knows them all.'

'Miss Greendew says now that John Ruskin's dead, your father is the greatest expert on Venice in the whole country. She says he probably knows more about it than most Italians.' Beatrice sighed and her blue gaze drifted to the window. 'I mean, it's all very well to be fashionable and have expensive things, but it would be nice to be *cultivated*, don't you think?'

What was it, I often wondered in the months that followed, that caused that tiny seed of longing to lodge itself in Beatrice's mind? It must have been something Hosanna said, some poetic description of the lagoon at dawn or of the glittering arches of San Marco, that caught Beatrice's normally commonplace imagination and convinced her she must see all these wonders for herself. Perhaps she was tired of having everything she'd ever wanted delivered almost as soon as she'd thought of it. The thrill of discovery, that first glimpse of something new and wonderful, was a delight no one could package and deliver. It had to be won; there was a sense of achievement in it. Perhaps that was what *culture* was all about; one must put oneself out to catch it – like chickenpox – in the most cultural place in the world, which, if Miss Greendew was right, happened to be Venice.

'It's in Italy,' Beatrice reported after consulting an atlas. 'On the right-hand side at the top, where that sea thing comes to an end.'

Beatrice had often told me she knew how to 'manage' her

father; but Alfred Dunstan caught on to the notion of *culture* and Venice with the zeal of a man who has seen the clouds divinely parted to reveal his way forward. It was true; elegant people were always dropping the names of Greek temples they'd seen, or Egyptian tombs. Their houses were full of stone heads and bronze urns attributed to this or that ancient Italian. To buy *new* was all very well, but old was much more refined. Beatrice was right; what was needed was culture, travel and that indefinable, world-weary gloss that comes from having one's mind broadened under a foreign sun. Within twenty-four hours, he had decided that Beatrice should certainly go to Venice, with me as companion and Hosanna Greendew as instructor and chaperone. By the following day he'd made up his mind to come with us and make an expedition of it and to bring his wife along with him.

Then, by chance, that afternoon my father's pony trap was held up by the same flock of sheep as the springmaker's enormous motor car and the Great Idea took its final shape. What better guide could they have than my father, Benedict Ascham, the country's greatest expert since Ruskin on the Italian Renaissance?

My father thought it was a frightful idea. When the spring-maker's note arrived, he put his elbows miserably on his desk and drove his fingers into the silver wings of hair above his ears, ruffling them up until he resembled a peevish cherub. The future was supposed to be Alfred Dunstan's stamping-ground; what business did he have with past civilizations? Until that moment, the past had been a comfortable place, preserved from the forces of change, and that was the way Par preferred it. Disturbance was change and change was wrong. At home, the country's Renaissance expert spent each day in the same old Norfolk jacket and what was then known as a cardigan-vest, with his spectacles dangling from his neck on one silver chain and a small silver-cased pencil suspended from another.

'Wouldn't you like to see Venice again?' Mar picked up a book which had fallen to the floor and restored it to Par's desk, where my father immediately pushed it back to the edge from which it had fallen already. 'I expect he'll do it in style.'

'But, for heaven's sake, I'm not a tour guide! He makes me sound like one of those fellows in the conical hats who take rich Germans up the Pyramids!'

My mother nodded placidly. 'Well, if you don't want to go, my dear, then Alfred Dunstan will just have to find someone else.'

'What do you mean, *someone else*?' My father swept up his spectacles on their chain, hooked them over his ears and regarded my mother severely. 'I can't imagine whom he'll find. My paper on the five Great *Scuole* was quite definitive. Dunstan will probably hire some rogue who'll point out "Desdemona's House" and tell him her great-great-granddaughter still lives there.'

'Very probably.' My mother folded her hands, unmoved. 'And then he'll come back and tell you all about it.'

'Oh, good heavens, I suppose he will.' My father gazed mournfully at his ink stand.

'Mr Dunstan says he'll pay for everything,' I pointed out, seizing my chance, 'and it's going to be a very grand affair. I told him only holiday people stay on the Lido, so now he's talking about taking a whole floor at the Royal Danieli.' Beatrice and I had been devouring Baedeker.

Par looked cautiously interested. 'A whole floor, indeed? And, of course, you're quite right, the Lido hotels are full of bathers and tennis players. The city itself is quite pleasant at this time of year, provided you take pastilles to burn for mosquitoes and insist on an iron bedstead.' He stopped speaking, realizing he was in danger of sounding enthusiastic.

'Mr Dunstan says we'll have a gondola of our own, even if it has to wait all day, and a whole first-class railway coach to travel there—'

'Really? Well, bless my soul.' For an instant, my father's eyes opened wide behind his spectacles and then he recovered himself.

'I must warn him that one gondolier is quite sufficient, unless he's out on the lagoon. 'They always want to bring a brother, or a cousin, you know—'

'And he's promised we can have churches and palaces opened up specially for us, no matter what it costs.'

'Then you must tell him one lira is quite enough for a church-keeper to light the candles.' My father sighed. 'But I don't suppose he'll remember. And the guides will cheat him and the cameo-sellers will rob his wife and he'll come back with nothing of that glorious city except a few tawdry glass beads and a sense of deep disappointment.' My father shook his head and sighed again. He glanced up at my mother. 'Do you know – I really think I shall have to go, if only to save that man from himself.'

My mother smiled. 'I'm sure that would be best.'

'And you'll come too, of course?'

'No, my dear, I have my index of *Saxifraga* to finish – and Chrissie will be there in Venice with you. Won't that do?'

My father looked glum for a moment; he hated being parted from her. Then his face brightened. 'A whole floor of the Danieli, Dunstan said? And a private gondola? Are you certain?'

Chapter Three

WE WERE TO go to Venice in May of that year, 1914, and Mar had expressed one small reservation about our tour. Wasn't Venice quite near the Balkan states and weren't there reports of fighting in Albania between the Serbs and the Moslems?

Alfred Dunstan dismissed her fears with his usual bland confidence.

'Dear lady—' I distinctly saw my mother wince. 'Albania is a whole five hundred miles from Venice, but in any case, in terms of politics, it might just as well be on the planet Jupiter. Wars are bound to happen in a place like the Balkans, but they're only ever little wars. Bang-bang for a few weeks, the president and his cabinet taken out and shot, and everybody's happy again.

'And yet, it's just as well these wars do happen, since it's my springs that go to make the guns and lorries on both sides! The way young Bea spends my money, I'd have to go out and start wars myself, if they weren't so good at starting themselves.' His lips drew back over his front teeth in a bright, aggressive semblance of a smile. 'But the Balkan peasants are only interested in killing each other, Mrs Ascham, I assure you. Venice will be as safe as your own garden and a good deal drier, probably.' The electric smile flashed again. 'I shouldn't think it rains half as much there.'

Easier in her mind, my mother returned to her *Saxifraga*. Wars weren't something she understood, except to deplore them. My parents were deeply distressed by violence of any kind; Mar had

33

been shocked by the suffragettes' recent slashing of the portraits of Wellington and Henry James and their attacks on Yarmouth pier and the British Museum. In Mar's view, women most certainly ought to have the vote, but as a force for peace-making, not for destruction. I saw her frowning at the door through which Mr Dunstan had just left.

'He didn't really mean what he said about making money from wars, I hope.'

I'd been too excited to listen. As far as I was concerned, the coming trip was a magical development. There was only one real disappointment and even that could be borne; Jack Dunstan wouldn't be with us.

'Father says he's to stay at school,' explained Beatrice bluntly. 'And Ida's too young to benefit. Which is to say, he couldn't be bothered with either of them.' Beatrice sucked her fingers; there'd been chocolate cake for tea. 'Mother wanted to stay and look after Ida, but, of course, he wouldn't have it. She's got to be with him.'

'Oh, I know, Par was awfully keen for Mar to come. He'll be lost without her.'

Beatrice's brows puckered a little over her prominent eyes and she licked her thumb thoughtfully. 'I don't think this is quite the same.'

Ah, Venice, city of masquerade – of masks upon masks – you were lying in wait for us, I believe, a glittering vision screening a swamp, a pall of brocade on a corpse. My unworldly father called you his greatest love, his childhood sweetheart. Yet you're really only an ancient courtesan, all things to all men, hiding your withered cheek behind the sweet images painted by your artist sons and veiling your subtle smile behind a Madonna's serenity.

On the day of our arrival, however, all I saw was enchantment. And nothing could be more ravishing than one's first glimpse of the sun-spangled Grand Canal, with wonder after wonder revealing itself on either side, fairy palaces built by djinns, jewelled with arches and fanciful balconies and attended by a swarm of firefly boats.

I'd already been hopelessly beguiled by our journey from Paris. My father had struggled against the overwhelming luxury of our private railway carriage for the first few hours and had then given in to its seduction. By Venice, we'd become accustomed to sumptuous food and constant attention. We were ready for marvels; anything less would have been unbearably disappointing. And the city of Venice, reading these expectations in our faces, generously obliged.

We were to live in a palace of our own – or, at least, a floor of it – right on the Riva degli Schiavoni, the Quay of the Slaves, where bronzed traders had piled the spoils of China, Afghanistan and Persia, defying the cunning of the Barbary pirates. The Royal Danieli Hotel had been the home of a duke; there was marble, frescoes and endless gothic arches – and Dickens had slept there, and Balzac, and Wagner.

Our private drawing room looked out over the perfect pink, white and blue confectionery of the lagoon. From its balcony we could see the peach-coloured islands of San Giorgio Maggiore and the Giudecca and, further to the west, the great pearly dome and pinnacles of the Salute. Below us the quay was alive with boats of all kinds, not just the silver-prowed, black-hulled gondolas nosing their way through the forest of mooring posts, but bluff-shouldered barges and fishing craft with short, businesslike masts and portly steamers snorting across the lagoon through a flock of bobbing *sandolo* skiffs. I loved the way the oarsmen stood smoking nonchalantly in the stern of their skiffs, miraculously balanced against the criss-crossing washes of the larger vessels.

'Look at that fellow painting the fishing boats, with his brushes stuck through the band of his hat! His easel's on the very edge of the quay.'

'Oh, and look at the dog, Bea, sitting right in the bow of that tiny boat! He'll fall in, for sure.'

Yet the animal didn't fall in. No one ever seemed to fall in, in that city on the water, not even the flowerpots balanced on the spindly balconies of the side canals or the children rolling down the steps of the humpbacked bridges.

'There'll be mosquitoes,' Mar had warned, as she supervised the packing of my cases.

Beatrice watched their unpacking with interest. 'You're so lucky, having red in your hair. Green doesn't suit me at all.' She pirouetted in the middle of our bedroom, a many-tiered afternoon frock crushed against her bosom. 'What do you think? Striped linen this afternoon, or muslin flounces?'

I watched her enviously, dismayingly aware of my green patent rain-proof coat, my green linen skirt and green tunic blouse buttoned from shoulder to waist. It had only just occurred to me that while I was looking at Venice, Venice would be examining me and finding me a little odd, to say the least. At home, in the past, I'd never cared what I wore. I'd always assumed my clothes were much the same as everyone else's and only the odd glimpse of our parlourmaid's fashion magazines had shaken my confidence. But since Beatrice's arrival, I'd taken to staring at myself for long periods in my looking-glass, glumly listing all the things that were wrong with what I saw. Now I was quite shocked when the Dunstans' maid opened Beatrice's trunks and a tide of chiffon and satin poured out. Beatrice's pyjamas were silk, not summer-weight flannel – and her petticoats were silk and her knickers too. Mar had said Beatrice would regret wearing Eiffel heels to tramp round Venice. I certainly hoped so.

When I confronted myself in the bathroom mirror that night, my hip bones stuck out like handles through my summer combinations. Buttoned up in bleached cotton, with my pale face and pale hands, I was as white as a bone all over. Only my hair was vivid with colour, pouring over my shoulders in a hot copper stream, which my mother refused to have shortened; my auburn hair, which permitted me to wear green.

Par had drawn up a meticulous programme for our tour of the city. First thing next morning, he marched us off to shuffle over the uneven marble paving of the Basilica of San Marco and peer up into shadowy vaults glimmering with the gilded agonies of Byzantine saints. From the outside, the papery grey shells of the cathedral reminded me of a wasp's nest, spiky and fragile. Somewhere inside, according to legend, one of St Stephen's ribs and a finger belonging to Mary Magdalene were kept among the great jewelled goblets of gold in the treasury. It was chilly in the Basilica; I didn't think I'd like to be a saint and be parcelled out, piecemeal, for worship.

'Splendid.' Alfred Dunstan gazed round with relish as we came out into the sunlight of the Piazza. He was just about to set off for the tables of a nearby café when my father called him to heel.

'Onward!'

The springmaker's face registered amazement. He was clearly astonished to find that vague, scholarly Benedict Ascham could be such a shameless bully where academic matters were concerned. My father had already wheeled about, a hand raised above his head and his beak of a nose aimed at the entrance to the Doge's Palace alongside.

With determination, he set off towards it, his spectacles and silver pencil rattling against his chest and his commentary flying back to us over one shoulder. 'Now, this gateway is late Gothic in style, already showing the influence of the Renaissance. It was designed for Doge Foscari by Bartolomeo Bon. Please note the putti round the bust of St Mark.' He waved a hand towards the scrambling cherubs and peered round to make sure we were all paying attention. 'This entrance to the palace is called the Porta della Carta because the decrees of the Republic were posted at the door. Ahead of us is the Scala dei Giganti—' Here Par pulled out his pocket handkerchief, scattering small coins over the paving and sending us all scurrying to pick them up.

Already we'd fallen into formation: Par in crumpled grey linen, setting a brisk pace at our head, followed closely by Hosanna Greendew in what looked like sackcloth, writing everything in her notebook the instant he said it, and then Beatrice and me walking together, our attention straying rather a lot. Alfred Dunstan and Letty were supposed to bring up the rear, but the springmaker kept stopping to test a piece of gilding with his thumbnail or feel the edge of a tapestry, so that Letty, in her rice straw hat, was usually left walking alone. Yet she didn't seem to notice; she seemed preoccupied, her eyes very wide, almost fearful of all she was seeing.

Her stunned expression returned as our gondola swept us through canals like dark tunnels where our voices echoed and re-echoed in the dankness, flying up to the narrow strip of sky overhead. Letty hardly seemed to look; she seemed dazed, as if she wasn't so much inspecting the city as breathing it in, from the rotting boards of the water doors to the crumbling iron grilles and the patches of coloured stucco clinging haphazardly to the brickwork. Only occasionally would she lift her eyes – curiously – towards the ranks of secretive arched windows barely a hand's reach apart, high above the water.

Alfred Dunstan sat squatly amidships, glaring at the decay.

'Don't they have any jobbing builders in this city? Plenty of work for them to do, that's certain. I'd send a gang of bricklayers out from England, if I didn't think the Italians would be too dozy to employ them. Look at that, over there—' He pointed to where a flight of stone steps was dissolving in graceful wreckage into the canal. 'Makes the place look untidy, doesn't it?'

In his seat near the stern, my father's panama hat swung round and he stared at the springmaker as though he'd suggested whitewashing over the Basilica's mosaics. 'You surely don't expect—'

'Yes, a gang of good English jobbing builders – that's what's needed.' Alfred Dunstan nodded with satisfaction. 'A bit of cement and a hoist or two; they'd have this place right in no time. *In no time*, I tell you.' He nudged Letty for confirmation; her head turned, but for a second or two she stared at him, uncomprehending.

Then her eyes dimmed from their glorious dream. 'Of course, Alfred, just as you say.'

She'd been recalled to duty. And for the rest of the afternoon her rice straw brim tipped this way and that, every inch the hat of a critical British tourist.

Par was in his element, buzzing with facts.

'Ah, now, the Palazzo Rezzonico.' He waved an abstracted hand at a towering pile of masonry knee-deep in green water. 'Browning's son lived here, you know – the poet's boy. A terrible painter, alas. He specialized in lumpish nudes and his wife had tantrums you could hear all over the canal. Luckily, she had money, but she didn't stay . . . took all the furniture with her . . .

'Now, that house over there—' He squirmed round, rocking the gondola. 'Do you see where I'm pointing? The house with the fifteenth-century balcony – that's where you might have found Byron's doctor's daughter. Her mother married again, a Turkish pasha, if I remember correctly, and wrote quite a notorious book . . . *Thirty Years in the Harem*, something of that sort.' A happy thought struck him. 'Though I dare say if one's married to a pash-*a* it's a relief that one's turn for his pash-*on* comes only once in a while.'

The springmaker cleared his throat in noisy embarrassment. Par, oblivious, chuckled at his little joke and swept on.

'Of course, Byron *himself* lodged, when he first came to Venice, with a linen-draper in the Frezzeria, the Street of the Arrow-makers, do you remember walking there yesterday? Byron

39

was soon sharing his bed with the linen-draper's wife, of course –
entirely with her husband's consent. English milord, d'you see?
Perfectly respectable lover. Not like the *gondolieri*, who were said
to take on anyone that paid them – man or woman alike. This is
a bit of a place for nancy-boys, I'm afraid. Good gracious,
Dunstan, that's a nasty cough you've got there. I should have that
seen to, if it's no better tomorrow.'

And the springmaker, who'd been trying to warn Par that two
eager sixteen-year-olds were absorbing every word, subsided in
mutinous silence.

In Venice, we gathered, a certain moral elasticity went hand
in hand with *culture*.

'You must allow the *essence* of Venice,' Hosanna Greendew had
instructed Beatrice and me, 'to seep into your souls.' She'd meant
the culture, of course, this taste for gilt frames and graceful loggias
which could be caught like a cold. But when you're actually in
Venice and your eyes and ears are propped open and your fingers
wriggle and your skin tingles with excitement, there are plenty of
sensations, I discovered, that reach the soul before culture.

I used to lie awake in the soft, grey dawn, listening for the
plash of oars and the groan and thump of rowlocks to herald the
day's first boat, slopping water on the flanks of our building.
Before long I'd hear the creak-clack of shutters being thrown
open nearby and then the slap of footsteps, down in the echoing
space below, as the Venetians began to go about their business.
Never mind the elegant foreigners in the Piazza, bowing to
acquaintances with the assurance of people used to being recognized by the crowd. I liked to pick out the native Venetians; I
liked the soapy sheen of their skin and their big, prosperous noses.
The people of the city had a polished, self-satisfied air, as if
business was good. The Dunstans, I thought, should feel at home
here.

Then I began to wonder if Letty Dunstan was lying awake at

her husband's side, staring into the half-light with those wide-open eyes of hers, thinking of . . . what?

It was strange, the way Venice popped disturbing ideas into your head. *Amore, amore* . . . I tried to imagine Lord Byron swimming home along the Grand Canal, his dark hair curling damply on his forehead, and had a sudden vision of Jack Dunstan instead, rowing up to the jetty at Waterside, full of pride and raw anger.

Oddly enough, I'd found myself thinking of Jack quite often since we'd been in Venice and in a rather startling, embarrassing way, as if he was standing very close and I could feel his presence through my skin; it gave me an odd little thrill in the pit of my stomach.

Perhaps it was the unaccustomed heat of the city that had made me feverish, or perhaps it was simply the daily sight of so many painted male and female bodies, well-nigh naked but so voluptuously moulded and so delicately tinted that you felt their flesh should actually be warm to the touch. I sometimes put out a finger, just to see. All of a sudden, I was surrounded by things that demanded to be stroked, great velvet draperies and bullion fringes, knotty carvings, marble as smooth as liquid, worn by centuries of curious fingers.

Was it the city that had disturbed me, that had sent me these strange, disquieting thoughts about Jack and Lord Byron? Alfred Dunstan believed it was paintings like Tintoretto's *Bacchus* in the Doge's Palace, with his naughty little garland of vine leaves. The springmaker was offended by that sort of painting. 'Far too many thighs and bottoms, if you ask me. I don't know how much they'd want for it, but I'd need a bit more in the drapery line before I'd put it on my wall.'

'Oh, no, Mr Dunstan!' Hosanna flung an anguished glance at Par. 'These pictures aren't for sale! You can't *buy* them. They're national treasures.'

'Are they, indeed?' The springmaker stared round, rocking on his heels, and stuffed his hands into his trouser pockets. 'Well, that's as may be, but if I can't find some clever Italian gentleman ready to pocket a few lira to have them taken off his hands, then they're the first treasures in this city that *haven't* been for sale.'

Certainly, Alfred Dunstan and his daughter had succeeded in buying up a remarkable amount of the place.

'I say, I do like those chairs.' Beatrice came to a sudden halt as we toured yet another cavernous palazzo. 'I don't care much for the vases, but I'd love one of those gilt armchairs with the red brocade upholstery. I can just see it in my bedroom in the new house.'

'But you've already bought those huge mirrors, Bea, and the chandelier, and all that lace, and the cameo belt, and the marble table, and the bronze candelabra—'

'It's just a chair, Chrissie. And it's awfully old, so it can't be worth very much.'

Beatrice promptly made her wishes known to her father, who spoke to the manager of the Danieli, who just happened to know a trustworthy dealer in antiquities. In a matter of hours, two very expensive red brocade chairs exactly like the one Beatrice had admired were being packed up for shipment to England.

'They always come in pairs, signor.'

And yet, at that moment I actually envied Beatrice her acquisitiveness. Beatrice's Venice – and her father's too – was so satisfyingly portable, so easily shopped for and sent home. With a flourish of lire they could shrink the whole experience of Venice and her mysteries into a hatbox and take it back to England to be shown off to visitors, exotic but safe; inspected, crossed off, conquered.

The Venice I'd discovered, like Tintoretto's *Bacchus*, was not for sale. It had crept up on me in the smaller, more modest palazzetti where Par's acquaintances offered us biscuits and marsala in tiny, gold-dipped glasses. It stole along the damp stone galleries, dappled with the light of the canal, and waited in the conspiratorial dark of the chapels, as rich and close as the inside of a jewel-box. After only a few days, I knew I'd never forget the musty smell of sun-rotted window hangings, or the soft skin-sheen of the tiled floors, smoothed by generations of feet, or the dark wooden ceilings glinting with gold, or the serenity, the cold, timeless, silent dignity of jasper and porphyry and marble, veined with the changing colours of the sea.

In my lonely confusion, I befriended a little striped cat near one of the cafés of the Riva and his shameless banditry reassured me. I used to find him in the mornings, chewing a pile of fish-heads someone had left, his cheeks gaily sequinned with scales and his ears pricked out like the ends of a carnival tricorne. He touched my heart with his lame hind foot, or perhaps it was simply that his wide golden gaze reminded me uneasily of Letty Dunstan. At any rate, we began to look out for one another every day, the cat and I, and made *amore* in our own way with purring and stroking and whatever high-priced morsels I could buy from one of the fishing boats.

He didn't need my friendship, that Venetian cat, and made his feelings plain, but for the gift of a few prawns or a piece of eel he was prepared to roll seductively on the paving, rumpling his stripes and baring his sand-coloured belly to be tickled. His fur was as soft as evening light and as yielding as velvet and it ran between my fingers like the trickle of a fountain. But my prawns bought only so much indulgence and the instant my time ran out, claws like poignards would fight me off and the little striped assassin would disappear down the *calle* to his next appointment, hopping awkwardly on his twisted toes.

Even the cats were dissipated! No one had warned me the city was so sensual, so wildly voluptuous. Here even the Christ-child was born among peacocks and thrones. In the churches, the saints met their martyrdom in luxurious silks and, outside, when we slid through the maze of canals, our prow seemed to cut through a floor of black Laconian marble. The whole city called out for abandon and excess, and I woke each day with my pulses racing, as if straight from a dream which had flooded my senses with sweetness and the taste of half-remembered pleasures.

I felt as if I'd like to be . . . to be . . . seduced. Is that so terribly shocking? I had a sudden, compelling urge to be caressed, and stroked, and laid siege to and made wanton; and for the first time I understood what I'd. wanted, truly wanted, from the coachman at Wickham, with his supple hands and his tight buckskin breeches.

I wasn't alone in my turmoil. One evening, when I walked out on to our drawing room balcony, I found Letty Dunstan already there, leaning silently on the rail in a silk kimono, her face lit by the reflected sparkle of the water. I stopped at once, framed in the doorway. Venice, I'd discovered, can play strange tricks with light, but at that moment Letty's face seemed transfigured by a kind of unearthly . . . *hunger*. That's the only word for it.

I'd never seen such an expression before on the face of a grown woman. The whole of Letty Dunstan's body radiated longing, the kind of inarticulate, bewildered yearning one sees in the faces of children left out of the games of their friends. As I watched, she closed her eyes and turned her face up to the sky, her breasts rising and falling under the silk of her robe. It was like the rapid beating of a bird's heart as it lies on the ground, stunned by the glass window it has mistaken for the limitless sky.

I almost ran to her. At that moment Letty Dunstan seemed the one person in that whole city who might understand what was happening to me. My father was obsessed by the Ginquecento, Hosanna's life was bounded by her notebook and her devotion to Par, and Beatrice was full of chairs and candelabra.

I must have stood there, uncertain, for several minutes. At last, silent as I was, some small sound must have given me away, because Letty suddenly turned her head, almost in fright. Then her expression changed as she caught sight of me.

'Chrissie! I didn't hear you.'

'I'm sorry. I didn't mean to spoil your peace.'

'It wasn't peace. Anything but that. It's this place.' She

indicated the city below. 'It makes one so restless. So ...
dissatisfied.'

'I know. As if something's missing. As if one's been half-
asleep until now—'

'Yes, only half alive.' She searched my face. 'Do you feel it,
too?'

'I wish I knew what was happening to me.'

'I wish – I wish I'd never come here. I was content at home.'
She glanced away again, twisting a strand of hair between her
fingers.

Par and Hosanna Greendew had tamed the city by boiling it
down to colour-analogies and horizontal composition. Beatrice
and her father had simply divided everything into what they
wanted to take home or couldn't abide. Only Letty Dunstan and
I seemed unable to cram the essence of Venice back into its
bottle. Our only comfort lay in the fact that we were half-way
through our tour. In another fortnight we'd be bound for home.

The next day my father carried us off to the Museo Civico in the
Fondaco dei Turchi to see Carpaccio's *Two Courtesans*, described
by John Ruskin as 'the best picture in the world'.

Beatrice's ankles were wobbling. 'Do we have to go? My feet
have swollen so much, with all this trailing round churches. I
couldn't walk another inch if my life depended on it.'

Par refused to be put off. He led us upstairs past a room full of
daggers and flags and on to the paintings. And there they sat in
their elaborate frame – two of the most famous women in Venice,
taking the air on the roof of their house among their pet dogs and
birds, shoes removed for comfort and an expression of infinite
boredom on their faces. I thought of Letty and me at the Danieli.
Why did women gaze from Venetian balconies with such
discontent?

'Nowadays, of course,' Par announced, 'we don't think
they're courtesans at all, but two women of the Torelli family.

And here—' He raised his spectacles and peered through them like a lorgnette. 'Here I differ from Ruskin. Inspired though this may be, it *isn't* the best painting in the world. And yet, when one considers how the eye travels so gracefully through the arm and shoulder of the first woman to the curved elbow of the second—'

My father stopped speaking, suddenly aware of another voice conducting a soft monologue nearby. He wheeled round, his eyebrows raised. Two men standing in the shadows nearby froze into apologetic silence. The nearer of the two was middle-aged and of middle height, his dark hair very silver at the temples.

'I do beg your pardon. I didn't mean to interrupt you.' His companion stood further back, giving an impression of younger, paler features. 'Please continue.' The older man inclined his head courteously. 'I was drawing my son's attention to some pearls in the picture, but I shall wait until you finish.'

'Pearls?' My father spun round to stare at the painting.

'I am a dealer in pearls.' The stranger smiled and made a small, dismissive gesture. 'Pearls are my business – and my passion, you might say.'

'Ah.' Alfred Dunstan bared his teeth in pleasure. '*Pearls*. Now that's something new.' He rubbed his hands. 'Pearls, how interesting.'

Beatrice beamed, her sore feet forgotten. 'I've always liked pearls.'

'So did the ladies of Venice.' The pearl merchant smiled again, shyly responding to their interest. 'They liked pearls so much that the Republic had to pass laws forbidding them to wear more than one strand at a time, or to wear pearls worth more than two hundred ducats.' He indicated the Torelli women. 'But as you can see from this picture, no one paid any attention. When the King of France came here in the sixteenth century, the Venetian ladies had pearls in their hair, in their ears and all over their gowns – everywhere.'

'Now these ones – excuse me – ' Warming to his subject, he stepped past my father to examine the painting. 'These are particularly spherical and perfectly matched. We talk about the "orient" of a pearl, the way it reflects light. They must have been very happy, these ladies, to own such jewels—'

'They don't look happy, though.' Letty Dunstan had been standing silently beside the picture. 'In fact, I think they look rather sad, in spite of their pearls and their pet animals, as if they feel they ought to be happy, to have so much, and yet they aren't.'

There was a movement in the shadows as the younger of the two men turned his head sharply to have a clearer view of the speaker. A shaft of sunlight from a nearby window revealed hair of startling blackness swept about by a tinsel of dust motes and a pair of intense dark eyes that seemed to consume Letty with a passionate fixity, searching for the source of her belief.

'It's true – pearls are no guarantee against loneliness.' His voice had an odd musicality, as if the words had been pronounced almost too perfectly to be a first language. 'I've often said this to my father, but then – pearls fill his life. They're like a family to him.' He smiled gently at his companion.

'Nothing is a guarantee against loneliness.' I was startled by Letty's vehemence. 'Not jewellery, or houses, or clothes—' Once more, the young man's dark eyes swept back to examine her.

'All this seriousness, just for a *picture*!' Alfred Dunstan's thick palms flew out in a gesture of impatience, shattering the melancholy. 'Good heavens, a dab of paint would soon put a grin on those women's faces and roses in their cheeks! Isn't that so, Dr Ascham? That's what painting's all about, a smudge of paint here, a twitch of the brush there, and you can have any kind of expression you like.'

'Ah, well now, my dear sir—' My father flew to the defence of art. 'You must remember this is a formal, classical composition! It has nothing to do with reality!' He took a deep breath and prepared to resume his lecture, but Alfred Dunstan had already turned back to the pearl merchant, determined to escape from Carpaccio.

'Pearls, now, I've always thought that must be an interesting line of business.'

'Consider the spatial control . . .' My father's thin, high voice trailed off into silence. Apart from the ever-loyal Hosanna, he'd lost his audience. The springmaker, his mind now entirely occupied by pearls, had begun to shepherd us away from the ranks of gilt frames.

The pearl merchant's name was Max Kassel and he and his son Philip had arrived in Venice the previous day on the steamer from Port Said, on their way home from a pearl buying trip to Bombay. I was surprised to hear that Philip Kassel – the owner of the dark, burning eyes – was only eighteen years old; from the gravity of his manner, I'd have guessed he was much older. There was nothing boyish about the narrow determination of his features or the deep, sculptural shadows that thrust cheekbone and brow into striking relief under the darkest of hair. He was looking forward, he said, to starting his studies at Oxford in the autumn. In the meantime, his widowed father had set out to show him something of the world.

'Golly,' whispered Beatrice in my ear as we trooped off to find a café. 'Isn't he utterly divine? Fancy finding someone like him in this musty old city!' And, sore feet or not, she sprinted forward to catch up with Philip, who'd fallen into step behind his father.

Par and Hosanna had been left with no choice but to follow, but they kept aloof. I saw Letty hesitate, glance back towards them, and then lengthen her step to catch up with the rest of us.

Chapter Four

ALFRED DUNSTAN, who'd had more than enough of museums, seized on the pearl dealer with relief. This was something he understood. This was commerce; this was trade. For his part, Max Kassel was enchanted to discover that the grumpy gentleman festooned with pencil and spectacles was *the* Benedict Ascham, whose books *The Renaissance Goldsmith* and *Some Gothic Altarpieces* had an important place in his own library. Before long even my father had thawed and the Kassels dined with us that evening at the Danieli.

They were staying at the Hôtel de L'Europe at the entrance to the Grand Canal, and the next day they insisted on taking us on a steamer excursion to the Lido followed by lunch at the Hôtel des Bains.

Beatrice's mind was fixed on pearls. 'Do you think Mr Kassel carries necklaces around with him? Would he show us, if I made Father ask? Or, perhaps Philip would mention it, if I asked him.' Beatrice smirked at herself in the mirror and fluttered her abundant lashes. The Kassels were dining with us again that evening and she was dressing for dinner in a satin gown caught round her hips with an enormous sash which she'd tried at least a dozen different ways.

In honour of our guests I'd brought out my one fashionable item, an embroidered 'Juliet' cap, which made the most of my long hair and which Beatrice coveted.

'Philip Kassel will do anything I ask, you know.' Beatrice

raised her voice. 'I do think he's awfully nice, and awfully handsome, of course.' I recognized the expression on her face; lips a little apart, her eyes very bright under their heavy lids. I'd seen her look at a cameo brooch in exactly the same way, and a chair, and a bronze candlestick.

It was an accident that finally made the Kassels full members of our party. It arose from the fact that all gondolas are black, something my father forgot near the steps of the Salute, when he climbed into what he assumed was the Dunstans' gondola, only to discover as it set out immediately from the shore that it was actually a *traghetto*, one of the gondola ferries which ply to and fro all day across the few dozen yards of the Grand Canal, swinging in mid-stream like elegant turnstiles to let passing traffic go by. Most Venetians scorn to sit down for the short crossing. I saw my father scramble to his feet as he realized his mistake and begin to scold the ferrymen in confused Italian which became shriller as the craft drew nearer to the opposite shore. He waved his arms wildly, rocking the boat. Clearly, the *traghetto* should turn round at once and take him back to his starting point.

'Oh, come back, you wretches!' Hosanna Greendew fluttered her notebook from the landing stage in a vain attempt to rescue her hero. 'Oh, dear Dr Ascham – oh, you fiends! You rogues!'

'Call out to him to stay where he is.' Letty Dunstan snatched at her husband's sleeve. 'The ferry will come back to this side in a moment, won't it?'

But as the boat whirled with a flourish against the far jetty, a heated argument seemed to break out on board. Soon, to my dismay, I saw the ferrymen manhandle my father ashore, knocking his panama hat into the water, where it floated away under the piles. Even on the jetty he went on shouting and shaking his fists, his hair ruffled round his temples like silver clouds on the brow of a painted Zeus.

'I think he's told them he won't pay for the crossing.' At my side, Max Kassel peered across the strip of green water. 'And now they won't bring him back.'

'But he'll be marooned! Mr Dunstan sent our gondola back to the hotel ages ago. He'll never think of walking round by the Accademia Bridge.' I gazed in desperation at the ranting figure on the far side of the canal. The *traghetto* had already set off again towards us; I could see the ferrymen chuckling over their little victory.

'Leave this to me.' Max Kassel walked forward to meet the boat as it arrived. I saw him bend down to speak to the nearest rower, pointing across the canal to where my father stood, now hatless and dispirited, staring dolefully in our direction. I strained my ears to catch what Max Kassel was saying, but his voice was too soft and, in any case, since he was fluent in the Venetian dialect I probably wouldn't have understood a word. After a few minutes, however, the ferry set out once more and the pearl merchant came back to my side.

'It's all settled, they're going to fetch him back right away. He wouldn't pay, you see, insisted he'd never meant to cross the canal and they'd no right to kidnap him. At least, that's what they think he was saying.'

'But they're going back for him now?'

'Oh yes.' Max Kassel's eyes sparkled with mischief. 'I told them I'd drag them in front of a magistrate and swear they'd abducted a British citizen in lawful pursuit of his business. I told them your father was related to the British royal family and their own King Victor Emmanuel, too, and I warned them their *traghetto* licence would instantly be cancelled, even if their great-great-grandfathers had been ferrymen on the same spot.'

Par maintained a dignified silence during his return crossing, sitting amidships with the prim dignity of Queen Mary herself. He even went so far as to allow one of the ferrymen to dust a spot of canal water from his coat before stepping ashore, but his panama hat, alas, was gone for good, no doubt already dissolved to a waterlogged pulp amid the bobbing rubbish of the canal.

Par's gratitude to Max Kassel was boundless. The pearl merchant had saved him from – from – well, from a long walk back, at the very least, and from countless lurking robbers and assassins on the way. Clearly, Max Kassel was a thorough gentleman as well as an enlightened scholar and the owner of two of my father's published books. All things considered, my father decided, Max Kassel was one of the pleasantest, most intelligent men he'd ever met. And since Alfred Dunstan and his family clearly approved of them too, the Kassels were instantly adopted into our little party.

We must have seemed an oddly assorted group, as we traipsed round the remaining sights of Venice. No matter how hot the day might be, Max Kassel always looked the same in his immaculately tailored black suit, complete with high, stiff collar and waistcoat; he was one of those people whose clothes miraculously never seem to crease. My father, on the other hand, could have crushed a bowler hat, never mind the clerical linen 'library' jacket he'd put on over his cardigan-vest as a concession to the heat. Alfred Dunstan and Philip Kassel were the only ones with any claim to fashion – the springmaker strutting in light tweed and a felt hat with a large gold Albert across his waistcoat, and Philip turning female heads in the Piazza in his well-cut grey flannel and straw boater.

By now, Philip's presence had put something of a strain on relations between Beatrice and me. I don't believe Beatrice had bothered to decide whether she liked or disliked Philip as a person: she used to describe him as 'deep', which meant much of what he said was too profound for her, though it impressed her hugely. No, she simply wanted to acquire him like all the other things she'd bought, and she certainly wasn't going to let such a find be stolen from under her nose. Her honour as a shopper depended on it. Before long we'd become locked in a kind of unofficial fashion contest which Beatrice, with her enormous – and non-green – wardrobe, was bound to win. I consoled myself with the thought that at least I couldn't look as odd as Hosanna Greendew, clothed like a medieval pilgrim in a brown linen poncho and a wide, flat, straw hat.

Only Letty Dunstan seemed to float through each day, cool, elegant and a little detached from us under her parasol, in a simple straight skirt and crêpe de Chine blouse which showed off her slender figure and made her seem far younger than her thirty-eight years. If we sat at a café table in the Piazza, complete strangers would bow to her and men would raise their hats. The springmaker flashed his growling smile and looked exactly like a guard dog showing his teeth. Where Letty was concerned, his eyes were always hard and wary.

It was fitting that we should have met the Kassels in Venice; father and son seemed wanderers by nature, like the old Venetian traders or Marco Polo himself. It's true they owned a house in London, but when Max Kassel spoke of it, the place was clearly just that, a house, not a home, merely somewhere to store a lifetime's belongings and an address for quarterly magazines.

Beatrice decided this was because Philip's mother had died six years earlier and she promptly surrounded him with all the sorrowful glamour of an orphan. Certainly, I'd seen him, sometimes, watching the Dunstans – Alfred, Letty and Beatrice – with a thoughtful expression in his dark eyes, as if the inner workings of a family were a puzzle he'd forgotten how to solve. I wondered if that was why they'd become nomads, he and his father, or whether there was simply an instinctive rootlessness about them, as if no particular country had a greater claim on them than any other.

Max Kassel had searched the world for pearls, travelling from the Persian Gulf to Ceylon, from Australia to Tahiti, to Venezuela and the Gulf of California, to any corner of the globe which might yield up treasure. I'd only read of such places in books, and his stories unfolded before me in dazzling colours. He used to amuse us with his adventures as we sat in the Piazza among the ranks of tables in front of Florian's café, drinking our morning chocolate and smugly watching the new arrivals having their photographs taken with the pigeons. What was the difference, he'd ask mischievously, between one of these fashionable ladies in their feathered hats and a New Guinea tribesman dancing in his plumes, except, perhaps, a bone through the nose?

I liked the way Max Kassel leaned forward when he talked, so that his sun-browned face seemed all eager dark eyes and winged cheekbones, while the upward-slanting lines at its corners gave him a fleeting, mercurial air. It was only when his gaze strayed to Philip that he seemed to fall back to earth, when he spoke of Julia, his dead wife, and the impossibility of being both mother and father to his son.

'He should have a proper home. A boy needs somewhere to belong to.'

That kind of remark brought a frown to Alfred Dunstan's brow. It seemed to strike him as feebleness. 'But you have a house in London.'

'That's all – just a house.'

'What? There's no furniture in it?'

'Oh, there's plenty of furniture. Much of it came with poor Julia. Some of her pieces are particularly fine.'

'Then that's your home, it seems to me. And if the place doesn't suit you, then you should move to another house that does. What more could you want?' The springmaker waved an impatient hand, as if the solution was obvious. Yet Max Kassel's gentle stubbornnness clearly annoyed him, and he kept returning to the subject of houses like a man picking at an old wound.

'The Venetians had the right idea, it seems to me. They took the profits of their trade – sordid, maybe – and they turned them into palaces full of as much culture as you could shake a stick at. What would your Titians and your Tintorettos have done, if these fellows hadn't sold enough silk and ginger to pay their inflated prices? You can't paint a fresco without a wall to put it on – isn't that so, Dr Ascham?' Without pausing, he added, 'You might even say it's a wealthy man's duty to build a monument to himself, if only to keep architects and painters in work.'

My father's chocolate cup halted an inch from his lips. 'So

you're about to become a patron of the arts, Mr Dunstan? Well, that's excellent news, I must say.'

'A patron of the arts? Yes, indeed – why not?' Alfred Dunstan seemed to swell until he overflowed his little wooden chair. 'Though you must admit I've been good to the architects already. My new house in the English Lakes, you know—' He nodded significantly at Max Kassel. 'Biggest place built in that part of the country for years. "Spare nothing," I said to the architect. "Let's make a job of it, if we're doing it at all."'

'We'll have fifteen bathrooms,' Beatrice informed Philip. 'And a luggage lift in the clock tower.'

'And a living hall,' added her father. A thought struck him. 'Dash it, Bea – we must have some frescoes up the staircase in the hall.' His dry palms whistled as he rubbed them. 'We'll have panelling up so high—' A hand hovered at table-height. 'And then the whole of the rest will be covered with paintings. People – animals – that sort of stuff.' His hand thrashed the air, conjuring up vast allegories of heaven and hell. 'Oh, yes, I can see it already.'

'And what does Mrs Dunstan think of all this?' Max Kassel glanced shrewdly at Letty. 'In my experience, a wife usually has her own ideas of how her home should look.'

Letty flushed delicately in the shade of her parasol. 'The house is really Alfred's, not mine. He's planned it all, down to the last doorknob and window pane.'

The springmaker rumbled his agreement. 'It's a waste of time, showing a set of plans to a woman. Much better to make the decisions yourself than pretend they understand anything useful.'

'So you always say.' Letty Dunstan folded her fingers demurely round the knob of her parasol, but the flush that clung to her cheeks made her eyes glow very bright in their pool of shadow. 'But then, you've never tried to explain, have you?'

Did the springmaker hear it – the defiance of the child singled out for criticism? It didn't seem so. Yet Philip Kassel noticed. I saw that sharp glance of his seek Letty out; Letty devouring her husband with her golden eyes as if she were seeing him for the first time. My little quayside cat had watched me with that same wild, wide-eyed stare when we were still strangers, wondering whether to vanish into the *calle* or to rip my hand with his teeth and claws, confused by his own savage instincts. Abruptly, Letty tore her gaze away to the grey arches of the Basilica, lowering her parasol as a screen.

'Just as well one of us has some sense,' observed her husband.

'Pictures on the walls are all very well.' Max Kassel returned to his earlier point. 'But to my mind, the only thing that makes a home is the love of a family, otherwise it's just four walls and a roof. Believe me, I've seen houses worth millions that were no more homes than museums and all because of the loneliness inside them.'

'Oh, I dare say you're right.' Alfred Dunstan drummed his fingers on the table top, then burst out, 'But don't tell me it isn't easier to be happy in a mansion than in a tumbledown cottage the size of a shoebox. Because it isn't. I've tried both in my lifetime and I *know*.'

From the far side of the table Beatrice stared at her father, startled. Without any warning, the springmaker's face had suddenly grown dark; his expression had become rock-like and the hairline at his temples had disappeared. For a few passionate seconds he was once again the Alfred Dunstan I'd seen on the day of the picnic, raging at his son near the growing walls of his new mansion.

'Let me tell you—' He stabbed the table-top with a finger, rattling the cups. 'Let me tell you, when you live in the back streets of a city, you're just so much dross, just another face in the crowd. But as soon as your house is big enough and you can pay your way like a gentleman . . . ah, well, all of a sudden people start to take notice. They step aside for you in the street. They're ready to listen to what you say, even if it's no more than you've been telling them for years. And what made the difference, my friend? Bricks and mortar, that's what.'

He threw himself back in his chair and took in the busy Piazza with a sweep of his arm. 'I tell you, I'm *glad* I came to Venice.

Really glad. Now that I've seen this place, I know I've been right all the time. Because the men who built Venice would have told you exactly what I say, that you haven't achieved a damn thing until you can prove it to the world in bricks and mortar. Lay it out in lumps of stone! Then they'll remember who you are.'

He stared round, challenging us to disagree. His face was still mottled with red where the blood ran hot and, wisely, Max Kassel let the subject drop. The springmaker took our silence for a sign that his argument had won the day and, with some satisfaction, signalled to a waiter to bring more chocolate. Yet it didn't seem to me that he'd convinced anyone but himself. Max Kassel, especially, appeared lost in sombre thoughts of his own. He was staring at his folded hands with the air of a man who wished life could only be as simple as the springmaker believed.

Such a useful little man. It was a phrase I'd picked up at Wickham, where my Uncle Hereward lived. The words still ring in my memory in Aunt Marchioness's nasal, disparaging tone: 'Such a useful little man, but, of course, *not one of us.*'

She was talking about the financier who'd just rescued her brother, the Duke, from looming bankruptcy, but who'd never be invited to shoot over the land his money had saved.

'Why not?' I asked my mother later and watched her struggle to explain Aunt Maud's rules of caste without calling her sister-in-law a bigot.

Max Kassel must have been an expert in such odious distinctions. I could imagine the sort of people who wore Kassel pearls as ropes and studs and quietly sold them back to the *useful little man* when times were hard. To those people – many of them far stupider and coarser than he was – Max Kassel was essentially a tradesman, barely promoted above the kitchen entrance.

And yet he was wealthy, and his London house was in one of the city's most exclusive squares, though I doubted if any invitations arrived there for country weekends. Imagine coming face to face with the man who'd relieved one of great-grandmama's necklace! No, decidedly, Alfred Dunstan was wrong. A large bank balance, even when translated into massive stone and mortar, simply wasn't enough.

The cups of steaming chocolate arrived together with ice cream for Beatrice, Philip and me. Diplomatically, Philip had placed himself between us two girls and I dare say we made an engaging picture, since I saw Max Kassel watching his son with approval. It was the one point on which he and Alfred Dunstan seemed to agree: that a university education – especially at Oxford, England's oldest and therefore most socially acceptable university – could free a young man from his family's past and let him begin life with a clean slate. Jack Dunstan had been told to keep away from his father's factories. Philip Kassel's father might wish him to see something of the world, but not with the purpose of becoming a pearl dealer. Both Jack and Philip were being sent off to Oxford to launder their ancestors in a tub of titles and ancient wealth.

And yet, for all his deep thinking, I couldn't help feeling there was something defenceless about Philip Kassel. He was too intense, too spiritual for his own good. His feelings were too profound, without any shell of cynicism to cover them. I kept thinking of Noël and the easy-going mockery between us that soon shot down any melancholy fancies. Philip had no one to tease him into silliness. He was like a highly-bred horse, showing each twitch of emotion like a flicker under the thinnest of skins.

I couldn't imagine him among the clever young men at Oxford. He had none of the flippant, slightly cruel banter which was fashionable among the young and which Beatrice carried off to perfection. Instinctively, with all the struggling maturity of my seventeen years, I found myself longing to protect him in a way I'd never wanted to protect Jack Dunstan, and yet at the same time the more warmth I felt for Philip, the more confused I became about my feelings for Jack.

Max Kassel's eyes grew soft with concern when he spoke of his son. Everything was for Philip – everything but the pearls. The pearls were simply a means to an end – a business – a trade like any other. Max Kassel held up his hands in a gesture of dismissal. Pearls, lamp-wicks; one might as well apprentice the boy to a butcher.

Yet the pearls, when at last we'd seen them, had been dazzling. We'd just finished dinner in a private room at the Hôtel de l'Europe when Max Kassel brought out a leather case divided cleverly into drawers and boxes and began to pour pearls on to the cleared damask cloth with the nonchalance of a child rolling marbles.

'How wonderful!' Beatrice clapped her hands as if she'd just seen a conjuring trick. 'Look at them! So many, all at once, just like bubbles.'

Hosanna pressed a hand to her bosom. 'The tears of the sea. The simple beauty of nature.'

'Well said, Miss Greendew.' Max Kassel selected one of the largest of the milky globes and rolled it in his palm, where its lustre reflected the deep colour of his skin. 'Pearls have nothing but their beauty to offer us, yet we still find them fascinating. We can't use them for drilling, like diamonds; we can't even spend them like gold. They're simply accidents, natural phenomena, a chance coming together of worthless substances to make something quite wonderful.'

He held up the pearl between finger and thumb. With every movement of his hand, subtle, dream-like tints passed over its skin, a sheen of blue or the faintest of greens melting into a sensation of pink.

'If you melt down a gold ring, it's still worth its weight in gold. But if you crush a pearl, you've broken its spell. There's nothing left but a spoonful of calcium and the speck of organic matter that was its heart. Its beauty is only a memory. No wonder the ancient Romans believed pearls were made by flashes of lightning.'

'What a lovely idea!'

Max Kassel smiled at my eagerness. 'I'll tell you an even better story. Long ago, people thought that at certain times of year all the oysters in the sea rose to the surface and opened their shells to catch drops of dew. Then they'd sink back to the depths to turn the dew into pearls.' He studied his pearl in silence, then let it fall back into his palm. 'I suppose it's hard to believe something as ugly as an oyster could have made such beauty all by itself.' His eyes rested for a moment on the pale intensity of his son.

Alfred Dunstan was holding a chocolate-coloured sphere up to the lamp. 'I suppose some of these must be worth a good deal.'

'Some of them, yes.'

'How much, precisely?'

'Oh, for that one—' Max Kassel shrugged. 'You could probably buy a medium-sized motor car. It came from Tahiti, like most of those dark-coloured pearls. The blue one by your hand came from California. It's probably hollow inside.'

'Valuable?' The springmaker picked up the slate-coloured globe and turned it in his blunt fingers.

'With those, it depends entirely on fashion. At the moment, the market's excellent for all kinds of pearls. Even these monsters—' Max Kassel opened a box and took out two large, uneven, opalescent objects like crystallized clouds. 'These are baroque pearls, for brooches. Look – this way up, you have the body and head of an elephant. Turn it round, and it becomes . . . oh, a cluster of grapes, perhaps.'

Beatrice wasn't listening. She was leaning forward over the table, her chin and throat palely reflecting the starched cloth. She couldn't take her eyes from the pearls. As she spoke, she sounded a little breathless. 'Which are the biggest pearls in the world?'

'The biggest? Good heavens! What a question!' Max Kassel searched the ceiling for inspiration. 'Certainly, there's a famous carpet of pearls belonging to the Gaikwar of Baroda which must be almost priceless. But if you mean one single pearl . . .' Absently, he manipulated the pearls in his hand. 'There's La Pellegrina, which weighs one hundred and eleven grains. That's about so big.' He indicated something the size of a large grape. 'I believe it's in Moscow at the moment. And there's a legend that Shah Jehan's throne contained a pearl almost twice as large, roughly one and a half ounces. But in terms of sheer size, I suppose the Hope Pearl is the biggest, though it isn't perfectly round. The Hope weighs nearly three ounces.'

'How much would a pearl like that cost?' The springmaker craned forward.

Helplessly, Max Kassel held up his hands. 'Strictly speaking it's a baroque pearl and, in any case, the price doesn't depend solely on size. Let's just say even you and I might have to think twice about buying it.'

He smiled and paused for a moment like a showman preparing for the climax of his act. 'As it happens, I do have some pearls in my possession which are virtually beyond price. Because of their history, you understand.'

From an inside pocket of his coat he drew out a black leather case, opened it, and held it out with something like reverence. Inside, nestling on a bed of cream satin, was a necklace of exquisite pearls, each one as big as a cherry stone, fastened by a diamond clasp.

'The Medici Pearls,' he said. 'These – and others – were given to Catherine de' Medici by her uncle, Pope Clement, on her marriage in 1533. She passed them on to her daughter-in-law, Mary, Queen of Scots and they were bought by Elizabeth of England after Mary's execution. Her successor, King James, sent them to Bohemia with his daughter Elizabeth, but they came back to England with the Hanover kings – still perfect, still unique.'

He tilted the case to catch the light. 'The old queen – Alexandra – had these thirty made into a necklace. You can see them in the Fildes portrait of her. And now—' Max wriggled his fingers to indicate the need for discretion. 'Obviously, I can't tell you who owns them at present, though I'm sure you can guess.'

Beatrice's eyes were so round I thought they might fall out of her head. 'And how do you come to have them?'

'I've been asked to find matching pearls to lengthen the

necklace – if I can.' Ruefully, he flung up his hands. "Match them!" they said, and like a fool, I agreed! If there are a dozen more pearls like these in the world, I'd like to know where! They are match*less* – that's their fascination. They're perfection – thirty individual miracles – and yet the greatest miracle of all is that thirty of them should exist, as exactly alike as the seconds of a minute. Not even a mirror could match them!'

Letty looked concerned. 'Then what will you do?'

'Oh, I'll search, search like a madman, all over the world.' He shrugged his shoulders. 'It's a matter of honour.'

Beatrice's hand was stealing across the white cloth towards the open case. Max Kassel closed it with a snap. 'In the meantime, these beauties go back to the hotel safe.'

'Well, I think—' Letty Dunstan spoke with such firmness that we all turned to look at her. 'I think it's a sacrilege to make a hole in something so beautiful. It's almost blasphemous, don't you agree?' She rested her chin on one hand, pressing the curve of her cheek into a soft, lustrous roundness.

'Silly!' exclaimed Beatrice. 'Pearls have to be drilled. How else could you wear them?' She snatched up a large tassel of white pearls, drilled and graded and bound with silver wire, and held it coquettishly at one ear. 'What do you think, Philip? Shall I ask Father to buy it for me?'

'You don't wear them like that.' Philip smiled indulgently, as she'd meant him to. 'That's how they're sold in Bombay – in those bunches. The Bombay pearl drillers are supposed to be the finest in the world.'

'But it's still a shame.' Letty gazed sadly at the shining strands. 'We're such perverse creatures, we human beings. As soon as we find something perfect, we have to spoil it for our own selfish pleasure.'

'But my dear Mrs Dunstan—' At the far end of the table, my father was moved to protest. 'It's only our need to live among beautiful things that lifts us out of savagery. The appreciation of form and elegance, that's all that raises us above the animals.'

'Well, I agree with Mrs Dunstan,' declared Philip suddenly. 'I think pearls are perfect as nature makes them. You might as well cut a rainbow into pieces and hang it round your neck.'

Letty's gaze warmed with gratitude. And Beatrice, who'd have snipped up a rainbow in an instant, if she could, scowled, but said nothing.

Hosanna had been working on verses describing Marco Polo's return to Venice from the land of Cathay and, on our final evening she stood before us, earnest in brown panne velvet, her open notebook balanced on one large palm and her free hand thrown out for dramatic effect. She had very large and expressive eyelids, ringed in the evenings with dusty kohl and, at the end of each verse, they rose up in mournful appeal like the lid of my father's roll-top desk.

> *Bearded, from the East came they*
> *Who had no need to ask their way*
> *Upon that dear, long dreamed-of day –*
> *Home, the wanderers!*

Out of Hosanna's direct view at the other end of the dinner table, Beatrice was grazing on a dish of grapes and trying playfully to pop one into Philip Kassel's mouth. Her lips glistened with grape juice and the half-glass of Madeira we'd each been allowed. She reached out lazily with her plump creamy arms, squashing her chiffon-covered breasts like a bolster on the damask tablecloth. Philip kept leaning back out of her reach, unwilling to make a fuss but reluctant to let Beatrice have her way.

> *Through the lanes at hasty pace,*
> *At last, to childhood's cherished place;*
> *'Sister – say you know my face!'*
> *Home, the wanderers!*

The poem was very long and, by the thirtieth verse, when the Polos were still trying to make themselves known to their family, my father's head was sunk on his chest in sleep and the rest of us were fidgeting wildly in our seats. Catching my attention, Beatrice rolled her eyes and then did the same to her father.

> *Bells rang out — the word was spread —*
> *'The Polos back! Not dead! Not dead!'*

At this crescendo Alfred Dunstan seized the opportunity to break into loud applause, pounding his stout hands with a noise like cannon fire. 'Splendid, Miss Greendew! You must give us the whole thing one day, when you've had time to finish it.'

'But it is finished. As good as.' Dismayed, Hosanna pressed the notebook to her bosom.

'It'll be none the worse for a polish, though, I'm sure.' The springmaker included us all in his breezy smile. 'Now, ladies, if you'll fetch your wraps, I think it's time for a trip on the water. I want to see if this Venice-by-moonlight business is all it's cracked up to be.'

It must have been the only escape he could think of. Romantic trips by gondola were hardly Alfred Dunstan's style.

Two gondolas waited at the water door of the hotel to carry us off on our moonlit tour. My father stepped aboard first — looking carefully over his shoulder to make sure he wasn't alone — but Hosanna Greendew was following so closely, so anxious to claim the seat beside him, that she collided with him amidships. The springmaker followed, dumping himself down heavily on one of the side seats, but Letty Dunstan had already stepped gracefully into the second boat, handed in by Max Kassel. Disconcerted, Alfred gazed round for his daughter. 'There's plenty of room in this one, Bea!' But Philip and I had followed Max and Letty and so Beatrice came with us too.

Before Alfred Dunstan could propose changing everyone round, the two boats set off into the night, carrying us along an inky gorge between high walls which compelled us to follow its sinuous path to the heart of the city. It was hard to recognize it as the same commonplace canal I'd looked down upon so often from above. Even the smell of night-time Venice was different; the dust had settled with the sinking sun and a cool dampness blended the ever-present, cloying scent of cooking oil with the green breath of the lagoon.

Earlier that evening, I'd looked out for the last time on the view from our drawing room balcony to the island church of San Giorgio Maggiore just as the low brick walls of the monastery were cast adrift, rose-gold in the last of the sun, on a sea of dark sapphire. This was the end, the last of the magic. I began to dread the feeling of emptiness that comes with the closing of theatre curtains, that dismaying return to the ordinary world, to the tawdry gilt of the circle stalls, the smell of crowded humanity and the realization that, after all, the play has been no more than an illusion of paint and canvas.

What of Venice and all the profoundly disturbing discoveries I'd made about myself? Was I really changed for ever, or had it simply been one more trick of the light?

Now, one behind the other, our gondolas slid with only the soft splash of oars between the houses and a kind of reverence kept us silent. From an open window nearby came the hesitant tinkling of a piano as someone fingered a tune. Couples, hidden in the shadows by the little bridges, murmured endearments as we glided below, yet we said nothing, afraid the walls might broadcast the echo of our thoughts.

At the other side of the gondola, Beatrice wriggled ecstatically and breathed excitement into the night air. 'Oh, it's all so romantic, don't you think?'

'Where are we?' whispered Letty suddenly. 'Does anyone know?'

'Somewhere near San Giovanni, I expect.' Yet even Max Kassel sounded unsure.

We emerged without warning on to the broad silver way of

65

the Grand Canal, a little beyond the Rialto Bridge and turned underneath it towards the Volta del Canal. Now the palaces fell back on either side like dancers at a ball: the rows of lighted windows were their collars of gold; from their knees, petticoats of shivering sequins trailed across the water towards us.

'Gosh – these insects!' Beatrice fanned herself with the end of her sash, a vigorous young animal scattering the ghosts of the night with one flick of her fringe. She leaned across to Philip, sitting by my shoulder. 'Do you know, I think I'd like to live in Venice for ever and ever. Then I could spend every night floating with a lover in my gondola, in one of these little cabin things with the curtains drawn. Wouldn't that be fun?'

'Not for me.' Philip's voice was firm. 'There are too many black shadows in this city for my liking. I prefer to see it in sunlight, from the deck of a *vaporetto*. Don't you find Venice rather sinister sometimes, Mrs Dunstan? All these gloomy side canals and mouldering buildings?'

'I thought I was imagining things.' I could hear the relief in Letty's voice. 'I kept remembering what Dr Ascham said about the old Venetians being forced to spy on one another and being dragged away at the least suspicion, to be blinded, or murdered, or shut up in a dungeon. Prison is such a terrible thing.'

Her voice had dropped to a murmur. Philip was gazing out over the bow of the gondola, his profile very clear against the moonlit water and as still as marble except for a faint tremor of his thick lashes. When he spoke, his voice was so low I realized his words were meant only for Letty; he'd forgotten me, just behind his shoulder.

'To be locked away from sight – it would be a kind of death.'

Letty's scarf rustled as she turned her head to whisper, 'I fear it will be.'

'To be crushed like a pearl until the spell's broken and the beauty's gone.'

'You understand.'

'What can I do? If there's anything—'

'Nothing at all.' I heard Letty sigh, as she'd sighed that evening on the balcony of our hotel. 'I never realized, you see. And now it's too late.' Impulsively, she stretched out a hand to touch Philip's. 'But you mustn't worry. We pearls can bear a great deal.'

Beatrice had been too far off to hear any of this, but she saw the gesture and leaned forward, pushing herself into the conversation. 'I really like pearls. Don't you like pearls, Chrissie?'

The two gondolas bumped alongside at that moment as we entered a lesser canal. Tactfully, Max Kassel picked up his cue, raising his voice. 'As a matter of fact, I was hoping to persuade all you ladies to accept a small memento of your visit. If you'll allow me, I'll have a pearl set in gold as a pendant for each of you and send them to England with my compliments.'

'But my dear fellow—' My father called across from the other boat to his saviour of the *traghetto* ferry. 'You must bring them to us yourself, if you insist on being so generous! Yes, you must, you and . . .' He groped for Philip's name. 'And . . . the boy. You must both come and stay with us at Windermere as soon as possible. My wife would be so interested to meet you, and my son Noël will be down from Oxford once his Finals are over. Do you know the English Lakes, by any chance?'

Before Max Kassel could answer, Alfred Dunstan butted in, 'And my house at Waterside should be finished by then. I'd very much like to have your opinion on it. Oh yes, definitely, you must come to the Lakes.'

Chapter Five

THE KASSELS had promised to come to the Lakes in the last week in June. By then, the Dunstans would have moved into their new mansion and it was the conjunction of those two events, I believe, that led to the springmaker's next Great Idea. It was born on the day following his return from Venice and excited him so much that he immediately rushed across the lane to Fellwood to share it with us.

It had been raining all day, typical Lakeland rain, short, soaking showers that pelted down without warning just as the sunshine seemed about to settle in for a while. Even so, I'd been out for a walk in Noël's old mackintosh with a hat crammed down over my eyes, simply for the sake of reassuring myself that my world had stayed as serene and countrified as I'd left it. I wandered down to the lakeside and stood sniffing the breeze, relishing the sharp note of green summer growth from the woodland on the opposite shore. And all the time, the rain dripped from the brim of my hat while from somewhere nearby came the familiar stuttering cry of a lamb parted from its mother.

It seemed incredible that I'd lived almost entirely without trees for a month; without trees, grass, reed-beds and scree, and dry sheep paths ridging the hillsides and waterfalls as sheer and straight as silver wire. So much of Venice had been covered in stone, its greenness confined to a few dusty trees and a creeper or two peeping sullenly over high walls. The memory of those dry alleys was so suffocating that I threw my head back to the rainy sky and filled my lungs almost to bursting. I shut my eyes and the cold drops drizzled through my lashes and over my cheeks, finding channels for themselves round my nostrils and lips. My hat fell off and I didn't care.

And yet it was, subtly, different from before. When had I ever abandoned myself to a rainy caress with such blind relish, such a greedy intensity of pleasure?

Mar examined me critically when I came in. 'I do believe you've grown up while you've been away. Or perhaps it's just that you're seventeen now and I hadn't noticed.'

In spite of the springmaker's assurances, Mar had been relieved to have us back. While we'd been away, life had gone on much as it usually did; but even Mar had begun to sense a growing unrest in the air, as if the world had become a simmering pot of grievances which kept boiling over into minor battles. The Army was being ordered into Ulster to prevent civil war; the Germans were launching warships as fast as they could; the Suffragettes had very nearly got into Buckingham Palace; now the miners and the railway workers had come out on strike. At such times, Mar's maternal instincts made her draw her family to her side like wayward chicks.

In contrast, across the lane in his rented house, newspaper reports of new German warships and Hungarian guns had simply made Alfred Dunstan rub his hands in pleasure. Busy shipyards needed springs and that meant good business for Dunstan's. A few small wars bubbling away could always bring a bright smile of satisfaction to the springmaker's face.

We'd come home to find the mansion at Waterside remarkably complete. It still squatted on its site like a gawky adolescent and its brickwork was as bright and raw as skin exposed too long to the sun, but the scaffolding had gone from its chimney pots and the house had a solid, permanent air at last. Down in the power house, mechanics were testing the engine which would drive the dynamos for the house's two hundred electric lights. The engine was large enough to pump well water to the upper floors, saw wood and run a buffing wheel for polishing knives; but its principal job was to transform the place by night into a constellation of specially imported American tungsten-argon lamps. The steamers on their way from Lakeside to Waterhead slowed down now as they passed. By day or night, 'Dunstan's Palace' had become one of the sights of the district.

It was almost ready to move into. Crates of furniture were arriving so constantly at Windermere station that the road to Waterside had become a continuous procession of carter's wagons. Beatrice was desperate for her red silk chairs and all the other things she and her father had bought in Venice, including a huge electric chandelier made specially in a workshop on Murano, consisting of three dozen orange and blue glass lilies on arching stems of gilded crystal. The springmaker hadn't forgotten his frescoes. On the day of his return, a letter was sent off to Hosanna Greendew's brother Jeremy, to ask if he'd spend his summer on the project.

The springmaker's Great Idea followed all this as naturally as day follows night. How better to show off his fine new mansion than with a Grand Venetian Ball?

Mar was examining a spray of *Hieracium Tridentatum* she'd discovered the day before by a stream near the village, and she was irritated by the interruption. Hawkweed had never been found near Windermere before and the possibility that it might be subtly different from Buttermere hawkweed or Coniston hawkweed had kept her comparing and sketching all morning.

The springmaker stared in disbelief at the plain green stems and then gave up any attempt to understand. 'About the ball, Mrs Ascham. I thought Dr Ascham's brother, the Marquess of Hornby, might care to come.'

Mar withdrew her eye from the microscope with a sigh. 'But there's no one at Wickham just now, Mr Dunstan. At this time of year, all the fashionable set are in London for the season. *Country* balls are always held in the winter.'

'Oh, are they?' With an effort, the springmaker diverted a scowl into one of his short, gnashing smiles. 'Well, I wouldn't know about that. All I know is, my house is finished at last and I intend to celebrate the fact. If fashionable people can't be bothered to come, then I'll just have to find some others that can. If I want a ball, Mrs Ascham, then I shall *have* a ball. It'll be the best ball ever seen in these parts and devil take the London season!' He brooded about this for a moment and then added, 'We'll wait until that man Kassel and his son are here.'

'It was almost,' Mar reported later, 'as if the whole thing was being arranged for the Kassels' benefit. He swears he's going to hold a ball for two hundred and fifty guests at the end of June – and all to impress a couple of people he met in Venice! The man must be mad.'

'He doesn't like to lose an argument, that's certain.'

The last of the plasterers, paper hangers, cabinet makers, glaziers, plumbers, upholsterers and carpet layers had vanished from Waterside by the last week of June, leaving the house startlingly empty and silent. I'd become so used to the sounds of sawing and hammering, to jaunty whistling or the cheerful exchange of insults between the tradesmen, that the house felt deserted, as if its rightful inhabitants had fled. In their place came an army of soft-footed servants sent by an agency, who did their work almost invisibly and kept their laughter behind a green baize door.

The Dunstans moved in – putting half a mile between our homes instead of just the lane where Beatrice had accused me of stealing her dog. I imagined I'd see less of Beatrice now, since our lessons with Hosanna Greendew had finished for the summer, but Mar and Par were invited to Waterside once or twice for dinner, so that I caught brief glimpses of the springmaker and his wife when the invitation was returned at Fellwood.

The change in Letty Dunstan since our return from Venice was alarming. She no longer skipped along on her little feet, but trailed beside her husband with a leaden step. Even illuminated by lamplight and her white silk gown, the flesh of her face seemed as dull as clay, and her eyes moved restlessly from side to side unless someone spoke to her directly. I could hardly believe the transformation. Only the previous summer, when the Dunstans had first come to the Lakes to oversee the building of their new house, Letty had clung to her husband's arm, blithely girlish and accustomed to being guided in all things. Now, when she walked by Alfred's side, her hunched shoulders and close-held limbs seemed to hoard the essence of herself obsessively, keeping it away from him.

I wondered if something awful had happened between them, or if the change was only in Letty. I'd never forgotten the desperate, bewildered hunger I'd seen on her face that evening in Venice on our hotel balcony, when she'd confessed to having been no more than half-alive until that moment. I remembered Philip's whispered remark, that night in our gondola, *To be locked away from sight – it would be a kind of death.* Letty had answered, *I fear it will be.* Was that what she'd seen, in all the passion of her newly aroused senses, a living entombment in Alfred Dunstan's country mansion? Had Letty wakened from a lifetime's dream, only to find herself married to a gaoler? Appalled, I followed every movement for clues and certainly, her avoidance of the springmaker's touch was total and meticulous. The instant Alfred moved near, she slipped back a pace like the repelling pole of a magnet.

Lingering in the shadows at the top of the stairs, I watched the elaborate minuet in the hall below as Letty subtly manoeuvred first Mar and then Par into place between herself and her husband, always finishing – as if entirely by coincidence – just out of the springmaker's reach whenever he tried to take her arm with one of his blunt pink hands. With my bird's-eye view I could see how the trick was done, but I wanted to know *why* – why this sudden, lonely revulsion at the heart of a marriage? And why, in Venice, had only Letty and I seemed to sense the city's sly seduction? In spite of the fact that she was Beatrice's mother, I kept thinking of her as someone of my own age, trapped by mistake among our dry, ancient parents. But, of course, Letty Dunstan was a married woman of thirty-eight while I was only a girl of seventeen and there was no longer a foreign city to bring us together.

Beatrice didn't seem to have noticed the change in her mother. Her bedroom was on the second floor of the new house, almost three minutes' walk from the front door, but once you were there, the view of the lake from her windows was striking. Without Philip Kassel to squabble over, we seemed to have become friends again. Beatrice could never have borne moving into her splendid new quarters with no one to admire them.

It was from Beatrice's window, idly staring out a couple of days before the ball, that I caught sight of a movement down by the jetty which roused my curiosity. As I watched, a tall male figure emerged from the alders by the lake, glanced round, then vanished suddenly down the overgrown path behind the old boathouse. It was all over so quickly that for a moment I thought I was imagining things. And yet, on reflection, the man's height and the quick, decisive turn of his head had plucked a familiar string in my heart.

It was summer, and the academic term was almost at an end. Noël had come down from Oxford, his Finals triumphantly over and had already hurled himself – to my disappointment – into archaeological investigations all over the Lake District. But the figure by the boathouse had been far too co-ordinated for my ungainly brother. With an unexpected lightness of the soul, I realized whom I'd seen.

I turned round from the window. 'Is Jack home from school already, Bea?'

Beatrice was experimenting with hairstyles for the ball and her mouth was so full of pins that all she could do was mumble. 'Came back last night – bag and baggage. He's finished with school now. Couldn't wait to get clear.'

She separated one lustrous strand from the remainder and skewered it firmly into a curl. 'He's in one of his moods, though.' She made a face in her mirror and took the rest of the pins from her mouth. 'He keeps going off on his own. I've hardly seen him at all today.'

'What's the matter? Doesn't he like the new house?'

'Doesn't seem to.' Beatrice shrugged her plump shoulders. 'But if you ask me, the real problem's all this Oxford business. Father started on him as soon as he got back, telling him all about Philip Kassel and how Philip was so quiet and serious and determined to make *his* father proud. He said the Kassels would be arriving tomorrow and then Jack would see how a young gentleman ought to behave and, please God, it would make him buck up his ideas before Father had to sort them out for him.'

She picked up her hairbrush again. 'Not that it'll make a blind bit of difference, except that Jack will hate Philip on sight, worse luck.' She considered herself in the mirror. 'I do wish the Kassels were staying here, at Waterside, instead of at Fellwood with you. It isn't as if we don't have room for them. And then—'

She was smiling, but her lips were curled and her large, lustrous eyes were half-veiled by their heavy lids in the old acquisitive look I'd got to know so well.

'And then I'd have Philip all to myself, wouldn't I?'

The Kassels were just as I remembered them. Powley fetched them from the railway station in the trap, and as they rounded the rhododendron bushes at the top of our drive and I caught sight of Philip's black, breeze-ruffled hair falling over his brow, and his father next to him, dignified in stiff collar, pearl tie-pin and black buttoned spats, the instinctive protectiveness I'd felt for Philip

wrapped itself round them both. Father and son, they were like
vagabond birds following a mysterious course of their own, driven
to our door by some whim of the weather but proud and
unsettled, as if they'd never quite acquired the habit of
domesticity.

They arrived on the day before the ball and when we paid a
courtesy call on the Dunstans we found Waterside restored to the
whirlwind of activity that had surrounded its building. At the
bottom of the steps, potted bay trees waited on the gravel to be
drawn up in ranks. On the terraced lawn beyond, a line of men
carrying plaster pillars and arches were marching, as single-minded
as ants, towards a great white marquee. I'd never seen such a
monster canvas. It lay between the house and the lake like a
gigantic, wheezing grub, its mottled sections bellying and empty-
ing in the breeze. Inside, Beatrice had told me without a
moment's self-doubt, they were reconstructing Venice's Piazzetta.
And why not? The Dunstans had already built a mansion; and
what was the city of Venice, after all, but a pillar and an archway
and a papier mâché lion or two?

The house itself was full of frenzied, scurrying people, some
with starched tablecloths under their arms, and others down on
their knees lovingly brushing the stair carpet.

'Which way to the china pantry, Miss?'

'I can't tell you, I'm afraid. I'm only a visitor here myself.'

Alfred Dunstan was standing on a tiger-skin rug in the middle
of his living hall, dwarfed by the towering marble fireplace behind
him. He greeted us with the brisk enthusiasm of a general in the
field. 'Look at the caterers' people, running about like headless
chickens! They wouldn't know how to wipe their own noses if I
weren't here to tell them. There's no chalk in the billiard room,'
he barked to the room at large.

One of the temporary waiters hurried past, his arms full of
plates.

'Did you hear what I said? There's no chalk in the billiard
room.'

'No sir. No chalk.' The man ran on his way, hugging his plates.

'Dammit, there's NO CHALK! Doesn't anybody listen to a word I say?' He made an explosive sound of contempt and lunged for the handle of his internal telephone system. 'Woodcock!' he roared into the mouthpiece. 'Dammit, where is the man when I need him?'

Somewhere in the house, no doubt, the Dunstan's recently appointed butler was going about his business. The springmaker could make bells shrill in pantries and kitchens, but the house was either too large or too full of flower arrangers, hired pâtissiers, fishmongers' delivery boys or lost violinists. To the springmaker's fury, it seemed to be nobody's job to answer.

Max Kassel was staring round, as amazed by it all as the springmaker could wish. 'You don't mean to say that balustrade is actually plated in silver?' He pointed to the glittering cascade of scrollwork and interlaced flowers that flanked the main staircase.

'As it happens, yes.' His billiard chalk temporarily forgotten, the springmaker smirked airily. 'It's the only staircase like it in the country – apart from one in Scotland,' he conceded. 'But mine's longer.'

'And the statues . . .?'

In truth, there were too many marble statues – dying slave-boys and nymphs and Spirits of Spring – all lined up as if they were queuing for an omnibus, headed by a stuffed bear rearing up to thrash its front paws in the air.

'Surprised? I should think you are.' The springmaker nodded in satisfaction. 'Venice has no monopoly of culture, my friend. That's something for you to remember in future.'

He led us out of the hall and we found Letty sitting on a drawing room sofa, a still, lonely figure. She rose up as we entered, composing her face into a formal smile of welcome which became dazed, like a sleepwalker's smile, when she saw that the Kassels were with us. Beatrice bounced in and hissed in my ear, 'I wonder if Mr Kassel has brought the Medici Pearls with him.'

'I shouldn't imagine so. They'll be locked up in a safe somewhere.'

'Oh.' She pouted. 'I thought he might let me wear them for the ball.'

'The Queen's necklace? Of course not.'

'Why not?' Beatrice's whisper was savage. 'The pearls would look just as handsome on me – better, probably. There's no point in having nice things when you're old.'

With some ceremony, Max Kassel presented us all with the pearl pendants he'd had made. Beatrice opened her little leather box and peered inside. For a ghastly moment I thought she was going to say 'How small!', but her eye met Philip's and she stopped herself in time. 'How lovely!' she said instead, but in such a flat voice that I thanked the Kassels several times over to make up for it.

The pendants were very pretty, each one a single pearl trapped in a web of gold.

'I chose the design myself,' Philip told Letty.

She fixed him with eyes as full of wonder as a child's. 'You couldn't have chosen anything better.'

'Dorothy Cole tells me her butcher's been invited to the ball.' Mar pulled her wrap closer against the imagined perils of the night air.

We were dressed to the nines, waiting in the hall at Fellwood for Powley to bring round the old landau to take us to the ball. Since there were six of us, Noël and I would follow in the trap, driven by young Powley, George's son. (I'd rather hoped to arrive with Philip instead, if only to annoy Beatrice.)

'Dorothy couldn't make up her mind whether to come or not. It's only a year since Edward died, but she'd like to find a wife for Christopher, now he's taken over the practice.'

A faint frown ruffled my mother's brow. Until Dr Cole's death the previous year, he and his wife had played bridge with my parents at least once a week. The only way I could tell if he'd called professionally was when he smelled strongly of ether. Mrs Cole had as keen an instinct for class distinctions as Aunt Marchioness and it had shocked her to think that the Windermere butcher might be tempted to ask her to dance.

Noël didn't like Mrs Cole. 'At least she'll be all right for sausages.'

Down on the dusky Waterside lawn, the marquee was now a giant firefly against the steel of the lake and the bay trees in their pots had been lined up as a black guard of honour along the terrace. The orchestra was whirling through a light opera overture as we went inside and its gaiety filled me with a wave of sudden, reckless excitement. Not being 'out', I was still only 'Noël's little sister', dependent for dance invitations on Uncle Hereward and Aunt Marchioness at Wickham, whose children were far older than me. This invitation had specifically said *and Miss Ascham*. Better still, Philip Kassel had waited at the bottom of the steps to offer me his arm and even if I couldn't quite bring myself to be in love with him, he was definitely the handsomest man in Windermere at that moment.

The Dunstans were receiving their guests at the door of the hall, the springmaker with beaming relish and Letty with the same sweet, absent smile I'd seen that morning. Alfred Dunstan's hair gleamed with well-being and his cheeks shone as if they'd been polished. 'Chrissie, my dear, so elegant tonight! Bea has been looking out for you all evening. My dear Kassel, welcome again.'

Since that morning, Venice had flowed into the house. At the foot of the great silver staircase, a rowing boat had been transformed into a cardboard gondola and filled with flowers. Bunches of striped mooring poles sprouted in corners, wound with coloured ribbon, and all the waiters and the caterers' men were dressed as gondoliers in broad-brimmed hats and white shirts.

And yet, if only because of the size of the house, the ball was in danger of being what Aunt Marchioness would have described as 'thin'. Apart from us, the Dunstans hadn't really made any friends, Alfred because he 'left all that sort of thing to Letty' and Letty because she didn't seem to know where to begin. In his determination to fill his house the springmaker had simply invited everyone — as Mrs Cole had discovered. Even so, there was a limit to the number of men in the neighbourhood capable of mustering white tie and tails and women in possession of satin or lace. Yet since everyone wanted to see the inside of the new mansion, they'd borrowed or sewed whatever they could. The first man I saw in the hall was Stringer Hesketh, the foreman of the gunpowder mill, with his wife and five blonde daughters, who confessed to having stitched frantically for a fortnight. By the door, the proprietor of the Coniston mail coach was downing a glass of champagne, the delicate goblet like a thimble in his enormous calloused fist.

I remembered to wave to Ida Dunstan, two floors above us, craning over the balustrade with her mother's maid at her side. Then I tugged at Noël's sleeve.

'Look! There's Hosanna Greendew! Good heavens, whatever's she wearing?'

Noël inspected Hosanna critically. 'It's either Hosanna or Boadicea, I'm not sure which.'

Beatrice was wandering round the hall, splendid in tulle and Venetian lace. As soon as she spotted our party, she rushed over with a squeal.

'Mr Kassel — and Philip, *dear.*'

Somehow, as she chatted, Beatrice's arm became linked with Philip's and she contrived to give him a quarter-turn so that he faced away from the rest of us.

'Have you seen the colonnade of flowers in the drawing

room, Philip? Oh, but you must! It's quite extraordinary. Imagine, absolute *fields* of blooms, cut just for our ball tonight. *Do* come and see it.'

It was all done so smoothly that Beatrice was actually dragging her captive away by the time I realized what she was up to. I was so indignant I might even have run after them, except that Christopher Cole asked me to dance at that moment and I lost sight of them both behind the decorations.

It was a habit with the Dunstans, to get what they wanted. I saw it at work again two hours later, when Beatrice's father cornered Max Kassel in the marquee. We were choosing ices at the time from the vast buffet set out under the yellow glare of the electric chandeliers.

'Well, Kassel, what do you think of my country retreat?' The springmaker made a great show of inspecting a cup of sorbet, but the back of his neck was pink-hot with glee. 'It's very comfortable, of course, but it's still a *family* house, do you see?' His cheeks were as round and cheery as apples, but his smile was relentless. 'It isn't a museum, nor yet an art gallery, as you feared. It's just a happy home for my wife and children and for all the Dunstans who'll follow us. Bricks and mortar, my dear Kassel, as I told you in Venice.'

'Oh, certainly, you've every right to be proud of it.' Max Kassel raised his glass in elegant surrender. 'I wish you and Mrs Dunstan and your family the best of good fortune and happiness in your new home.'

Yet after the springmaker had gone on his way, Max Kassel's face assumed a thoughtful expression. 'I'm pleased to see our friend looking so happy.'

'You are?' My father peered in the direction his host had taken.

'Oh, indeed. Perhaps, after all, it isn't true what they're saying in London: that Alfred Dunstan has spent more than he should have on this house of his. Even the richest men have limits.'

My ears were burning. I buried my nose in my sorbet and shamelessly eavesdropped.

Par was struggling with the idea of Alfred Dunstan as a pauper. 'Are you saying he's run up debts he can't pay?'

'The banks are pressing him, I believe. His creditors won't wait for ever. The word in London is that only a major war can save him.'

'But that's jealousy, surely!'

'You'd think so, to look at him, wouldn't you? Not a care in the world.'

At that point I was carried off to the dance floor by one of the Childewood boys from Holt Hall and I didn't hear any more. Over my partner's shoulder, I looked round for Philip – Beatrice had only allowed me one short dance with him all evening and I'd have liked another – but more particularly, I was searching for Jack. I'd been counting on his being there; yet it was well after midnight already, almost time for the 'musical entertainment' planned as the final highlight of the evening, and there was still no sign of him.

Letty Dunstan waltzed past with Mr Childewood himself. Her face was flushed and she was smiling – so much like the old Letty that I was quite cheered. Francis Childewood obviously found her enchanting. As they danced, his head was bent constantly towards hers with an expression of delighted amusement. The springmaker was standing on the second step of the staircase, clearly displeased with what he could see from this vantage point. His smile was still in place, but his eyes were like shiny pebbles as they followed his wife's progress round the dance floor.

At his signal, the orchestra brought the waltz to an end, laid down their instruments, and went off to snatch a little supper. The 'gondoliers' began to set out chairs in rows, while in a cleared space before the fireplace, a large man with oiled hair and a princely manner began a conference with his accompanist at the piano. Alfred Dunstan clapped his hands to make sure of everyone's attention.

'And now, dear friends, if you'd like to take your seats in the next five minutes or so . . . As a *very* great favour to me, Signor Enrico Arnoldi has agreed to desert the stage of Covent Garden Opera House for one evening, to entertain us with a selection of arias by Mozart and—' He glanced down at the scrap of paper in his hand. 'And Verdi. As soon as you hear him, I'm sure you'll think, as I do, that Covent Garden's loss is our gain.' He bowed towards the brilliantined gentleman, who ceremoniously bowed back.

There was a general buzz of activity as people began to find themselves seats. I saw Christopher Cole being shepherded towards a chair by his mother and his sister Irene.

'But I don't like opera, Mother. You know that perfectly well.'

'Perfectly well!' echoed Mrs Cole. 'That may be, but you'll still sit and listen to it like everyone else.'

'Suppose I tell them I've been called away to an emergency.'

'An emergency! I should think not.'

Four gilt chairs had been set out for the Dunstans on the first landing of the staircase, as if for a royal party. On the floor of the hall, I saw Francis Childewood and his wife edging along a line of chairs. Beatrice hurried towards us.

'You haven't seen Jack, have you? Father'll be livid if he doesn't turn up for Arnoldi. He reckons Jack's spent the whole night in the billiard room.' Beatrice grimaced and bustled off to join her mother.

Letty's face was still bright with the elation of dancing and her new-found excitement as she made her way through the crowd towards her husband. She was wearing one of the fashionable brocade gowns with a light chiffon bodice that seemed almost to fold diaphanous wings over her naked shoulders. The springmaker stepped down into the hall as she approached, stared at her for a moment, and then, in a calculated gesture, stretched out one of his solid red hands to clasp her shoulder and the back of her bare neck.

'Letty, *my dear.*'

His coarse, blunt fingers lay on her white flesh like horrible worms, declaring to the room at large that this golden woman who'd presumed to enjoy herself in another man's arms was *his* – Alfred Dunstan's – and everyone should take note of the fact.

'Alfred, please, you're hurting me.' Letty twisted her head; her husband's hand was forcing it forward, turning her eyes to the floor. A crimson flush had begun to spread out from the bulbous ends of his fingers.

'Now, Letty. Let's not make a fuss. You can't spend the whole night dancing, you know.'

It was all perfectly public. The ball-goers standing nearest to the stairs glanced at one another unhappily, but didn't dare to interfere.

Then all of a sudden, a tall figure in evening dress materialized from the crowd – Jack – pale and intent. 'Leave her alone. Take your hand away.'

Alfred Dunstan thrust out his chin and stared at his son with contempt. 'Don't speak to me in that insolent manner, you young pup. How dare you! While you're under my roof, you'll oblige me by minding your own business.'

His hand tightened, forcing a soft cry of pain from his wife.

'Let go of her, I said! Leave my mother alone, or so help me . . .'

All over the room, the expectant chatter had died away to silence. Along the rows of seats, heads swung round, trying to identify the site of the drama.

'Get away, Jack!' I heard Beatrice's voice. 'You're showing us all up.'

Instead, Jack lunged forward, seized his mother by the arm and forcibly tore his father's fingers away. 'I said leave her alone, damn you!'

The force of the movement threw Letty behind him. In that instant, father and son faced one another across the space of two feet. I saw Alfred Dunstan swing back his arm with the full power of his thick shoulders and slam it forward again. I called out 'Jack!' only to hear, in the same second, the sharp, dreadful *crack* of a fist meeting flesh and bone. The blow spun Jack round so that his back was towards me. I saw him lift a hand to his face and then turn away, to be swallowed up in the crowd.

Beatrice's fists flew to her cheeks. At the foot of the stairs, Letty gave a wild shriek, swayed and reached out, suddenly stricken, for support. Philip Kassel was there to catch her as she fell; he must have been making his way through the throng as the drama unfolded.

'Stay back. Give her air.' Christopher Cole cleared a path for himself along a row of seats and hurried to where Letty was surrounded by a ring of downturned heads. As suddenly as it had fallen silent, the hall began to rustle with the sound of whispering as those who'd had the best view passed the news to the rest.

My father had missed all the excitement. 'Is this tenor fellow going to sing, or not?'

'Shh, my dear.' My mother hated 'scenes' of any kind. 'Poor Letty . . . Her first ball in the new house and this is what happens . . . Look – they're helping her upstairs now. There's Christopher Cole and Beatrice and Philip.' She fixed me with a glare. 'And where do you think you're going?'

'I thought, perhaps . . .'

'Just stay where you are. The polite thing is to pretend nothing's wrong.'

I was concerned about Letty, but I was just as concerned about Jack, who'd vanished as abruptly as he'd appeared. The sound of that sickening blow was fresh in my mind. I didn't like to think of Jack all alone somewhere, with no one to tell him how brave he'd been.

The little procession escorting Letty Dunstan disappeared upstairs and for a few moments the audience and the oiled maestro stared at one another uneasily. Then a familiar sturdy figure in evening dress appeared near the fireplace, tramped across to the piano, held a brief consultation with Signor Arnoldi, and turned back to face the company, adjusting his shirt cuff. The spring-maker's smile was firmly back in place.

'Ladies and gentlemen.' He waited for silence. 'Ladies and gentlemen, I must apologize for this little upset. The fact of it is, my wife suddenly felt a trifle faint. It's a very warm night, I'm sure you'll agree. But Mrs Dunstan is most anxious not to spoil your enjoyment of the evening and so we're going to carry on, just as before.'

In the front row, somebody coughed rather obviously. There was an outbreak of loud whispering and then three or four rows back, Stringer Hesketh, the gunpowder maker, got to his feet. He ran a finger round the inside of his stiff collar.

'If you don't mind, Mr Dunstan, I think it's best if we go now.' He faced his host squarely over the rows of heads. 'I'd appreciate it if you'd convey our apologies to Mrs Dunstan.' Mrs Hesketh and her daughters were already edging out of the row of seats and other people had begun to stand up. There was a scraping of chairs and a rumble of general agreement.

'Best if we go – aye.' The proprietor of the Coniston mail coach hauled himself to his feet and stared round for an exit.

They'd no intention of 'carrying on' as before. Stringer Hesketh, the butcher, and the mail coach man would have been ashamed to sit where they were politely pretending nothing had happened. They might not know anything about the London season, but they knew what had taken place in front of them that night and they didn't hold with it. In a few moments Alfred Dunstan was lost to view behind a wall of shuffling people escaping from their seats as rapidly as long gowns and boiled shirts would allow.

I heard his upraised voice, 'But I'm sure, if Signor Arnoldi doesn't mind . . .'

Servants ran about everywhere with coats and wraps and shouted on the steps for carriages. The Childewoods were already in the hall doorway, murmuring a perfunctory goodnight to their host, who'd darted round the flank of the crowd to bid his guests some semblance of a farewell. Philip Kassel ran down the stairs to join us.

'Mrs Dunstan's feeling better. Just shocked and sore where that brute was holding her.'

Par peered through his spectacles. 'Is it over already?'

Mar took his arm. 'All over, dear, I think.'

The springmaker nodded uncertainly to us as we passed and for the first time, I noticed that the knuckles of his right hand had been bound up in a handkerchief which, even at a distance, showed a stain of bright red.

Chapter Six

THE DAY AFTER the ball, Mar sent Powley to Waterside with some early strawberries and a note for Letty enquiring after her health. She received a brief reply from Mr Dunstan thanking her for her concern for his wife, but indicating that no help was required.

'Or wanted,' added Mar, folding his letter again and pinching the crease. 'Not that I'm surprised. Poor Letty. She's so alone there.'

Philip had been standing with his hands in his pockets. Now he took a decisive breath. 'Perhaps we should call.'

'Oh, yes . . .' I was more worried than ever about Jack, shut up in that house with his father.

'No,' said Mar. 'Not yet, anyway. We might easily do more harm than good.'

Yet her fingers folded the springmaker's letter once more and a third time and a fourth, absently making it smaller and smaller. My father, who spent every waking hour among Machiavelli and the Borgias, refused to be surprised by anything that went on in other people's families. But Mar had wished Waterside well for Letty's sake; now a faint frown of disapproval began to appear on her face whenever Alfred Dunstan's name was mentioned.

If Waterside had drawn in upon itself, our house at Fellwood was positively under siege. It began on the morning after the ball, when goodness knows how many girls arrived at our door with notes from their mothers. They were followed by Irene Cole bringing an ice cream mould Mar had once admired, then one of the Hesketh girls looking for a recipe for witch hazel tonic and, later on, the Curate's unmarried sister bearing a pair of kid gloves she thought Mar might possibly have left in church on Sunday.

'I'm almost sure they were in your pew.' But she blushed as she said it and suddenly discovered a stray lash in her eye. 'At least, I *think* I'm sure.'

'This is what comes,' complained Mar, 'of having a young Adonis in the house. Even the Curate's sister has taken to fibbing. Imagine having that on your conscience.'

But neither the Curate's sister's fibs nor Irene Cole's ice cream mould made any impression on Philip – it wasn't the kind of thing he noticed. He was pleasant to them all, but cool and abstracted, as if he had something more important on his mind. I'd seen him after the first few words had been exchanged, with his eyes fixed determinedly on some distant object, quite silent while his visitor tried desperately to make conversation, blushing and chattering, gossiping about the previous night's excitement.

Philip's father, meanwhile, was proving a big success with my parents. Already, Mar had made up her mind to study the natural history of the pearl in all its shapes and sizes, while Par and Max Kassel would sit for hours, discussing the massive jewels given by kings to their wives and mistresses, later to be sold and broken up, bartered or stolen a thousand times in their long history.

'Do you know what footmen used to do, a hundred years ago, after a ball like last night's?' Max Kassel regarded me quizzically, his winged eyebrows soaring. 'They'd have hunted out all the pearls that had dropped from the ladies' gowns, and stamped on them. The ones that didn't break were real and could be picked up and sold.'

I remembered Beatrice and her preoccupation with the Medici necklace. 'Have you found any pearls yet to match those enormous ones you showed us in Venice?'

'The Medici Pearls? No, unfortunately, not yet. I heard of one owned by a dealer in London, but when I compared it with the others, the colour was wrong. And now that the Austrian Archduke's been shot in Sarajevo, I'm afraid borders are going to be closed all over Europe and it's going to be impossible to travel.'

His genial expression had faded to one of concern and I realized how isolated a life we led in our corner of England, cut off among our mountains and our lakes.

'I met a Russian Duke in the Venice Accademia one day. He called the Austrians bandits and swore they'd be cut down like dogs, with their friends the Germans, too, if they tried to steal something for themselves from the Balkan war.' His eyes strayed to where Philip was politely listening to Irene Cole and his troubled expression deepened.

'You don't think there could be a big war in Europe, do you, Mr Kassel?'

He gazed at me sadly. 'I hope not, my dear. But Alfred Dunstan's counting on it.'

Philip was determined to go back to Waterside. 'We haven't heard a word from there since the ball. Mrs Dunstan might really be ill.'

I was amused by his little deceit. I'd never thought Philip capable of deviousness. 'You're sure it's *Mrs* Dunstan's health that concerns you? You aren't hoping to see Beatrice, I suppose, on this little jaunt of ours?'

By now I felt sure enough of him to tease and, besides, I was surprised and slightly put out to find he'd fallen so quickly for Beatrice's wiles. I'd rather hoped he'd have been clever enough to see through her. He stared at me, his black eyes very wide and opened his mouth as if to object. Then, he thought better of it and his lips curved into a wry, apologetic smile. (How I envied Bea that mouth!)

'You've found me out.'

'Of course! You can't hide anything in this house. I thought you'd have discovered that by now.'

In fact, I was madly anxious to visit Waterside on my own account, even if it did mean watching Bea make sickening sheep's eyes at Philip, but my mother was adamant. 'Not yet, my dears. All in good time.'

In the end, it was Beatrice who called on us, terrified, I suppose, of losing Philip to me, or to one of the other girls who revolved round him like planets round a sun.

'Father's gone back to "weekly boarding",' she announced. 'The factories are going like billy-oh, so from now on he'll be off to Manchester every Monday morning and only here at weekends.'

At once, the hollows of Philip's face were lit with bright expectancy. 'Does that mean we can come and see you at Waterside?'

'Of course.' Beatrice fluttered her eyelashes. 'Come whenever you like.'

We went back to Waterside the following day and since Philip was with me, I was allowed to drive our little spindle-back gig all by myself – much to George Powley's disapproval. He held the mare's head as I climbed into the high seat, but his beard stuck out in a scowling tuft and his woolly brows were pressed down so far that his eyes glittered through them like weasels in a hedgerow.

'Canny wi' the beast, now. It's a warmish day.'

'Don't worry, I'll take care. We aren't in any hurry.'

We genuinely weren't in a hurry and yet, somehow, in another way, we were; subtly aware of running out of time in spite of being young and having our whole lives ahead of us. I couldn't forget what Max Kassel had said about a possible war in Europe; I didn't really believe it, but I couldn't forget it either. The mare ambled along through the fragrant shade and molten specks of sunlight dripped through a net of oak and chestnut leaves to splash on our heads, yet the peace and contentment had gone.

Beatrice was in the conservatory with Ida and her mother, who was propped up on cushions on a long cane settee. Ida was curled up at Letty's feet, immersed in *The Railway Children*, while Beatrice, in a chair nearby with Topsy dozing on her lap, idly turned the pages of a fashion journal.

'Oh, look! It's Chrissie and Philip.'

The three female faces turned towards us, a trio of Dunstan women sitting close together in that large space as if they found comfort and security in one another's company. Then Beatrice put on her coquettish 'social' expression for Philip's benefit and the unity of the group was broken.

'I hope we aren't disturbing you . . .'

'Not a bit – it's a delightful surprise. We haven't seen a soul for days.' I was disconcerted by Letty's wide, tremulous gaze and the transparent hand she laid, almost weightless, on my arm. 'Sit here, by me, please.'

But Philip had already taken the place between Beatrice and her mother and so I sat down next to Ida. An awkwardness remained and we seemed fated to chat about trifles: about the warmth of the summer and how long it might last; about a yacht that had capsized during a race on the lake; and why there was no railway tunnel at the bottom of Ida's garden where she could have heroic adventures like the children in her book. And all the time, what I really wanted to know was what had become of Jack. No one had even mentioned his name. All at once, my patience ran out, though even then I tried to be diplomatic.

'How is Mr Dunstan?' I enquired as if the idea had just occurred to me. 'And how is Jack?'

'My husband's in Manchester.' Letty glanced at me almost

gratefully and pronounced the words with care, as if she wished us to be absolutely sure of the springmaker's absence. 'He won't be back until Friday evening.'

'And as for Jack . . .' Beatrice sniffed her contempt. 'Nobody knows where he gets to these days. Not that anyone cares. The less we see of him the better.'

'Bea!' Letty looked reproachfully at her older daughter. 'You know that isn't true.'

'Well, *I* certainly don't care where he hides all day. He can stay there for as long as he likes, as far as I'm concerned.' Beatrice tossed her head. 'He deliberately set out to make Father angry in order to spoil the ball. I'd been looking forward to it for ages and he knew that perfectly well. So I don't care if he absolutely hates Oxford. The sooner he goes there, the better it'll be for all of us.'

At Letty's feet, Ida scowled at her sister. 'At least you *went* to the ball, which is more than I did. You all said I was too young to stay up, which is nonsense, because I was still awake when the ball finished and everybody went away. You just wanted to keep your precious Philip all for yourself, because you're so selfish.' Ida began to snivel and knuckle her eyes and Letty reached out wearily towards her.

'Now look what you've done, Bea. That was thoughtless.'

Beatrice raised her chin combatively. 'She's just being silly.' She leaned forward. 'You're a silly little baby, Ida. And Philip thinks so too – don't you, Philip?'

This produced real howls from Ida, who clung round her mother's frail neck, her face buried in her shoulder.

Vainly, Letty patted her younger daughter's back. 'If you're going to be like that, Bea dear, you'd better go out into the garden and leave us in peace. Go on, all of you. Ida's really very upset.'

'Oh, this is too pathetic.' Beatrice bounced to her feet. 'Come on, Philip, come and see the summer house Father's built in the old rose garden. It's got the sweetest little leaded windows – you'll adore it.'

Philip stood up, but lingered uncomfortably, glancing from Beatrice to her mother.

'I really am sorry, Mrs Dunstan . . . we seem to have spoiled your afternoon.' He ran a hand through his black curls, reluctant to leave and, certainly, Letty and Ida made a touching scene, both pale-faced, with Ida's dark hair cascading over her mother's shoulder. 'Are you sure there's nothing I can get you?'

Letty's golden eyes lifted to his, flecked with trembling light. 'We shall be perfectly all right, Ida and I. Don't worry, Philip dear.' She disentangled a hand from under the midnight web of Ida's hair and held it out to him. 'Come back and see me before you leave. In fact . . .' For an instant she hesitated, then added in that same tone of eerie clarity, 'I hope you and Chrissie will come here often while the summer lasts. Waterside needs young people to fill it with sunshine. Will you promise to come and keep the summer alive for me?'

'Of course.' Philip had agreed to it almost before she'd finished speaking. 'We'll come as often as you like. That's true, isn't it, Chrissie?'

'Oh, certainly.' Yet I felt a rising jealousy. What was it about Beatrice that fascinated Philip so much?

'Come on, Philip!' Beatrice had been waiting in the glazed doorway; she stepped back into the room to catch his arm. 'The summer house – remember?'

I noticed she didn't say 'Come on, Chrissie.' Well, if that was how the land lay, I certainly wasn't going to play gooseberry in the *adorable* new summer house. I had a place of my own to visit – a dear, timeless place where I'd always found space to think alone and where there was no echo of the clamorous, bad-tempered scramble of the world.

The boathouse and jetty at Waterside had been built in the middle of the previous century, in a cove on the lake shore where fishermen had once hauled their nets in the dawn. If you knew where to look, you could still see the ancient, blackened hearth-stones where they'd made a fire to keep themselves warm and to boil a kettle for tea. The cove was enclosed by a low escarpment fringed with alders and bracken. It had been our pirate head-quarters when Noël was ten and would only let me go with him as a Red Indian prisoner. He used to frighten me out of my wits with stories about the cliff at Blake Holme, further down the lake, where the outlaw Cornelius had lived, and about Calgarth Hall near the village, where the skulls of the wicked squire's victims kept coming back to the scene of their murder. But when he really wanted to terrify me, he'd wait until dusk was falling and pretend to see the phantom ferry boat, the ghost of a vessel lost three hundred years earlier with all her passengers, including a wedding party, it was said, returning from Hawkshead Church.

'Listen!' He'd hold up a finger. 'Can't you hear it? That thin cry. That's the fellow who missed the boat and was doomed to wander up and down the Claife shore, calling for the lost ferry to come back for him.' And sure enough, as I listened I'd hear a thin wail – no more than the whistle of a sandpiper or the fluting of a reed bunting – and with a shriek I'd take to my heels across the turf, heading for the safety of home.

This particular afternoon was too bright and calm for ghosts. The wooded heights on the far shore were standing on their heads in the lake. From the jetty I could match individual trees to their upside-down selves in the water and, all round the boat-house, bright tortoiseshell butterflies were flickering through their nursery among the nettles.

The boathouse itself was too fanciful a structure ever to be taken for a Lakeland building, although the years that had mossed its pagoda roof and peeled and bleached its wooden sides had made it less of an oddity. At its western end, where the building stood up to its knees in the lake, double doors had once guided pleasure craft out on to the water, gaudy with awnings and parasols and highly polished brass. The General had often talked about the house-parties of his youth, when everyone sailed off for picnics in secret bays – the butler and several footmen having set out hours earlier by dog-cart to lug hampers and silverware down to the shore.

Now, half a century later, the boathouse had a derelict air. If it wasn't for the fact that the Dunstans so seldom went near the lake, the building might already have been pulled down or taken over by Beatrice for a tea-house. Its derelict state had probably helped to save it, aided by the thoroughness with which the alders round the cove had swallowed its oriental eaves into their mysterious undergrowth. Nowadays long-legged harvestmen ate their picnics under the sills of its boarded-up windows and the wooden piles on which it stood made a pleasure-ground for scuttling, rat-sized voles.

In fact, if it hadn't been for a faint sound – the puzzling scrape of metal on metal – I wouldn't have bothered to go near the place that day. I'd certainly never have thought of pushing through the nettles to put my ear against its warm, splintery side between the tattered flakes of green paint. That was where I heard the noise again, quite clearly this time, the harsh song of steel upon iron, so regular that I'd almost convinced myself it must be the rasp of a mooring ring nudged by the water rippling under the doors, when the sound stopped, started again, then stopped, to be followed by the hollow *chunk* of a file falling on wooden planking.

Tearing at the bindweed stems which kept knotting them-selves round my ankles, I struggled through the bushes at the rear of the boathouse to find that the path leading down to its small side door was less overgrown than I remembered. More than that, the brass doorknob, though still stained with age, was as shiny as if the hand of a regular visitor had polished it, and the inner edge of the keyhole was worn to a glitter, like a metal eye. For a moment I forgot I was no longer a Red Indian whose camp had been invaded. Indignantly, I pushed open the door and went in.

After the brightness outside, it took several seconds for my eyes to adjust to the dim interior. All I could make out was that the double doors overlooking the lake had been pushed open a crack, letting in just enough light to trace the edge of the wooden pier which ran round three sides of the building and the stairs to the sail-loft above. Above my head, the meagre strip of sunshine had skewered the rafters with a shivering lance of light thrown up by the black water that sucked and slapped between the piers.

At the far side of the boathouse, just as I remembered, the shadowy form of an old launch took up the entire length of the building and about a third of its width – a long, narrow slice of a boat from her sharply raked bow to her skimming, spoon-shaped stern. Ten years earlier, when Noël and I first discovered her, her silence had struck us as sinister. Then, as we got to know her better, she seemed a sad old thing, furred with dust and woefully neglected, her brasswork black and her leather cushions gutted by rats. Nevertheless, she was the pirate ship of our dreams and we sailed her through countless adventures on the Spanish Main until a gardener found us and chased us out. After that, the place was locked up and the only way inside was to take a lung-bursting breath and dive underneath the great double doors into the spider-webbed darkness. We did it a couple of times for the sake of defiance, then regretfully went back to our jetty-stockade.

And yet something about the old launch was different. As my eyes became accustomed to the soft dimness, I could see a dark figure motionless in the passenger well behind the funnel, staring suspiciously into the gloom. Noël's ghosts must have lingered in my mind because when the phantom called out across the water, I jumped.

'Who the devil's there? Beatrice, is that you?'

I took a step forward on the wooden pier, swallowing my fright. Already I'd recognized the voice and was ashamed of my fears. 'No, it's me. Chrissie.'

I heard a short, exasperated exhalation of breath. 'Damn! Damn and blast.' This was followed by another furious sigh. 'Oh, confound it! Why did you have to come snooping round here?'

'I wasn't snooping. I just came to see what was making a noise. This was my private place, once, and Noël's, too.'

In sullen silence Jack Dunstan and I confronted one another. I was resentfully aware that this wasn't how I'd wanted to meet him. I was hardly at my fascinating best, but under a cloud, accused of spying. I felt foolish, stupid and terribly childish.

'I'm sorry if I'm spoiling your afternoon. Since I'm obviously interrupting something, I'll go away again and leave you alone. You don't have to be so rude.' I turned to sweep out of the boathouse and the planks underfoot creaked alarmingly.

'For God's sake, be careful where you put your feet, there's a rotten bit just where you're standing. Yes, there. Keep to your right, towards the back of the shed.'

'This way?' I stretched out an arm.

'Just don't drown yourself. I'm in enough trouble as it is.'

'You needn't worry about me.' I turned back to face him. 'For your information, I'm a pretty good swimmer and I've been here before – often.'

'Rubbish. This place has been locked up for years.'

'That's why they locked it, because Noël and I used to come here when we were children and play in the launch. General Milnes was afraid we'd fall in.'

I could see Jack quite clearly now, watching me across the watery width of the boathouse, thigh-deep among the blackened valves and gauges of the old engine, with his hands loose by his sides and the thin gleam of a spanner in one of them. I still wasn't sure if he believed me. It seemed best to offer proof.

'The launch used to have an awning to keep off the sun. It's that roll of canvas under the stairs. You can still see the stripes, but mostly it's rotten.'

I began to feel possessive again. I didn't like the idea of someone raiding the place for souvenirs.

'What are you doing to the boat, anyway?'

He ignored the question. 'How did you know I was here?'

'I didn't know. I was down by the jetty and I heard a scraping noise. I just came to see what was making it.' Now I knew where he'd been going on that afternoon before the ball, when I'd watched his disappearing-act and assumed he'd wandered off for a quiet cigarette. 'Why are you taking the engine to pieces?'

'This isn't the engine, it's the boiler.'

'Isn't that the same thing?'

'No, of course it isn't.' There was such scorn in his voice that I wondered why I'd ever found him attractive. 'The boiler makes steam to run the engine. This is the fire box. *That's* the engine.' He pointed with his spanner. 'Those things are the cylinders. The steam expands in the cylinders and drives the pistons that turn the crankshaft.'

'I know that,' I lied. 'Everybody knows.'

'You didn't.' He considered me sourly for a moment. 'I suppose if you know I'm here, then Bea knows too.'

'I've only just found out myself.'

'But you'll tell Bea as soon as you see her. Best friends, aren't you?'

I thought about this for a moment and remembered Beatrice leading Philip Kassel away, clinging to his arm and giggling.

'I haven't got a best friend.' This sounded feeble, so I added, 'I've never needed one.'

He leaned against the funnel, blending his long silhouette into its shadow. 'But you'll still tell Bea you've seen me here.'

'Not necessarily. Not if you don't want me to.'

He snorted. 'Girls always tell tales. Bea always does.'

'I don't. Not if it's important.' With an effort, I gave him a level stare. '*Is* it important?'

'It is to me. Bea will go straight to *him* if she knows and that'll be the end of all this.'

I presumed he meant his father, but I was still concerned about the launch. 'Tell me first what you're doing to the *Siren*.'

'Is that her name, *Siren*? It suits her.' He glanced along the length of the launch and then back to me. 'I'm not taking her to pieces. At least, I am, but only because I'm going to put her back together again. In a couple of months I'm going to have her running under her own steam. Across the lake, just like the old days.'

He threw it out like a challenge, as if he expected me to tell him it was impossible.

'Can you really do it?'

'I reckon so. With a bit of hard work.' He inspected me obliquely, trying to decide where my loyalties lay. 'Well, Chrissie-all-alone? Are you going to tell them what I'm up to? Because my father will stop me, if he finds out.'

I lifted my chin. 'I've kept this place secret for years, you know. Long before you found it.'

'Swear. Cross your heart and hope to die.'

'I will not! That's blasphemy. If I say I won't tell anyone, then I won't and you'll just have to take my word as a lady.'

He snorted again at that, but didn't insist. Instead, he glanced down at the boiler as if wondering whether I could be trusted. It seemed to me that we suddenly had a common cause.

'Can I come round and see what you're doing? Nobody knows I'm here. Bea's gone off to the rose garden with Philip, so she won't care where I've gone.' Before Jack could object I began to make my way along the wooden piers that skirted three sides of the building.

He twisted round the funnel to watch my progress. 'So my sister's run off with the handsome Philip, has she?' A harsh note of amusement had entered his voice. 'Well, I can't say I'm surprised. That's the Dunstan way of doing things. Bea wants Philip, and whatever Bea wants, she gets.'

I was much closer to him now, by the launch's stern-lines, and my eyes were accustomed to the gloom. He was wearing an old flannel shirt with a narrow stripe, stained with oil and rust; his dark hair had fallen over his brow and he looked like the pirate I'd once wanted to be.

'You're a Dunstan, aren't you?' I was tense and the question came out sharply. 'Do you get everything you want?'

He stepped away from the funnel and for the first time I saw the blackish stain of bruising that spread from his lower lip to his chin, with an angry red scrape at its centre where his father's fist must have landed.

'I will get what I want.' He scrutinized me slowly. 'One day.'

For a strange, disconnected moment I was afraid he'd stop looking at me and turn away, and I suddenly couldn't bear that. I swung my hips, exactly as Hosanna Greendew had told me never to do. 'Go on, then. Tell me what it is you want.'

His left hand rose to explore his damaged jaw. 'That's a dangerous question.'

'I'd still like to know the answer.'

'You'd be shocked.'

His eyes had never left me; he had blue eyes like all the Dunstans except Letty, and in the gloom they seemed as intense as indigo, the vivid blue cores of gas flames. I wasn't sure any more what we were talking about. In those seconds of staring we seemed to have passed into deeper and wilder territory than I'd intended. For a moment I felt real alarm at what I might have led him to say. Then the panic itself became intoxicating, and I didn't care any more.

'Say what you like. You can't shock me.'

A slow smile twisted the corner of his ravaged lip. 'We'd better not take that chance.' He turned back to his beloved engine; and, with nothing else to do, I sat down on the bottom step of the loft stairs to watch him in silence. After some time, he glanced up again.

'You don't have much to say for yourself, do you?'

'I prefer thinking, I suppose. Noël says I think too much.'

'I'm not complaining. Think all you like. Bea never shuts up unless she's asleep.'

It seemed to me that I'd been invited to speak. 'How do you

know so much about boats? I saw you rowing, once, last year. You row very well.'

'I've rowed for years. I was in the school eight.'

'But that didn't teach you about steam engines.'

'No. I've learned most of that from hanging round the Dunstan factories. I talk to the turners and the fitters and watch the coppersmiths working.'

'Bea says your father's forbidden you to go there.'

I saw his shoulders stiffen. The thin light deepened the stain of the bruising on his face. 'My father can forbid as much as he likes – I'll still do it. And even if you run off and tell him, it won't stop me.'

'I said I wouldn't tell anyone and I won't.'

In spite of his swift hostility, there was something thrilling in the thought of sharing such a secret with Jack Dunstan; or perhaps it was thrilling precisely because of that hostility. Whichever way, I didn't see why I should be any more polite than he'd been. What I wanted to know, I might as well ask.

'Did it hurt much, when your father hit you?'

He bent over the rusty boiler, avoiding my glance. 'It didn't bother me.' He fitted the spanner over a bolt. 'It's happened before.'

I watched him throw his strength behind the spanner, his head down and one knee jammed against the fire box for leverage. His shirt strained as the muscles of his back rose along his spine and massed on his shoulders. There was something raw, almost brutal, in his determination to conquer the unyielding metal.

'Actually . . . I thought it was pretty terrific, the way you tried to look after your mother.'

'Did you.' It was an exhalation of breath, not a question. 'Damn!' He leaned back, breathing heavily, and wiped a hand over his forehead, leaving a smear of dirt. 'It's stuck fast. I'll have to try something else.' He glanced up and saw me watching. 'What's the matter? Think you can do any better?'

'Maybe it just won't move. It's awfully old.'

'I'll shift it – don't you worry. Throw me that hammer, will you? The one at your feet.'

I tossed him the hammer. He caught it easily and bent over the valve once more.

'Why is it so important to get the *Siren* running again? Just because your father wouldn't like it?'

'Because I'll have done it all myself. That's what he can't stand.' Jack's voice echoed round the engine well. 'Because it'll be my achievement – something he's had no part in. No power over.'

He was speaking to the launch as much as to me, to the obdurate engines and the stubborn iron, explaining why they had to give way before his will.

'When I was about six or seven years old, I made a toy boat. It wasn't much of a boat – just an old piece of wood I'd cut to shape, with a stick glued on for a mast and some cardboard for a sail. But I'd made it myself, and I was proud of it. I wanted to see if it would run right across the pond in the park.'

Once more, he jammed the spanner into place. This time he swung the hammer against it with a hard, ringing blow.

'My father saw me setting off for the park with my nurse, carrying the boat in my arms. He went mad with anger, tore the boat away from me, broke it over his knee and threw the pieces into the fire. No son of Alfred Dunstan's was going to be seen playing in the park with old sticks and carpenter's rubbish. If I wanted a yacht, I could ask him. He might – or might not – give me one.'

Jack lifted the hammer and swung it hard, twisting with the force of the blow, but the bolt stayed firm.

'My nurse burst into tears. She was scared to death of him, like everyone else. But I didn't cry. I just wanted to kill him. Six years old, and I wanted to kill my father – not because he'd burned my boat, but because he'd robbed me of the chance to do something of my own.' He straightened up for a moment and spat on his fingers. 'Now he's bought me this place at Oxford. He wants to boast about his son who's studying Latin and Greek – and in a few years' time he'll boast about how he's bought me a degree, too.'

Once more, he raised the hammer. It seemed to halt for a second, motionless at the top of its curve, before flashing down in a mighty explosion of power that sent echoes ringing from the rafters. This time the spanner swung through a quarter turn.

'Did you see that?' Jack glanced up at me, grinning. 'I knew it would give in the end.'

He battered the spanner again, then flung down the hammer and heaved the bolt clear by main force. When he stood up again his chest was heaving but his eyes were bright. He indicated the launch with an oily finger. 'That's why I need this boat so much, because for the first time in my life I've got the chance of something that's *mine*, something I can finish by myself, without his money or his interference. When the *Siren* steams across the lake again, I'll know it's only because of what I've done. And he'll know it, too. By God, he'll know it.'

I wanted to say something profound, something to match the passion of his dream. But I had nothing remotely important to offer – no sacrifice worth the white-hot intensity of his resolve.

'Jack, I swear I won't tell anyone what you're doing.' I took a deep breath and prepared to pawn my immortal soul. 'Cross my heart and hope to die. On my mother's life – everything.'

I was conscious now of being a hopeless renegade, of having thrown in my lot with his. And I didn't care. All I knew was that I'd never seen such wonderful, embattled single-mindedness – such lonely courage. If the gates of hell had swung open at our feet, I'd willingly have followed him into the furnace.

'I'd like to help, if you'd let me.'

He held up a hand and cocked his head, listening. From somewhere outside I heard a faint voice calling 'Chrissie! Christ-a-bel! Where on earth have you got to?'

'I don't want Bea coming down here to look for you.'

'No. I'll go back and head her off.' I got to my feet and brushed at my skirt. 'She'd better not see me covered in dust and cobwebs.'

'Give me a moment to change my shirt and I'll walk back with you.'

He reached down to gather the flannel shirt round his ribs, and stripped it off over his head in a single, easy movement, presenting me, suddenly, with an anonymous male torso stretched out – no, *exhibited* – for my inspection in all its faintly shining nakedness. He'd done it quite deliberately. Even my brother Noël changed his cricket shirt in the privacy of his own bedroom. I'd never before been close to such an area of warm, tactile, potent, breathing male flesh and I was sure Jack Dunstan knew it. He was playing a game with me – a dangerous Dunstan game – with my embarrassment as the prize.

He was actually grinning as he vaulted out of the launch towards the laundered white shirt he'd tossed over the rail of the loft stairs. He was still tucking the tail of it into his trousers as we left the boathouse and dragged some long stems of bramble across the path behind us.

'Chriss—ee! Oh, where have you got to?' Up on the terrace, Beatrice was becoming impatient.

As we crossed the turf, Jack gripped my elbow. 'Not a word, remember? You swore it. You crossed your heart.'

He crossed it again, with his finger, on the bodice of my dress.

Hell's gates were gaping so wide I could smell the sulphur, but I wasn't going to let him win again. 'There's dirt on your forehead. You'll give the secret away.'

I reached up to rub it off and felt his breath, warm from our running, beating on the hollow of my palm.

Chapter Seven

WHAT WIDER world did I need than Fellwood, Waterside, the village, the boathouse and the great, still lake that united us all? When I look back on the last few unshadowed weeks of that summer of 1914, they exist for me behind a veil of gold, like a bright window behind a thin muslin hot-season curtain.

It was the last summer of my youth and I was sure I was in love. The glory of it dazed my mind and the thrill of it heightened my senses. I became aware, as never before, of the fingertip patter of breezy leaves and the warm, hard edges of the jetty planks under my bare toes. The smell of scorched grass beneath my cheek enchanted me as we lay dozing on the lawn and the inky softness of a midnight windowpane chequered with tiny, anxious moths. And when the dawn chased a yellow floss of mist from the valley, releasing, one by one, perfect black-tasselled trees – though I felt a sharper melancholy than I'd ever known in my life before – I clasped even that to my starving, rational heart.

I gave up thought that summer and learned instead the song of rhythm and inflexion in which words themselves are only a distraction. I spent hours curled up on the loft steps in the boathouse while Jack laboured on the entrails of the *Siren* and talked in fits and starts to no one in particular. Before long I'd realized that even when his words were curt and defiant, the echo I heard in my heart was less self-assured. Perhaps the darkness of the boathouse encouraged him to speak, or perhaps it was simply because I had so little to say for myself. I was a human presence, an indistinct sympathetic figure, except for those moments when he recognized me for my seventeen-year-old self and deliberately set out to rouse me in that taunting, physical way of his.

'No, I can't tell you, you're too innocent.'

'I am not innocent! At least—' feeling the blood rise to my cheeks, 'I'm not ignorant, if that's what you mean.'

He'd lean on the boiler, grinning, as if it was highly amusing to see me wrenched one way by fear and another by fascination. He'd glance away, then back again, a sideways grin this time – *Oh, if you only knew!* – before returning, smiling and whistling softly, to the work in hand. Perhaps he tolerated me because, in spite of everything, I refused to be frightened away. Something – instinct, or a sixth sense made up of tiny, half-observed clues – assured me there was no real need to be afraid, and that the very things about him which were most alarming, like the fierceness of his spirit and the raw, swift intensity of his passion, were exactly those things that could strike fire from my own uncertain soul and should be explored and cherished.

Beatrice was in the throes of a frenzy for Philip Kassel.

'Do you actually like my brother?' she asked one morning, screwing up her face as if the prospect was hard to believe. At the time, we were being driven to Windermere village in one of her father's motors. Fortunately, it was the kind of vehicle where the chauffeur drove out in the open, in front of the private, glass-windowed compartment where we sat, shut up together behind a tawny curtain of dust. It must have been this odd, unexpected intimacy that had started her talking.

'I mean, do you like him a lot – in the way I like Philip?'

I had to think for a moment. My feelings about Jack were too mixed up to explain, even if I'd wanted to share them with Beatrice. It was easiest to lie. 'I'm not mad for him, if that's what you mean.'

'I'm not mad for Philip.'

'Of course you are! I saw you in the summer house yesterday afternoon, with your head on his shoulder, looking all dreamy and not saying a word.'

Beatrice blushed crimson and turned her face away, but she was smiling, happy to be caught out. After a moment she even sighed and clasped her hands in her lap; now that I'd torn the secret from her, she couldn't stop talking about her longing for Philip. The words poured out of her describing the wonderful cleverness of the things he said, the narrow knees which made such interesting shapes under the fabric of his trousers, the heart-breaking story of his mother's death which Beatrice had extracted with crashing thoroughness ... Every mound and hollow had been secretly inspected and guessed about and sighed over. Beatrice was as tireless in her love as she was in her shopping. She fell silent for a moment, staring at her feet. Then she raised her head.

'I wonder what it's like to sacrifice your virginity – to offer it to someone you know you're going to love for ever and ever. To say, "This is all I have to give you. I only wish it could be more."'

It wasn't often that Beatrice achieved dignity, but at that moment she seemed unexpectedly solemn and determined. Her new-found humility was quite embarrassing.

'This isn't like you, Bea. Whatever have you been reading?'

'"A meeting of souls." That's what it said in Miss Greendew's poem about Anthony and Cleopatra. "A mating of eagles," she called it.' Beatrice leaned back on the slippery leather seat and trailed her fingers down its upholstered channels. 'I'm sure Philip would be so passionate, so serious and intense. You can tell, can't you? His hands are so sensitive.' She sighed wistfully. 'I expect he's had lots of lovers already. He's been to so many romantic places, and he's almost foreign, isn't he?' Her fingers continued to trace their sinuous path along the leather seams. Her eyes were closed now and she was breathing softly through her mouth. 'I touched his throat and his ear, once, and his skin was so smooth, I can't tell you ...' She flexed her spine in a languorous undulation and sighed again. 'I'd go to bed with him tomorrow, if he really begged me. I just couldn't help myself.'

'Bea – you wouldn't dare. Think about *babies*.'

'You don't have to have babies. Philip would know how.' She whispered Philip's name again like an incantation and her eyes flew open, brilliant with moisture. For several seconds she stayed like that, unmoving, with her head thrown back, studying the fan-pleated silk above our heads with an expression of dreamy contentment.

I wasn't as shocked as I should have been. Sometimes in the darkness of the boathouse I'd wondered what I'd do if Jack made a serious attempt on my honour – and almost wished that he would. But Beatrice's brow had already gathered itself into a frown, as if the first thorn of suspicion had appeared in her Eden.

'Chrissie . . . do you believe it's true that young men some-times get so's they absolutely must have a woman and if a girl won't let them, they'll find another one who will?' She bit her lip and glanced down into her lap. 'Because I bet Irene Cole would let Philip do it with her, if he wanted. She's so *obvious*.' Her hands flew up to push hair back from her temples in sudden frustration. 'Besides, it would be special with Philip. It would be . . . oh, like the biggest, sugariest, squashiest, most glorious ice cream sundae ever. Utter heaven.'

'How can you possibly know that?'

'I just do.' Beatrice looked desperate. 'It would be heaven.'

'Better than millefeuille with Grand Marnier?' By now, I knew most of Beatrice's weaknesses.

'Well, of course.'

'Better than chocolate pudding with almond cakes, or rasp-berry charlotte?'

'Much, much better. Chrissie, I'm serious!'

'Oh, you certainly are.'

'You see—' She clasped her hands across the bosom of her shantung motoring-coat and assumed an expression of seraphic joy. 'I think I'm probably in love with Philip.'

And when I couldn't help smiling, she rounded on me at once, as furious as if I'd accused her hero of infidelity. 'Well, I'll tell you something I *am* sure of, shall I? Jack's done it with a girl. I know he has, though I'm not supposed to. I overheard him having a row with Father about it, something to do with a maid at school, and Father saying Jack was damned lucky not to be sacked for it and it was only because he'd given the headmaster money for his blasted library that Jack could finish the year at all.' She stopped and studied my face, her eyelids half-lowered, lasciviously curious. When she spoke again, her voice was husky. 'Do you think that's awful, the thought that Jack's been with a woman?'

Confused, I murmured, 'No, not specially. Oh look, here's the church! Tipper will want to know where to drop us and we haven't even decided ourselves yet.'

Later, the motor took us back to Waterside for lunch, and by then the knowledge of Jack's sinfulness had become oddly exciting. He had a way of lounging in a chair in an insolent curve which thrust out his hips and long legs, regarding us all with careful, detached curiosity. He was prepared to be among us, said his bearing, but not one of us; and the thought of that detachment being set aside to accommodate the hot body of a school maid and that careful curiosity satisfying itself on soft, obliging female flesh, was enough to send a tingle through my bowels like the kneading of a thousand determined fingers.

To Mar's dismay, Max Kassel was talking of going to Amsterdam, while he still could, he said. When she suggested that Philip, at least, should stay on with us, his father readily agreed.

'It's good for him to live among a family again. All this travelling round the world, never staying anywhere for long – it's a lonely life for a young man. I'm almost the only friend he has, poor boy.'

Oh, lucky Beatrice! The god of expensive parcels and

109

grasping, ardent little fingers was surely looking after her. I could imagine what lonely Philip saw in robust, down-to-earth Beatrice. She'd take him shopping and fill his arms with all those parcels whose contents she'd forgotten by the time she got home. 'The round one with the red string? Did I buy that? Give it here.' She'd tear it open with squeals of astonishment. 'The little powder-puff, of course!' And the tiny thistledown ball would be carried upstairs to join a dozen others in the drawer of her dressing table. Yes, it would be good for Philip to stay with us for a while.

That was the sum of my thinking. Yet I'd misunderstood Philip quite badly and only realized it one afternoon at Waterside, when I found him in the new summer house, taking solitary refuge from a shower. I bounded in, brushing raindrops from my shoulders, and looked round.

'What have you done with Bea?'

Philip was slumped in a rustic armchair with his head thrown back against the rail, staring moodily out at the rain-drenched roses.

'Bea's run off, up to the house. I said something crass.'

'Oh.' I settled myself in the chair beside him. 'Well, never mind. She'll get over it soon enough. She's terribly fond of you.'

Philip made a sound of irritation. 'I wish she wasn't.'

The rain was drumming on the summer house roof. I stared at him, taken aback. Beatrice must have offended him with her over-confidence. I tried to tease him out of it. 'A girl's hopelessly in love with you and you'd rather she wasn't?'

Philip's right hand formed a fist and beat heavily, twice, on the arm of his chair as if the stupidity of fate was beyond endurance. In the oblique light he might have been a Renaissance martyr, ready for the arrows of torment. His white linen jacket fell in soft pleats round his body, like milk poured from the lip of a bowl, all creamy folds round his ribs and mysterious hollows where his wrists emerged from his sleeves. All that was missing was a thin, fatal trail of crimson.

'Not Beatrice – not *her* – especially not her! That's what's so sickeningly cruel about the whole business!' He shook his head and glanced away, despairing, as if the game of life wasn't worth the candle.

'Well . . . if it isn't Bea . . . and yet, I can see there's someone . . . Then who is it, Philip?'

He turned back to me, astonished, almost outraged that I hadn't realized. 'Letty. Mrs Dunstan. I thought you'd guessed.'

'*Letty Dunstan?*'

'Well, of course! Oh, if you were a man you'd understand.' He leaned towards me. 'When I saw Letty there, in that gallery in Venice . . . Chrissie, it was as if my life had suddenly begun to make sense. All the travelling, always being among strangers, living in one hotel after another and then, suddenly, just as if it was the most natural thing in the world, Letty Dunstan was *there*, waiting for me by that picture in the Museo and I realized I'd known her for ever, as if she were a part of me.' A black curl fell over his brow as he shook his head. 'I can't explain it, perhaps we were lovers in a previous existence, who knows? All I'm sure of is that I was meant to find her, or never be whole again. I need her as much as the air I breathe. If I sleep at all it's only because I'm dreaming of her. And yet she's helpless. She's been abandoned to a brute of a man who's locked her away from the world in this prison of a house.'

His fist fell again on the arm of his chair. 'When I remember how he treated her on the night of the ball – I could kill him for it! She's like a child; so gentle. She gazes up at me with those great eyes of hers and she seems to be looking to *my strength* – mine – to rescue her. And yet I can't be sure. Perhaps she thinks of me as hardly more than a boy – eighteen years old – a year younger than her own son.' He fell silent for a moment. Then I heard a long despairing, sighing breath that seemed to weave itself into the breeze that stirred the roses. 'How can I tell her? How can I explain what I don't even understand myself – except that I know it's true?'

'Oh, Philip dear . . . I don't know what to say.'

'Just don't say *Beatrice*.' Philip leaned back into his chair. 'Beside her mother, Bea Dunstan is a peasant. A clod. Her father's daughter. A greedy, self-seeking clod.' He stared furiously round the summer house. 'And the worst of it is, I have to pretend to make up to her, because it's the only way I have of being near Letty.'

'Perhaps you should have gone to Amsterdam with your father and tried to put it all out of your mind.'

'No!' It was a cry of pain. 'How could I possibly leave her?'

I had no comfort to offer. We sat silently in our ridiculous rustic chairs while the rain slowed to a regular patter, then to a drizzle, and finally died out altogether as the clouds blew away towards Kendal. I stood up.

'I'm going to the house. Are you coming?'

'No. I need to be on my own for a bit. I couldn't bear running into Beatrice just yet.' He ran his fingers through his hair. 'You won't say anything, will you?'

'Of course not.'

The heady scent of rain-washed blooms was blowing in great gusts from the rose beds as I walked back towards the steps leading to the terrace. Ordinarily, I'd have noticed nothing but tremulous petals, as soft as the lobe of an ear, and tightly furled, virginal buds. Now Philip's melancholy kept bringing me an image of funeral flowers and the over-sweet smell of faded wreaths.

I'd been so wrapped up in my own voluptuous happiness. I'd been walking on air in a state of rapture and had assumed in my bliss that everyone shared it. Not Philip, it seemed. And not Letty, either. When I entered the house by way of the conservatory, she was curled up among the cushions on the cane settee, one arm stretched out languidly, her cheek resting on her shoulder. At first I thought she was asleep, but her eyes were open, listlessly contemplating the clutter of lemonade glasses we'd left on the table half an hour before.

She glanced at me without interest and returned to her brooding.

'Has the rain stopped, then?'

'Yes, a few minutes ago.'

'Oh.'

It seemed best to leave her. I turned away towards the door that led to the dining room.

'Won't you stay?' She'd raised her head again; her cheek was rosy where it had been pressed against her shoulder. 'I have such sad thoughts when I'm all on my own. I used not to mind, but it's different now.' She drew up her shoeless feet, tucking them under the hem of her skirt and patted the sofa. 'There's room for you here.'

I sat down on the creaking cane and folded my hands on my knees. 'Shall I ring for them to take away these glasses?'

'No.' Her eyes showed alarm. 'No, leave them, please. I like to look at them.' She smiled faintly. 'You must think me very strange . . . I think so myself, sometimes. I look back on my life and I wonder how it ever came to be like this.' She reached out to draw back the hair that threatened to hide my face from her sight and hooked it behind my shoulder. 'Pretty hair. Tea-coloured. I like it when you turn your head and the sun catches your hair as it flies out.'

Her attention drifted back to the table and her hand, wandering, strayed out to one of the glasses, alighting like a moth where the rim was printed with the cloud-image of the drinker's lips.

'I'll give you a blessing, pretty-hair. That you may never wish yourself young all over again.'

Beyond the door, in the dining room, a clock counted the seconds in velvet steps. 'Is that what you wish? Surely not. You aren't old—'

'Old enough. Too old already.' Her finger followed the rim of the glass, lingering on a trace of sugar. 'The years pass while your back is turned and suddenly all you're left with is longing. No more hope.'

The glass was empty. All the others contained a drying debris of lemon slices, and Ida's several inches of abandoned lemonade. But one of us, I remembered, had carefully fished out all the lemon with a long spoon and left the ghost of his kiss for Letty to cherish.

Philip.

I could have screamed aloud. Why did I have to think so much? Why couldn't I have sat there, admiring my fingernails, paying no attention to the glasses, and stayed cheerfully ignorant? Instead, the happiness of two people had been thrust into my hands – a barbed, dangerous happiness that could only draw blood. I knew more than either of them. I was God for a day.

By rights, I should do nothing. And yet if I did nothing, I'd never forgive myself. How could I deny Letty the bubbling thrill that filled my own veins?

'Philip's in the summer house,' I said.

Letty's head rose at once and turned towards me like a flower following the sun.

'He was pretty miserable when I left him.'

She blinked. 'He's fallen out with Bea. That's what she said when she came in.'

'No – this had nothing to do with Bea. It was something else.'

'Why tell me?'

'Because I think you know it already. You suspected in Venice.'

She drew in a breath. 'I did nothing, I promise you. Nothing.' *Help me*, pleaded her eyes. *I am weak. Tell me it has to be.*

'Philip's making himself wretched.' I couldn't look at her any longer, I couldn't bear the terror in her face. 'Perhaps you ought to go and talk to him.'

'Chrissie . . .'

'Yes?'

'Look at me.'

I had to turn back to her. Those great, imploring eyes swallowed up the whole of her face. She laid a hand on my arm, lightly, like a bird descending – a trusting, despairing bird.

'Are you sure?'

'You ought to go. It's all he wants.'

Her dress rustled as she scrambled to her feet and searched for her discarded shoes. She was all movement and yet, for an instant, she was still, fixed to the spot, uncertainly sweeping a fair curl from her forehead. Then, in a moment, like a creature of the air, she was off without a word, just a single, frightened backward glance as if the whole of her past life lay there, full of reproach, among the pleated silk cushions of the conservatory.

Chapter Eight

THE PREVIOUS year, my brother Noël had come back from Oxford with a motorcycle. This was most unlike Noël, who never took much interest in anything less than five hundred years old – though he kindly made an exception for me. At heart he was a pedal bicycle man. His long, bony wrists stuck out of his coat sleeves very much like bicycle spokes; he used to fly happily through the streets of Oxford with his sharp knees rearing up in front, one after the other, and the ends of a long scarf streaming out behind. If an American friend hadn't graduated that year and sold his more awkward possessions in preparation for going home, Noël and the motorcycle would never have been united. It was an everlasting miracle to my parents that he'd ridden it all the way from Oxford to the Lakes without once falling off.

At Fellwood it was given a home in the old wood store beyond the stables where Powley cordially hated it because it smelt and upset his horses.

'Goodness *knows* what Noël was thinking of,' Mar used to say. I doubt if Noël could have explained it himself. It had been a second's infatuation – swift, intense, and rapidly over. And now, as often as not, when the metal beast was dragged out of its lair for a short run on a sunny day, I was the one in the saddle.

Jack Dunstan looked envious when I mentioned it. 'It's a Triumph,' I said with casual pride. 'It's got a 550cc engine and three-speed gears.'

'Side valve?'

'I've no idea. You'd have to ask Sam Powley, George's son. He looks after it. Or . . . you could come and see it for yourself.'

There weren't many things capable of diverting Jack from his work on the *Siren*, but a Triumph motorcycle was one of them. He squatted down and examined it with something like awe, running his fingers over the chain and the carburettor and the flanks of the grey and black fuel tank. In turn, his hands fascinated me, with their fingernails as curved as spoons and the pale, prominent joints that gave each finger the elegant waist of a woman. There was something like reverence in his touch. No doubt the springmaker viewed motorcycles in the same light as home-made yachts and steam launch engines.

There was a pillion saddle fixed to the luggage rack over the rear wheel; its American owner had been in the habit of taking friends out to an oak-beamed tavern at Garsington. Strictly speaking, of course, I shouldn't have dreamed of going anywhere alone with a member of the opposite sex, but Noël had cycled into Windermere to collect some books from the London train and, in any case, our country ways were more casual than those of city drawing rooms. Besides – I happened to know Mar had gone 'botanizing' that morning at Ambleside.

'Do you want to take the machine for a spin? We could run up the track to Moor How behind the plantation.'

'Only if you let me drive it back.'

I'd gone up there before, with Noël in front. It was entirely different when Jack sat behind me with his long thighs embracing mine along the sides of the roaring, leaping machine and our bodies pressed together in a kind of swooping dance as we leaned into corners. The hill track was steep and, more than once, as we bumped and skidded our way along it, Jack threw an arm round me to steady himself. The muscles of my stomach went tight with excitement under his hands. I couldn't remember ever feeling such pure, unadulterated joy before. On that motorcycle we were reckless – we were possessed – we were surely immortal. I heard a crazy laugh, and realized it was mine.

117

Then we were as far up the hill as the track would take us and had to clamber up among the rocky outcrops until we'd reached the top and could fling ourselves down on the grass and look out, breathless, over the sweep of Windermere. But I'd viewed the lake on countless occasions and, before long, I'd turned to envying the ease with which Jack could lie, limbs sprawled, one knee bent and his body curved to the contour of the ground, an unconscious harmony of relaxation. As a girl, I'd always been taught to be aware of how I sat, or moved, or lay down. The result had been to make me disappointingly aware of my own body which still seemed so boyish, compared with Beatrice's effortless lushness. I tried lying back on my elbows in the hope that what bosom I had would stick out, but the result was unsatisfactory.

How I longed for voluptuous curves and dimpled corners, for a sumptuous counterpane of flesh to cover the narrow angularities at my shoulders and knees! Sometimes at night I tried to weigh my breasts, cupping them in my hands as I imagined a man might — as Jack Dunstan might, I suppose — and found that, like wavelets on the surface of the sea, they refused to be weighed. They remained soft cones with no solid existence of their own. Only the nipples pleased me, rosy as coral and vigorous as pursed lips.

In Venice I'd become a secret connoisseur of bosoms, amazing my father with my new-found enthusiasm for Renaissance art. Tintoretto's Ariadne had rounder breasts, but she had nipples like hard marbles, I was pleased to see. When the sun went down, throwing its rose-gold through my bedroom window, that's when I could tolerate my reflection in the mirror, when my narrow, tree-climbing thighs and my bony toes, almost as long as my little finger, turned fondant-soft and I could just about imagine someone wanting me in the same way as a flirtatious school maid.

Today, however, Jack had something else on his mind. He lay for a long time, propped on one elbow, shading his eyes with his hand. Then he lowered it, absently, to finger the half-healed scar at his lip.

'Your brother Noël – he's going to be an archaeologist, isn't he?'

'He already *is* an archaeologist. He's been one since he was seven years old. That's when Mar took him up to Hardknott Castle – the old Roman fort between Ambleside and Ravenglass – and he somehow managed to find a coin with the head of Marcus Aurelius. Since then he's never wanted to do anything else but dig up history. I expect he gets it from Par.'

Jack broke off a long stem of grass and examined it. 'That's the whole point, though, isn't it? If your father's a historian, no one's surprised when you want to dig up old coins. If he's an artist, then you can probably paint. If he plays the violin, then you can usually sing, at least.'

'I suppose that's true. So what?'

Jack aimed the grass stem like a lance and sent it off into the rocks. 'What if your father's a brute and a liar? What does that make you?'

The parallel had never occurred to me, but then, I never knew what to expect with Jack. Whenever I thought I'd succeeded in circumnavigating the whole Jack Dunstan and knowing all there was to know, he still managed to take me by surprise. Once, in the middle of some fiddling task, I'd seen him give up a whole precious afternoon to trap and gently release a tortoiseshell butterfly that had blundered into the boathouse to batter itself hopelessly against the black walls. Time after time, he crept up to where it had settled, tick-tocking its wings in alarm, and I heard his voice in the shadows, hardly above a sigh. 'Stay there, now . . . Don't be afraid . . .' And those skilful hands would reach out – only for the creature to dart like a spark from their supple imprisonment, starting off the whole painstaking hunt again.

'What does it make you?' I said. 'It makes you determined to be different, that's what.'

'Do you think so?'

'That's what it's done to you.'

'Maybe.'

'And besides, what about your mother? You must have inherited something from her.'

'That's hardly likely. My mother's a saint. Any ordinary woman would have left my father long ago, but she's absolutely loyal. She's the only truly incorruptible person I know.' He lay back on the turf and folded his arms under his head. 'Thank God there's one in the family, at least.'

For the first time, I felt a pang of doubt about what I'd done – which I swiftly dismissed. In the few days since our conversation in the conservatory Letty had begun to look happier than I'd ever seen her. Her skin was as bright and firm as the crimson-splashed buds of the Snow Queen roses pinned to her wide collar, and her hair shone in its neat coils. She looked like a wind-blown blossom, flitting across the lawn in her favourite tiered skirt of cornflower blue, her arms held out like curled sepals. As often as not, when she reached us, I'd hear her singing to herself under her breath. It was such a delight to be near her that we'd taken to spending a great deal of time at Waterside, Philip and I, and still she begged us to stay longer.

She didn't seem to have made any friends of her own age, in spite of my mother's efforts to draw her into her own circle of 'suitable' women. Perhaps she didn't want any. Clearly, that summer, she'd decided to remain cast away with us 'young people' on our green and unworldly island in the sun, where the light sparkled on her silvery lashes when she laughed and a dusting of peppery freckles masked her thirty-eight disregarded years.

'I think it's charming of Letty to bother with you all,' said my mother, not understanding. She was laying out little scrawny pencils and scorecards for an evening of bridge. My father didn't play; the ritual made him nervous and he could never remember which suit was trumps.

'It can be a perfect bore, you know, chaperoning active young women. One can't turn one's back on the flighty ones for a moment and yet the others send one to sleep with their dreary tattle about frocks and novels. Not that you're either flighty *or* dreary, my dear. I expect Beatrice gives her mother far more cause to worry than you do.'

I don't believe Letty worried about either of us for a second. Far from dampening our fun, she was always the centre of it, the sparkling well-spring of our enjoyment, anxious only that we should keep returning to share her happiness.

On most fine days we lunched under a canvas awning on the terrace, all except Ida, who, to her fury, still took her meals in the nursery. The breezy damask cloth was weighed down by enormous white plates with fennel-green borders and antique yellow vaseline glass goblets; massed bowls of sulphur-coloured achillea, standing amid the heavy silver, brought sunshine even into the green shadow of the awning. There was always wine, too, and no limit on how much we should drink, none of the usual 'just-half-a-glass-that's-quite-enough'. Beatrice and I could have gorged ourselves every day on honeyed, golden Burgundies and the finest champagne, if we hadn't had such a weakness for lemon squash.

I even persuaded Jack to join us. If I couldn't find him in the damp obscurity of the boathouse, crouching over the *Siren*'s steam valves, he was usually in the powerhouse, where there was a lathe and metal-working tools.

'It's a waste of time. I'll get something to eat in the kitchen.'

'I should turn up for lunch, if I were you. Beatrice is beginning to ask questions.'

In truth, Beatrice was far too absorbed in Philip to care about anything her brother might do, but the threat was enough to draw Jack out of hiding for an hour or two. And having discovered the soft web of sensual indulgence which had begun to wind round us all, he came again, curious, the next day and the day after that.

It took me by surprise, this new and rather disturbing freedom. Yet a little of the springmaker's Montrachet, as intense and lustrous as Mar's yellow beryl beads, made it seem as natural an instinct as drowsiness or hunger − even the sprawled limbs and the immodest laughter that went with it. Out of the corner of my eye, I saw Beatrice lolling over Philip's arm like a starving dog. And all the time Letty Dunstan watched us with her golden eyes, amused by our intemperance.

But on Friday evenings, it was understood, everything changed. At six o'clock we said our goodbyes and parted for two days, for that was when Alfred Dunstan came home to his family.

It amazed me that Beatrice hadn't noticed any change in Philip and her mother, or deduced anything from it. I arrived for lunch one day in time to see her showing off a pair of silk evening stockings she'd bought that morning in Windermere, baby-pink with a fashionable mother-of-pearl sheen. She kept dangling them coquettishly in front of Philip's nose, still radiant and bouncy from shopping, having lugged home her morning's spoils to be admired.

In the chair next to Philip's, Letty was drowsily watching the fun, her left arm stretched out in its georgette ruffles so that a couple of languid fingers – apparently by accident – rested lightly on Philip's wrist, her wedding ring glinting with each flourish of the pink stockings. Below her long lashes, her glance slid over us with lazy amusement. She ate very little, I noticed, as if she'd already fed, but her lips were swollen and, under some hastily applied powder, her cheeks were softly vivid with the flush of over-indulgence, like the glow of scarlet silk through chiffon.

That was when I realized how she and Philip had passed their morning; Ida had been with her nurse, Beatrice in the village, and Jack either in the boathouse or working at his lathe. Philip had been with Letty – eighteen-year-old Philip, with all his urgent, headlong passion and thirty-eight-year-old, golden-eyed Letty.

Now that I'd guessed their secret I noticed more: fleeting smiles full of shared understanding, quickly veiled by lowered eyelids; a trick of standing together, not quite touching but intimate enough to sense one another's warmth; an excess of concern that was as cloying as a kiss, 'Take my bread roll, it's softer. Let me fetch your wrap – a cushion for your poor head.' And once, when they thought no one could see, I caught them with their hands intertwined, Letty's as wiry and quick as a monkey's, Philip's boyish and resolute.

The discovery was unexpectedly disturbing. It shouldn't have been. I knew perfectly well in theory what men and women got up to in the privacy of the bedroom and I had no reason to suppose that Philip and Letty would behave any differently. But until that moment there'd been a misty, fairytale quality to my imaginings, very possibly involving a string orchestra and a cloud of fluttering angels. Now I'd been presented with incontrovertible evidence of something coarse and furtive; I felt as if my ethereal Letty had failed me in some way, though I couldn't logically think how.

Other eyes, perhaps, understood more.

'Are you sure Mrs Dunstan is to be painted as Venus?' My father was shocked by Jeremy Greendew's choice of subject for the Waterside walls. 'I mean, I do realize Venus was supposed to be Vulcan's wife, but she was rather . . . *flighty*, to say the least.' Par made her sound like a giddy parlourmaid. 'I mean to say – Mars – Mercury – that scoundrel, Bacchus – she *kept company* with them all, you know.' His fidgeting drew a squeal from the chair castors. 'And Venus is so often painted naked, like Botticelli's *Birth* or, heaven forbid, like Venus Genetrix, hitching up her skirts and beckoning with an apple, or Venus Callipyge, Venus of the Delightful Buttocks . . . Oh dear, oh dear.'

The springmaker had been absolutely specific about the style of painting he wanted in his frescoes (his murals, I should say, since the plaster had long since dried on the walls of the living hall – my father had carefully explained the difference). There was to be nothing remotely *modern* about the pictures, none of Greendew's Vorticist nonsense or those stick-figures that a babe-in-arms could have drawn. No – what was required were old-fashioned scenes full of Roman mythology and giants and heroes of the sort Alfred Dunstan had seen in Venice. There'd been no green heads or three-nosed women in the Accademia, that was certain, and what was judged great art by the Italian masters was quite handsome enough for the walls of Waterside. Ask Dr Ascham, if any proof were required.

My father was following the project with a kind of fascinated horror.

'Vulcan – is that what Dunstan's chosen to be?' Par pressed down his brows, ridging his forehead. 'The blacksmith of the heavens? How extraordinary!' He tapped his teeth with the leg of his spectacles like a railwayman testing the wheels of his loco-motive. 'Well, I suppose Vulcan was the nearest the Romans had to a maker of springs, but, you know, Vulcan was supposed to be hideously ugly – and hairy and crippled into the bargain. I wonder if Dunstan's aware of that?'

It didn't seem likely. Greendew's Vulcan had been designed to flatter, a blacksmith-god whose face wore a distant, abstracted expression I'd never seen on Alfred Dunstan's. It suggested aristocratic concern and weary nobility, much like the look I'd seen on the face of the Marquess, my Uncle Hereward, when someone told him a hen harrier had been seen among his nesting grouse.

This giant Vulcan was to dominate the staircase wall, sur-rounded by groups of admiring labourers and piles of Patent Coil Springs in various sizes. High above the staircase, cherubim would flutter round his head like moths, trailing patents and testimonials, while nearby, before a romanticized version of the house at Waterside, three female figures would gaze at him in adoration, trussed up in the floating, billowing draperies so dear to the springmaker's heart. To my eye, the women looked as if they'd been hit by an earthquake while hanging curtains. This was where Letty came in, as Venus, Vulcan's wife, and Beatrice and Ida as two of the Graces. Personally, I couldn't see what was wrong with turning Letty into Venus. It seemed far more of a cheat to let Beatrice and Ida stand for purity and benevolence.

Greendew, the artist, turned out to be as tall and spiky and mustard-coloured as his sister, Hosanna. He even walked with the same giraffe-like swoop of the neck and though he carried the large Greendew nose and bony features with rather more style, I'd never seen a man before who wore kohl round his eyes. By ten each morning he was up on his scaffolding, hurling paint at the wall and, since scarlet turned out to be one of his favourite colours, this frenzy gave him by lunchtime a blood-spattered, murderous air.

I only found out later that he'd taken Philip, whom he'd noticed whispering in Letty's ear, for the son of the house. By the time he'd realized his mistake, he was too enchanted by Philip to change his plans, and Letty's lover remained as a striking Narcissus on the wall of her husband's mansion.

Venus was recognizably Letty, but with an odd light in her eyes that amounted almost to invitation. Her fingers were folded modestly over her chest, but her loose hair flew out like a banner and her mouth had fallen a fraction open. The artist had put in the little cinnamon-coloured mole on Letty's upper lip that she'd only recently given up hiding with a dab of lanolin and pearl powder and which gave her mouth the provocative crimson curl of a split-open fruit. The whole effect was sharply, inescapably voluptuous, and made me wonder if Jeremy Greendew had understood more than I ever had.

One day, walking back from the boathouse, I noticed a movement among the trees that grew thickly beyond it. Thinking it was probably Topsy getting herself lost again, I pushed my way through the undergrowth and saw one black and one golden head low down amid a circle of scattered petticoats and, under the tail of a rumpled shirt, pale buttocks clenching in such a rhythmic frenzy that great hollows appeared in their sides, and lolling knees and ecstatic, clutching hands – I hurried away, shocked to the core.

Was this what Letty had yearned for? It was as if a spirit of the air had suddenly slumped ignominiously to earth, as if a beautiful child had shown herself gross and knowledgeable beyond her years. It had been those awful thrusts, brutal and squalid. It had been the sheep and the ram pick-a-back behind the drystone wall. It had been bestial and demeaning – and it was all my fault.

Now, as we lunched in the milky green shade of the canopy on the terrace, I watched the lovers together – Philip's darkness against Letty's amber-and-ivory brilliance. It seemed so obvious to me now that they were lovers. Crossing the lawn with Philip, Letty strolled with a loose-jointed carelessness I'd never seen before, swinging her hips and trailing her sun hat by its ribbons as if her life was too engorged with sleepy pleasure to be over-precise. Philip, in contrast, seemed to have grown more serious, tugging his fingers in slow perplexity and smiling only when his solemn glance met hers.

Sometimes, impulsively, Letty would reach out to rumple his black-lacquer curls as if he were a fretful puppy, drawing a squeal of protest from Beatrice. 'I've just made him comb it!' Then she would draw back her lips to show square white teeth and laugh, tilting up her face to the almond-coloured belly of the awning.

And still it seemed the artist and I were the only ones who'd realized.

In the late afternoons, Letty would wind the handle of the springmaker's prized hornless gramophone, filling the air with waltzes for us to dance to, or 'slow drags', the languorous, rakish band music born in smoky cellars across the Atlantic.

Still not quite believing, I studied Letty and Philip on the odd occasion when they danced together and learned more, almost, from their elaborate show of indifference. They must have agreed that Philip must still – officially – belong to Beatrice. They danced as two women will dance who've been left without partners, in absolute silence and looking steadfastly in different directions.

Sometimes Jack would dance, too, but often he preferred to listen to the music, tapping his fingers lightly on the arm of his chair and observing us with that cool, detached expression of his. When he did dance, I suspected he understood the havoc he could cause by crushing me against his hard, spare body and enjoyed making mischief. We always started off at a formal distance, but before long, somehow, we were pressed close enough for each step of the dance to have become a shared movement, a rhythm that tugged at something so deep inside me that its stirrings actually made me afraid. The Dunstan's chauffeur sometimes used to start up the engine of his motor with the smooth metal side of the bonnet folded back to show the shivering, pulsing bowels that lay behind it. That was how I felt inside, as the gramophone scraped out its slow syncopation, as if every organ in my body had claimed the right to a throbbing, shuddering life of its own. And when the lunchtime wine had lingered in my head, stifling my fear and making me reckless, I loved it, that feeling of helpless disorder and never wanted it to end.

Beatrice used to cling to Philip with her head against his shoulder and I wondered how Letty could bear to see her lover held close in her daughter's arms. Yet Beatrice was necessary to their deception and the only clue to Letty's thoughts was the faintly hungry expression that tightened the delicate skin round her eyes and made her chin look pointed with strain. Beatrice herself was blind, her eyes closed. Cradled on Philip's shoulder, she seemed wrapped in a soft, pious benevolence which drew out the corners of her lips in a cat-like smile. For the time being, Beatrice could see nothing but Philip.

I suppose I should have felt guilty because of Beatrice – but I didn't. I certainly didn't suffer any pangs on behalf of Alfred Dunstan, though it would have helped if he'd been a great 'ladies' man' himself, like the travelling stone-wallers, those brown and sinewy vagabonds with the fine moustaches and roguish eyes who came once a year to maintain our garden terracing and steal the hearts of our housemaids, even while the girls claimed to despise them.

From observing the wallers I learned there's a subtle cocksureness about a man who's kissed many women, not necessarily a swagger, but an underlying ease, a confidence in his own attractiveness. Alfred Dunstan stood too far away from the women he spoke to, so that he had to lean forward, stiff-shouldered, with his eyes on the ground, to hear what they said. It wasn't the behaviour of a man who believed himself irresistible.

No, if I felt uneasy – and I did, more often now – it was on Letty's behalf. I'd wanted so much to do something for her; now I'd begun to wonder if I'd done something *to* her instead.

It was Beatrice who suggested, one evening, that we swim in the lake. It had been suffocatingly hot all day and between the sticky heat and the wine at lunch, our nerves were on edge and the smallest remark was enough to cause a quarrel. Beatrice had even started an argument with Jeremy Greendew about the exact colour of her eyes, which she claimed he'd got wrong in the mural. 'If anything, they're cobalt blue, and you've made them cerulean.' Beatrice had invaded his paintbox to make sure.

'Surely their colour depends on the light.'

'It does not. Look at them now! Isn't this bright enough for you?'

'All colour's an illusion anyway, Miss Dunstan. Nothing's really one shade or another. It's all to do with refracted light.'

Beatrice drew herself up. 'I'm not talking about *science*. Don't you know a question of art when you see one?'

And while we buzzed like an angry hive, we drank like bees in a tub of nectar. By the time the quarrel had been exhausted, we were all quite tipsy and half the afternoon had gone.

'Stay for dinner,' begged Letty. 'I'll send a message to Fellwood. I refuse to let the party break up on such a sour note.'

But the ugly mood continued at dinner. Beatrice's cheeks were a hectic pink and she wriggled so much in her seat that I suspected her of trying to stroke Philip's leg with her toes under the table. Heaven only knew where Jack had been all afternoon, but he brought a tension like a drawn bow to the dinner table with him. When Philip made a feeble joke he killed it with a word and then snapped at Beatrice when she scolded him. A hard stare challenged her to try again. She tossed her head, but said nothing.

Afterwards, all four of us walked stiffly out on to the terrace, where the long shadows were fading to an impartial lead-blue dusk and the landscape already lay under the stillness of night. Letty had gone upstairs to see to Ida and we were temporarily without our presiding deity.

'Let's swim.' Beatrice's expression was mulish; her eyes had a hard glitter and her lower lip bulged over a chin as round as a hen's egg. She looked so like her father that I felt afraid of what I knew.

She persisted. 'I've never swum in the lake. Let's swim.'

My discomfort remained, a nagging pain. Suddenly, all I wanted was to have the evening over and done with. 'The water's jolly cold, you know, even in summer.'

'All the better. It's such a hot night.' Beatrice turned to Philip and raised her voice. 'Philip wants to swim – don't you, Philip?' And when he made some non-committal murmur, she seized on it for agreement. 'There you are – I told you he did.'

By now we'd left the terrace. We were strolling, four abreast, down the lawn towards the lake and, with every step, it became more difficult to say, 'That's far enough. Let's go back.'

Beatrice had already linked her arm with Philip's, taking him captive. 'I say we swim.'

Only now, I remembered my blue alpaca bathing dress, folded in a drawer at home. 'What are we supposed to swim in, Bea? We can hardly walk into the lake in our petticoats.'

So much for swimming! Then I heard Beatrice's voice in the dusk, coolly provocative.

'I don't see why we should have to wear anything at all. Men often bathe naked, don't they? Why shouldn't we?'

There was a long silence, broken only by the rhythmic whisper of our four pairs of feet over the parched grass stems.

'What – swim with nothing on at all?'

'Why not?' Beatrice's blouse rustled as she shrugged. 'It's almost dark now. Nobody's going to see anything. Besides, I've always wanted to know what it was like to be absolutely naked in the water, without yards of skirt and stupid black stockings. Don't you want to try it?'

We were all, I have to say, three parts drunk, but not sleepy drunk, or confused. Ours was a dangerous, clear-headed derangement; we were brilliantly, inventively, recklessly drunk. And we were hot, as hot as the thick air which barely satisfied our lungs and which lay like a damp, stifling blanket over every inch of our skin.

'Of course, if you're going to be prudish about it, Chrissie, then you needn't come in.' Beatrice's scorn was blistering. 'I'd forgotten how old-fashioned and narrow-minded country people can be. But Philip and I are definitely going to swim. What about you, Jack – are you a scaredy-cat too?'

'I'll swim.' It was the first time Jack had spoken since we'd left the house.

'I'm not a scaredy-cat,' I heard myself say. *Country people* had stung. It reminded me of the sixpence Beatrice had given me at our first meeting. 'I've swum in the lake since I was little. I bet I swim better than you do, Bea.'

'Prove it, then.'

It wasn't the icy blackness of the water which disturbed me – though I dare say it should have. It wasn't even the possibility of being seen without a stitch of clothing; in my drink-exalted state the idea of sliding into the water as naked as a savage was exhilarating. What did it matter if I was seen? That night had so obviously been made for glorious risks – for shamelessness, for experiment, for the breaking of sour old rules – for the headlong indulgence of the senses. Not for thinking, and certainly not for guilt.

'Oh, *come on*, Chrissie!' This, Beatrice had clearly decided, was to be the night when she annexed Philip Kassel once and for all.

We stripped off among the alders by the jetty, Beatrice and I, racing not to be the one left behind, tearing clumsily at unseen hooks and eyes. Beatrice lost her brooch in the long grass, dratted it, and then insisted she didn't care. Beyond the lowest leaves, the dusk was a haze of silver-grey; in our ghostly refuge white garments split open to reveal flushed, humid skin, flickered, and were discarded in the blackness at our feet.

Somewhere nearby, a gurgle of disturbed water indicated that Jack and Philip were already in the lake, but separately, still not speaking to one another. Beside me, Beatrice took a deep breath and stood up, straightening her back and raising an uncertain hand to sweep hair from her damp forehead. She was completely naked, as rounded and ripe as a heavy bunch of grapes, all shoulders, breasts, hips and knees, and the soft, dark, fuzzy shadow between her hips given a pearly bloom by the night.

'Ready?' Her voice was tight and nervous. She flung me a glance, wildly resolute, gulped another breath and pushed through the branches towards the lake.

Jack and Philip were chest-deep in the shallows where the chill was bearable, their faces hovering like lesser moons over the midnight surface of the water. I heard Beatrice gasp as the coldness engulfed her thighs, and saw her lean forward to swish the water like a day-tripper at the seaside, forcing a brazen laugh. I hoped Philip realized it was all done for his sake. I wondered how far he'd let Beatrice go.

'So you came in after all.' As I lowered myself into the lake and felt its cool, dispassionate fingers explore my skin, Jack's voice cut through the darkness and, a moment later, I heard the first ripples of his approach. 'I didn't think you'd dare.'

Somewhere beyond, Beatrice was swimming round after Philip. The thought made me bold. 'You've no idea what I'd dare.'

'No.' His head and shoulders resolved themselves into a pale island, reassuring in the blackness. Droplets of water clung like glinting beads to his hair and trickled down into the wells where his collarbones rose, delicately bird-winged, when he rested his hands on his hips. 'So why did you?'

'Why did I what?'

'Change your mind.'

'I don't know. I was hot, I suppose.'

'You were hot.'

'Isn't that a good enough reason?'

'I don't know.' There was silence for a moment. 'I don't understand what goes on in women's heads.' The words flew bitterly into the night among the tiny, milling insects.

'It's much the same as goes on in men's heads, I should think.'

'No.' The denial was swift and absolute. He swung his hands, pushing the idea away, driving the water into great whorls. 'I used to think so. But it isn't the same at all.'

'All right, then – it isn't.'

Crossly, I turned my back on him and swam away for a couple of strokes. A short way off, Beatrice and Philip were thrashing the lake into a ghostly foam, soaking one another and shrieking. With nothing better to do, I swam back to where I'd left Jack. From that angle a trick of the light made the skin of his face look dark and exotic; he'd tanned quickly in the few hours he'd spent away from the *Siren*. I swam slowly, admiring the harmony of his head and shoulders, the clean line of muscle and bone. By now my eyes had become accustomed to the night and I noticed a pulsing shadow under the angle of his jaw, one – two – three, tapping intently.

'For instance . . .' He spoke as if I'd been there all the time, tightly, as if he'd been losing his temper little by little. 'For instance, *you* should be able to tell me—'

He pushed violently against the engulfing water, his fingers spurting strings of seedpearls through the glassy black-green. It occurred to me how much more vivid he seemed in the dusk or in the shadows of the boathouse, as if full daylight dimmed him like a flame. His intensity needed the night as a foil.

A scream split the darkness – Beatrice, squealing with excitement.

'Damn it—' The words suddenly burst out of him as if they could no longer be contained. 'What kind of madness turns a decent woman into a whore?' Frustrated, he beat the water with the flat of his hand. 'What makes a woman throw herself at a man she hardly knows? Not a man – a boy – a fool. For God's sake, what does she see in her looking-glass each morning, if it isn't something vulgar and worthless?'

Startled, I thought he was talking about his sister. 'It's so hot, I suppose she just wanted to swim. There didn't seem any great harm in it—'

'*What?* Who on earth are you talking about?'

'Bea, of course—'

'Not her, for heaven's sake!'

'Oh.' A great drum was banging in my ears. It seemed impossible that he couldn't hear it.

'Why do you keep moving away from me?'

'I didn't know I was.' Yet I'd been drifting towards the shore; my buttocks grounded on shingle and I began to tip over on to my back. Jack's hand, swimming, skimmed my thigh.

'You haven't answered my question.'

'How can I, if I don't know who you're talking about?'

My fingers scrabbled for a hand-hold in the loose grit of the lake bottom. By now we were both in the shallows, where the wavelets washed and sucked at our bodies, bubbling between us.

'Just a woman! Here—' He reached out to draw a strand of wet hair from my eyes with a kind of distracted tenderness. 'All right – a married woman.'

Now I knew he'd been watching them, Letty and Philip, and had seen everything I'd seen, and – knowing his mother so much better, I suppose – had realized what was going on between them. Even then, I tried to deny it.

'You can hardly expect me to answer a hypothetical question—'

'I do.'

'But if I don't know who you mean—'

'Don't play stupid games! You're no more of a fool than I am!'

The hand which had touched my hair suddenly reached out to cradle my jaw, keeping my face turned relentlessly to his. Whatever he saw there increased his suspicions.

'You do know something.'

'I don't know anything at all.' I squirmed from his grasp and scrambled, splashing, to my feet. 'Now, leave me alone!'

He made a grab for my leg. It was too wet and slippery for him to hold, but he was up in a moment and running, and managed to catch me where the ground rose at the jetty by hooking my arm, and pushing me against the weather-worn planks. The wood was cool now and the edge pressed into my naked back.

'Please – you're hurting me.'

'I'm sorry. I didn't mean to.' He released his hold, but kept me imprisoned by leaning his hands on the wood on either side of my shoulders. How bizarre to be there, pressed as close as a couple on a dance floor, brute-naked and trembling, yet instinctively saying *please* and I'm sorry! He was breathing as hard as I was. We were so close that every couple of seconds my nipples brushed his chest, sending little darts of sensation down through my belly, all the way to my knees. I wondered if he was aware of it. We'd turned our faces aside and yet we remained cheek-to-cheek so that our damp skin almost touched and water dripped from his hair to trickle between my breasts. I felt his lips convulse against my ear.

'Tell me.'

Beatrice's voice drifted in from the lake, 'Phi–lip . . .'

'Philip Kassel.' His voice was almost a growl. 'Well?'

'You mustn't ask me.'

'Philip Kassel and my mother.'

134

'Please, Jack . . .'

Please again. I didn't want to touch him, to push him away; I couldn't bring myself to press my hands against that frightening, raw reality. His skin was warmer now and the smell of it, mingled with the faint scent of my borrowed cologne, reminded me of empty cigar-boxes, sweet and woody with an acid edge.

'Philip Kassel and my mother.'

I could have screamed at the animal nearness of him, the urgency, the throb in his voice. All I wanted was for him to let me go. 'Yes, they're lovers – yes, of course they are. Since you know it anyway.'

He let out a long, whistling sigh which tickled the hair by my ear and left a stillness where it passed. 'I was sure. It was impossible, but I was still sure.'

He hadn't let me go after all; I was afraid and I became angry. 'What has it got to do with you, anyway? Does it matter, if she's happy? I wouldn't expect you to understand—'

'Why not?' He tilted his head back to stare wildly at me. 'I've had nineteen years in my father's house, when I wasn't away at school. And my mother's been shut up with him, all that time – with his cruelty and jealousy. Believe me, I understand! What I can't do is *forgive* her! God help me, she's my *mother!*'

His face was too close to mine for proper focus. All I could see was a blurred mask of pain – Jack Dunstan, stripped raw, uncomprehending, flayed and laid open to the last agonized nerve – and I couldn't bear to watch. I forced myself to look away, to where a bat was zig-zagging among clouds of insects in the navy-blue void; he took it for indifference.

'Dammit, have you any idea what *he'll* do to her when he finds out?'

'Your father?' I turned back, startled. 'But why should he ever find out?'

'Because she'll give herself away! She's like a child, she can never keep a secret. If she'd left him – run away to something better, somewhere safer . . . But to ruin herself with *that*—' He flung back his head in desperation. 'With a pretty boy from Venice!'

'But Philip cares for her, I'm sure he does. Otherwise, I'd never have—' Too late, I swallowed the rest.

'What?' Like a wolf, he was searching my face again. When I stayed silent he almost shook me. 'What did you do?'

'I was the one who told her.' I forced up my chin, trying to recapture my belief in what I'd done. But something had changed. Now the only things I could remember were the swollen lips, the swaying, voluptuous walk and that frantic, greedy coupling among the trees. 'I told Letty that Philip was in love with her. He wouldn't say anything himself.'

'You helped him? You helped that bastard Kassel to ruin my mother?'

'Let me go!' Inches away, I could feel the hoarded anger welling inside him, searching for a focus. Philip and Letty were elsewhere; I was there, trapped – within reach.

'You helped him! You did his dirty work for him. You . . . bloody – little – *pander.*'

I had no idea what a pander might be. All I knew was that I was crushed between the jetty and a vigorous, tormented male body – that Jack's face was against mine, his mouth was searching furiously for mine, and his hands were tangled in my hair, snaring me, imprisoning me helplessly against him. From the distant terrace windows the scratching of a gramophone began to tinkle out into the night as someone – Letty, perhaps – wound up a waltz, saluting our bizarre dance of destruction.

'Speak to Letty!' I twisted my head, trying to escape. 'Say all this to *her*, for heaven's sake!'

'Damn you! How can I?'

The pain of it was like a sob in his voice. We were all knees and hips and hard, struggling, desperate flesh – a lifetime, now, beyond *please* and *I'm sorry* – and yet I could feel the seduction of that shared rhythm, that instinctive fusion of our striving bodies.

All at once, out of the felted air it started to rain, splashing us with warm, compassionate drops that smelled of honey and faded summer blossom, sprinkled over us like an absolution. I turned my face up to it, suddenly no longer afraid, understanding at last in some calm central core that this was how it was meant to happen and that I was meant to be part of it all, part of life and death, a small element in the eternal lake and the weeping sky. In that instant it seemed perfectly natural that Jack's rage should find deliverance in me and his despairing need find a release. But I'd no sooner thought of it than the heavens opened with a roar, engulfing us in a chilly torrent, a bombardment of water that battered our bare skin, ran into our open mouths and beat our eyelids closed, shocking us into immobility. A lump like a boulder rose in my chest, cold and dispossessing. In my despair I pressed my lips against the still, wet smoothness of Jack's shoulder and encountered sweetness. Over our heads, the thunder rolled again.

Then, quite nearby, I heard Beatrice calling out 'Chrissie! Jack! Where are you?' just as a mighty flash lit everything, Beatrice's wet head and Philip's, bobbing like footballs in the lake, eyes and mouths in a frozen *oh*, and Jack Dunstan, standing apart from me now, white as bone, the god of creation made flesh.

Out in the lake, Beatrice was weeping and calling my name.

Chapter Nine

THE NEXT DAY was Friday, and I stayed away from Waterside. Philip went back on Monday, but I didn't. I claimed to have a head cold, but I wasn't so much ill as sick to my soul. My chief symptom was a crawly self-loathing that made me wish I could slough off my skin like a lizard and step out in bright new colours, completely cleansed of the soiled, uncomfortable past.

For once, I was grateful when Par read out the significant parts of his newspaper at breakfast, covering my silence with his high, querulous monotone. It was August 3rd, and I remember the fact that Germany had declared war on Russia two days earlier being tut-tutted over as something that had happened in unruly Europe, safely beyond our shores. The discovery of an unknown fresco by Paolo Veronese excited my father far more and made me pass over, in my preoccupied state, the full importance of what was happening across the North Sea.

I spent most of the morning sitting silently in the drawing room window with my feet curled up on the upholstered seat, hugging a cushion. Everything was going wrong and not just between nations. I could see now that where I'd tried to bring happiness, I'd simply opened the door to pain and distress; worse, I'd encouraged Letty Dunstan to put herself in real danger. I hated to think what the springmaker might do if he found out about Philip – this man who'd ruin a rival without a moment's hesitation. What would he do to the mother of his children? Throw her out? Divorce her? Keep her youngest child from her?

I could see it all with horrible, unsentimental clarity now it was too late to undo the damage.

The world was a hostile place. I tried my old childhood trick of escaping to the looking-glass room reflected in the big overmantel mirror, where I imagined myself walking upside-down on the back-to-front ceiling, round and round the plaster rose – an effort of concentration that almost always took my mind off my troubles. This time, it didn't.

And because I hadn't turned up at Waterside, Beatrice came to seek me out.

'Are you all right?' She gazed at me suspiciously from under her smooth brow.

'Just a bit of a sniffle, that's all.' To prove it, I sniffed. 'It'll be gone tomorrow.'

'No, I mean *all right* – after Thursday night when we went swimming. You were terribly quiet when you went away. I thought maybe Jack had been stupid and you were in a huff or something.'

'No.' I gave an airy little shrug. 'No huff.'

'It did get rather . . . out of hand. I suppose we'd all had too much to drink. And then there was that terrible thunderstorm. I couldn't remember which was worse – to be struck by lightning in the water or on land.'

Beatrice plumped herself down in an armchair by the fireplace and smoothed her skirt with critical care. Silently, I started to count the Chinese plates in the alcove behind her, determined to keep the conversation on safe, trivial ground.

At last she raised her head and fixed me with solemn eyes. 'Chrissie – can I speak to you? In confidence, I mean?'

'Don't you always?'

'No. This is important. It's about Philip.'

'Philip?' I took refuge in teasing. 'Now, what has Philip done, I wonder? He's usually such a perfect gentleman.'

'That's just the point.' Beatrice kept up her sombre stare, defying me to make fun of her. 'He is – always – a perfect gentleman. Even when I give him every chance not to be. That night, in the lake, for instance – I mean, most men, if they really liked a girl, would at least try to kiss her, or do something. There we were, without a stitch on . . . actually, it's just as well it rained, or Mother would've wanted to know how we got our hair wet.' Beatrice rolled her eyes. 'But the point is, I did think that for once – for *once* – Philip might get sort of carried away. But there was nothing at all, Chrissie, he didn't try to touch me, or get 'familiar', or do anything. In fact, if it didn't sound so silly, I'd almost say he seemed frightened of me. You'd have thought I was his maiden aunt!'

'Oh. I see.' I groped for an explanation Beatrice might accept. 'Perhaps he isn't as much of a Casanova as you think.'

Beatrice tucked in her chin and inspected her hands. 'Or maybe there's another explanation.'

'It's always possible he's taken a vow of chastity.'

Beatrice's head snapped up; her expression was savage. 'Don't make fun of me, Chrissie! I know I'm not as clever as you are, or sarcastic, like Jack, but I'm not totally stupid. I do have *eyes*. I can see things that are going on.'

'Look, Bea . . .' I was becoming nervous. 'Maybe Philip's just a little shy. Have you thought of that?'

'Or maybe he's in love with my mother!' Beatrice leaned forward, snapping out the words. Her teeth gleamed as her lips drew back, spitting out her suspicions with cobra-like malice. For a moment, she stayed like that, immobile. Then, having made her point, she settled herself upright again. 'Haven't you seen the way Philip trails after Mother like a little dog, fetching her parasol, keeping her glass filled, gazing at her with those big black eyes of his as if he'd like to eat her up? Oh, yes.' Beatrice stretched her neck as if the smell of the evidence offended her. 'I can see it all now. He was never really interested in me at all. It was Mother all the time and I've let him take me for a real fool.'

'But surely you aren't suggesting . . .' I stopped, cautious.

'What? That Mother's encouraged him? I haven't seen her

doing anything to *dis*courage him – have you?' She fixed me with a righteous stare. 'I mean, she must know perfectly well how I feel about Philip and yet she's kept him dangling round her like a little slave-boy.'

'Indulged him, you mean. In his infatuation.' I suddenly realized I'd been holding my breath. 'I suppose it's quite flattering. She is a lot older, after all.'

'But that just makes it worse, Chrissie. It's disgusting! She *is* old. She's married. She's got Father, hasn't she? Why should she have Philip being soppy about her, too?'

Beatrice hadn't used the word *lover*; I put up a silent prayer of gratitude. 'It's always nice to be admired.'

'Well, I think it's ridiculous. And I think Philip's an idiot. In fact, I'm going to tell him so, the first chance I get. I've a good mind to tell Father when he gets back.'

'Bea – I wouldn't do that, honestly.'

'Why not?'

'He might not understand. He might easily – well – jump to the wrong conclusion. See more in it than there is.' I was beginning to wish I hadn't spoken. 'You know how possessive he is.'

'Well then, he'll know exactly how I feel about Philip, won't he?'

I could only see one solution: for Philip to leave Fellwood – and Waterside – as soon as possible and give up any thought of Letty Dunstan. I cornered him as soon as he came home and manoeuvred him into the dining room.

'Philip – have you spoken to Beatrice?'

He shrugged. 'Not since yesterday.'

'Thank goodness for that. Something awful's happened.'

'I know.' His brow furrowed, and he thrust his hands into his pockets. 'The Germans have declared war on France now. Mrs Dunstan got a telegram from London. I'd no idea things had gone so far.'

'Oh, dear. I mean, have they? There was something in Par's newspaper this morning, but I didn't pay much attention. It all seemed to be diplomats sending official letters.' Now I could read the seriousness of the situation in his face. 'You don't think there'll really be fighting, do you?'

'Goodness knows.' He stared at me, abstracted, and then looked down at the carpet. 'All I do know is that it's ruined everything I'd planned.'

'Going up to Oxford? Why should this make any difference?'

'No, no. Forget Oxford. That's all in the past.' Irritably, he brushed the suggestion aside. 'The vital thing now is to find a place where Letty and I can live, where she'll be safe. I had thought we could stay in the south of France for a bit, until the fuss died down. But as things have turned out—' He chewed his lower lip. 'We'll just have to wait, that's all. I expect the war will be over soon enough.'

I couldn't keep the shock out of my voice. 'You're planning to run away with Letty Dunstan? For good? You're going to run off with *Alfred Dunstan's wife*?'

'Well, of course!' A black curl fell forward like a question mark over his astonished eyes. 'Chrissie, I *told* you! This isn't a passing infatuation. I couldn't live without Letty now, any more than I could exist without the sun or the stars. I'd be like one of those poor devils in the dungeons in Venice, locked away from the light because someone had betrayed them to the Council. It would be a living death – and it's the same for her, I know it is.'

'She's agreed to go away with you?'

His left hand stole up to tug at his ear-lobe and he laughed, a fond, indulgent laugh, old before its time. 'Letty's such an innocent. She likes to pretend that if she doesn't worry too much about the future, everything will take care of itself. It's one of the things I love most about her.' He drew himself up, a young warrior facing a hostile world. 'That's why I have to take care of everything.'

'Philip, this is crazy – you're only eighteen years old!'

'So?' His stare was disdainful. 'I'm not a child, you know. Or are you going to trot out all the sniggering rubbish you hear about young boys and older women? What is it they say? Everything goes merrily along until the day he notices the chicken-scales on his lady-friend's neck and she catches him going through her purse. Is *that* what you think we are, Letty and I?' Outrage gave his voice a hard, defiant edge.

'Of course not! Far more than that—'

'Nothing like that at all!'

I gaped at him, speechless. This was much, much worse than I'd feared. Surely the whole world had taken leave of its senses.

'But, Philip, this is all impossible! Beatrice already suspects there's something going on and I'm afraid she may tell her father. That's what I was going to say to you. For Letty's sake, if not for your own, you have to put an end to this affair.'

'Ah.' His dark brows lowered again. 'Beatrice. Yes, that's a nuisance. Never mind, I'll find a way of keeping her quiet.'

'No, Philip!' I tried to bring my face directly before his. 'The only way out of this mess is for you to go away and forget all about Letty Dunstan, Waterside and everything.'

He caught hold of my arms just above the elbows; I could feel the determination in his grip. 'Now, Chrissie, I'm grateful for your concern and for the warning about Beatrice, but I'll deal with this in my own way.' His dark eyes raked my face, as if searching for some hint that I understood the immensity of his love. 'How could I possibly forget about Letty? You might as well ask me to give up breathing. You can't expect it. What else do I have *in this world* but her?'

I left Waterside to itself the next day as well. I was too afraid of what was going to happen and that Jack would hold me to blame. I kept thinking if I could only explain to him about Venice, and the balcony, and how everything had suddenly changed there . . . But I couldn't banish a vision of that dreadful, agonized face,

143

furiously imploring me for something I couldn't give him because I didn't understand what it was.

There was no relief to be found anywhere. The newspapers reported that if Germany invaded Belgium, ignoring Britain's warnings, our country, too, would be at war.

Philip came back from Waterside just after lunch, his face pinched and set, and ran upstairs to pack a bag.

'They're saying it wouldn't be a long war,' said Mar. 'No longer than Christmas, probably. But Philip's quite right to go up to London, just for a few days, to see if his father needs him.'

'Just for a few days?' I asked Philip, hoping faintly that he'd taken the coward's way out.

'One week at the most. There's something I have to do there.' He glanced up from a note he was writing and smiled grimly. 'Don't worry, Chrissie – everything's taken care of.'

'And what about Beatrice? If she says something to her father—'

'Beatrice won't say anything. I told you. It's all taken care of.'

Powley drove Philip to the station in the trap – and my father and young Sam Powley, too, on a particular errand that was enough to clear thoughts of anything else out of their heads for the afternoon. Some months earlier, Par had received an astonishingly large cheque from an American foundation for a monograph on *The Renaissance Capitalist: Cash and Conceit*. In a moment of madness, prompted by his hatred of the trap and the obvious comfort of the springmaker's motor cars, Par had ordered a Ford Model T tourer, which was now awaiting collected in a Windermere motor garage.

But first Philip Kassel had to be taken to the railway station. As he climbed down from the trap, Philip handed my father an envelope – a pearl-grey rectangle taken from the rack in his bedroom – and asked Par if he'd make sure it was delivered, by hand, to Letty Dunstan.

'As soon as possible? Well, of course, my boy. Safe journey to you.' Par leaned down to shake his hand. 'Now, Sam, where's this garage of yours?'

Three days later, Par and the Ford were back in the village for a tightening of brakes, Sam Powley's driving having already made my father nervous, when Par spotted his fellow motorist, Alfred Dunstan, boarding his vehicle outside the station.

'Friday afternoon, of course!' Par hurried over. 'Dash it! Just the man! I've been carrying this letter in my pocket for days. I completely forgot about it, in all this bother about the new motor. It's addressed to your wife, I believe.' Par pulled out the envelope and peered at the inscription. 'Yes, that's right. It's from the Kassel boy – Philip. He's gone off to London for a few days, to see about this war. Here, you might as well have it.' He gazed enviously at the springmaker's tasselled upholstery. 'Tell me, Dunstan, don't you find this motor of yours swings about a bit on corners?'

I met Beatrice in the haberdasher's the following day, buying a silver chain-link purse, just in case they were all commandeered for the war.

'Why haven't you come back to Waterside?' She examined me sourly. 'I'm angry and fed up and I've no one to talk to.'

'Has Jack said anything about me?'

'No, he hasn't.' She pouted. 'But then, Jack doesn't say a word to anyone these days. He turns up for meals in a filthy mood, and the rest of the time I never see him.' Her eyes narrowed. 'I was right, wasn't I? You two have had a quarrel.'

'No – nothing like that.'

'Oh no?' Beatrice's eyebrows rose in twin arches of disbelief. 'I've told you before, Chrissie – I'm not blind. I may not say anything, but I do *know* what's going on. And there's been plenty of that recently, let me tell you!'

'You mean . . .' I tried to read her meaning in her face. 'Philip?'

'Of course, Philip, who else? Rat that he is,' she added furiously. 'If I told you all that's been going on in our house – under our very noses – behind Father's back . . . Oh, it makes me sick to think of it!' She blew out her lips in exasperation, and then eyed me shrewdly. 'You don't seem very surprised.'

'Philip . . . dropped a few hints before he went off to London.'

'Oh, he's told you, has he? The whole sordid story. About how he and my mother have been having an affair?' Beatrice's expression was stony. 'He ought to be ashamed of himself, but he isn't. He seems to think Fate arranged the whole disgusting business and he isn't to blame for any of it. He has to follow his destiny, or some such nonsense. I think he's a double-dealing swine.'

'Aren't you sorry for him – even a bit?'

Her face seemed to shrivel and grow hard before my eyes. It was like an indrawing of the spirit, a withholding of compassion and humanity and tenderness, all the instincts that go to making the soul wholesome and generous.

'Sorry for Philip Kassel?' She gave a contemptuous sniff. 'Of course not. I'm just glad I saw through him from the start. I always thought there was something *foreign* about him. I was absolutely right not to trust him and I think Mother's taken leave of her senses.' She clasped her hands in front of her bosom and drew in her round little chin. 'He wormed his way into our house and I blame you for that, Christabel Ascham. If you hadn't invited him to stay – him and his weaselly little father – none of this would have happened.

'Now he actually believes Mother's in love with him. You should have heard the nonsense he told me!' Beatrice's gaze was relentless and unblinking. 'He's got some idea they're going to run off together in a month or two, once this war's over and they can go to the south of France.' She curled her lip. 'It's pathetic, isn't it?'

Her scorn was almost tangible, her disgust as powerful as her passion had been only a few weeks earlier. The force of it disturbed me. 'Poor Philip. You're right, he should never have come here.'

'Mother won't go anywhere with him, of course. Why should she? He's just a little schoolboy she's using to pass the time. If I told Father what's been going on, he'd break Philip Kassel in half.' Beatrice spoke with such relish that I began to panic.

'But what about your mother? You don't want her to suffer, do you?'

'It would be her own fault, wouldn't it? Carrying on with a boy young enough to be her own son? It's no more than she deserves.'

'Bea, I know it isn't any of my business, but—' I laid a hand on her sleeve. 'Sometimes it's best to say nothing, for everyone's sake.'

Beatrice looked at me speculatively for a moment, as if wondering where my loyalties lay.

'As it happens, I'm not going to tell Father.'

'Oh, I'm so glad—'

'I've made a bargain with Philip. He was quite desperate, in fact, absolutely begged me to keep his secret.' Her lips formed a grim line of satisfaction. "Give me one good reason for keeping silent," I said to him. "You and Mother took me for a fool. Well, now you can pay for it. See what it's like when *you* want something you can't have."'

Beatrice's eyes kindled at the memory. She'd wanted Philip, in spite of all her denials, but Letty had taken him from her. I knew in that moment that Beatrice would never, ever, forgive either of them. Whatever had ensured her silence, I guessed it hadn't been compassion.

Beatrice's voice broke into my thoughts. 'When did Philip say he was coming back from London?'

'On Wednesday, as far as I remember. Why do you want to know?' An inexplicable chill crept round my heart.

'Because he's bringing me something.' She thrust out her chin and surveyed me coolly.

'What?'

'The price of my silence. I think it's time he was taught a lesson, you see.' Her face became suddenly savage. 'I'm not a fool, Chrissie and I won't be taken for one.'

Monday morning came, but the springmaker wasn't at the station to catch the Manchester train. On Tuesday our parlourmaid, Annie Steadman, reported that her sister, who worked at Waterside, had heard raised voices from Mrs Dunstan's bedroom – Mr Dunstan's voice, mainly – after which Mrs Dunstan had taken to her bed with a migraine and her husband had emerged holding a pearl-grey envelope, which he'd locked in his desk.

Philip came back after lunch on Wednesday, looking pale and drawn. In London everything was war and confusion. Kitchener was said to be looking for 100,000 volunteer soldiers and the Navy to be searching for enemy vessels. In our village, the butcher had put up a notice: 'No German Sausage for the Duration of the War'.

Philip left his bag in his room and came bounding downstairs. 'I have to go over to Waterside right away.'

I stopped him at the door. 'Alfred Dunstan's at home. He hasn't gone to Manchester this week.'

I saw Philip's confidence waver. 'Oh, well. It doesn't matter. As long as I can have a few moments alone with Letty.'

'Philip, why not leave it until tomorrow – please? I don't trust Beatrice.'

His face became bleak. 'Don't worry about Beatrice. I've got something here that will keep her quiet for a while.' He touched the pocket of his coat. 'It had better.'

'Why? What do you mean – it had better?' The expression on his face frightened me. He had the violent, hunted air of a fugitive, a desperate man risking everything on the turn of a single card. 'What on earth have you done? What has Beatrice made you do?'

His eyes met mine, black hollows, empty of shame or defiance. He'd passed beyond such things: nothing existed for him now but the wild, overpowering need which drove him, for good or ill – it no longer made any difference.

'When I got to London I discovered my father was still in America. His ship had been delayed because of the war.'

'So?'

'So—' The words ripped out like bullets. '*So* – I opened his safe and took the Medici Pearls.'

'For *Beatrice?*'

He shut his eyes, and a kind of shudder passed through his stiffened shoulders. 'What else could I do? I had to buy time to speak to Letty – to arrange things, to make plans.' He ran a distracted hand through his hair. 'There must be somewhere we can go, where that man Dunstan can't find us. I'd thought, perhaps, Italy. But now Italy's being hauled into this damnable war. Maybe America – I don't know.' He gazed at me fiercely. 'Compared to what I've done here, does it matter if I'm a thief? I'm beyond pity – I know it. This will break my father's heart when he finds out. But Chrissie—' He took hold of my hands. 'I'd murder for her, if I had to, without any hesitation. Believe me. And now I must go.'

'Philip!' I called after him as he hurried towards the top of the drive. But I was too late. Either he didn't hear me, or his mind was too full of thoughts of Letty and what he'd done for her sake. He vanished behind the rhododendrons without turning his head.

Chapter Ten

MY PARENTS had gone to Grasmere in the Ford. Noël had set off by bicycle to Boot, where he planned to put his machine on the train and travel down to Ravenglass for a couple of days to make drawings of the Roman villa at Walls. I thought of going down to the kitchen for a chat with Mrs Hall, our cook, but my heart wasn't in it. My heart and my mind were with Philip at Waterside; and after more than an hour had gone by, I decided that where my heart and mind had gone, the rest of my body might as well go too. Not that I meant to go all the way to the house; I just couldn't stay at home, staring at the meaningless lines of a book. It had started to rain – it rains a good deal in our part of the world – and dark squall-lines were travelling across the distant surface of the lake. There was nothing for it but to snatch a macintosh and an umbrella and set off along the road in the direction of Waterside.

I was hoping to meet Philip coming back. I hadn't thought what I'd do if I covered the whole distance to the gates without meeting him. As it happened, just as I turned the last bend that revealed the iron gates with the lodge beside them, a figure in white ran out from the opening, stopped, gazed round, thrust a hand crazily through his hair and started off at a peculiar half-running, half-stumbling pace away from me towards the village. I was sure it was Philip. I shouted his name, but I was too far away for him to hear. I couldn't imagine why he'd set off in the opposite direction to Fellwood. He had no hat or waterproof. He

was going to get wet through and he hadn't even fastened his
jacket, which was flapping open.

'Philip! Wait!'

I slipped off my shoes, stuffed them into the pockets of my
macintosh and took off after him like a hare, the umbrella
bobbing. The road was stony and hurt my feet, but I didn't care.
He didn't hear me flying behind him until the last minute. He
kept on stumbling and trudging towards the village, dragging his
feet, running a bit, and all the time gasping in great uneven
breaths that seemed pumped by the arms that flailed at his sides.

'Philip!' I caught up with him at last and wound my arm like
an anchor round one of his. 'Where on earth are you going?'

He stopped, swayed, and stared at me, I swear, almost without
recognition.

'What?'

'Philip — what's happened? Why didn't you come back to
Fellwood? I've been worried to death about you.' I tried to hold
my umbrella over us both, but he kept pushing the edge away as
if its black arch was unbearable to him.

'Here, under this tree, then. That'll give us a bit of shelter, at
least.'

I had to drag him to the trunk by main force. He kept shaking
his head and staring round, as if there was something vital he had
to do, if he could only remember what it was.

'Waterside—' I pulled his damp jacket together across his thin
chest, but he pushed me away impatiently. 'What happened,
Philip? What about Letty — and Beatrice?'

The names seemed to rouse him. He drew a hand across his
eyes.

'Finished. It's all finished. Everything.' His eyes filled. His
face was the colour of putty, with great leaden hollows under his
cheekbones. 'Here—' He dug in his jacket pocket, holding the
edge of the garment with scrabbling fingers, pushing the pocket
out of shape. Without a word, he handed me a crumpled sheet of
writing paper and I smoothed it out against the bole of our tree.

Philip

I have promised my husband never to see you again.
What occurred between us was dishonourable, but it was
also brief and meaningless. Alfred understands this and has
generously forgiven me.

You were wrong to believe I would give up my
marriage for you. My husband has, and will continue to
have, all my love and my loyalty. Do not try to
communicate with me again.

Letty Dunstan.

Philip was staring at the paper. He traced the outline of a
word with a finger. 'Meaningless.' He shook his head slowly.
'No. That isn't true.'

I read the note again swiftly. 'Alfred Dunstan must have
forced Letty to write this. I can't believe she'd be so cruel. But
how could he have found out?' I glanced at him. 'Beatrice? Did
Beatrice tell him?'

Philip's shoulders gathered in a despairing shrug; it no longer
mattered. His anguished eyes rose to meet mine. 'It wasn't all
meaningless – was it?'

'No, it wasn't.' I tucked my arm into his and pulled him close.
'Letty would never have sent you away like that if you'd seen
her.'

'Oh yes.' He nodded bleakly. 'She did.'

'You saw her? You actually spoke to her?'

'Dunstan brought her into the room. After I'd read the note.
She seemed . . . quite strong, quite determined.' Philip's gaze slid
away from my face towards the dripping fringe of leaves that
bounded our shelter, but I doubted if he saw it.

'He said – Dunstan said – "Well, wife, there's your lover. He
can't believe you don't want him any more – he wants to hear
you say it yourself. So here and now I'm giving you your
freedom. Go off with him if you want. Go on, I won't stand in

your way. The two of you can walk out of this house together and I won't lift a hand to stop you."'

Philip's face grew avid and he thrust out his hands. 'I told her to come away with me – not to be afraid – that there were places we could go to where she'd be safe.' His gaze dropped to his fingers, clutching the empty air. 'But she wouldn't leave him, even when I begged her. She said her place was there, in his house, and I actually think at that moment she believed it.'

'Oh, Philip . . .' I slid my arm round his back, but he pushed me off and took a step away, in the direction of the village. 'Where are you going? Fellwood's this way.'

He swung round and considered the alternative for a few seconds. 'No.' He shook his head. 'I have to go. I can't stay here.'

'But it's pouring with rain and you've nothing but the clothes you're wearing. Please, Philip – come back to Fellwood, until tomorrow, at least. You'll feel better after some sleep.'

'*Sleep?*' He stared at me for a moment, then gazed up into the branches overhead as if he'd discovered them for the first time, and lurched abruptly out into the rain.

'But where are you going, for heaven's sake?'

He threw out an arm in a gesture that embraced the whole universe. 'Away. Somewhere. Anywhere but here.'

'Oh, Philip – take care, please . . .'

But he'd gone, stumbling off towards the village, determined to escape from my concern. For the second time that day I watched him disappear towards his future without a backward glance.

Beatrice had warned me, 'She won't go anywhere with him, of course.' Perhaps Beatrice, for all her silliness, was wiser than I was in the ways of the world. I'd believed Letty had loved Philip, just as he'd loved her and still did, I imagined, in his hopeless, bewildered heart. I'd seen her finger trail like a tear down her lover's cheek and her fond, golden glances. I'd come to believe with Philip that, given the freedom to choose, Letty would follow her lover out of the prison of her husband's house. Now, I simply didn't understand. I wouldn't have treated a dog in the way Letty had treated Philip.

I had to find some explanation to give Mar. I told her there'd been a row of some kind at Waterside and that Philip had needed a few days away from us.

'He's desperately unhappy,' I said.

Mar made a so-so face. 'Ah well. He's young.'

I didn't remember the Medici Pearls until I was undressing for bed. Perhaps Philip would have time before his father returned to put the necklace back where it belonged. I only hoped he hadn't given it to Beatrice.

Sometime that night, the enormous iron gates to the main drive at Waterside were swung shut and – according to the butcher's boy who told our cook next day – they could now only be opened by the lodge-keeper by prior arrangement with the house itself. Annie Steadman passed on a report from her sister that Mrs Dunstan was ill and not receiving visitors. Mar sent an experimental gift of strawberries, only to have them returned with the message that Mrs Dunstan 'regretted that she couldn't accept them'. Waterside had drawn in upon itself.

'Curious people,' Par concluded. 'Do you know, when I gave Dunstan that letter for his wife, you'd have thought I'd handed him a bomb. "It's just from Philip Kassel," I said, but it didn't make any difference. There was no pleasing the man.'

Now, at last, I understood how the lovers' secret had been given away. I had no idea what Philip had written to Letty, but I could guess. And I could picture the springmaker's iron-grey head bent incredulously over the protestations of love, the silly private names, the reminders of passionate moments and the promises to return soon with a plan for Letty's freedom. It said a great deal about the man that he must have read all this on Friday night and bided his time. Cuckolded – no doubt with the knowledge of his staff and therefore of half the district, too – he'd nevertheless kept his temper and silently made his plans.

Later that day Hosanna Greendew arrived at Fellwood, waving a note. The Dunstans were returning to Manchester. Hosanna's services as tutor to Alfred's daughters would not, after all, be required in the autumn.

Hosanna's bosom swelled with indignation. She hissed in my ear, 'Those girls would be a great deal better off filling their minds with solid geometry than *other things* I've heard about.'

The following day, a farm cart loaded with her brother's paints, scaffolding, bottles of turpentine and rolled-up sketches arrived at the Greendews' cottage together with a cheque for the balance of Jeremy's fee. The painter of murals was no longer wanted. I wondered if, even then, one of the gardeners was covering Jeremy's wayward Venus with whitewash.

Max Kassel had more determination than the rest of us. Two days later, desperate with concern for Philip, he simply presented himself at the door of the lodge at Waterside and refused to go away until he was let in. Philip hadn't returned to London after all. Max had come back from America to find a note several days old explaining that Philip had left for the Lakes to begin a new life with Letty Dunstan, the only person who made his existence worthwhile. Now, at Waterside, Max discovered that Letty had stayed with her husband, while Philip had fled in a state of despair. The springmaker had no idea where the young man might have gone and couldn't have cared less. As far as he was concerned, he hinted unpleasantly, if it turned out that Philip was never seen again, the world would have lost a dangerous troublemaker.

As for the Medici Pearls – all thirty of them, with their diamond clasp – he claimed to know nothing about them.

★

'I doubt if anything that went on in that house would surprise me.' By the time Max Kassel had finished his story Mar was wearing her severest outraged-lizard expression. I guessed I was in for a long interrogation once the pearl merchant had gone upstairs for the night.

'I haven't told the police yet that the pearls are missing.' Max Kassel sighed gloomily. 'I should have told them, I know. But, you see, if Philip comes back in a day or two and still has the pearls, no one need know they were ever missing. Then no one will call him a thief – or me along with him. But, obviously, I can't wait for ever.

I stared at him indignantly. 'But nobody can blame you, surely! And the pearls must be insured.'

'They are, of course. But you don't lose the Queen's pearls – irreplaceable, historic pearls – and expect to stay in business.' The pearl dealer shrugged. 'Word will soon get round that Max Kassel is not fit to be trusted. And yet—' His eyes grew round with injustice. 'Who else should know where my safe keys are kept, if not my son? And Philip is simply a young man in love.' He shook his head. 'I don't even blame Mrs Dunstan. No one can say "You must fall in love with this one, but not with that one."' He held out a hand to right and left. 'If it's anyone's fault, it's Alfred Dunstan's and mine, for not giving enough attention to people who had a right to expect it.'

'But you have important friends, surely.' Mar searched for scraps of comfort. 'All these wealthy people who've bought your pearls. They'll understand that you've done nothing wrong.'

'My dear Mrs Ascham, I've had a pair of pearl earrings pass through my hands and the owner cut me dead at the opera a week later. These people are business acquaintances, not friends. But, never mind.' He pulled up his shoulders, and his voice became firmer. 'What does it matter if the pearls are lost for ever, as long as I know Philip is safe and well?'

★

The following week, two strangers called on us from London, two men who described themselves as policemen 'of a sort' and gave an address in the War Office. One was small, with slicked-back hair, a thin moustache and the clipped manner of the professional army, as opposed to a gentleman officer. His companion was heavy-set and more silent, but I noticed his colleague called him Commander, and waited respectfully whenever he asked one of his slow, unexpected questions. What really made my hair stand on end, though, was their identical raincoats: loose, buff-coloured macintoshes with prominent rubbery seams, worn with identical black bowler hats. They were like men accustomed to a King's uniform who couldn't quite shake off the habit of conformity, no matter how hard they tried to pass for ordinary folk.

They'd already been to Waterside, asking questions about the Medici Pearls. Beatrice had admitted they'd been intended for her, but claimed they'd never been handed over. I wondered if that was true. If Alfred Dunstan was as deeply in debt as Max Kassel had said, the Medici Pearls, sold in secret, might have made a considerable difference. And yet Max had insisted that with pearls such as those, secrecy was impossible.

The men from the War Office specialized in secrets. They kept asking why Max had waited for almost a week before telling the police about the theft of the pearls.

'Well, naturally, he thought Philip would bring them back at any moment.' Mar's tone indicated impatience. 'What else would a father have done? They boy isn't a thief, you know.'

'But that's just what he is, in the eyes of the Law.' The small man balanced his bowler precisely on his knees. 'He's a thief, Mrs Ascham.'

'If he *was* the one who took the pearls, of course.' The heavy-set man stared round our drawing room as if he was on the look-out for stolen property. His face seemed uncomfortably flushed; both men had refused an invitation to remove their waterproof coats.

'Perhaps,' the large man added, 'we've been led to think the boy has the pearls, when, in fact, they're somewhere quite different.'

'But surely Philip left a note, confessing to the theft.'

'Anyone can write a note, Mrs Ascham.' The small man showed his teeth in a ferrety smile. 'You – me – even Mr Kassel, I dare say, though he claims he didn't.'

My father snorted. 'For goodness sake, man, don't tell me you suspect Max Kassel of having a hand in this? Why on earth should he want to ruin his own business?'

'He might – if someone made it worth his while.' The small man leaned forward significantly. 'You see, we've had our eye on Mr Kassel for some time now as he wandered round the world. Here today, gone tomorrow, always on the look-out for pearls – *so he says*. Who'd suspect him of looking out for bits of information at the same time, to pass back to his German masters?' He tugged at his moustache. 'For instance, did you ever notice anything a bit furtive about him while you were in Italy? Meetings on street corners? Callers arriving late at night?'

'But this is utterly preposterous!' My father swung his arms in disbelief and his spectacles flew out on the end of their chain. 'You can't think Max Kassel is a *spy*! But, my dear fellow, spies are supposed to keep hidden, not to advertise themselves by making off with bits of royal trinketry!' He appealed to the ceiling for the blessing of sanity. '*O, quis custodiet ipsos custodes?*'

The heavy-set man's eyes narrowed. 'So you speak foreign languages too, do you, sir?'

'That,' said my father succinctly, 'was Latin. It means "Who is to police the police?"'

'Does it, indeed?' The spy-catcher looked interested. 'And Mr Kassel speaks Latin, does he?'

'As an educated man, I imagine he does.'

'As well as Italian, German and French, like a native, a bit of Slovak here and there and a smattering of Arabic – that's an unusually wide education, wouldn't you say?' The small man looked meanly triumphant. 'Oh, don't worry, we know all about Mr Kassel and his accomplishments.'

He leaned forward again. 'And, speaking of foreigners, I'm sure I don't need to tell you – being an educated man, as you are, sir – that with this war on, there are small countries, too, who'd be only too pleased to get their hands on a bit of cash.' He tapped the top of his bowler. 'The pearls could be in the Balkans by now, waiting to be exchanged for guns and explosives. Use anything for money, those fellows.'

Mar wriggled indignantly in her chair. 'I've never heard such nonsense! Max Kassel is trusted by some of the most important people in Britain. Why on earth should he want to buy guns for the Albanians or the Bulgars?'

The small man whistled through his teeth. 'Enemy aliens, Mrs Ascham. Saboteurs. Anarchists. You might sit next to one in a railway carriage and never notice a thing – very polite, some of these exotics. And then, one day – *bang*!' He slapped a fist into a palm.

'Remember Sidney Street?' demanded the heavy-set man suddenly. 'Royal Horse Artillery brought up two 13-pounders, and they still couldn't root out those three. They might have been there yet, if the place hadn't burned down. Letts, they were.'

'Well I can assure you,' Mar informed him icily, 'that Max Kassel is neither an anarchist nor a spy.'

The small repeated his ferrety smile. 'No, ma'am. Course not.'

'He *isn't*. He just isn't. And neither is poor Philip, though I agree, he seems to have got himself into a silly mess.'

'More than a mess, ma'am, I'd say.' The small man explored the edge of his moustache with a finger. 'It's a matter of national security now. Which is why I'll have to ask you not to say a word about it outside this room, you two and the young lady. And if you do hear anything from young Kassel – here's my card.' He fished a piece of soiled pasteboard from an inside pocket, knocking his signet ring against something bulky and metallic. 'Any little details about the Kassels, anything you think I ought to know, that's where you can find me.'

We sent them back to the railway station in the trap, sitting side by side like pots of salt and pepper. I hoped the mysterious lump under the ferrety man's macintosh hadn't been a revolver. How could we have come so far from a few glances exchanged across an art gallery in Venice? I tried to push the image of a gun from my mind, but it lingered for a long time after the men had gone, like the smell of warm rubber in our drawing room.

By the time I saw the Dunstans again, the Germans were forcing their way through Belgium and the first British troops had landed in France. Par's newspaper announced that the New Zealanders had thrown out the German governor of distant Samoa. In the village, the baker's window had Union flags and coronation mugs set up among the tea-cakes.

I'd gone into Windermere to post some botanical specimens of Mar's which had to be dispatched with explicit instructions, and when I came out of the post office I saw the familiar long shape of Alfred Dunstan's motor drawn up nearby. There was no sign of the springmaker. Tipper the chauffeur was sitting, half-turned, in his driving seat with the air of someone who'd soon have to get down and open doors; behind him was a silhouette that looked very like Letty's. I was seized with a desire not to speak to her. I felt like a fellow-culprit in what had happened to Philip and I hadn't forgiven her any more than I'd forgiven myself. I'd have crossed the road to avoid her if she hadn't opened her door a little way and called my name.

'Chrissie.' Her gloved hand appeared in the opening, beckoning.

I walked over to the motor. 'Good morning, Mrs Dunstan.'

She'd leaned forward in her seat and now she pushed the door wide. 'Oh, I'm so glad. Won't you step inside for a moment and talk to me? The girls insisted on stopping at the sweet shop and they've been so long that Jack's gone to find them.'

Reluctantly, I climbed into the motor and she pushed Beatrice's dog off the seat to make a space for me, still chattering. 'We're going to Manchester today and I did hope to see you before we left, but – I had no way – Alfred only left this morning.'

'I understand.'

She closed the door behind me, giving us privacy. Even so, she'd dropped her voice so low that I wondered if Tipper had been paid to listen. At a few inches' distance, Letty looked more fragile than ever; her skin had the same transparent quality as the glass of a skeleton watch, as if there was nothing to hide each beat of her pulse and each spasm of her nerves. Her eyes devoured my face.

'Philip—' she whispered. 'Have you heard anything? I know his father was looking for him.'

I shook my head. I was tempted to demand *Do you care*? but I couldn't have flung such an accusation into that haunted countenance. 'No one's heard a thing. He's completely disappeared.'

'Oh, my God.' She hid her eyes in her gloved hands for a moment, recovered herself and, with a glance at the glass partition, clasped her fingers in her lap. 'I know you blame me for all this.' Her eyes met mine once more. 'You think I selfishly encouraged Philip to believe we had a future together. But I didn't.' She shook her head sadly. 'I only encouraged myself. I let myself dream, Chrissie – was that such enormous wickedness?'

'But if you loved Philip, why didn't you go away with him? He'd have looked after you. He adored you.'

'And in ten years' time?' Her eyes flashed with sudden moisture. 'Have you forgotten how old I am? In another ten years I'll be forty-eight and Philip won't even be thirty. My hair will be grey and I'll be trying to hide the lines on my throat with scarves and necklaces. Do you think Philip would still have adored

161

me then? Why should he, with women from all over Europe throwing themselves at him and wheedling themselves into his bed?'

She smiled grimly. 'So much for my dreams! Alfred finished those off in his own brutal way. He never forgets how old I am, even if I do.' Her hand rose like a bird from her lap, fluttered and fell. 'He doesn't have time for make-believe, my husband. But perhaps I should be grateful to him. There was truth in his cruelty. "He'll leave you." That's what he said. "He'll leave you in some broken-down *pension*, selling yourself to wealthy Englishmen taking the cure. And that's exactly what you'll deserve."'

'Philip would never do that!' I was outraged on Philip's behalf. 'You were everything to him—'

'Everything *now*. But young men change. You may find that out for yourself one day. In a few years' time – who knows how much of a burden Philip would have found me?' She straightened her shoulders. 'At least I know Alfred will still want me as his wife. I've damaged him and he won't ever forget that, but at least he hasn't lost me. In the end, you see, I chose Alfred over Philip and so he's beaten his rival, which is what matters most to him. Alfred never lets go of anything that's his, so I shall always be his wife. I shall always have a position and a roof over my head.'

Her eyes travelled slowly over my face. 'You don't understand any of this, my poor Chrissie, do you? Jack doesn't understand it, either. "You could have left him," he keeps saying. "If you wanted Philip Kassel, why on earth didn't you go?" I've sinned twice, you see, in Jack's eyes: once by being an ordinary woman who was tempted and gave in, and then by not having the strength to finish what I'd begun.' She shook her head. 'I've always been weak – Jack knows that. Time after time when he was a child I should have rescued him from Alfred, but I always found an excuse to look the other way. He had to manage on his own.'

A few feet away, the shop door opened. Letty laid a hand on

my arm. 'Philip will get over it, Chrissie, I promise you.' She smiled sadly. 'I'm the one who will suffer.'

'Ida wants Fry's chocolate and Bea's insisting on liquorice and humbugs. That's the problem, apparently.' Jack's voice faltered as I opened the door and stepped down. 'Oh! Hello, Chrissie.'

I'd never seen him in city clothes before, in a formal suit, highly polished shoes and a shirt-collar with the stiff shine that comes straight from the maker. On his tall, angular frame, the effect was so austere and correct that he seemed like a stranger. Perhaps he felt the same about me, since his eyes flicked down at once to consult a gold watch he'd taken from his waistcoat pocket.

'Those girls are a menace, aren't they? At this rate we shan't see Manchester today.'

Alongside us I heard Letty's door swing shut with a click, leaving us with no escape. Trapped, I studied the post office window beyond Jack's shoulder.

'I hear you're going back to the city. Will you be away for long?'

He gave a slight shrug. 'I don't know. Father couldn't wait to get away from here. After what's happened, he hates the place.'

'You mean, you might never come back at all?' I turned to look at him in surprise. He'd been examining me intently, but his eyes slid away at once.

'It's possible.' There was a pause. 'I thought you'd be pleased to get rid of us.'

'No, of course not.'

'No? I thought perhaps you were angry. When you didn't turn up again after – well – after all that business at the jetty.'

'It wasn't that at all. As a matter of fact, I don't remember a great deal about it.'

This was a complete and deliberate lie. I remembered every detail of what had happened, but wild horses wouldn't have made me confess to it. Not that anything had actually *happened*; nothing of the kind that anxious mothers mean by 'happen' when they question their wayward daughters. *Did he . . .? Did you . . .? Did anything happen?* No, it wasn't so much the memory of the physical nakedness that hurt. The real, unbearable indecency was the way Jack and I had stripped ourselves emotionally naked, without the least saving shred of a compassionate veil of affection. I had to pretend to forget that. I couldn't have endured hearing him say a commonplace 'sorry', a cheap, kitchen-drawer, sticking-plaster sort of admission that something not quite proper had occurred. Because a cataclysm had occurred, something so profound, and moving, and frightening that an entirely new Christabel Ascham stood before him now, without blushing or biting her lip, or twisting a strand of her hair round a finger in the sheer thrill of his presence.

'I don't remember much of it either.' He looked me directly in the eye, the steadiness of his stare exposing our joint lie for what it was — a pact between us, an agreement to keep the discoveries of that night to ourselves and pretend to the world nothing had ever taken place.

'Too much to drink.'

'I expect so.'

'Yes.'

Deep inside, I wanted to whoop and shout and fly down the street with my arms held out, spinning like a whirlwind. Instead, I stayed where I was, groping for something conversational to say. 'So . . . you'll be staying in Manchester for a bit.'

'Mother and the girls will.' He pointed to an army recruiting notice in the post office window. 'I'm going to join up. And before you ask — no, I haven't told Father. He can say what he likes, but I've made up my mind. I did a spell in the Officers' Training Corps at school, so maybe I'll get a commission, but I don't really care.' He gave me another of his direct stares, and once more I sensed that odd combination of hunger and defiance.' After all that's happened, I just want to get away from here and do something on my own account.'

It wasn't very different, I reflected, from what Philip had told me.

At that moment, Beatrice and Ida tumbled out of the sweet shop, bickering and snatching.

'Oh. Hello, Chrissie.' Beatrice surveyed me without enthusiasm. 'Has Jack told you? We're going back to Manchester today.'

'So I hear.'

'Father says we have to go. And after everything that's happened—' Beatrice glanced contemptuously over her shoulder at her mother, 'I really can't say I blame him. So you can have Waterside all to yourself if you want.' She shrugged and popped a humbug into her mouth. 'I expect we shall have a new house in Manchester soon.'

The chauffeur slid down from his seat to open the door, hold packages and restrain the excitable Topsy. Ida clambered into the motor and began to make a place for herself.

'Goodbye, Chrissie.' Beatrice wiggled her fingers. 'I'd promise to write, but I probably won't. Letters are such an effort – I can never think of anything to say. You'll just have to think of us all when you go for walks by the lake.' She followed Ida into the car.

'And the boathouse,' I murmured.

Jack heard me. I saw him glance back over his shoulder as the motor pulled away.

Chapter Eleven

AFTER THE DUNSTANS had gone, the house at Waterside seemed to fall into a deep sleep. Blinds of buff holland were drawn over its multitude of windows, the butcher's and provisions merchant's carts no longer trundled through the arch to its kitchen quarters and most of the staff were sent away. Annie Steadman's sister went off as maid-of-all-work to a schoolmaster's family in Cockermouth, a post which, Annie told us, she didn't like half so well as the large and bustling servants' hall at Waterside.

As the sun lost its warmth and the trees showed the first splashes of their autumn tints, I often walked by the lake shore and the jetty, drawn back to the deserted mansion as if it was only in the presence of its extravagant turrets and balustrades that I could believe what had happened there during that turbulent summer. If it hadn't changed me so profoundly, I'd almost have imagined it all as a dream of the sleeping house. Like some fairytale princess under a spell, Waterside slumbered on, while all around it the hedges and lawns continued to be trimmed and the gravel and the paving of the terrace to be swept free of weeds against some distant awakening.

The Dunstans' departure had entertained the neighbourhood for a few days, but it was quickly overshadowed by news of the war. At first, it had been presented to us as a noble undertaking. Great Britain, we were told, was like a fair-minded uncle chastising his upstart nephews; the whole thing would be over as

soon as Germany and Austria had been shown the error of their
ways – a job the *Daily Mail* boasted the Navy could do single-
handed. Then came reports of the bloodbath of Mons and the
humbling of the British Expeditionary Force. Suddenly it seemed
that the war might not, after all, be 'over by Christmas'. Yet this
only seemed to make people more determined. Shop windows
bloomed with Union Jacks and Lord Lonsdale's recruiting posters
were everywhere: *Are You a Man, Or Are You a Mouse?* All over
the district, young men who didn't want to be mice kissed their
mothers and sisters goodbye and solemnly shook hands with their
fathers – as many joining the army each day, it was said, as had
formerly signed on in a year of peace.

Noël had been invited by his former Oxford tutor to join an
expedition to the Anatolian Mountains, searching for the tomb of
one of Alexander's generals. But before very long we learned that
the Ottoman Empire had joined the war and archaeology was out
of the question.

At first, no one really knew what being 'at war' was supposed
to feel like. During those initial few weeks, if it hadn't been for
the newspaper reports and the flags in the shop windows, being at
war would hardly have felt different from being at peace, though
some cautious souls began to lay in stores of tea, coffee and sugar,
just in case. Then rumours began to spread. Mrs Hall, our cook,
heard that if the Germans invaded, we might have to flee into the
countryside with nothing but a blanket and a little food. George
Powley started to sleep in the stable. He knew a farmer near
Kendal whose best plough horses had been taken by the Army,
right in the middle of the harvest. The local newspaper claimed
that Boy Scouts were being sent out to patrol bridges and
reservoirs, and that two fourteen-year-old schoolboys from Keswick had run away to be soldiers and had got as far as France
before they were discovered and sent back.

Par began to fear for his Ford motor car. But in the end it was
young Sam Powley, who drove it and nursed its jiggling innards,
that went off to war, leaving Par so downcast that I decided my

contribution to the national effort would be to learn how to drive and maintain the thing myself.

Patriotic fervour spread like an infection. Even Hosanna Green-dew, who'd objected at first to the idea of British soldiers fighting on the same side as the unspeakable Tsar, ended a poetry-reading with a triumphant version of 'God Save the King' in which she was joined by the whole audience. A couple of days later the local newspaper published a whole column of her rousing verses, ending with a stirring call to arms:

> *Let the shepherd leave his gentle flock*
> *And the fowler quit his lakes!*
> *Where is the man whose conscience sleeps*
> *When tyranny awakes?*

Max Kassel, to judge from the melancholy letters we received, had been a stranger to sleep for some time. Nothing, still, had been heard from Philip, and Max was greatly afraid his son might be caught up in the war, or might fling himself recklessly into it. As for himself, people with the slightest German connection were now being attacked in the streets of London and he expected at any moment to be interned as an 'enemy alien'. The Medici Pearls had never been found and he suspected – no, he was certain – that the gentlemen of the Home Bureau of the Secret Service were following him wherever he went, in the hope of picking up clues. 'And yet, if I only knew that Philip was safe . . . I could bear it all, and more.'

By December, reports of freezing mud, barbed wire and death had begun to filter back from the Front to silence the music hall jokes and anxious families learned to live in fear of the yellow telegram envelope. By the spring of 1915, our own east coast towns were being battered by shells and Zeppelin bombs and the first mutilated survivors of the dreadful fighting at Ypres were beginning to fill the hospitals.

That was when Noël decided he couldn't stay at home any longer. I found it impossible to imagine my gentle, bookish brother firing a gun at anyone – he could hardly picture it himself – but the fact remained that other chaps were fighting for their country and Noël insisted it was only right that he should go and 'do his bit'. Secretly, I think, Mar hoped that the recruiting officers would take one look at her gangling, hollow-chested, visionary son and send him back to her at once; but they didn't, and Noël vanished into the Army in a uniform which hung even more loosely on his shoulders and hips than his Oxford undergraduate garb. He sent us a postcard-photograph of himself from his training depot, Private Noël Ascham, very solemn and determined, with his cap balanced uncertainly on his ears and his neck emerging like a slender stem from the over-large collar of his uniform.

Lots of houses in the village now seemed to have a square of white card in their windows showing that they'd 'sent a man to fight for King and Country'. Even Jeremy Greendew had set off for France at his own expense to paint and sketch the slaughter, and his sister, who could do little more against the Hun than burn her Goethe translations and paste sticking-tape over the name 'Bechstein' on her piano, was becoming more and more frustrated by her desire to do something practical for the cause.

One bright May morning she arrived at Fellwood rubbing her long, narrow hands with satisfaction.

'There you are – it's done! In a fortnight's time I shall be in training and a couple of months after that, with any luck, I shall be in France with our fighting boys.' She dominated our drawing room, a six-foot warrior-queen. 'Better to die in battle than in bed, as they say! By heaven, I could never love a man who didn't do his bit for his country.'

Par stared at her, astonished. 'You're going to be a *soldier*, Miss Greendew?'

'Well, of course not, Dr Ascham! Though I hope I'll do my best with a rifle if I ever have to. No, no, I've been to London, to call on Mrs Hilda Ellice Browne. Perhaps you saw her advertisement in the personal column of *The Times*? She's looking for ladies to make up a women's ambulance corps to transport the wounded in France. And when I told her I spoke French and had some knowledge of nursing, she kindly agreed to let me join her group.'

'You're going to drive an ambulance?' I couldn't imagine Hosanna at the wheel of any kind of vehicle.

'Oh, I shan't drive! I shall look after the wounded.' Hosanna clasped her hands together in the manner of a Rossetti angel. 'Our young men are *dying* over there. How can I stay by my fireside and do nothing?'

I felt thoroughly ashamed of myself. It had always been so easy to laugh at Hosanna behind her back – at her clothes and her verses and her odd manner of speaking – yet she'd been the first to find a way of making herself useful. I was fully aware that having now passed my eighteenth birthday, I'd have been expected to go and fight if I'd been a man. It was 'the decent thing', the duty of every unmarried man, to join up. Mothers wrote to the papers, boasting that they'd sent six or seven sons to the war and would send six more if they had them. And if any young men still hesitated, there was talk of conscription. Before long, men of fighting age mightn't have any choice in the matter.

I thought of Noël and Jack – and Philip, too, perhaps – in some weary, mud-caked corner of the war. Noël's letters were censored: all we knew was that he was now in France with his battalion and had been made a lance corporal in recognition of the way he'd written letters home for those who couldn't do it themselves. He was particularly good at letters to sweethearts, who wrote back to their menfolk with gratifying passion, earning him quite a reputation. It had rained a good deal, he reported, but fortunately he was used to that. Nearby, he'd heard, were the remains of a Roman fort, tantalizingly, since the previous week, behind German lines. I knew he was trying, in his own Noël-ish way not to worry Mar, which made me even more anxious. I wondered if Jack was sending similar letters to Letty. I tried to imagine him alive and well, at least. Par didn't like to see women reading a newspaper, but I used to borrow his *Times* anyway and scan the lists of casualties until my eyes swam.

When Hosanna left that day, I caught up with her at the gate and asked for Hilda Ellice Browne's address. I slaved over my letter of application until the evening, rejecting one version after another, concerned that Mrs Browne might take one look at my age and dismiss me out of hand. Yet I could drive the Ford quite well by now and I'd developed impressive muscles in my right arm from swing-starting the engine. I could deal with a puncture and look after the lubrication and I knew all about retarding and advancing the spark in the magneto to hit the right point to fire the mixture. In those days women drivers were scarce and women mechanics scarcer still; I was sure I was just what was needed – the problem was to convince Mrs Browne.

In the end, there seemed only one way, though my father, particularly, was horrified by the idea. Wasn't it enough, Par wanted to know, that Noël was somewhere in France, being shot at by Germans? And now here I was, proposing to set off for London on my brother's Triumph motorcycle, with the object of joining a team of no doubt well-meaning but undoubtedly rather brazen young women who were determined to risk their lives in that same country! To my surprise, Mar supported the idea. The threat of war had made her pull her children closer, but now that the war was real and Noël and other mothers' sons had been drawn into it, it was the duty of their womenfolk to look after them. Besides, she argued, if women wanted to vote like men, they must be prepared to labour alongside them. Far better to make oneself useful helping wounded soldiers than to chain oneself to railings or blow up exhibits in a museum.

Par retired, defeated, and I set off in riding breeches and Noël's leather waistcoat, leggings and cap (complete with goggles), bearing a list of Mar's friends with whom I could stay on the way. Uncle Hereward and Aunt Marchioness were to have the pleasure of my company in London.

The capital was buzzing with the business of war. In spite of my motorcycle I felt very much like a country mouse come to town. One of the first things I saw in London was a woman in a proper silk top hat, driving a hearse with four black horses; no doubt her brothers or her father were in France, or Turkey, or at sea. There were women manoeuvring enormous horse-drawn railway wagons and patrolling with the police at the main railway stations. They claimed the right to go where they pleased, these splendid new women, alone and after dark, without being taken for streetwalkers.

Mrs Hilda Ellice Browne turned out to be a wiry little woman in her fifties with a Roman nose, a high linen collar and the imperious manner of a queen. I stood at the foot of her Belgravia steps in my dusty leggings, with my hair – dishevelled from my leather cap – tumbling over the shoulders of my brother's too-large waistcoat and doubted if she'd have taken me on as an under-housemaid. She looked me over in silence for a moment and then observed, 'Side-valve engine, I see. Chain drive?'

I was so taken aback that I answered automatically, 'It's a belt, actually.'

'Any problems on the way here?'

'Nothing really, except a damp magneto, sometimes.'

'Ah. Dashed nuisance.' She peered at me sharply. 'You'll have to go off to learn first aid, stretcher drill and field cookery. You're no use to me without those.'

'I'd be happy to do it.'

'Excellent. Come back here first thing on Monday. And if I were you, I should throw away that carbide headlamp and get one of the new dynamos. Good afternoon to you, Miss Ascham.'

Mrs Browne, I learned later, had been the first woman to travel from the Cape to Cairo in a single journey, complete with porters and medicine chest, following her engineer husband.

Compared to that, it must have been child's play to beg or borrow an assortment of private cars and lorries, have them fitted out for the transport of the wounded and arrange for them to be taken across the Channel with her little troupe of volunteers. By the time we left, we reckoned we'd learned all there was to know about beef tea and emergency wound dressings, and we looked thoroughly military in jackets, caps and ankle-length khaki skirts. There'd be plenty of work for us, Mrs Browne had been assured, among the gassed and the wounded from the trenches.

Yet to her amazement, as the women's First Aid Nursing Yeomanry had already discovered, the British Army refused to countenance the idea of members of the female sex driving ambulances in France. Even the Red Cross would only have us on sufferance and proposed so many restrictions that Mrs Browne swept out of their offices in a temper, vowing to have nothing to do with them. We might have remained unemployed for the duration of the conflict, if it hadn't been for the war's unrelenting hunger for men at the Front. With male ambulance drivers becoming a luxury the Army could ill afford, Mrs Browne at last persuaded the authorities to let us work in Calais alongside a group of FANYs from Lamarck Hospital, ferrying wounded soldiers from trains at the Gare Centrale into hospital-ships bound for Britain.

Until that moment, all I'd seen of blood and wounds had been the diagrams and lantern-lectures we'd been given during our training and the rabbit I'd persuaded George Powley to skin and cut up for me before I left home. I'd thought I was prepared for anything; and yet what possible preparation could there be for the shocking butchery of war — for the empty faces of the blinded, the tormented gargling of those whose jaws had been blown away, or the bloody stumps where young limbs should have been? I was horrified by the sight of these broken men, sometimes shivering uncontrollably and reduced to tears by the slam of an ambulance door, sometimes held together, it seemed, by no more than a binding of white bandages under their drab brown blankets, just shrunken shapes on the wooden stretchers with their trailing canvas straps.

They were far more accustomed than I was to the presence of sudden death. 'Shall I shift 'im for you, Miss? Come on, old lad, you're in the lady's way and it won't make much odds to you now.'

For a while, I woke each morning in our wooden hut with the dry tracks of tears trailing into my hair. I'd wept in my sleep from sheer exhaustion and the nightmare of helplessness in the face of such stupid, senseless waste.

I was one of the youngest in our group. For once, I wished I'd been to boarding school instead of being educated at home; the atmosphere in camp must have been very similar, a kind of brisk cheerfulness in the face of adversity. Since we were unpaid volunteers, we were all — to be blunt — from what Mar would have called 'good families' where earning a living wasn't a consideration, and the general attitude was one of hearty stoicism. 'Come on, Ascham! Buck up! Don't look down! Just be glad it isn't you on that stretcher!' The girls who hunted, I noticed, seemed particularly unmoved by the sight of injury. I had to un-learn all my lessons of the previous summer: to shut down my eager emotions, to swallow my outrage, to pay no attention to the dreaded smell of gangrene or the yellow faces and greenish buttons of the gassed men. Feelings were treacherous, unstable things, best kept locked up behind a front of sturdy good humour.

As the weeks passed, a kind of numbness set in, not indiffer-ence, but a splitting away of one's cheerful, efficient khaki self from the timorous creature within, until little by little the tender kernel withered and shrivelled away. I was distressed, it's true, when Mar wrote to say that poor Max Kassel had been sent to a camp for internees at Alexandra Palace, still under suspicion of being a spy; but pretty soon my khaki identity reasserted itself, a stoical, cheery presence who handed out cigarettes and shared the men's bitter jokes without flinching at their burned flesh and mutilated faces.

Hosanna Greendew was a favourite with our patients, striding around with her cap askew over her large nose, quoting bits of Shakespeare or music hall doggerel. The men liked her oddness and she realized it, and generously made herself ridiculous for their sakes; a small piece of good old British eccentricity reaching out to them on the shores of France.

Mrs Browne dashed back to Britain and returned with more vehicles and a handful of pink-and-white young women, all earnestly ready to 'do their bit'. Was that what we'd looked like ourselves, hardly a year earlier? Since then we'd endured air raids, gales and bombardment from the sea. During the winter we'd had to deal with frozen lorry engines that needed to be swing-started every hour of the night to keep them from seizing up. We'd dragged dead men from the canals and distributed food to air raid victims and, as a little welcome light relief, had occasionally been invited to dances or to dine at army messes nearby.

By now I was quite proud of my fortitude. The wounded soldiers were patients – *cases* – to be helped as sympathetically and efficiently as conditions allowed. As long as I didn't let myself think of Noël, or Jack, or Philip huddled on a stretcher or shuffling along in a row of broken, bandaged men, I was confident I could deal with whatever came my way.

Then, one day, down at the railway station, Mrs Browne beckoned me over to where the duty medical officer and a couple of nurses were bent over a newly unloaded casualty, their voices a concentrated murmur and their hands moving with the urgent, dexterous haste that indicated a sudden emergency.

This one will have to go straight to the hospital. He's started to haemorrhage again, cut up by a rifle-grenade, poor boy. He needs surgery right away.'

They carried the wounded man, unconscious, through the station yard, trying to balance haste with carefulness. I hurried ahead to throw open the doors of the ambulance. By now the casualty was surrounded by so many stretcher-bearers, nurses and anxious, helping hands that it was only when they hoisted him

175

up, shoulder-high, towards the dark mouth of the lorry, that I suddenly caught sight of his face, so still and leaden white against the rough brown of his pillow.

'Wait – oh, wait! I think I know him—'

But the doors, with their great crimson cross, were already closing, and Mrs Browne was speaking in my ear, 'As quickly as you can, dear, but try to avoid the bumps, won't you?'

For a moment, I couldn't move. Then my training reasserted itself. Speed. I tried to fix my mind on that, to blot out the sight of black curls matted with blood and ominous grey shadows gathering like rain clouds round a young brow and cheekbones. It was Philip Kassel on the stretcher. I was certain of it in a way that went beyond reason, as if from the very start of the war I'd carried the expectation of disaster in my heart like a ghastly inevitability and had only waited for the day it should seek me out. Noël, Jack, and Philip. Why should they remain safe, after all, when so many others had gone? And what about poor Max Kassel, interned and under suspicion, without a word of news from his missing son?

I gripped the wheel like a maniac to stop the shaking of my hands and set off like a rocket through the narrow streets, all the time trying to avoid potholes and bicycles and spine-jarring tram lines. Speed. It was all I could offer Philip at that moment, all I could do for him.

I wished I could tell him it was me at the wheel. *Hang on, Philip!* He didn't wait for us. He died, the nurse said, barely a mile from the railway station, with a gasp and a sudden flashing open of his eyes. By the time we arrived at the Military Hospital, there was nothing the surgeons could do.

There was official confusion over his name. Philip Kassel, I'd told them, and yet his papers were in the name of Private Peter Castle. Would I go to the mortuary and make a formal identification?

Philip's face was more radiantly peaceful in death than I'd ever seen it. His features were quite unmarked. With the sheet drawn up to his chin, it was almost possible to believe he was sleeping, delivered for a while from the torment of a world which held no place for him. I wondered what had brought him such peace at the end. The dusty roof of a makeshift ambulance could hardly have inspired such unearthly calm.

'Right enough – according to this, his next of kind is a Mr Max Kassel of Chester Street in London.' The orderly was examining Philip's dog-eared paybook. 'Picture of a lady. Blonde – very nice. Probably his mum.' The orderly slid the tiny rectangle back under the book's cover and went on searching the pockets of Philip's bloodstained tunic. 'Comb, pocketbook, jackknife, spare laces. I suppose he'll want it all sent back, this Mr Kassel, whoever he is.'

Philip's death all but destroyed my hard-won strength of purpose. In the days that followed, I kept telling myself that he was simply another tragedy among a multitude of lost husbands, sons and brothers – another name on the casualty list. Yet all I could think of was how desperately vulnerable were the people I cared about, just sparks in the wind of war, extinguishable in a second as thoroughly as if they'd never existed. If Philip had died, then Noël could die – could even be dead already – a nameless corpse half-drowned in a shell-crater. And if not Noël, then Jack Dunstan. It was the sheer *unfairness* of Jack's dying I wouldn't be able to bear. Philip, I suspected, would have understood death in a way Jack would not. I began to search every bandaged face, to examine each huddled form with an intentness bordering on obsession. I had to be ordered to stand down at the end of each shift, so terrified was I that I might miss a glimpse of the last two or three casualties brought in.

'Buck up, Ascham! Don't look down!' Ashamed, I mastered my fears, locked them away in the same seldom-visited part of myself as my tears and my youth, and carried on as before.

And then, in mid-April, not long after Philip's death, I became a casualty myself. I'd been sent out to the camp at Audruicq, about fifteen kilometres from Calais, with a load of blankets, stretchers and other medical supplies in a big Vulcan lorry. For some reason, unloading had taken ages and darkness caught us when we were still on our way back, a couple of kilometres short of Calais. By sheer bad luck the Germans had chosen that night to launch an air raid, but thanks to the roar and shudder of the Vulcan's engine, the first we knew of any enemy action was a blinding flash somewhere ahead that seemed to turn night into day. At the same time, our windscreen burst into a thousand pieces and the road seemed to buckle like a crumpled carpet. Some blessed instinct made me turn my head aside, or I might have been blinded. As it was, the steering wheel wrenched itself, spinning, from my grasp; I could only haul on it, frantically stabbing at the brakes, as the lorry careered towards the side of the road, pitched drunkenly off it, and swayed on two wheels into a farm building before toppling over on to its side. When we were eventually extracted from the wreckage, both bones in my lower right leg turned out to be broken; the only thing that had saved it from being hopelessly crushed, said my cheerful surgeon, was the high, stout leather boot I'd been wearing under my skirt.

Now it was my turn to be sent home to recuperate. At least Mar was pleased to have one of her chickens home to be fussed over, though after the clatter and bustle of our Calais camp I found it hard to sleep in the peace of the Lakes. Fellwood itself had grown noticeably quieter, with one housemaid instead of three and an odd-job man who was well over seventy. Mrs Hall was still in the kitchen, but Mar had mastered the art of egg-scrambling at her fourth attempt, and Mrs Hall now went to visit her daughter in the village on Sundays and Wednesdays. Annie Steadman, our modish parlourmaid, had gone off to be a telephone operator, while her sister was no longer a maid-of-all-work in Cockermouth, but a well-paid lorry-tyre studder in Manchester. Sam Powley had come home with gassed lungs and a bayonet wound you could put two fingers into, only to find our Ford laid up without petrol and our pony and trap back in service.

Now he was busily courting his old sweetheart, a publican's daughter in Keswick, and helping behind her father's bar, where his bayonet wound had become something of a local institution.

It was all part of the new world I'd glimpsed in London at the start of the war – and it was proving uncomfortable for some. At Wickham, my Uncle Hereward's house, where the butler and the housekeeper had been accustomed to being waited on by servants further down the domestic order, many of the rooms were now closed up whether the family were there or not. Archer, my magnificent coachman, had long since gone the way of his kind and was rumoured to be the owner of a motor garage in Torquay. Worst of all, Aunt Marchioness had actually been informed by the girl instructed to take letters to the post that she'd no intention of licking the stamps herself, 'on account of the taste of the gum'.

Some new institutions had established themselves. Christopher Cole – now 'young Dr Cole' to the whole community, even though his father had been dead for three years – had been delivering babies and coping with diphtheria and other medical crises almost single-handed since the start of the war; the Army had scooped up so many of the newly-qualified doctors. He came regularly to check on the progress of my leg and, if there was time, often stayed to chat. I suppose my months spent transporting wounded men gave us something in common; at any rate, before long I found myself wondering why I'd ever found Chris Cole difficult to talk to and began to look forward to his visits. His sister Irene – who'd been one of Philip Kassel's most fervent admirers – was working as a VAD nurse in a hospital converted from a large country house near London.

Max Kassel weighed heavily on my conscience. Philip's death in France had made no difference to his father's treatment: Max was still under suspicion as a spy, still locked up at Alexandra Palace, and no one seemed to have lifted a finger to help him. If nothing else, I could at least visit him. As soon as I was able to walk with the aid of two sticks, I put the idea to Chris.

179

'I could travel down to London by train. That won't do me any harm, surely.'

Reluctantly, Chris conceded that it wouldn't. 'But for heaven's sake,' he added, 'take care. I want you back safe and sound.'

Uncle Hereward was minding a desk in the War Office and easily got me permission to visit Max at the Alexandra Palace camp. The visitors' area was a bleak room with wooden tables and benches and, on the day I went, it had the hushed, desolate air of an abandoned gymnasium. Somewhere outside in the June sunshine, the internees were exercising in their fenced-off area of the park, watched through the wire by curious sightseers. The visitors' room was high-ceilinged and echoing, and Max Kassel came into it like a small, immaculate ghost, almost without leaving a shadow.

The authorities had sent him 'Private Castle's' pocketbook and his battered paybook, its pages rimmed with a brownish stain that looked very like blood and filled with the scribbled signatures of lieutenants and captains. In the cardboard pocket inside the front cover was the photograph I'd last seen in Calais, the picture of Letty Dunstan on the lawn at Waterside, her head tilted back and her hands held out in laughing invitation. Gently, Max removed the little book from my fingers, slid the photograph out of sight again and closed the cover. I wished I could have told him that Philip had murmured a message at the end, but it would have been a cheap deception. Philip had abandoned himself to strangers. He'd meant to disappear.

Max looked thinner and older than I remembered and the veins of his hands stood out like blue cords under his tissue-paper skin.

'Perhaps someone in Philip's regiment would know more – someone in his unit.'

'I know so little about the army. I wouldn't even know what to ask.' Max buried the paybook in the darkness of an inside coat pocket. 'Besides, it wasn't Philip who died. It was a boy called Castle who had to hide himself away, even from his own father.'

Twelve months earlier, I'd have reached out to take Max's emaciated hands in my own, impulsively offering him my warmth and my strength. The desire to do it still stirred in me, but Max's dignity was so perfect and so fragile, and I was no longer impulsive. I folded my fingers together and glanced out of the nearest window.

'I can't see why they won't let you go free. They know what happened to Philip now. They must understand you were never a spy.'

'Ah, but you see, the Medici Pearls have never been found. If Philip didn't have them, then where can they be? Every so often, they come back and ask me, these secret policemen. They can't believe I don't know.' Max Kassel raised his hands in a gesture of hopelessness. 'I say "Why don't you ask Alfred Dunstan how he's managed to pay off all his debts? Perhaps he knows where the pearls are. It's no use asking me."'

'Alfred Dunstan has paid all his creditors? But then, he always said he made money out of wars. I suppose this one has been as good for business as the others.'

'It must have been very good, then.' The pearl merchant shrugged. 'He owed a great deal of money and now, suddenly, he doesn't.'

The patch of sunlit floor in front of each window intensified the shadows beyond its edge, a sharp reminder of confinement. Max Kassel's high, formal collar was as stiff as ever, but his neck was loose inside it and I could imagine what effect each succeeding day of imprisonment was having on his health. If only I'd been able to speak to Philip, just for a few moments.

'It's the only wish I have left.' Max Kassel spoke with a vehemence that startled me. 'Before I die, I'd like to give the pearls back. For Philip's sake, so that no one could call him a common thief. That's what the gentlemen from the Secret Service call him, you know.' He smiled faintly, relishing the irony. 'I say "Very well, go and ask Philip where the pearls are."'

Uncle Hereward wasn't in charge of aliens. And even if he had been, he said, there was nothing he could do for Max Kassel. If the Medici Pearls turned up and Kassel's hands were proved to be clean – well, that might be another matter, but as things stood . . .

Par was luckier than Max Kassel. Noël came home on leave, awfully thin after a spell of bronchitis, but trying bravely to make jokes about life in the Army. I only realized how truly and deeply Noël and Par loved one another when I saw them shake hands on the railway platform at Windermere, briefly and formally, as if anything more might have led to an unmanly scene.

'Are you better, my boy?' Par peered at Noël over his spectacles, twitching his nose to keep them from sliding down it.

'Oh, much better thanks.' Noël smiled fleetingly. Then they both looked away in opposite directions, Noël scratching his ear and Par suddenly seized by the need to polish his spectacles on the lapel of his coat. Abruptly, Par swung back.

'Ever get to it, did you? Your Roman fort?'

'Ah. No. Bit of a disappointment, in fact.' With a shrug, Noël dismissed twelve months in the trenches. 'By the time we got across there, our own artillery had shelled it to blazes. Rotten luck, after all our efforts.'

'Oh, my boy—' At last Par allowed himself to show emotion. 'I really am *so* sorry.'

I'd written to Mrs Browne, asking if I could return to driving duty in Calais. The new offensive on the Somme had begun with appalling slaughter and I knew the trains with their huge red crosses would be crowding into the Gare Centrale, putting a fearful strain on the medical facilities. While I waited for an answer, I tried to limp each day as far as I could, to strengthen the muscles I'd need for driving the heavier vehicles. I made Waterside my goal and every day managed to walk a little nearer. I wanted to see what changes the months of emptiness had brought.

The last of the staff had long since gone. According to Mar, the place was now looked after by a caretaker, a single man who lived in the lodge and spoke to no one. I wondered if he was expected to look after the gardens. For the first time that I could remember, a straggle of grass had sprouted on the drive beyond the iron gates and, when at last I worked my way round through the adjoining meadow to view the house from the lakeside, I could see weeds springing up between the stones of the terrace, and the lawn shaggy with lush summer growth.

All along the terrace wall, wind-blown roses lashed at the balustrade, and the cupola of Beatrice's beloved summer house, ripped off by a gale, lay upside-down in a flower bed, half full of green water, a playground for pond-skaters and damselflies.

I couldn't believe the neglect was accidental. Alfred Dunstan could never have forgotten Waterside, the house he'd built as a celebration of his own achievements. There was only one other explanation: that the springmaker had deliberately abandoned the place – had decided to punish it with neglect for being the scene of his humiliation, 'Dunstan's Palace', where his wife had made love to an eighteen-year-old boy behind his back. He wouldn't sell it, because that wasn't Alfred Dunstan's way. Just as he'd never divorce Letty or make it possible for her to live apart from him, he had no intention of letting Waterside pass out of his control. Instead, he would allow it to wither and decay, as Letty would grow old in his home, secure from any possible rescue.

There was no one to see me as I limped across the untidy lawn and made my way up the steps to the terrace. Spiders had taken over the space between the blinds and the windows, weaving scraps of greyish lace over the buff linen. Bird droppings splashed the upper sills and dock plants had found a rooting-place at the side of the steps. That's when I remembered another, unintended victim of the springmaker's malice. Silent beyond the chained and padlocked doors of the boathouse, the old *Siren* must be lying in her black dungeon with only the lapping of the lake for company. *The only thing I've ever had entirely of my own,* Jack had said of her. But now Jack had gone and the *Siren* had been left to sink gently into the dark water, mouldering plank by plank, no doubt, until the neglected eaves of the boathouse fell in on top of her to become a vast, waterlogged, weed-infested tomb.

A few days later I mastered the sloping lawn and walked out along the jetty; no one came to challenge me, or ask what I was doing on private property. This was where we'd slid, naked, into the lake, the four of us, excited by wine and quarrelling. And precisely here, Jack and I had fought in the darkness and I had discovered a new and soul-stealing kind of madness. It frightened me now, the sheer intensity of the feelings I'd known: the unbearable, fizzing triumphs, the catastrophic glooms and the helpless, irresistible compulsion to submit, to become the creature of his savage desire, a bitch for sale. Never again. I'd learned, in painful lessons, to ration myself for my own good, to lend myself out little by little, never to give myself entirely. If I ever wavered, I only had to recall Philip's anguished face as he ran from Waterside, leaving his heart behind to be ripped and trampled on.

Jack Dunstan was gone. Rational now, I could afford to think of him with sentimental regret – a piece of my growing up I'd never see again. I wished him well. I shut my eyes tightly and tried to send out the essence of that peaceful place, far across the lake and beyond, just in case he was thinking of it – wherever he was. I constructed an image in my mind of the *Siren* in her prison, of the uncontrolled, earth-smelling growth all around, of the black lacquer of the lake, scraped with peacock blue and of the silent air, disturbed only by the rushing whirr of mallard wings ... It was my world once again, but I offered it to him in his exile.

Chapter Twelve

'YOU'RE OVERDOING IT,' Chris warned me. 'It's too early for all this cycling business. You'll just have to be patient and wait for your leg to get better. It's only – what – three months since you broke it? Well, then. You can't expect to be back to normal overnight, not with the muscles as wasted as they are.'

'You're just making work for yourself, Dr Cole. You don't want me to get well again, so you've always got someone to visit.'

I'd been teasing, but Chris suddenly chose to take me seriously. 'Do you mind my coming to see you? You always seem quite pleased, but it's hard to tell, sometimes.'

I'd gone down to the front door to see him off and halted with my hand on the doorknob, disconcerted. 'I'm always delighted to see you, Chris. You know that.'

'Do I?'

'Well, yes. Of course.'

'It's just that you seem awfully anxious to get back to this ambulance of yours in Calais.'

'I feel useful there, that's all. I hate moping around at home when there's so much work to be done. Have you seen how many men have been wounded since this new push began in France?'

'Well, you can't go back there just yet. But—' He hesitated. 'If you really want to make yourself useful, you can always do some typing and filing for me. My medical records got into the

185

dickens of a mess during that last outbreak of influenza and I've never caught up. If you'd like to, of course.'

I found I rather enjoyed organizing Chris. I'd known him for so long, I suppose, that we were perfectly relaxed in one another's company and after a morning spent in the surgery I often stayed for lunch with Chris and his mother.

He'd already made a name for himself in the district. 'Dr Cole always comes out,' people said and I could see from Chris's accounts that there were several patients who were never sent bills, no matter how often the doctor 'came out', and others who were left to pay when they could.

'You'll never be a rich man, Chris,' I told him.

He just grinned. 'Like Alfred Dunstan, do you mean? I think I could bear that.'

Old George Powley swore he was 'a good'un'.

'He was puttin' things back in his little bag, just about to go, when he happened to say summat about that old rifle wound of mine – about the difference between close-up an' far off, an' I said "You don't know the half of it, my lad. You want to see what the Boers could do with a Mauser .276," an' he said "Tell us, then. Let's hear it." An' so I told him.'

'What – all of it?' I knew from experience how long George Powley's South African War reminiscences could take.

'Every particle. I give 'im the lot. Even the story about Steinaecker's cow an' the Bitterenders. "There's been wars afore this'un, you know," I said. *And*—' He stabbed the air with a knobbed finger. 'He listened till I'd finished.' Powley leaned back in his chair and inhaled significantly. 'I reckon he's better with rheumatics than his father was. My old knees haven't been so good in ages.'

★

'You're a good doctor, Chris, do you know that?'

'I'm pleased to hear it.' His square, boyish face flushed with pleasure. 'Especially from you.'

'That's kind, but I'm not much of an authority, I'm afraid.'

'I didn't mean it medically.' He was taking me into the village in his little two-seater Austin and the need to keep his gaze fixed on the road ahead seemed to make it easier for him to speak. 'What I was trying to say . . .' He changed gear with deliberation. 'What I was trying to say was that it means a great deal to me that you approve. Of me. As a doctor – well, as a person, really.' He pulled out to avoid a bicycle pedalled madly by something resembling a bag of washing on spindly legs. At the last moment I realized it was Hosanna Greendew – Hosanna, whom I'd left in the thick of the Calais convoy.

'Good heavens! I wonder why Hosanna's back?'

'Chrissie—' He sounded reproachful. 'Are you listening?'

'Yes, of course.'

'And am I making any sense?'

'You're saying you'd like us to stay friends.'

'More than that.' We'd already passed the first houses of Bowness and would soon be in Windermere proper. Realizing our journey was nearly over, Chris began to speak more quickly. 'It just seems to me that you and I feel pretty much the same about life – about the war and the future and all that. We even like the same things. Living here, for instance, and having the hills to walk in.'

He changed gear again as we rounded a bend and I thought how dependable he was. I liked the way nothing distracted him from the task in hand.

'Anyway, I've been doing a bit of thinking and . . . Oh, dash it all – to be perfectly blunt, I thought we might do rather well together, you and I. I don't suppose this is the most elegant way of saying it, but I do know you're an absolutely marvellous girl and pretty, too, and if you could see your way to spending the rest of your life as a doctor's wife you'd make me the happiest man in the world. You probably think I've got the most awful cheek, but I had to say it all the same.'

He finished in a rush of words, but still managed to bring the car to a perfect standstill in the crowded square. I couldn't imagine Christopher Cole ever losing his head or becoming embarrassingly sentimental. Perhaps it was because he often seemed older than his twenty-seven years; it may have had something to do with the half-spectacles he wore for his patients, with their gold wire rim. It always surprised me, when he took them off, to see the freshness of his face; he looked like a schoolboy caught playing with his grandfather's glasses. It was typical of Chris to be neither particularly old nor particularly young. Everything about him was moderate — even the light brown of his hair, golden at the temples, exactly the shade that matches the complexion so well it's hard to be sure of the hairline.

Chris, I knew, would never demand to know what was going on in my head. There'd be no emotional pressure, no dramas, no distressing outpourings of the heart. Instead, he'd be trustworthy, sensible and affectionate, a man respected by his patients for doing his job well. I liked the way he hadn't said *love*, as if we were a pair of spooning adolescents.

There was complete silence in the car. Chris continued to stare through the windscreen.

'You're offended.'

'Not at all. I'm very flattered. In fact, I can't think of anything I'd like more than to be a doctor's wife.'

'Oh!' For the first time, he turned to look at me. 'My goodness.' There was something like relief in his face, mingled with pride. After a second's hesitation, he reached out to take my hands in his. 'That's wonderful, honestly.' He glanced at the window behind me, where heedless shoppers trudged to and fro. 'I ought to kiss you, but — you know — it's a bit public, isn't it?'

'Absolutely. Make up for it later.'

'Right.' He squeezed my fingers and gazed at them as if he

were seeing them for the first time. Then the practical, dependable Chris slid back into control.

'Now – what you need is a ring.'

Mar was pleased, but uncertain.

'Darling, you won't be twenty until next year. You're still a girl, really. I mean, Chris is a fine boy and I was very fond of his father, but . . . are you absolutely sure?'

I was absolutely sure I was no longer a girl. One thundery night by the Waterside jetty had brought me a woman's wisdom, the war had taught me carefulness and Philip Kassel had shown me the danger of loving too much. The perfect solution was to be moderately in love with thoroughly moderate Chris.

Our only disagreement was over the date of the wedding. Chris wanted us to be married as soon as possible, while I still hoped to go back to Calais for a while, at least.

'They need me there, Chris.'

'But I need you here just as badly, for all sorts of reasons. There must be other women who can drive.'

Mrs Cole, Chris's mother, didn't want any delay. She'd been trying to marry Chris off for years. 'Christo*pher* and Christa*bel*! Isn't that perfect? You were obviously made for each other. When is the wedding to be, then, my dear?'

'Actually, we haven't decided.'

'Haven't decided,' she repeated automatically. 'But what's that boy thinking of?'

'It's me, I'm afraid, Mrs Cole. I feel I ought to go back to France for a bit first.'

'To France for a bit first.' She gazed at me in concern. 'But are you well enough? Is your leg strong enough yet? And who'll help Christopher in the surgery?'

As things turned out, Mrs Browne wrote back to say the convoy was overwhelmed with work, but thanks to a new wave of volunteers, it currently had as many drivers as it needed. She'd

love to have me back in the future, but just at the moment . . .
So Chris got his way and the wedding was set for October.

Par was relieved. Now there was only Noël to worry about –
Noël and Par's beloved Venice. It had seemed inconceivable to
him that anyone would fight a war near such a cultural treasure,
but the Austrians had nevertheless sent their Tauber planes to
bomb it in May of 1915 and four out of eleven had hit their
target. Since then, the Italians themselves had used Venice as a
base for their retaliation. My father was outraged. 'Why didn't
they turn the Basilica into a dynamite factory and have done with
it?'

At least the famous bronze horses of San Marco had been
crated and carried off to safety in Rome and the best paintings
spirited away. Anti-aircraft balloons were now anchored in the
lagoon and important buildings like the Doge's Palace hidden
behind walls of bags stuffed with seaweed. War-time Venice
sounded very much like Aunt Marchioness in the leather motoring outfit she'd adopted as part of her personal battle-readiness;
her best diamonds might have been sent to the bank, but she still
looked like a rich old lady in an eccentric hat.

I'd never forgotten the smells and sounds of Venice, that
muddy breath shot through with bitter green and the scent of oily
cooking pots, or the morning *creak-clack* of shutters. I thought of
it whenever tawny shadows formed in the corners of tall, cool
rooms, recalling dark windows that framed rectangles of brilliant
terracotta, the sunlit wall of the building behind. But Venice was
in my past; I'd never know it in that way again, like Philip, and
Jack, and recklessness.

News of it was hard to come by. Par hoarded every scrap of
information, following the fate of the city, piece by piece, like a
man feeling his limbs after a bomb explosion, anxiously counting
his fingers and toes. The palazzos, the pictures, the churches, the
statues – as soon as he'd reassured himself that one favourite was
safe, he'd remember another and be unable to rest until he'd
satisfied himself that it, too, had survived. The Scalzi Church, we

discovered, had lost its roof in a bombing raid and many lesser buildings had been destroyed.

I finally became impatient with him. 'There's a war on, for heaven's sake! What do the pictures matter, as long as the people are safe?'

He gazed at me, astonished, and took refuge in his usual argument. 'But this is precisely the time when we need these pictures most! Without them man is no better than a beast. This—' He indicated a water colour of San Giorgio Maggiore which hung on his study wall. '*This* is proof that we're not entirely depraved. Even while we kill one another, we can still create the sublime.'

Poor Hosanna Greendew might not have agreed. She'd been sent home on compassionate leave. Her brother, Jeremy, had been killed by a stray shell near Amiens while he sketched a group of men rigging up a field telephone in a support trench. She'd kept a photograph of him with her in Calais, a dim little rectangle showing him leaning casually on a captured German gun, a broad-brimmed felt hat pulled down over his eyes and the collar of his open-necked shirt turned up by the breeze. I could never imagine waspish, fastidious Jeremy in the din and filth of war, and yet he looked happier than he'd ever done when he painted gods and goddesses on Alfred Dunstan's wall.

'Reville and Rossiter,' Aunt Marchioness pronounced firmly when she heard I was soon to be married, 'obviously. They made Henrietta's wedding gown, if you remember – perfectly heavenly. Or you could go to Redfern, of course. They still make for the Palace too, but I fear they're a little *démodé* these days. Yes, I know there's a war on, but that's precisely why one must keep up standards. Perhaps Christabel would like one of my tiaras?'

It was hard to convince her I was about to be the wife of a country doctor and intended to buy the rest of my trousseau in the rather less expensive surroundings of Manchester. That's why

I happened to be in St Anne's Square one day in August; I'd just bought a dressing-gown in Hankison & Sankey's, and when I came out into the sunshine I caught sight of a figure I was sure I recognized pushing a lady in an invalid chair towards the edge of the pavement. Something about the woman's positive, emphatic walk struck a chord in my mind – and the way she wore her jet straw hat so squarely on her brow, with its brim bearing down on her rather fleshy features like a candle snuffer on a festoon of wax. It was Beatrice Dunstan, I was certain, pushing what I took to be an elderly relative.

'Bea – it is you, isn't it? Bea Dunstan! Don't you remember me?'

The jet straw hat twitched round. 'Chrissie? Good gracious, how extraordinary to see you.'

As she spoke my name, the face of the invalid turned round to examine me. I was shocked to see it was Letty.

'Look, Mother—' Beatrice bent forward over the rubber handles of the chair. 'It's Chrissie Ascham. Isn't this a surprise?'

'I can see for myself who it is. Chrissie, my dear, you've put your hair up, but otherwise you've hardly changed at all.'

I couldn't believe the change that two years had wrought in Letty Dunstan. She was only forty and her face was still largely unlined, though the freckles which had given her such an air of girlishness had either faded or been hidden under a layer of pearl powder. What was so shocking was her wasted body and the thin, hunched shoulders supported by the cane back of the chair. Most startling of all, though, was her hair, no longer golden, but almost entirely turned the straw-grey of an ageing blonde.

'Mrs Dunstan . . .'

'Now, don't tell me *I* haven't altered. The mirror shows me the truth of that every morning.'

I could imagine her staring into it with her faded eyes, searching for some trace of the woman Philip Kassel had worshipped.

'I'm sorry to see you've been ill.'

She'd tugged off a glove and her transparent hand rose absently to her brow. 'I have headaches. They leave me very weak.'

'This is one of Mother's good days.' Beatrice's tone was brisk. 'But we'll have a headache tomorrow, I expect, after coming into town.' She leaned forward again like someone speaking to an aged idiot. 'The nurses will make you rest with the curtains drawn.'

I saw her eyes flick to a point behind me and heard a masculine step. I turned quickly, afraid it might be Alfred Dunstan swooping down on us, but it was the chauffeur, Tipper. A large Rolls Royce motor car waited by the kerb.

'Time to go home, Mother.'

'Already?' Letty craned round.

'You'll only make yourself ill, if you stay too long. You know what Father said.' Over her mother's head, Beatrice made the face adults use to signal a fractious child.

Letty stretched out her hand to me as if she accepted there was only enough time for the formalities. 'Are your mother and father well? I do hope so. And your brother's safe. I'm so glad.' She glanced at Tipper, who'd come round to take over the handles of her chair from Beatrice. 'I must go, my dear. Bea looks after me so well.' The hand touched mine and clutched there for a moment. 'I do think of you, sometimes.'

'Goodbye, Mrs Dunstan. I'll tell Mar you were asking for her.'

Beatrice made no move to follow her mother, but watched stolidly as the chauffeur levered Letty carefully out of her chair and helped her into the rear seat of the Rolls.

'I'd no idea your mother was so ill.'

'The headaches are the worst part.' Beatrice's eyes remained on her mother. 'They started soon after we came back to Manchester, just the odd one at first and then more and more often. The doctors keep examining her, but they haven't much idea, really.' Beatrice puffed through her lips as if she'd had enough of the medical profession. 'I didn't think she needed a proper nurse at first, but Father insisted, and I suppose he was right. She has nurses day and night now. Father says she mustn't be allowed to do anything at all.'

I'd been examining Beatrice while she spoke. I was sorry to see she'd lost the wonderful sheen of plump health which had been her chief attraction. She no longer glowed with that greedy *joie de vivre*, that cheerful, honest lust for the good things in life which had made her silliness forgivable. Now her lower eyelids had developed a hound-like curve of discontent and the two incised channels flanking her lower lip suggested that she was more often sullen than not.

Together, we watched the chauffeur manoeuvre Letty's invalid chair into the motor where she waited, a still, pale face at the window.

'Father's devoted to her,' Beatrice assured me, 'in spite of . . . well, all that business at Waterside. You can see how her looks have gone,' she added brutally. 'Mother used to dye her hair, you know. Father made them take the hair dye away, in case it made her headaches worse.'

Personally, I couldn't think of anything more inclined to bring on a headache than to be cruelly deprived of one's beautiful hair, but I kept silent.

'She mustn't excite herself, you see, so no one comes to the house now. Father meets his business friends in town.'

Uncle Hereward swore Aunt Marchioness got a headache whenever it looked as if the Bishop might stay to dinner. I wondered if Letty had taken refuge from her husband in illness, and if Alfred had pursued her there, making her a prisoner of her own frailty. Beatrice had the grim air of a gaoler.

'And what about you?' I asked her. 'It must be livelier here than in the Lakes. Do you have a young man away at the war?'

'No, I don't.' The old mulish look had returned to Beatrice's face. 'Mother's seen to that, and no mistake. I have to stay at home, don't I, because Father says so. I did think I might go and nurse, or learn typing or something, but Father said no – Mother needs a companion and Ida's too young. It's all *her* fault, as usual.' Her expression defied me to find fault with this logic.

'Ida must be thirteen now. How is she?'

'Well enough.'

I was beginning to run out of conversation, though Beatrice seemed in no hurry to join her mother in the Rolls. Simply for something to fill the silence, I said, 'I'm engaged to be married, believe it or not. In October. To Christopher Cole. The doctor – do you remember him? He took over his father's practice. His sister Irene was awfully in love with—' Just in time, I stopped myself from uttering Philip's name. Then I decided to, anyway. I'd hated the relish with which Beatrice had discussed her mother's fate. 'Philip Kassel's dead,' I said. 'In France. A rifle-grenade.'

'Oh.' She blinked a couple of times, quickly. 'I never saw his name in the casualty lists.'

'No. He was calling himself Peter Castle. That was the name on his papers. They brought him up to Calais, but he was very badly wounded and he began to haemorrhage.' Beatrice was staring into the distance and I wasn't even sure she'd been listening. 'Will you tell your mother?'

'No.' She met my gaze with sudden scorn. 'Why should I tell her? She was to blame for everything that happened. We wouldn't have had to come back to Manchester if she hadn't wanted Philip in the first place and I wouldn't have had to stay at home, looking after her. No, if you don't mind, I shan't tell her.'

I didn't argue. If Beatrice wanted to keep that one small part of Philip for herself, I could hardly blame her. Yet it made me realize how bleak her existence must be, if she found pleasure in keeping such a forlorn secret from her mother.

Beatrice was straightening the belt of her tailored suit. 'After all, if Philip's dead, there's really nothing more to say, is there?' I'd forgotten how she sometimes looked and sounded exactly like her father. 'I must go.' At last she made a move towards the waiting motor. 'I can't offer to drop you anywhere, I'm afraid. Mother's chair takes up too much room.'

'Bea . . .' I reached out to detain her. There was something I still wanted to ask, and I might never have another chance. 'What about Jack? Is he well? He said he was going into the Army—'

Beatrice lifted her chin with something of her old spirit. 'Jack's a Captain now. He's just been home on leave. He picked up a bit of shrapnel when the Somme offensive started last month, but it wasn't much.' That had been Jack's account of it, I was sure: I could almost hear his voice tossing out the words. 'He's gone back to his battalion now, but he was going to spend a few days in London first.'

She put her head on one side to regard me and a certain mean triumph slid into her expression. 'I shouldn't be surprised if he hasn't got a girl in London. More than one, probably.'

'Well, I'm pleased to hear he's safe and not seriously hurt.'

Beatrice gave me a critical look. 'Don't you mind?'

'About what?'

'About Jack. Seeing girls in London.'

'Oh. No, of course not.' I hadn't expected her to be so direct. 'I hope he enjoys himself, that's all.'

'Oh, I expect he'll do that, all right.' Beatrice gave a bitter little laugh. 'As for Ida and me, we're like those two women in that picture in Venice, just sitting at home, bored to tears, getting older and older.' She eyed me for a moment, almost in pity. 'Goodbye, Chrissie. Have a nice wedding.' Then she turned and began to walk to the car.

'Bea! Wait! What about Waterside? Will you ever come back there, do you think?'

She stared round at me, frowning, as if I'd raised an unwelcome ghost from the past. 'Waterside? Oh, no.' She shook her head. 'Never. Not back to Waterside. Oh, I shouldn't think so – not ever.'

★

After that I couldn't pass the mansion at Waterside without thinking how much it resembled Letty Dunstan herself. As far as the springmaker was concerned, Letty had shamed him and Waterside was a memorial to that shame. Now he'd shut them both up behind iron gates to moulder and die, little by little, far from the sound of laughter. Letty was in Manchester, surrounded by nurses; at Waterside the gardens were half-way to a wilderness and it was said in the village that the caretaker drank from the sheer boredom of being tied to the place.

On the twenty-first of August Chris was called out to an emergency at the police station in Windermere.

'It was the caretaker from Waterside,' he reported when he came back to the surgery. 'Apparently he's been hitting the bottle pretty hard recently and this morning he decided there were man-eating crocodiles coming out of the lake, or something of the sort. It took Sergeant Naylor and six other men to get him to the police station, he was in such a state. I've had to send him to hospital to be dried out.'

At Fellwood, I found Mar in a state of some annoyance. 'Isn't that perfectly maddening! Just fancy being left with the keys to *that place.*'

'What place?' I tried to follow the direction of her furious finger. 'To Waterside?'

'Of course, to Waterside! Would I mind taking charge of the keys until the Dunstans can make other arrangements? Sergeant Naylor asked me himself. What could I say?' She stared resentfully round the room. 'It's really too bad of them. It isn't even as if we knew the Dunstans for very long. Suppose the roof falls in while we're in charge of their house? What will we do then?'

Chris pricked up his ears when I mentioned that the police had left us holding a large and rather awesome baby.

'Do you think anyone would mind if we took a look round inside? I've only ever been in the place once, for the Grand Venetian Ball. Do you remember? When old Dunstan decided to beat the daylights out of his son in front of everyone?'

I didn't share Chris's amusement. 'He only hit Jack once, actually.'

'Really? Oh well, it was years ago.' Chris grinned. 'But I definitely think we should go and check the house over, if you've been left in charge of the keys. What if this caretaker fellow's left a window open and some robber makes off with the art collection?'

'Par said none of their pictures were very good.'

'The furniture, then. You can make an official inspection, and I'll come along as bodyguard, to look after my lovely fiancée.' He swept up my hand and kissed it. 'Come on. It'll begin to get dark in an hour or two, and I don't suppose the power's switched on.'

We let ourselves in by the main door to the kitchen quarters, after taking several minutes to find the right key on one of the two huge rings we'd been given. Inside, the larder corridor smelled of emptiness. The air was chilly and faintly sour and our footsteps rose up from the concrete floor to rumble round the white-tiled walls as if a whole regiment had invaded. Chris lifted the receiver of the household telephone and held it to his ear.

'Will you be wanting your tea now, sir?'

'Don't.' Even with Chris there, it was eerie to be all alone in that enormous house.

Chris peered into the funnel-shaped telephone mouthpiece and tapped on the square wooden case. 'Dead as a doornail, as we medical men would say.' He hung the receiver back on its hook and wandered further along the passage past a row of brass coal scuttles waiting patiently to be filled. 'What's in here?'

'That first door is the kitchen.'

The huge tiled hall must have been left ready to roar into life again if the family ever required it. I remembered how proud Alfred Dunstan had been of the specially imported French range in the centre of the room which vented its smoke through under-floor flues. Its multitude of hotplates were covered in dust now and the handles of its ovens were tarnished, but the enormous kettles and saucepans still waited in their towering racks for a dinner hour which had never come. At the far end of the kitchen, the coffee mill which had once grumbled its way through pounds of beans stood silent in the dusty deal dresser. The flour bin had been taken over by a colony of spiders. Its lid was missing, and the copper moulds above it were dulled brown with neglect.

There's a dead mouse down here.' Chris crouched down by the door, his scientific curiosity aroused. 'Died of cold, I should think. Or starvation.'

In the fish larder, the great zinc-lined ice cabinet stood open and empty, yet the cupboards in the china pantry were still full of the gilded, highly-coloured Minton and Coalport services the springmaker had preferred.

'They didn't even take their china with them.'

As far as I could see, Alfred Dunstan had left an entire household behind, everything he'd bought for treacherous Waterside. Yet why blame teacups and spoons for his disgrace? On a shelf of their own, I saw the green-bordered plates and yellow vaseline glass goblets Letty had kept for the terrace when her husband was away. Even in the dimness of the pantry they seemed to glitter with captive sunlight, with reckless golds and viridians, ochres and limes, with all the bud-bursting vigour of that summer long past.

'If you've seen enough, we should lock up and go back, Chris. It certainly doesn't look as if anyone's broken in.'

'But we've only just got here, for goodness' sake. Come and look at this.' Chris was moving about behind the frosted-glass door panels of the pantry next door. When I went in, he was examining a tarnished toast rack clamped over a little silver spirit stove. 'What on earth do you do with it?'

Reluctantly, I joined him. 'It's a crisper. It keeps your toast from turning into leather.'

'Not really? My God! There are four of them here. How much toast did they need?' He lifted the lid of a chafing-dish. 'If only country doctors lived in this kind of splendour!'

'You don't mean that. This was never a happy house.' I was

longing to say *Let's go home*, but Chris was clearly enthralled by each new discovery.

'I can't wait to see the rest of the place.' He pointed to the passage beyond the door, with its garnet and brown linoleum. 'This way, I presume.'

I didn't know what to expect beyond the heavy door that divided the pantries and kitchens from the rest of the house. I'd last seen the place after dinner, on the night Beatrice had insisted we all swim – Philip, Jack, Beatrice and I. Then, as usual, the electric bulbs had filled the house with their brassy blaze, gleaming from the varnished wood and the curling silver of the hall staircase like flares in a showman's tent. It had been a relentless light, as brilliant and aggressive as the springmaker's smile, projected across the lake. In those days the house didn't simply belong to Alfred Dunstan, it *was* Alfred Dunstan – his spirit in bricks and mortar and uncompromising stone – and it filled me now with the same unease as the springmaker's actual presence had always done. But after the first few minutes I was reassured. This was Waterside asleep, without its dynamos and electric power, a dim, silent cavern of drawn blinds, where dust-sheeted shapes floated like icebergs in the gloom. The cue racks in the billiard room had been emptied and the table shrouded in a shaped canvas cover. The drawing room chairs were a range of white stalagmites; above them hung the electric chandelier in its linen bag. Only the statues in the living hall seemed to have defied wrapping, leaving their noses, breasts and chins to be redefined by dust, along with the stuffed bear, sad and mouse-ridden, who still pointed the way to the stairs.

That was when I saw them floating high above the silver staircase, ghostly figures struggling back through a vengeful layer of distemper: Vulcan with his springs; Letty as Venus; Beatrice and Ida as Graces, materializing faintly as if through a fog, just as Jeremy Greendew had painted them. It would have taken several coats of paint to cover Jeremy's triumphant scarlet beyond hope of return, and the work had been botched. Philip Kassel's Narcissus lurked in the mist, not quite blotted out, but not quite present either. The last figure, unfinished, had been meant for Jack; it remained an indistinct presence in that house of shadows, as if the artist had never been quite sure of the substance of his model.

'Good heavens!' Chris halted, his mouth open. 'I don't remember seeing a mural on the night of the ball. I'm sure I'd have noticed.'

'Jeremy Greendew only began it a few weeks later. Alfred Dunstan must have had it whitewashed, after—'

'After the great scandal.' Chris gazed up at the wall. 'I remember. The whole of Windermere was talking about it. Mrs Dunstan ran off with a young boy, didn't she?'

'She didn't run off with him, that was the trouble. It might have been better for everyone if she had.'

Even clouded in distemper, Letty seemed to swim towards us with her extravagant hair, her voluptuous curves and the eerie glint Jeremy Greendew had put in her eye. Chris could hardly stop staring.

'She certainly looks like a goer, Mrs D. I wish she'd taken a fancy to me.'

'I don't know why Jeremy painted her like that. He made her look like the landlady of a particularly cheap pub.'

'Or the madam of a very expensive brothel.'

'Chris!' I gazed at him, astonished.

'Come on, I want to see where it *all happened*.' He grabbed my hand and set off for the staircase. 'What an incredible place this is!'

At the top of the stairs, the door to Letty's little sitting room stood ajar, her 'boudoir' as her husband had called it. Still clutching my hand, Chris pushed his way inside.

'More dust sheets.' He glanced round. 'Spiders' webs in the fireplace and a damp patch on the wall.'

Letty's bedroom was next door. 'This looks more promising.' Without hesitation, Chris pulled me through the connecting door.

The bedroom, for some reason, had escaped the shrouding of white that had enveloped the rest of the house. It was just as I remembered – as if, instead of a doorway, we'd passed through the barriers that seal the past from the present. I could have been exploring that shadowy space in a dream, strange but entirely familiar, with its cream walls shaded to soft grey and the blue of its furnishings to deep indigo. The air was still and musty with decay, and yet perfumed, even now, with a faint trace of Letty's Parma violets. The carpet under our feet was as soft as when Letty and Philip had walked over it, but damp had begun to spot the tall gilt mirror and spread a bloom on the polished wood of the bed. There was mould on the window sills, as velvet to the finger as the peacock-blue stitching of the bedcover and, when I lifted a straw hat that had been left, forgotten, on the dressing table, I found it was stained with mildew and part of its brim had been gnawed away. And yet now that its gloss had gone and decay had given it an unexpected poignancy, one part at least of the springmaker's mansion had become beautiful.

Chris was excited by the expense of it all. His eyes shone as he held out the rotting edge of a curtain and worked a finger into the gilded scrolls of the console table. 'Can't you just imagine Mary Pickford waking up in a room like this? Or Gloria Swanson lying in that bed, waiting for a lover?'

He sat down on the end of it with his knees apart, wriggled a bit, and then patted the place beside him. When I sat down he slid an arm round my shoulders, trying to pull me against him and, without meaning to, I felt myself resisting.

'Doesn't it . . . do something to you, this kind of place? It does, doesn't it?' He drew back my hair and spoke softly, close to my ear, caressing it with his warm breath. 'It's so unreal, like a palace in a movie. It's so . . . *seductive*. I keep thinking of Letty Dunstan in this bed, making love to her young friend.'

'You must have a very lively imagination, then. You only ever saw them at the ball.'

'You'd be surprised what I can imagine.' Softly, he touched my cheek. 'You know, you have skin like a pearl. It's quite beautiful.'

He leaned over to kiss me, gently at first but then with a determination that parted my lips, exposing my mouth to his probing tongue. His eyes seemed like those of an enormous predator and I closed mine hastily. Little by little, he was pressing me down on Letty Dunstan's peacock-blue bedcover. Taken aback, I allowed myself to be pushed into its dusty comfort. This was a Chris I hadn't encountered before, a determined lover whose lips brushed my eyelids, murmuring soft words of need. His hand slid down inside my dress as his mouth returned to mine; his exploring fingers found a nipple and began to tease it gently. I willed myself to relax, to lose myself in his eagerness. This was my future; to be loved by this man. I made my mouth soft against his, offering him possession. After a moment his hand left my breast and slid down to my thigh; I could feel him drawing up the fabric of my skirt and then the heat of his palm skimming the bare skin above my stockings.

All at once I sensed another presence, watching us, not in anger, but in sadness. Panic engulfed me. My hand flew down to catch Chris's, brushing against his trousers, feeling his stiffness.

'Not yet – not here—'

'There's nothing to be afraid of, honestly darling. It won't hurt if I'm careful—'

'Oh, Chris, not here, please—' I squirmed away from him and sat up, tugging at my skirt. 'I just couldn't, I'm sorry. Not in this house.'

'Oh.' Flushed and tousled, he eyed me like a truculent schoolboy deprived of a treat. 'Well, of course, it's up to you. If you want to wait . . . the wedding's not much more than a month away, I suppose.' Like a disappointed child, he added, 'I thought you wouldn't mind. I thought you felt the same way I did.'

'I do. And I wouldn't have minded, I promise. Anywhere but here.'

'Oh well, you're probably right.' He still sounded peeved. 'I suppose we ought to wait until we're married and do things properly.'

'Chris, darling, it has nothing to do with you, or not being married. It's this house—' I made up an excuse. 'You said yourself, Waterside is full of cobwebs and echoes.'

Chris considered me for a moment with the searching expression he kept for patients whom he suspected of malingering. Then he suddenly grinned as if he'd caught me out in a secret weakness.

'So you believe in ghosts, do you, Chrissie Ascham! I'd never have guessed it. Well, well – my terribly sensible fiancée, scared by a house full of ghosts!' He leaned forward to kiss me on the lips with proprietorial amusement. 'I wonder how many more of these surprises I'm in for?'

I gave a shamefaced little laugh, which seemed to be what was expected. I knew the next line of the fiancée's part. 'You'll just have to wait and see. I might have all kinds of horrible secrets.'

A couple of evenings later, cycling laboriously back through the gathering dusk from a late and melancholy supper at Hosanna's cottage, I happened to notice the iron gates of Waterside standing a little way open. I was almost certain Chris and I had locked them behind us when we left, but perhaps we hadn't. At any rate, we were, in a way, responsible for the place, so I wheeled the bicycle over to investigate. The rusty chain which had fastened the gates was now broken in two, while the padlock – still closed – swung uselessly at one end.

Burglars? I glanced at the lodge, empty since the caretaker's departure. I couldn't expect any help from there. The road was empty in both directions. Yet I'd be safe, I decided, as long as I stayed on my bicycle; no one would hear me and I could make a wide circle past the back of the house, looking for any sign of a break-in. If I saw anything suspicious I'd go straight to the village and tell the police. I pushed the gates open a little way against their barrier of weeds and cycled silently up the dark, leafy tunnel of the drive. As soon as I reached open ground at the top, I switched off my cycle lamp.

As far as I could see, the front and the nearest side of the house were utterly dark. All the same, the pounding of my heart seemed loud enough to alert an army of burglars as I turned under the archway that led to the kitchen entrance and pedalled at a good speed across the courtyard.

I was just swinging the cycle round when I saw it: a definite light behind the frosted glass of the kitchen windows. Yet it wasn't the wavering beam of a torch, but a steady yellow lamplight. And burglars surely don't light lamps, not even in deserted houses.

I brought the bicycle to a standstill, put my toes on the paving, and considered what to do. As far as I knew, the only keys to the house were in Mar's bureau at Fellwood. Had the drunken caretaker escaped from his hospital bed and let himself in without telling anyone? It seemed the most obvious explanation. Chris always said alcoholics could be very determined in their drinking; the caretaker had probably come back to search for a bottle he'd hidden in the house before he was carried off to hospital. Indignation banished my nervousness. How dare the man break into the house after the police had entrusted us with the keys! Propping the cycle against the laundry wall, I strode up to the door, twisted the handle, and, when the door opened quite easily, marched inside.

There was no light in the larder corridor, but the kitchen door was open and the white tiles in the passage glittered in the reflected light. The heels of my shoes clacked loudly on the concrete, alerting someone in the kitchen beyond; I heard a chair scrape over the floor. Then the kitchen doorway was filled by a large male silhouette, arms spread wide like a crucifixion, gripping the frame on either side. This was no caretaker. I almost turned to run. And then, even though the light was all from behind, I realized I knew the defiant set of that head and the chin, lifted in silent warning.

Chapter Thirteen

PLENTY OF people saw ghosts during the war. Aunt Marchioness's sister saw her son, a lieutenant in the Fusiliers, standing quite clearly in the hall of their house in full uniform and smiling, on the morning he was cut down by machine-gun fire at Gallipoli. And a whole battlefield claimed to have seen the heavenly host that scattered the German cavalry at Mons. Now I was sure it was my turn. I could have sworn, in that half-lit larder passage, that I could see Jack Dunstan filling the kitchen doorway, demanding to know by what right I was there.

'Chrissie? Good God! Of all people.' The vision shook its head, lowered its outstretched arms and turned back into the kitchen. 'For a moment there, I thought you were the drunk that looks after this place.'

This was no vision from the hereafter; ghosts don't concern themselves with the state of the staff. This was Jack Dunstan, unmistakably flesh and blood, as alive as I was. And yet, idiotically, I found myself answering him in the same flat, unemotional tone.

'The caretaker was sacked a few days ago. Mar has the keys.' I even raised my voice, so he'd hear.

'And you saw a light and came in.'

'You left the gates open a bit.'

'Ah! Stupid.'

Was he waiting for me to join him in the kitchen? I went in anyway.

The kitchen looked quite different by lamplight. In its watery luminescence the enormous chamber resembled nothing so much as the Basilica in Venice, with its arches and glittering walls. A single, workaday oil lamp stood on the heavy table near the range. Eighteen feet overhead, where the white tiles curved inwards, the ceiling was lost in shadow. The lamp glass was stained, or it might have shed more than a circle of yellow on the smooth deal of the table. As it was, beyond that pool of brightness there was only the occasional pinpoint of a brass handle or the glint of a white enamel bin.

I wondered what Alfred Dunstan would have said if he'd seen one of his prized Coalport dessert plates tossed down on the scrubbed pine beside a jar of ox tongue, a tin of condensed milk, a bag of sugar and a badly-sliced loaf. A knife and fork had been left at right-angles, as if the meal had been hastily interrupted.

I stared at it all, baffled. Jack Dunstan – of all people, as he'd said himself. I couldn't begin to imagine what he was doing there. Beatrice had told me he'd been promoted to Captain and had gone to London on his way back to his battalion. So why in heaven's name was he at Waterside, living like a fugitive? Then an explanation occurred to me, one so dreadful that a cold fear wrapped itself round my heart. If Jack was hiding, he must have deserted – quit the Army, run away from the war. Was it possible?

When I finally risked a glance at him, he was standing by the range with his arms folded across his chest, watching me in such silent distrust that I could almost believe he'd read my thoughts. I found myself gabbling, trying to explain my presence.

'I thought someone had broken in. I suppose you still have a key.'

'No.' He unfolded his arms and transferred his hands to his pockets. 'But the lock on the fish-larder window was never any good.'

The whole situation was so bizarre that this didn't surprise me. The new, fugitive Jack Dunstan didn't look like the kind of man who'd be stopped by a locked door if there was something he wanted on the other side of it. Two years had passed since our last meeting outside the post office in Windermere; now the lamplight picked out the bones of a face that was starker and more desolate than I remembered. His dark brows pressed down on eyes narrowed by a habit of weariness, scored deeply at their corners by arrows of disillusion. Two more fissures ran vertically from cheekbone to jaw, enclosing a mouth whose lower lip curved up and out, constantly on its guard. He didn't look as if he'd shaved in two days. There was no sign of his uniform – he was wearing workmen's canvas trousers held up by a heavy belt, and a flannel shirt. I could well believe he'd broken into the house by way of the fish-larder window. But that didn't explain why he was there.

'What on earth . . . I mean, *why* on earth—' My gesture of hopelessness must have given him some idea of my confusion, but he deliberately turned his back on me.

'I can't offer you coffee or tea. There's no fire in the range.' His hand rose, hovered a moment, then reached past the lamp to where a bottle of whisky waited, three-quarters full. 'Will you have some of this?'

'Fine.' I didn't want to drink, but I had the distinct feeling that I'd have to, if I wanted to stay.

'Sit down, then.' He hooked a toe behind the leg of a nearby wooden chair and slid it towards me, then went over to the dresser and came back after a moment with two small tin pudding moulds. 'This is the best I can do. There are glasses somewhere, but it's too dark to find them.'

'Those'll be fine.'

He tipped a little whisky into one of the moulds, swilled it round to collect the dust, opened the fire door of the range and tossed the muddy liquid inside. Then he refilled the mould and held it out to me. 'Just to prove I'm not totally dissolute.'

I noticed he didn't bother rinsing his own. He'd given me a dismayingly large amount of whisky. I indicated the abandoned plate. 'I've interrupted your meal.'

'I'm not hungry. I just eat out of habit.' He pushed the plate aside and perched on the edge of the table in its place. The toe of one well-travelled boot appeared briefly in the lamplight.

'Jack—' I struggled for words to convey the shock of his reappearance. 'You do realize I thought you were in London, or on your way back to France? I saw Bea in Manchester and she told me you'd been home on leave, but you'd gone back again.'

'She was right. I should have gone back.' He stared at me defiantly for a moment, then let his gaze wander away among the shadows. 'But, as you can see, I didn't go, I came here instead.' His eyes swept back to engage mine, intensity suddenly driving out weariness. 'You aren't to tell anyone you've seen me.'

'You've *deserted*? Jack – I can't believe it!'

'Swear you won't tell anyone.'

'But, for heaven's sake—'

'Swear it!'

'But, Jack, they *shoot* deserters, don't they?'

I stared at him, stiff with horror. Only that morning, George Powley had told me that in his opinion, deserters sent to the firing squad got off lightly. 'A man's lower'n a worm,' he'd growled, 'if he don't stand by his comrades. What's left to him after that? I wouldn't feed him to the pigs, for fear they'd get bellyache. Chop 'im up small and put his head on a stick. That's what they used to do.'

'Jack, you've got to go back, at once. You must turn yourself in.' In my anxiety, my hands flew about like startled moths. I almost seized hold of him, there and then, to push him towards the door. 'Tell them your train was delayed – tell them anything – but for heaven's sake go back.'

'I will go back!' He shouted the words in my face. 'But not yet. I have to stay here for a while and lie low. If I'm found, then . . . I won't be the only one in trouble, not by a long way.' He took a long, uneven breath and lowered his voice. 'That's why you have to go out of here tonight and forget you ever saw me.'

'How can I possibly do that? What do I say to your mother, if I meet her again? You can't ask me to keep a secret like that!'

The sudden ferocity of his anger took me utterly by surprise. He swung towards me and slapped his palm down hard on the table, making the jars and tins jump. His face was hard with rage. 'It's none of your business what I do! This is my life – *mine*! And if I decide not to go back to France for a bit, then it's my choice and nothing to do with you. If I'd closed those bloody gates properly, you'd never have known I was here.'

There was a horrible, embarrassing silence – embarrassing, not because I'd been afraid, although I hadn't relished being frightened, but because of that sudden, almost indecent loss of control. It had been such a raw, brutish explosion of anger, the fury of an infant or a baited animal. The expression on Jack's face indicated that he realized it and might have tried to salvage the situation if he'd known how. Clearly, it was far beyond him.

I put down the unfinished whisky and got to my feet. 'You're quite right, of course. If you want to sit here until the police find you and haul you off to be shot, then, as you say, it isn't any of my business.' I turned towards the door. I felt a lightness, a relief, as if his anger had released me from any obligation to worry. 'Goodnight, Jack.'

'Where are you going?'

'I'm going home.'

'Why?'

'*Why?*' I stared at him incredulously.

He avoided my eye and methodically poured himself another whisky. The bottle rattled faintly against the rim of the mould. 'It didn't take you long to get sick of me, did it?'

I hesitated, still half-turned towards the door. 'Are you surprised? All this time, I've been worried about you, away at the war. And now you turn up out of nowhere, and frighten the wits out of me . . . Don't you want me to go? Isn't that what you said?'

'I can't help it.' He ran a hand swiftly through his hair, his fingers rigidly spread. 'It just happens, sometimes. Sit down – please – now that you're here.'

I sat down again, slowly, on the edge of the chair. 'Jack, are you sure you want my company? Or would you rather be alone?'

'I'm not fit for company, that's the trouble.'

It was something like an apology and I decided to take it as one. 'You look worn out. You need to sleep for a while, then you'd feel better.'

'I suppose I might – if I did sleep. But I don't, much. Not without this.' He reached out again for the whisky bottle, then glanced up warningly. 'Don't say it.'

'Say what?'

'"You're drinking too much." Do you know something? I wish to heaven it did make me drunk – falling-down, belly-up, blind drunk. But it doesn't even do that.'

'Then why drink it?'

He looked at me over the tin rim, and I had a sudden sensation of gazing into a deep, deep well. 'It makes the guns stop.'

I watched him in silence as he drained the measure. It occurred to me then that two years in the trenches were enough to wreck any man's nerves. Three months, they said, was as long as many young officers lasted. If he survived for a year, an officer could lose the capacity to estimate danger and begin to take ludicrous risks with his men. I'd seen other soldiers with the same sleepless, haunted eyes. I wanted to ask Jack how he'd been wounded and how long he'd had to recover, but I was afraid of setting off another outburst. What Jack wanted me to know, I suspected, he'd tell me.

He'd been examining me critically. Now he pointed to the solitaire diamond on the third finger of my left hand. 'Engagement ring?'

Of its own accord, my right hand slid to cover my left. When I realized what I'd done, I deliberately pulled my hands apart again and smiled brightly, a confident, bride-to-be's smile. 'I'm getting married in October. To Chris Cole – do you remember him? Irene's brother, the doctor? He took over his father's practice that last summer you were here.' I felt obliged to add, 'He's the only doctor left for miles, poor thing, apart from a seventy-year-old fellow in Keswick.'

'I expect he's been kept busy, then, bandaging fingers and dosing croup.' Jack managed a bitter smile. 'And what about you? What have you done since the war started? You've been going to church, I suppose, and praying for us all? I bet you've even knitted some socks. No – don't tell me – ' He held up a hand. 'You had to drive the baker's van after the baker was gassed at Ypres.'

I waited in silence, letting him finish.

'I've been driving an ambulance, actually. In France.' Briefly, I told him how I'd spent my time in the Calais convoy and how I'd come to break my leg. 'It wasn't the Somme, I know. But I did do something.'

'So you did.'

Once again I sensed his discomfort, as if he understood he'd gone too far, but didn't know what to do about it. After a moment he slid the whisky bottle along the table towards me, an awkward peace-offering. 'You aren't drinking.'

'I haven't finished this yet.' For once, I knew I had the advantage of him and decided to risk everything. 'Why don't you go back to your regiment, Jack, and ask them for help?'

'What kind of help?' His expression defied me to go any further. I watched suspicion dawn in his face. 'A doctor? Some kind of do-gooding psychologist? Is that why you think I'm here, because I'm a head-case?'

'It's nothing to be ashamed of. Lots of men go down with shock and you've been out there longer than most—'

'You mean, I've been there for two years and I haven't had the common decency to get myself killed.'

'I never said—'

'All right then, if you want a dead hero, then I am dead. Dead *here*.' he stabbed a finger against his temple. 'Dead *here*.' He pointed to his chest. 'Empty. Cleaned out. Finished. Nothing left but bad dreams. Is that enough for you?' His eyes were alive with furious resentment. 'Oh, what the hell do you know about it? You sit there with that ring on your hand, *nearly* a doctor's wife, and suddenly you know what's best for everyone—' He stabbed the table with a finger. 'Listen to me. I have a good reason for being here and it has nothing to do with shock or neurasthenia, or whatever name they give it. There's nothing the matter with my bloody mind, except I'm in the middle of a war. I'm trying to stop a disaster in the only way I know how – and it's no one's business but mine. I'll turn myself in when I'm ready and not before, and if they do shoot me for deserting it won't matter a damn, because nobody bloody well cares.'

'I care.'

That stopped him. For a few seconds there was silence, except for the sound of our breathing.

'More fool you,' he said.

I hadn't meant *care*, of course, not in the way I realized it had sounded. I was sorry for him, naturally, but I didn't care as I once would have done – more than reason, more than my own life. I'd never care like that again for any mortal creature, but the words just flew out before I could stop them. I'd have liked Jack to understand the difference, but it didn't seem the moment for explanations. Chris, I was sure, would have understood.

Instead, I said briskly, 'By rights, the best thing I could do would be to go straight to the police station tomorrow morning and tell Sergeant Naylor where to find you. You say you aren't ill, which means you're a deserter and a coward. But since I don't believe for a moment that you *are* a coward, then you must be ill and I should turn you in for your own good, so that you can get proper help.'

He'd raised his head; he was staring at me with an expression of such wild apprehension – such tigerish alarm – that I felt a stab of fear.

'Don't.' It was a warning. 'Just don't do that, though I don't believe you would. Because if I did believe it, I'd have to get out of here tonight and find somewhere else.' He gripped the table and leaned towards me. 'For God's sake, Chrissie, don't you know me well enough to trust me? I will go back. Look, I'll make you a promise, I'll turn myself in on the last day of September. That's just over a month – it's all I need – time enough. But I can't risk being found until then.'

He was sick – deranged. He had to be. He'd simply had more than he could take of the shelling and the mud and the sight of casual death. It followed that part of his sickness was this insistence that nothing was wrong, or that something inside him had died, as if that could possibly happen to a man and leave him sane and whole.

'All this business about being dead inside—' I put on my brisk ambulance-driving voice. 'If you feel like that, then you must be ill, but at least you're still in one piece, physically. That's something, isn't it? Not like thousands of other poor devils who didn't have your luck.

'Philip Kassel's dead, you know. Cut up by a rifle grenade. They sent him up to Calais because they thought he might pull through, but he didn't. The last time I saw him, he was in a shed they were using as a mortuary – Philip, exactly as I remembered him, and yet . . . nothing. That's why it makes me so angry, to hear you say you don't need help.'

Jack was staring into the blackness of the floor. 'You don't have to listen.' Then, trying for once, perhaps, to make up for his rudeness, he added, 'I didn't know about Philip.'

'I went to see Max Kassel in London. They've locked him up in one of these camps for enemy aliens and he's become little and old, just a shadow of himself. He's lost everything in the world that mattered to him: his son, his business, everything, and yet he's being so brave about it. The police still think he was spying; they think he stole those pearls himself – the ones Philip took – and sent them to Bulgaria, to pay for guns. And yet Max won't hear a word against Philip. All he can think of is clearing his name. Jack—' I leaned forward abruptly, because my words didn't seem to be having any effect. I found myself fighting a desire to hit him. 'Don't you care at all?'

He lifted his haggard, weary eyes to meet mine and I wished I hadn't been so brutal.

'Oh, I care.' His fingers had curled tightly round the tin mould. 'I care that Philip Kassel was cheated, like all the rest, first of all by my mother and then by the politicians who let this war happen. Do you know what he died for? Not for justice – just for greed and power and the ambitions of a handful of old men. That's the squalid truth. I've watched good men die for no more than a few yards of ground.'

'They're still heroes. That's what their families believe.'

'Oh, it's true! They're heroes to go on fighting, once they realize the truth.'

I kept seeing the faces of the men on stretchers at Calais. 'And so you've left them to go on fighting without you, these heroes.'

'No.' He shook his head in weary despair. 'I've told you – just for a month or so. After that I'll go back, I swear it, and they can do what they like to me. By then it won't matter.'

I wanted to believe him. He seemed to believe it so firmly himself. Like a coward, I made a show of glancing at my watch. 'Goodness, it's almost ten. I said I'd be home by half past nine.'

He folded his arms and studied a rack of kettles. 'Mustn't worry Christopher, I suppose.'

'This has nothing to do with Chris. It's Mar who worries. It's this leg of mine. She always expects me to crash my bicycle into something.'

'Which, of course, you won't do. Having driven a big, powerful ambulance.'

'Jack, I can change a wheel, scrape sooty plugs and clear an airlock in a fuel pipe. If you give me enough time, I can clean out a carburettor and grind-in a leaking valve. I've even mended a punctured petrol float with the edge from a sheet of stamps. And no, I'm not going to crash my bicycle.'

This seemed to amuse him. 'You're going to make a useful

wife, I can see that. I hope Chris Cole knows what a bargain he's getting.'

'In case you hadn't realized,' I blurted out, 'Chris loves me.'

'And you love him?'

'Well, of course.'

There was an instant's silence. 'Best of luck to you, then.'

'I really must go.' I stood up and, after a moment, Jack seemed to accept the fact and got to his feet. Then he took a couple of steps and I realized he was blocking my path to the door. I couldn't tell whether he'd done it deliberately or not, but I felt the hair prickle at the nape of my neck.

'Chrissie . . .' He sighed and passed a hand over his eyes. 'I'll ask you again. Will you swear not to tell anyone I'm here? All that business about going to the police – did you mean it?'

'Suppose I did mean it? Are you going to try to keep me here?'

'No, of course not! What do you take me for? But I'd have to get out of this house and find somewhere else to hide.'

'And even if I do swear not to tell anyone – what makes you think I'll keep my word?'

He held my gaze until I thought I saw a glimmer of amusement in his sleepless eyes. '"Cross your heart, and hope to die" – remember? You never told anyone about the *Siren*.'

The *Siren*. Had I kept my promise for two years? It felt more like two lifetimes. I wished he hadn't reminded me.

'Very well. I swear it. I won't tell anyone.' I moved towards the door.

'There's something else.' He held out a hand. 'Will you come back tomorrow?'

'Tomorrow?' I stared at him, disconcerted.

'I need your help. I'll need food – oil for the lamp. I can't risk being seen in the village.' His eyes searched my face. 'Will you get them for me?'

'No! Absolutely not!' I was horrified by the idea and my indignation poured out. 'You've no right to ask me such a thing!

217

Maybe you do have a reason for being here, or maybe it's all a pack of lies but, either way, I don't want anything to do with it. You said yourself this was none of my business, and it isn't – and I don't want it to be.'

'Of course.' He nodded. 'It was stupid of me to expect anything else.' He pushed the kitchen door as wide as its hinges would allow. 'Why should you want to come back here, after all? I'm hardly sparkling company.'

My throat was tight with fury. 'I really must go.'

He followed me into the passage. 'I'll come out with you.'

'There's no need.'

'Politeness.'

'I tell you, there's no need. I *can* manage a bicycle without help.'

'Oh, I'm sure you can.' His bitterness suddenly spilled over. 'You can do anything you damned well want, you and your precious Chris. Heal the sick, walk on water. It must be a great satisfaction to you.' For a moment, his eyes held mine. 'Oh, go away and leave me alone.' He turned and began to stalk back along the passage towards the half-light of the kitchen.

'Jack!'

'*Get out*! For Christ's sake, leave me in peace! Go and oil an axle, or whatever it is you do.'

'Fine! I will go, then. And I hope you stew in this mess you've made.' With as much dignity as my limp would allow, I turned about and set off rapidly down the passage.

He halted and turned, just short of the kitchen door. I could sense his eyes on me as I marched away.

'You said you cared! Didn't you?'

I didn't bother to respond. I simply kept on walking, my head down.

'You don't give a damn! It was all just so much bloody talk.'

Then I heard his voice like a groan behind me, a mixture of surrender and despair and exhaustion. 'Chrissie . . . they're here, if you want to know.'

I stopped marching. 'What are here?'

'Philip Kassel's pearls. The ones you're so concerned about. They're here, in this house.'

'I don't believe you!' I swung round. Jack filled the passage, a dark silhouette. 'The pearls can't have been in Waterside all this time!'

'Why not?'

I was sure he was lying, snatching at any excuse to keep me from leaving. At the back of my mind, I could picture Mar in a panic, phoning Hosanna to ask where I was and then launching a search party. I tried to ignore the image. 'Why should I believe you? How do you know the pearls are here?'

'Philip told me himself.'

'*Philip* did?'

Jack's silhouette moved its arms, stiffly. 'I ran into him last summer, in a training camp at Le Havre. They'd sent me on a technical course, something to do with trench mortars and percussion bombs. Philip was hanging around the docks, waiting to go up the line.'

'And he just came out with it? "By the way, this is where I left the pearls."'

'Among a lot of other things, yes, more or less. It seems a long time ago, now.' Jack put his shoulders against the wall, pushed his hands into his pockets and tipped his head back against the cool tiles. 'Once he'd started, he just kept on talking. It was mainly rubbish, but I couldn't stop him. I would have stopped him, if I'd known how. He kept going on and on about my mother – how she'd looked and the things she'd said to him . . . How he kept smelling her perfume – Parma violets – and how she used to take her hair down and let him run his hands through it. It was all embarrassing stuff like that. Not the sort of thing you want to hear about your mother. He was totally besotted, poor bastard – off his head. I was sorry for him, in the end.'

'And he told you he'd left the pearls here?'

'He said he'd brought them back from London. Bea was

threatening to go to Father and she made him steal them, the bitch. Shows you how mad he was. But then, of course, everything went wrong and Father got hold of him and threw him out with the damn pearls still in his pocket – and he just wanted to be rid of them.' Jack rested the sole of one foot against the wall. 'He said he hated the sight of the things, after what had happened – after my mother gave him up. They were just so many useless beads.'

'And you never thought of telling anyone?'

I heard a hollow laugh. 'If you're out in No Man's Land working on the wire, a string of pearls is the last thing on your mind, I assure you. I hadn't thought of them until you mentioned them tonight.'

'But you do know where they are?'

'I'm pretty sure I can remember.'

'But that's wonderful!' I stifled a desire to run back along the passage and start searching at once. 'Think what this means to Max Kassel – freedom, maybe! You could almost say Philip gave the pearls back himself.'

Jack shifted his position, unhurriedly. I could feel him watching me, calculating. 'You want me to find them, then?'

'Well, of course! Is that difficult? Where exactly are they?'

'Hidden.' He allowed a short silence to fall. 'You'll have to come back tomorrow. I'll need daylight to find them.'

'Tomorrow.' I remembered our earlier conversation.

'If you can square it with your conscience, of course, with these high principles of yours.'

Something in his voice made me uneasy. 'You will still be here tomorrow, will you?'

'Are you afraid I won't be?' There was another short pause. 'You must want those pearls pretty badly.'

'Well, yes.' Stupidly, I added, 'I'd probably have come back tomorrow anyway. To see if you were all right.'

'That's a damned lie! Five minutes ago, you didn't want anything to do with me. "Stew", wasn't that what you said?'

'I was angry.'

'You were afraid.'

'Nonsense.' I wished it sounded more convincing. 'Jack . . . I will come back here tomorrow.'

'For the pearls. Yes, I'm sure you will.'

'Not just for them.'

'No. Of course not.' He raised a hand in ironic farewell and turned back towards the kitchen. 'I'll look forward to your visit.'

And then he was gone, leaving me alone in the half-darkness.

Next morning, my first thought was to cycle over to Waterside before Jack could have second thoughts and disappear again. I'd gone over our conversation a hundred times in my head and I no longer doubted that the pearls were at Waterside. Jack's account of his meeting with Philip had been too painful to have been made up on the spur of the moment.

I tried to believe I might have gone back without knowing about the pearls. If I'd thought I could help, if he'd been prepared to let me – that might have made a difference; but in his present bitter, restless mood . . . I wasn't afraid; he made me uneasy, that was all.

Unfortunately, I'd promised to put in an hour's work at the surgery first thing, which meant that I wouldn't reach Waterside much before half past ten. I bought some bacon and eggs as a peace offering, but by the time I'd finished making out orders for the various pills and ointments on Chris's list, it was more like a quarter to eleven when I slipped my bicycle through the gates at Waterside, closing them carefully behind me. By now I was quite worried that Jack would have gone and as I cleared the top of the drive and saw the house as silent and closed-up as ever, I was almost certain he had. Then, as I rode through the archway into the kitchen courtyard, I saw him leaning on the wall by the kitchen door.

'This is a bit risky, isn't it? What if I'd been the police?'

'I saw you from the billiard room window, coming up the drive.'

'You were looking out for me?'

'I was playing billiards.'

Without another word, he turned away towards the kitchen door. Uninvited, I followed. Day had filled the kitchen with a cream-coloured light that thinned to milky green shadows round the corners of the huge dresser and the arched opening where the dumb-waiter had once whisked breakfasts to the upper floors. A couple of mattresses had been dragged in and piled with blankets. I assumed that was where Jack had spent the night. The whisky bottle on the table was now almost empty, though Jack himself looked more purposeful. All the same, there were smudges of fatigue like dusty fingerprints round his eyes, and grey-brown hollows under his cheekbones that suggested he ate when he happened to remember, if at all.

I was desperate to find out about the pearls, but I knew better than to ask.

'Bacon and eggs.' I put my parcels on the table. 'If we can light the range, I'll cook you something hot to eat.'

I thought at first Jack was going to refuse. He passed the back of his hand defensively across his lips and then found an excuse for accepting. 'Why not? It'll give you some practice for married life.'

I forced a smile. 'Always useful.'

I unwrapped my packages while Jack went in search of kindling and coal. He came back with a bucketful and opened the door of the fire chamber.

'Here.' I gave him some of the greasy paper from the bacon and watched him lay the fire with a deftness I hadn't expected. I'd forgotten the fascination of those strong, supple hands with their oddly vulnerable fingers, the fingers that had confounded me whenever I'd tried to call him unfeeling.

He was wearing the same flannel shirt as the night before,

open round the soft well of his throat. I found I'd forgotten that too – that velvety hollow cradled by the roots of the muscle supporting his stubborn head. Always that mixture of strength and small, private weaknesses he'd have died sooner than acknowledge.

He dug in his pocket for matches, then stood up and stepped back to watch the progress of the flames. After a few moments, satisfied the coal was dry enough to kindle, he went round to inspect the brass knobs that operated the flues and dampers.

'Main oven. We don't need that.' He slid the knob in its slot and I heard the grate of a shutter closing somewhere inside the iron entrails of the range. 'Main flue open – that should keep the fire drawing – and this one half-way, maybe.'

He stepped back again suddenly and his leg caught the edge of the open fire door, hurling it shut with a clang that echoed like cannon fire round the tiled walls. When I glanced up, Jack had gone perfectly rigid, his eyes pressed shut, his face contorted in an expression of agony. In a couple of seconds the spasm had passed, but when his eyes blinked open, the lids were scarlet from the fierceness of the pressure. Heaven knows what he read in my face.

'Are you going to fry that bacon or just stand there staring?'

'I'll have to rinse a pan.' I lifted one of the smaller skillets from the rack and took it through to the scullery, to the huge glazed fireclay sink, grateful for an excuse to leave the kitchen. Now I was sure I knew why he hadn't gone back to France. I'd seen men fresh from the trenches weep like children at the slamming of an ambulance door, or throw themselves flat as if shells were already hissing through the air. I'd seen sixteen-month veterans scramble back into a hospital doorway when the scent of sun-warmed flowers smelled like a gust of deadly gas. Goodness knows what suffering passed before their eyes in those moments – but it was real enough.

Jack ate quickly, scooping up the bacon fat with slices cut

from a pound loaf as if the meal might be his last for a while. I tried not to hang over him, sensing he might resent having an audience.

He glanced up once. 'Aren't you eating?'

'No thanks. Chris is coming over for lunch.'

Immediately, I was glad I'd said it. *Chris.* Even his name was enough to put everything back where it belonged, to restore sense and order to my life. It made me confident enough to add, 'We're going to look at a house at Troutbeck Bridge that Chris thought we might take for our first year or so. The owner's been posted abroad and didn't want to rent to just anyone, but apparently, when he heard it was to be "Young Dr Cole" and his wife, that made all the difference.' I gave a carefree laugh which came out like a nervous whinny. 'I can't think why it should matter. We aren't exactly saints.'

Now that I'd started, I couldn't stop myself. The words 'us' and 'our' poured out like a kind of release.

'At least we've managed to stay out of any arguments about the wedding, no matter what our families said. Chris's mother is desperate to have "Jesu, Joy of Man's Desiring", but the Rector says the choir can't manage it, although Mrs Cole thinks the real problem is that the Rector's wife – who plays the organ – can't cope with the twiddly bits in between. And Par says if we have anything by Wagner he'll walk out, right in the middle of the service.'

Jack pushed his empty plate away, scraping it across the table, and reached for the last of the whisky.

'Oh, Jack, not again.'

'I knew you'd say that, sooner or later. *Oh, Jack, not again!* I hope Chris Cole knows what he's in for. If he isn't a saint already, he'd better learn.'

'It won't do you any good, you know.'

'On the contrary.' He tipped some of the whisky down his throat. 'It does me a great deal of good. Particularly when I start to remember things I'd rather forget.'

'Nightmares, you mean.'

He moved the bottle through an arc. 'Not always at night.'

'You don't have to go through all this alone. What if I were to bring a doctor here—'

'The saintly Chris, I suppose.'

'He might be able to help. You're hardly unusual. Lots of men have the same problem after years in the trenches.' Without realizing it, I'd slipped into my Browne's Brigade manner again, cheerfully solicitous. 'It can be treated, you know. It's no disgrace.'

He snorted scornfully. 'My dear girl, after two years, this is *normal*. Nothing out of the ordinary. You should see some of the others.'

'Then why all this?' I swung an arm, taking in the makeshift bed and the squalor of the table.

'I told you. I do have a reason. And anyway, it makes no odds, since your doctor friend is never going to know I'm here – because you've promised not to tell him.'

'I won't tell him. Not unless you say so.' I watched Jack drain the last of the whisky, conscious that time was ticking away, minute by minute. By now, I'd guessed what he wanted. He wanted me to ask outright for the pearls; until I did, he wouldn't even tell me whether he'd found them or not. He was absolutely convinced they were all I'd come back for and now he wanted me to prove it.

'I wish you'd let me help. I am worried about you, you know.'

'Oh, I'm sure you are!' He pushed the cork back into the empty whisky bottle and smacked it with his open palm. 'Do you honestly expect me to believe that, when you couldn't wait to get away from me last night? Look—' He leaned forward. 'Since I know you're bursting to ask, I found your blessed pearls this morning, as soon as it got light. They were exactly where Philip said they'd be.'

He rooted in a pocket, and stretched out his hand. When he

opened his fingers, there in his palm was a single, perfect pearl, not quite pure white in colour, roughly the size of a cherry stone and disfigured by a small hole.

'But there were thirty of them!'

'There are thirty, and a diamond clasp. They're quite safe, don't worry. The question is – do you want them?'

I stared at him. 'Well, of course I want them! Or rather, the police want them. Don't you see? This will mean everything in the world to Max Kassel. He's been so ill in that camp, and now they may actually let him out.' I reached out to take the pearl but Jack closed his fingers over it and withdrew his hand.

'Of course you want them. That's the only reason you came back here, after all.'

'Not just for that.'

'Don't take me for a fool, Chrissie.' Unhurriedly, Jack laid the pearl beside him on the table, where it sat, large and greenish-cream in the reflection of the tiled walls. He let several seconds pass in silence.

'You see, I did a bit of thinking last night, after you'd gone. And then I slept . . . better than I've done for a long time. I don't suppose that means anything to you. I expect you fall asleep the minute your innocent head touches the pillow. But I don't. And even when I do—' He shrugged. 'Too many memories.'

'I'm pleased to hear you slept. But what does that have to do with the pearls?'

'Wait.' He held up a finger. 'Now, it occurred to me that if I simply hand over the pearls – just like that – you'll have got everything you came for and, while I'm sure you'll be very grateful for at least five minutes, you'll be off like a dose of salts to see about this wedding of yours. Because you don't give a toss about me. Not really.'

'Jack! That isn't—'

'Wait, I said.' Thoughtfully, he propelled the huge pearl in a circle on the tabletop. 'That's why I broke up the necklace. I thought we'd start with one pearl, just for a beginning, and then see how we get on after that.'

'One pearl?' I stared at him, trying to follow what was in his mind.

'One pearl today. And tomorrow you can come back for another.'

'*What*? Oh, no.' I shook my head. 'Not on your life.' Now I was certain he was mad. Not just haunted and nightmare-ridden, but utterly mad. 'And what if I don't come back tomorrow?'

He regarded me steadily across the few feet that separated us. 'You won't get another pearl, then, will you?'

'I don't believe this. You're going to *pay* me to come back here, day after day—' My voice began to rise up the scale. 'By handing over the pearls, one by one?'

'Look, Chrissie – I need your help. I told you that last night, if you remember. I can't risk being seen in the village, but you can buy whatever I need.' He gestured towards the empty frying pan. 'This is – what – the twenty-fourth of August? Thirty pearls, thirty days, that would take us to . . .' He made a quick calculation. 'The twenty-second of September. I'd settle for that; it should be long enough. The next day I'll go back, turn myself in, whatever you want. That's a fair bargain, isn't it?'

'*Fair*? How can you even suggest such a thing?'

'Why not?' He leaned forward, his expression suddenly intent. 'All I want is your time. That shouldn't matter to this doctor of yours – Chris, or whatever his name is. I'm not trying to spoil your life. If he makes you happy, then I wish you both all the luck in the world. But I can't stand being alone. I realized that last night. Just having you here – just *talking*, the two of us, even squabbling like fishwives – it kept the ghosts away for a while.'

He took a long breath. 'But you wouldn't have come back today, if it hadn't been for the pearls – you made that quite clear. And why should you? I'm a deserter, after all, rude, bad-tempered, and . . . oh, other things you know nothing about. You're right,

I probably will shock you and offend you – because I know how bloody I can be. Much, much worse than you've seen.' His fingers curled on the table top, scratching faintly. 'But this way, I *know* you'll come. You'll keep me fed and if I want to talk, you'll have to listen, because you won't have any choice.'

I leaped to my feet. I was actually shaking with fear and disgust. 'You bastard! What kind of woman gets paid for keeping a man company?'

'A dead man – I told you.'

'You aren't dead. You're just contemptible! Disgusting! You've always been an evil bastard, Jack, ever since I've known you.' By now, I no longer cared what I was saying. It was pure, raw emotion, a passionate outpouring of the kind I'd denied myself for years. Gutter language I'd heard in the war sprang instinctively to my lips. 'You louse! You *shit*! You absolute *fucker*!'

I suddenly heard myself and stopped, appalled. I couldn't believe I'd said such things. Chris would have been shocked to the core.

Jack was staring at me with burning eyes and something like approval. 'Go on – it's true! You might as well say it. What else do you expect from Alfred Dunstan's son but a bastard's bargain?'

'You weren't his son years ago, before the war?'

'Oh, I was. I just didn't realize it, that's all. Once a Dunstan, always a Dunstan. You can't change that.'

He snatched the pearl from the table and held it up between finger and thumb. 'Well? One at a time, or none at all. If you don't want them, they go into the fire.' He kicked open the door of the range.

I was outraged by the cruelty of his bargain and by its sheer, downright shamelessness. 'If Chris knew for a second—'

'Max Kassel would never see his pearls again, I promise you.'

'My God, you're vile!'

'And you'll come back here for thirty days and be . . . what's the word? My *sin-eater*. The one who shares the vileness, the one who gets paid to save a dead man from hell.'

'I won't be anything of the kind! If you won't give the pearls back out of common decency, then burn them, or choke on them – I don't care which!' I turned on my heel and marched out of the kitchen, slamming the door loudly enough to send an echo like a gunshot round that great tiled room.

From inside I thought I heard what might have been a cry of pain.

Chapter Fourteen

I MUST BE working you too hard.' Chris glanced at me critically as I got into the car. 'You look dead beat. Or is it the wedding that's tiring you out, arranging all the flowers and invitations and so on? I know how you girls like to have everything absolutely right, even with a war on.'

Ordinarily, I'd have objected to 'you girls', but this wasn't the moment. I'd had to toil for fifteen minutes over a basin of cold water to cool the flaming cheeks caused by my confrontation with Jack and even then I still looked shocked enough when I went downstairs for Chris to notice something amiss.

For a moment I toyed with the idea of telling Chris the whole story and letting him take charge. He was a doctor, after all; he was used to illness. This business with the pearls – this *blackmail*, to be blunt about it – was surely the product of desperation. In that case, for Jack's own good, shouldn't I forget my promise and find him some help?

As soon as I'd framed the thought, I knew I'd no right to take such a risk. Suppose Jack wasn't ill and all I achieved was to have him dragged away and shot? Even if that meant he'd set out, quite shamelessly and cynically, to force me into doing what he wanted, I couldn't bear to have his death on my conscience. Not Jack's. In any case, what on earth would Chris think of me? At the very least, I'd been stupid to put myself in such a position. To be paid, day by day, for my 'company' like a . . . why not say it? Like a common whore! I was furious with Jack – *furious* – but

I was also ashamed for him. No, I couldn't bring myself to tell Chris.

I was left with an image of Max Kassel, ill and alone, in the aliens' prison in London. What was I supposed to do? Jack was desperate; Max Kassel was just as desperate. Jack was probably more than a little mad. How much could I be expected to risk for Max's sake?

I was vaguely aware of the house at Troutbeck Bridge being unexpectedly pleasant, with light, airy rooms overlooking a wooded slope and a little gabled porch almost hidden under a mass of old roses. As we went round, I tried to keep my mind on the location of water boilers and stopcocks and whether the current 'tween-girl would stay on to 'do' for us, but my thoughts kept wandering back to that cheerless kitchen at Waterside and the tormented, animal moan I'd heard as I slammed the door.

'What do you think, darling?' Chris took my arm as we went downstairs again, temporarily out of earshot of our guide. 'It looks just about perfect to me, apart from that awful picture of dead pheasants in the hall. I can just see you pouring tea for me in the breakfast room, in some sort of frilly *peignoir*. Chrissie . . .' He gave my arm a gentle squeeze. 'Are you listening?'

The house did seem ideal in every way. Chris clearly thought so and he was usually right. The interior of the Austin was filled with his happy humming as he let in the clutch and we began to roll off down the hill. I wished uneasily that I could share his satisfaction.

Half-way home I began to fish for information.

'Chris – do you know anything about these men who have nightmares because of the war? Shell-shock. That sort of thing?'

'Neurasthenia, you mean. I've read about it, certainly. The Army doctors occasionally publish papers on their cases. Some men have apparently been so badly affected they've been shocked into dumbness or paralysis.'

'What about drinking? Can that be a cause?'

'Drink's a symptom, rather than a cause, a man hitting the

bottle after a long time under fire. Why?' He threw me a side-ways glance. 'Don't tell me Noël's been draining the sherry decanter.'

I grasped at a half-truth. 'It isn't Noël. It's someone he knows. An officer who's pretty badly shaken, but refusing to see a doctor about it.'

'Afraid he'll be told he's mad, I suppose. That's common enough.'

'And is he, do you think? Mad?'

'Doubt it. Though if he's using the bottle as a cure, he could be on the way to dipsomania.'

I considered this in silence for a bit. 'What could a doctor do for a case like that? I mean, how would he be treated?'

Chris sucked in a sternly professional breath. 'Oh, some medical men would go as far as electric shock therapy. But at the moment, the most effective treatment seems to be simply to listen. These chaps often believe they've somehow got out of step with normal life. Nobody understands. Nothing makes them feel any better. There's a psychologist near Edinburgh who thinks it's a form of thyroid poisoning – doped-up nerves that have just taken too many shocks.'

I didn't respond at once: I was thinking. After a few seconds, Chris began to fidget. I'd noticed it made him uneasy, sometimes, when I thought.

'I should leave it all to the experts, darling.' Without taking his eyes off the road ahead, Chris patted my knee. 'I don't want my bride looking thin and worn-out on her wedding day! Just worrying about me will keep you quite busy enough.'

I lay awake for a long time that night, not thinking of Jack but of Max Kassel, thin and misused and yet somehow keeping up a heart-rending dignity in his lonely prison. His sole purpose in living, he'd said, was to keep alight the flame of Philip's memory. Philip had been cursed to love where there was no hope. Once the Medici Pearls were recovered, the world would see that this had been his only fault.

'For myself, I will never lose hope. Surely we have a right to justice, at least, after all our sadness. Are we not to believe in justice?'

The other part of the *we*, I realized, was Philip. And yet, thanks to me, by now the vital pearls were probably charred lumps among the ashes in the Waterside kitchen range. They meant nothing to Jack Dunstan, except as a means of buying my co-operation, and I'd made it quite clear that wasn't for sale.

By lunchtime the next day I'd almost convinced myself it was too late to do anything. The pearls were gone, Philip Kassel would remain a thief forever, and there was, in truth, no justice left in the world. And yet how could I face his father and say so?

By three o'clock in the afternoon, I knew I couldn't − not without making sure there was no hope at all. I reminded myself sensibly that the whole unpleasant business was a symptom of Jack's illness. Chris had explained everything, and Chris was a doctor. I'd coped perfectly well with the countless casualties in Calais and Dunkirk; there was no reason why I shouldn't deal with Jack Dunstan in the same positive, cheerful manner. Viewed in that light, his bargain was more ridiculous than sinister. I could even pretend to go along with it at first and gradually persuade him to go back to his regiment and seek help.

I limped round to the woodshed and wheeled out my bicycle. I only hoped I hadn't left it too late.

Jack was still at Waterside. He must have seen me from the billiard room again, because he appeared at the kitchen door as I cycled up, and leaned his shoulder against the door frame.

'Hello, Chrissie.'

I stayed where I was, on my bicycle, balancing with one toe on the paving. I'd planned exactly what I was going to say. 'The pearls. Do you still have them?'

'Yes.' He examined me carefully. 'Do you still want them?'

'On three conditions. You aren't the only one who can make bargains.'

'Go on, then.'

'First, I'll buy food and whatever you need in the village and I won't tell anyone you're here. But I'll call here when it suits me to come and not otherwise.'

'That's fair enough.'

'Second, even if I only stay for five minutes, that still counts.'

There was an instant's hesitation. 'I won't stop you from leaving.'

'And the third thing—' I took a deep breath and brought out my final condition in a rush of words. 'You must understand I'm in love with Chris and we're going to be married. He's a good, decent man who trusts me not to do things behind his back and I won't put up with you sneering at him or criticizing. Or anything.'

He raised his eyebrows and I saw the ghost of a smile.

I persisted. 'You know what I mean.'

'I'm hardly in a position to criticize anyone, am I? A louse like me? A bastard – and all those other things you called me yesterday.' I felt the hot colour rise into my cheeks, but before I could protest, he'd raised his hands in a gesture of peace. 'I'll agree to anything you want – as long as you keep my secret. Do I take it we have a bargain?'

'I suppose so.'

'Then come inside. Let's not talk out here.'

I leaned my bicycle against the wall beside the door, relieved that he'd agreed so easily. It wouldn't do to assume anything, of course. In Jack's erratic state of mind he could easily disappear again, or destroy the pearls in a fit of temper. All the same, it was hard not to feel a tingle of excitement at the idea of the secret policemen having to apologize to Max Kassel when the pearls were handed over. Thanks to me, there might – just might – be some justice in the world after all.

Jack stood aside for me in the doorway, but I waved him on. 'You go first.'

'Why?'

'Because that's what I want you to do.'

He shrugged. 'As you please.'

I followed him into the house, taking care to keep a formal distance between us. In the kitchen, Jack dropped into the chair beside the range. The faint, bitter smile had reappeared.

'Now—' He stabbed a finger towards the dresser at the end of the room. 'You go over there, and I'll sit here. That way I can't ravish you, which is what you seem to be afraid of.'

'Oh, how dare you! It never crossed my mind.'

He leaned forward. 'Chrissie, if I wanted a woman I wouldn't be here, making polite conversation with you.'

I lifted my chin with frigid dignity. 'I see.'

'God in Heaven! Don't tell me you're offended because I *haven't* lured you here to have my wicked way with you!'

'Of course not.' I swept my hair out of my eyes.

'I thought you wanted all the rules settled between us.'

'I do.'

'And you're going to marry Chris, whom you've just told me you love with a passion.'

I examined his expression for any hint of mockery, but found none.

'And, as I said to you yesterday, I've no wish to interfere in your engagement.'

'You couldn't, even if you wanted to.' I heard my own voice snap out the jibe, as spiteful as a child's in a school playground. I was left with a distinct feeling of having been out-manoeuvred, of having made myself ridiculous, and lost the moral superiority I'd counted on. Then on the table beyond the range, I caught sight of a new, unopened bottle of whisky.

'I've thought of another condition.'

'That's four. You said there were only three.'

'Well, this is a new one. You have to stop drinking. I won't come here if you're going to be half-drunk all the time.'

'And if I don't want to stop?'

'You want to get well, don't you?'

'Why are you so certain I'm sick?'

'Because you are sick, in a way. And I intend to help you get better.' Without giving him a chance to protest, I snatched up the bottle and the corkscrew lying nearby, swept off to the scullery and emptied the contents into the sink.

When I went back to the kitchen Jack was sitting exactly as I'd left him, with his elbows on the arms of the chair and his steepled fingertips resting lightly against his lips. He must have heard the whisky going down the drain with its dreadful glug-glug, yet he hadn't said a word. I glanced at him curiously, wondering if I detected the faint glitter of battle in his eye.

'Are there any more?'

'Do you honestly expect me to tell you?'

'I'll probably find them anyway.' I made an effort to sound like the nursing sisters on the hospital trains. 'You must try to eat properly and drink less. I'll do some shopping tomorrow, before I come along here. You can either make out a list, or I'll buy whatever I think you need.' I rubbed my hands together briskly. 'Well, that seems to cover everything.'

I glanced towards the door, wondering if Jack was going to make me ask for the first pearl. But he stood up and produced it like a conjuring trick.

'I expect you want this.'

In spite of my best efforts, my fingers trembled as I took it from him and rolled it in my palm. The pearl stared back at me like the pupil of an ancient, knowing eye. It was warm from Jack's touch and long accustomed, its glinting sweetness implied, to being employed in transactions between men and women. It lay in the cushioned hollow of my palm, naked and softly radiant, exactly as it must have lain on countless scented breasts. Somewhere in the recesses of my mind, it struck me that pearls so large were never earned by virtue.

'I'll see you tomorrow,' Jack said.

At home, I hid the pearl away in an old stud box of Par's at the back of my stocking drawer. It gave me an odd little thrill to have something so ancient and valuable among my lisles and clocked silks: Catherine de' Medici; Mary, Queen of Scots; Elizabeth; and now Christabel Ascham. I recognized the tingling awareness of something alien and slightly dangerous, like finding a wild, wicked cat-face watching me from among the creamy frills of the roses.

That evening, Chris took me to see Buster Keaton in *The Balloonatic*, bought me a box of Turkish delight and kept my hand warm in his own, like a mouse in its hole, until the incomparable Buster and his girl had sailed off in their canoe, hitched to the runaway balloon.

I went back to Waterside next day with potatoes, strawberries and some chops from the butcher, for which Jack insisted on paying me.

'I won't be in your debt. That wasn't one of your conditions.'

He'd broken up the summer house roof to use as kindling in the range, and perched on the table to watch me deal with the chops.

'When did you learn to cook?'

'In France. We had to look after ourselves a lot of the time – we even had to cut one another's hair. I always cook at home now, when Mrs Hall isn't there. Chris will only come for Sunday lunch if I promise him jam roly-poly.'

A few minutes later I wished I hadn't said that, when Jack wanted to know why I wouldn't eat with him, lost his temper, and guessed, with merciless accuracy, that it was because of how I wanted our relationship to be.

'I feel like that damned dog of Bea's, like a mindless animal that has to be kept in its place. Is that how you see me?'

'You're imagining things.'

'No, I'm not.' He leaned towards me. 'All this rubbish about "getting well". You're trying to turn me into an invalid, a good cause, some rather disgusting specimen you've found by the roadside. "Poor Jack, *such* a shame. The war, you know." And then you tap your head, like this.' He put a finger daintily to his temple. '"He scratches the furniture, but he's no real bother."'

'I've never heard such nonsense!'

'I won't be a good cause, Chrissie, I warn you. I won't be some wretched dog you can feed and then forget.'

'You're the one who's forgetting, surely. "Buy what I need, and don't tell a soul." I've done all that, exactly as we agreed—'

'And never missed a chance of letting me know how much you despise me. By God, there's nothing colder than charity! You must feel *something* for me, even if it's only loathing. Look at me, Chrissie – not at the wall. So help me, I will not be ignored!'

'All right, then!' I gave him a level stare. 'Have you ever thought of shaving and taking a bath?'

He took a bath the very next morning, right in the middle of the kitchen floor, in the marbled tin tub that hung on the back of the scullery door, with water boiled up in enormous stock pots on the range. I know this, because he waited to get into the tub until the time he guessed I'd be arriving, so that my first sight of him that day was an insolent arrangement of steaming flesh and long, dripping limbs dissolving into soapy puddles on the tiles.

'Pour in some more hot, will you?'

'I will not!' Incongruously, it struck me that I'd never seen such elegant knees, domed and delicate as birds' skulls, tapering gracefully into the long muscles of his calves. I'd never seen Chris's knees, nor anything like as much of Chris as I was seeing of Jack at that moment. All the tall length of him seemed broken in three to fit into that sud-swirled pool; I was left with an impression of indolent, sinewy strength, all sleek and glittering with streamlets of water. A memory stirred of a hot summer night when I'd seen as much, and more, of a boy turning into just such a man. I swiftly dismissed it.

'I'll wait for you in the garden.'

'As you please.' An airy hand rose from the suds. 'Just don't slam the door.'

It was a brazen challenge, of course. I could imagine Jack lying there, grinning, as I crossed the courtyard, guessing, with that maddening instinct of his, that whatever else Chris might do, he would no more dream of taking a bath in front of me than of stripping naked at our wedding. Par would have called it a middle-class fetish, the idea that making hurried, fumbling love in a deserted house was excusable, but being seen in the raw by one's fiancée was disgustingly obscene. After the wedding – that would be different – but not before. I gritted my teeth and made up my mind to say nothing about the bath. In three days, Jack had already made me lose my temper more often than I'd done in years. I was astonished at myself.

Still, I'd discovered that all I had to do to get my own back was to demand, 'Don't you want to get better?'

'I'm not *ill*, for God's sake! Take your hypocritical, moralizing charity out of here, if that's all you can give me!'

But he was ill, otherwise why would he be hiding himself away? Chris had explained the treatment: Jack needed someone to listen. And certainly, when he was busy at some task and his face was turned away from me, he could speak about almost anything, without spite, without resentment, but with an intensity that sometimes disturbed me. I simply had to be there, silent, a human presence that neither judged nor criticized.

After two days of restlessness and excuses, he managed to bring himself to go down to the boathouse to look at the *Siren*. And having seen her once again and inspected her, he decided that she wasn't so far from being ready to sail and that, having time to spare, he might as well occupy himself as sit in the kitchen.

Two years had passed since we'd been together in the boathouse. Once, its damp shadows had been a sanctuary. Then, with the incident at the jetty, we'd destroyed its innocence, Jack and I, in our new and inconvenient awareness. Now we were alone there again in the soft light of the half-open doors.

This was a shadow-time for Jack, when his mind would wander back to people and places I knew nothing about. If I brought him a newspaper, he'd read about the Zeppelin raids or the war in the Balkans and start talking about the Western Front, much as one might speak about a distant, only partly-understood country of baffling cruelty. Sometimes while he worked he'd talk about the summer we both remembered, 1914, that last high carnival of Waterside. Out of habit, I'd taken up my old position on the loft steps with my knees drawn up and my arms wrapped round them, and only my gentle breathing and the rustling of my skirt to remind him of my existence. We often came back to something that seemed to puzzle him, the intensity of his mother's affair with Philip Kassel.

'Philip used to say he died each night and only came alive again next day when he saw her.'

Jack straightened up for a moment and gazed at the sliver of lake visible between the edges of the black doors. 'Philip was eighteen years old – a whole year younger than me. I used to watch them together, touching, always touching each other – their hips, their shoulders, a finger brushing a cheek, lips to an ear – as if they couldn't hold anything back from one another, as if they'd no pride, no dignity, nothing secret. As if they'd made themselves as defenceless as sleepwalkers – as children, even. *Why?* What could bring them to that?'

'Love. Trust. Need, too, I suppose.'

The sound of my voice seemed to remind Jack I'd been there all along. He twisted round to look at me with the strange, unsettled eyes of the dreamer waking to an unfamiliar reality.

'You understand it?' The eyes devoured me. 'Yes, I can see you do. You know all these things instinctively – without pain – when all I see is a passably pretty boy and the mother of three children who couldn't keep her hands off him. Was he so wonderful in bed, do you think? Was that what attracted her?'

'No, I think it was simply tenderness – that's what Philip gave her. She'd never known it before and then suddenly there he was, aching to love her. Does that make sense to you?'

He squinted at me for a moment longer, then wiped his hands on a rag and climbed out of the launch. 'And that's what you have with Chris, is it – tenderness?'

'Well, yes.' It seemed the easiest thing to say. How could I explain that we were *comfortable* together, Chris and I, in a way that carried so much less risk than any flaming passion? We were reassuringly alike, familiar and dependable, perfectly well suited. Unfortunately I couldn't think of any way of describing our love that didn't seem drab or half-hearted.

When Jack and I left the boathouse, clouds like tufts of rose-coloured innocence were drifting above our heads in a celestial breeze. Jack stared speculatively over his shoulder for a moment.

'You told me you could cut hair.'

'Cut hair? Oh, up to a point, I suppose – not very well. In France, we girls used to cut one another's, and the patients' too, if they asked. But that was only because there was no one else.'

'Then cut mine, will you? Now, this afternoon.'

'Oh, hold on, I'm no expert. And I haven't any scissors.'

'I found some this morning in one of the kitchen drawers. They're stained with rust, but they're sharp enough.'

He must have planned it, hours before. I snatched at another excuse. 'The kitchen will be too dark by now. And lamplight's no good.'

'Outside, then. On the terrace. No one will see us up there.' He was already bounding up the lawn to fetch what I'd need, beyond the reach of my reluctance.

In France, we'd sometimes been asked to trim the hair of the convalescent soldiers in their slings and bandages and I'd quite enjoyed it. We'd made an occasion of it, full of teasing and bantering remarks about lonely sweethearts at home and the charms of the French mademoiselles. But this was different and I was sure Jack could sense it, with that quick, instinctive understanding of his. His hair was so like himself – dark and vigorous, springing up defiantly from his head and only when its first fierce energy was spent, consenting to fall in disordered waves.

He was determined I should cut it, and sat down on the lichen-splashed steps leading down from the terrace to the overgrown rose garden, among the pearlwort and dandelions that filled the cracks between the stones. I could feel the strength of his hair between my fingers as I selected each strand for my shears: it fell softly over my hand, covering my engagement ring and curling, before I'd realized it, round my fingertips like a subtle, silken net. It was still warm from the sun, and the smell of whatever hairwash he'd used transferred itself faintly to my palms. As I snipped, Jack stretched his head back, little by little, like a snake uncoiling to enjoy the sun's warmth on its skin, drowsily stretching out his long body and those brown, wiry, bare feet of his – I'd hardly seen him in shoes since he'd arrived. I began to feel each rasp of the blade against that dark mass of hair like a release, the strong beak of the scissors plunging forward again and again until the snippings tumbled over my fingers, suddenly free, weightless as curled shadows.

'You did that well,' he said when I'd finished.

That was the evening of the seventh pearl. He no longer put the pearls into my hand, thank God, but left each one on the dresser for me to take when I pleased. That way I could pretend that simply by coming to Waterside I'd completed our bargain. But as I took that seventh pearl after cutting his hair I knew that once again Jack had won something from me I hadn't intended to give. He'd told me he didn't mean to be ignored. Now I

suspected he'd declared open war on my indifference. I made up
my mind not to touch his hair again.

The following day Chris had a free afternoon and took me rowing
on the lake. We let the boat slide into the shallows where low
branches of alder swept the water and in that dappled haven kissed
like parched travellers in a desert.

'Hey . . .' Chris was the first to pull away, leaving me clinging,
unsatisfied. His eyes were shining, but puzzled, and he was
breathing unevenly. 'What a ferocious creature I've taken out
today! Not a bit like my usual sensible Chrissie. Much more of
this and there'll be no more talk of waiting for the wedding.'

He slid his arms round me again and I lay back, moving my
breasts against him, trying to pull him down to the bottom boards
and recapture the desire that had filled him in the dusty grandeur
of Letty Dunstan's bedroom. As I strained up towards his mouth,
I was suddenly filled with such a sharp longing that it seemed to
split me to the core, a narrow lance of pure, ravenous desire, a
perfect spear-point of lust, breathlessly urgent and utterly, wan-
tonly indiscriminate. I'd never known such tormenting need; in
that instant, I'd have done anything – anything – to satisfy it. All
I could think of was that Chris should save me, should answer the
craving and reassure me with the strength of his love. But he
rested on his elbows, keeping his smiling lips out of my reach.

'How blue your eyes are! Just like the strong clear blue of
glass bottles.' He touched my lips with a playful finger. 'No, my
darling, if I kiss you again all our good intentions will come to
nothing and I won't be able to look your mother in the face
when I take you home.'

'I don't care. What does it matter?' I raked his flanks with my
fingers, aching and humiliated, reaching desperately for his mouth
with mine.

He lowered his head to kiss the tip of my nose. 'Besides, it wouldn't be very sensible, at this precise moment. We've agreed we don't want babies for a year or two, so we'd better take care.' This time, he kissed my forehead. 'You'll just have to be patient, you greedy little hussy.'

I don't believe he ever really looked at me; the signs of that racking lust must have been printed on my face and in the hollow defeat of my empty arms. Instead, he sat up and combed his hair with his fingers.

'Better not scandalize any patients we happen to come across. Some of these old hens can spot a hair on your collar at a hundred yards. Now—' He shaded his eyes. 'I reckon there's just about time to row round the point before surgery.'

Jack gave me the tenth pearl on the third of September.

Often, now, if there was time, I left my bicycle at home and walked along the lake shore to the trees bordering the meadow that had been the Waterside lawns. I'd become terrified someone would see me cycle in at the gates and begin to ask questions.

I never knew quite what to expect. If Jack had spent a night among his ghosts, he could be savage in his loathing of everyone and everything, but principally of himself. On days like that, if I tried to persuade him to give himself up, he'd repeat what he'd said about 'having a reason' and revile me for not trusting him. 'The day after the pearls run out – that's what we agreed. Or isn't that soon enough for you? Can't you stand my company until then?'

On the other hand, if he'd slept, he might be ominously calm. He'd watch me intently as I tidied the kitchen and cross-examine me about my engagement. How long had I known Chris? How long had we been engaged? And one day, after I'd given him two or three short, off-hand answers, had Chris and I become lovers yet?

'That's none of your business! What a thing to ask!' I felt my cheeks warming with embarrassment.

244

'Ah . . .' He levelled a forefinger in my direction, his eyes full of triumphant amusement. 'That's more like it.'

If he still drank, I was never aware of it. I neither smelled whisky nor discovered any bottles and, after a while, I began to believe he'd given it up overnight, simply decided he could do without. I was his whisky now — his diversion — his defence against his memories.

On September the eighth I reached the fifteenth pearl, the mid-point of the necklace. Chris and I had spent the morning at the rectory, making a final choice of hymns and anthems for our wedding. I'd had dinner with the Coles the previous evening to celebrate Irene's arrival home on leave, and at first Chris blamed the late night for my wandering attention.

'I can see I'll have to keep her under control, once she's my wife,' he joked to the Rector.

The Rector glanced at my face and smiled, I thought, rather thinly.

Afterwards, outside the rectory door, Chris reproached me for the first time in our engagement. 'I don't know what's the matter with you these days, darling. You're miles away, half the time. You called poor Aunt Dora "Aunt Doreen" all through dinner last night, even though I'd told you all the names in advance. I know she asked you to treat her as family, but you might have tried to get her name right.'

'I'm sorry, Chris. There just seems to be so much to remember. I'll write to Aunt Doreen — I mean Dora — and apologize. Will that help?'

'Well . . . tell her you have a cold and it's affecting your hearing. But, honestly, Chrissie, this morning, with the Rector—'

'Yes, yes, I know!' The protest was sharper than I'd meant it to be. 'I've said I'm sorry. What more can I do?'

Chris's Austin was parked at the rectory gates. He opened the passenger door for me, but the little motor suddenly seemed like a cage and I couldn't bear to get in.

'I'll walk into the village, if you don't mind. I have things to do.'

'What sort of things?'

'Just things. My business. Nothing to do with you.'

I'd never been so sharp with him before. For a moment Chris leaned on the car door and regarded me with his 'medical' face.

'I expect you're feeling a bit down, darling. Pre-wedding nerves and all that. The chemist will give you something for it, if you ask him. A herbal pick-me-up, or something, just until the big day.'

Across a distance of a yard I examined my fiancé. Chris was certainly showing no sign of nervousness; if anything, impending marriage seemed to suit him. He'd begun to look rather handsome in a seasoned, responsible kind of way, as if the prospect of having a wife to support had given him a rather dashing gravity. Old Dr Barnes in Keswick had begun to complain that he hardly ever saw a woman patient under fifty any more, since they'd all started going to 'young Dr Cole'.

But then, they probably hadn't been scolded as I had. I must have overlooked the signs of Chris's rising annoyance; they were easy to miss. No one ever heard raised voices in the Coles' house. It was regarded as terribly bad form to 'make a scene'. Chris didn't become angry, I'd discovered, so much as *displeased*. He became displeased if some small annoyance ruffled the logical routine of his day, but you only knew it from a slight tightening of the muscles round his eyes and a sharpening of the pale edge of his nostrils. On the other hand, I'd never seen him lose his temper, not even when the butcher let his hand-cart run away in Church Street, making a large dent in the side of Chris's Austin and covering it in tripe and pork sausages.

And now I had earned Chris's displeasure. I hadn't enjoyed it; I seriously resolved to do better in future.

I was still humming 'O God of Love, to thee we bow' as I walked over to Waterside in the afternoon. I sang it under my breath as I crossed the kitchen courtyard. 'When stormy winds fulfil thy will, and all their good seems turned to ill . . .'

Jack must have been working on part of the *Siren*'s engine. He came across from the powerhouse as I arrived, wiping his hands on a piece of rag, his feet bare as usual. For some reason it immediately infuriated me to see him, as if he alone had been the cause of my falling-out with Chris.

'Well, here I am again!' I managed such a caricature of cheerfulness that he immediately looked suspicious.

'I can see that.'

'And how have you been?'

'Since yesterday?'

'Did you have a good night? Did you sleep well? Have you had anything hot to eat today?' This was exactly how Chris catechized the elderly farm workers. His next question, I knew, would be 'Bowels moved today, have they?' Just in time, I stopped myself from asking.

'What's all this about?' Jack frowned at me. 'Something's upset you, that's for sure.'

'Upset? Nonsense! It's a beautiful day. It couldn't be more perfect.' What a lie; I was still writhing under Chris's displeasure. 'Goodness, you are a mess! Have you been oiling the *Siren* or oiling yourself?'

'Stop it, Chrissie!'

I was vaguely aware that Jack was losing patience with me, but I didn't care. I'd made up my mind he was the sole cause of my row with Chris and that my promise to keep his secret had made things quite impossible.

247

He lengthened his stride to intercept me at the door. 'Why don't you come down to the boathouse? There's a valve I want to replace.'

'I'd rather sit on the steps by the rose garden, if you don't mind.' I set off at a vigorous pace towards the side of the house, with Jack in pursuit.

'This is something to do with Chris, isn't it? I can always tell when he's been lecturing you. You start behaving like a clockwork doll, as if you'd no mind of your own.'

I wagged a finger at him. 'I won't hear a word against Chris. That was our agreement.'

'Chrissie!' He sprinted ahead in order to look me in the face. 'For heaven's sake stop this nonsense. If there's something wrong, then tell me.' When I didn't answer, he fell into step beside me. 'Didn't you hear what I said?'

How strange, I thought to myself, that's exactly what Chris keeps asking. 'I've got a cold,' I told him airily. 'It's affecting my hearing.'

'*What?*'

We'd reached the shallow steps that led down from the terrace to the wilderness of grass and roses. I plumped myself down on a convenient slab of stone and clasped my hands on my knees. It was exactly the way Hosanna had taught me to sit when she read poetry to me as a child.

'Oh yes, this is nice.'

I heard my own voice, thin and vindictive, disturb the peace of that tangle of blossom and instantly felt ashamed. Spread out at our feet, the honeyed sea of breeze-stirred grass-heads threw up great silver waves that surged across the half-acre, tossing the roses in their swell. In the very centre, a stone dryad was swimming, her lichenous arms garlanded with bindweed, a mermaid princess with a court of aphids, bees and tortoiseshell butterflies.

Jack stared down for a moment as if to be certain my anger was spent and then stretched himself out beside me. Neither of us spoke. I still didn't trust myself to say anything and Jack wisely left

248

me to simmer down. I lay back on the shallow steps, letting the drowsy sigh of grasses soothe my vexation, and determinedly built a mind-picture of my wedding day. The sun would shine – I had no doubt of it – and all thought of pearls, whisky bottles and nightmares would be behind me. The Rector's wife would miraculously find the skill to manage 'Jesu, Joy', Hosanna's flowers would be a thing of wonder, and Chris's aunt would decide she preferred the name Doreen to her own and would thank me for bringing it to her attention. 'When days are filled with pure delight, When paths are plain and skies are bright, Walking by . . .'

Dimly, I realized Jack had begun to speak. He must have been speaking for some time before I became aware of his voice describing another neglected garden, years earlier, during the war. It had been very much like the one at Waterside, more like an English garden than anything you'd expect to find in France. But the house had been shelled to pieces and the family were long gone, leaving a child's wooden chair smashed in the rubble and a Noah's ark surrounded by scattered animals. For some hours, Lieutenant Dunstan and his men had rested among the weeds and the struggling roses, taking pleasure in the familiar scents of home. Their idyll hadn't lasted long.

'The village was shelled again the following day.' His tone gave the fact a drab inevitability. 'We lost eight men trying to hold the place. Later on, we found the platoon sergeant's hand still in the trigger-guard of his rifle, just his hand, nothing else. It had his wife's name tattooed across the knuckles. A-N-N-E, that's how we knew it was his. She'd got the last word, someone said – just like a woman.'

There was a short silence while Jack stared out over the embattled roses. 'They keep coming back to remind me, these men. But not when you're here.' He turned his head to examine me curiously. 'Why's that, do you suppose?'

My head was still full of something borrowed, something blue and Hosanna's white tobacco-flowers. I turned on one elbow and gazed at him, puzzled.

'You haven't been listening to me, have you?' His dark brows drew together. 'You have to listen, or they'll start coming back again. You have to *care*, Chrissie.'

We stared at each other, hopelessly at odds. Then, with his eyes still fixed on my face, Jack suddenly reached out, caught my right hand in his own and slid it between the buttons of his shirt to lie over his heart. So swift was the abduction that my hand was imprisoned against the warmth of his naked skin before I realized it. He held it there for as long as I tried to pull it away and then, when he felt my fingers relax against the low, steady beat of his heart, he left them to their own devices. His skin was as soft as a bird's wing and firm across the muscles of his chest, dusted below his breastbone by a net of fine hair. My trailing fingertips raised a faint electrical charge like the sparking of a glass of champagne, a curious tingling which instantly penetrated all the primitive little hollows of my being, fluttering there like a hundred tongues.

He unfastened another two buttons for me and I hardly noticed; my fingers simply understood that they'd been invited to travel on towards the hard, swollen knot of a nipple and beyond it to where the skin became warm and secretive under his arm. For a few moments they rested there, deliciously at peace, before greedily gliding on, over his ribs, to where a strip of scar, as slippery to the touch as fluted satin ribbon, led to the tight hollow of his stomach and a puckered groove like a second, discontented mouth.

It was the mouth of that newly healed wound, pursed in disapproval, that jerked me to my senses. Jack was still watching me, his eyes raking my face as if trying to read in me something crucial about himself.

I snatched back my hand. 'That was unfair of you!'

'Not what you expected of me.'

'I should think not!'

'Then your expectation was wrong.' He leaned towards me and promised softly, 'I won't let you ignore me, Chrissie. I did warn you.'

'Then I can't possibly come back here.' I scrambled to my feet.

'Where are you going?' There was a note of alarm in his voice.

'Away. For good.'

'And what about the pearls? You want those, don't you?'

'Damn the pearls! *Help me*, you said, *help me to hide*. That was all. But now you're asking for my soul—'

'No!' He shook his head like a dazed man. 'I didn't mean to frighten you.'

'But you want too much, Jack. Too much!'

'I want—' His hand combed the air and fell again, defeated. 'I don't even know what I want. For you to care a bit, perhaps. To feel the hurt – to weep for me, even. Can't your precious Chris spare me that?'

'*I* can't spare it, Jack. It isn't Chris, it's me. *I* can't spare it.'

That night, I spilled out the fifteen huge pearls on my bedcover, precisely half of the Medici necklace. I marshalled them in a row, then rolled them with my finger into a softly glowing heap. Either way, they profaned the plain little bed I'd slept in since childhood. No fairytale dewdrops could have seeded these giants. They were trollops among pearls, too sumptuous for purity, too voluptuous for innocence. They were powdered sisters, their virginity long since drilled and threaded, white and coquettish like the tyrant Elizabeth who'd flaunted them. They trickled slyly over my palms, cool and caressing, whispering of joyful fingertips on warm, responsive skin in a breeze-blown rose garden, earlier in the day. They were sensual beyond belief, those pearls and, before I knew it, they'd conjured up a thundery night down by the jetty and two overheated, unconstrained bodies flooded by sudden physical need. Alarmed, I fought down the gross ghosts of the past and put the pearls back in the darkness of their box.

Fifteen pearls – fifteen more days. No. No one could expect

that of me. Jack must either give me the remaining pearls all at once – immediately – or the Queen and her secret policemen would have to be satisfied with half a necklace.

He refused outright. 'We had a bargain! You knew the terms. You'll have the last pearl on the twenty-third of this month and after that I'll go to the police, or back to my regiment, or wherever you want. Isn't that what we agreed?'

'Yes, that's what we *said*. Nothing about – well – anything else.'

'All right.' He held up his hands. 'I apologize. I went too far, and I upset you. I realize that. If I promise it won't happen again – will that do?'

I went home that day with the sixteenth pearl. I'd sat by the dresser while Jack had stayed near the range.

Sixteen pearls. Seventeen. Eighteen. Nineteen. Twenty.

It was the fourteenth of September. A couple of days earlier a letter had arrived from Noël to say he'd been posted home to take up troop-training duties at the regimental depot. Reading between the lines, I suspected his unit in France had given up trying to make an effective rifleman out of my brother. If anything, his eagerness to 'do his bit' would make him even more of a liability. A soldier who can't tell you whether his weapon's loaded or not because his mind is running on the Sumarian word for 'trench' is worse than useless, and shouting at Noël would have no effect whatsoever. He'd just apologize profusely and then forget all over again.

Mar, however, was convinced that Noël had received some deadly wound and the truth was being kept from her. Nothing would reassure her except to inspect him with her own eyes and she immediately made arrangements to travel south with Par.

'Mrs Hall will cook dinner for you tonight and leave something cold for tomorrow, when she goes to her daughter's. I'll ask Powley to make sure everything's properly locked up. You will be all right, Chrissie, will you?'

When the sun began to move towards the west and the light in the boathouse became too dim to see, we'd got into the habit, Jack and I, of walking along the lake shore at the foot of the overgrown lawns, moving out of sight among the trees if we heard the *tup-tup* of a steamer. The flower spikes of sorrel had turned rusty brown in the long grass; earlier in the summer the lawn had seemed almost blood-spattered with their crimson heads. But there were still a few pink-white mops of yarrow, yellow ragwort and purple, honey-smelling thistles, so that the terraced meadow was altogether a more cheerful place than in the days of its green velvet dignity.

'How many gardeners used to work here, Jack?'

'Four or five, maybe. There always seemed to be someone shaving away at this lawn.'

'And now it's almost as high as my waist.' I'd taken my shoes and stockings off. My feet were turning almost as brown as in the days of my girlhood. 'Do you know, I think I prefer the place this way. I like to feel the grass stems sliding between my toes.'

There was something about the lake shore that always brought me a feeling of peace. We were both content that evening. Jack had been testing the boiler and cylinders of the *Siren* – the first time she'd had steam up for decades – and had declared her ready for her all-important trial run the following afternoon.

We sat down among the stiff stems of a patch of cow-parsley overlooking the lake – as usual, significantly apart. Ever since that day in the rose garden I'd been careful to keep my distance, though I knew my vigilance annoyed him.

'It's all right,' he said. 'I won't touch you.' And then, a few minutes later, 'What are you thinking about, Chrissie?'

I was thinking, as I often did now, about that thundery night down by the jetty, just yards away from us, when I had not been so cautious. I was puzzled by the reckless, sentimental creature I saw there, with her naked back pressed painfully against the planks, so willing to cast herself into the uncharted waters of a man's desire. For years, that impulsive child had embarrassed me. I'd never breathed a word to Chris about that night of storms, and yet now, strangely, I couldn't think of it without a pang of jealousy. She'd had courage, that girl; all I had now was prudence.

Jack's gaze had wandered back to the jetty; he hadn't really needed an answer. In profile, the outline of his lashes dropped lower over his eyes, as if a certain bitterness was attached to the memory. And yet, for the first time, oddly enough, I felt no embarrassment in speaking about it.

'That night . . . it's just as well none of us knew what was going to happen so soon afterwards.'

'Why do you say that?' His glance searched my face. 'Would you have come away with me among the trees somewhere, if you'd known there'd never be another chance and we'd all have to go and fight a war?'

'I don't . . . expect so.' They were the fastidious, dainty tones of Chris's fiancée. I wondered if I should believe her. 'Would it have made things very different, if I had?'

'Maybe.' He looked away across the lake, and I heard a long, regretful sigh. 'No, that's wishful thinking. And anyway, in those days I still believed I could go out to France and prove I was – not a Dunstan, at least.' He drew up his knees and encircled them with his arms. 'Not *his* son. Not a monster.'

He spoke the words so quietly – so softly – that for a moment they hung in the air, transparent of meaning. Jack's gaze was still fixed on the watery mosaic of light and shadow, as if searching for a clue to the insoluble puzzle of his life. When he spoke again, I had to turn my head to catch the words.

'When the Germans marched into Belgium I really believed someone had to stand up for honesty and decency and honour – all the old-fashioned things my father despised.' He shook his head, dismissing his innocence. 'Then, when I got out there, I found there was no high-minded, noble cause after all. There were just young soldiers coming out, brave and idealistic, and getting cut down – and another lot coming to take their place and the same thing happening all over again. And safe behind the lines, a few grasping, pitiless old men like my father were sending them out to die.'

A sudden squall from the lake rattled the brittle stems of the cow-parsley, and he rested his chin on his folded arms.

'Even if you survive, I've discovered that war has a way of scraping away at your notion of yourself, scraping away until it's laid bare whatever was underneath, raw and frail and mortally terrified. Day and night, it becomes a waking nightmare where there's no *you* any more, just a mindless creature of slaughter. I saw men who'd have stolen bread from a blind beggar, and yet there were others who were decent all the way through, to their last breath. That's when you find out about yourself – which kind of man you are.'

A cloud like torn muslin dragged across the sun and I seemed to hear the bleakness of winter. He held a hand rigidly before my eyes, the fingers splayed.

'See that? That's the test. After two years in the trenches, some of the men who'd been there from the start were shaking too much to get a fork into their mouths, but not me. If you give me a rifle with a telescopic sight, I can still hit a cap badge at six or seven hundred yards. Steady hands, you see – a killer's hands. Because it makes no difference to my score, one corpse more or less. I know there isn't any hope for me.'

I stared at him, horrified. 'There's always hope, Jack, of course there is. One day this war will end—'

'No.' The wintry eyes regarded me without emotion. 'Not for me. There's no point in my having hopes or dreams, because of what I am. I'm Alfred Dunstan's son, and there's no escape from that, if I live to be a hundred.'

I opened my mouth to protest, but he cut me short. 'You said it yourself. *Contemptible*, you said. A piece of shit. A bastard.' He smiled faintly, and touched my cheek with precision, his lips a little apart. 'I'm even blackmailing you. Doesn't that prove something?'

'No, it doesn't. This neurasthenia—'

'I've told you – I'm not ill.' He scrambled to his feet and began to walk back through the long grass to the house. 'I just know what I've inherited.'

I had to run to keep up with him. 'That isn't true! Jack! Wait for me.'

He didn't answer. He went on, marching so determinedly up the slope that by the time we'd reached the top of the lawn we were almost racing. If I hadn't been barefoot I'd never have kept up. Minutes before, I'd scrupulously preserved a distance between us; now I scurried at his heels as he strode through the rose garden towards the kitchen courtyard. I was afraid he'd go indoors and slam the door in my face, simply to be alone with his wretchedness. By this time my breath was coming in gasps and I caught his arm to slow him down.

'Wait for me – please!'

He tried to shake me off, but I held on and forced my way into the house at his side.

'God in Heaven – just leave me alone!' He put his forearms against the tiled wall of the passage and leaned his head on them, turning his back to me and to the world.

'Jack—'

'Get out!'

'You wanted me to care. That's what you said. Well then, you have to listen to *me* sometimes.'

There was a long, obdurate silence.

'Very well. I'll go away, if that's what you really want. My shoes are in the kitchen.'

Silence again. I took a couple of steps away from him towards the kitchen door, my feet slapping on the bare cement. Then, all at once, I heard his voice echoing from the tiles like a soul calling from the vaults of hell. 'All right, if you must know, I've found out my father's been selling to the Germans.'

I turned back, stunned. 'To the *enemy*? Are you sure?'

'I found papers in his desk at home. Springs – gun parts – supposedly shipped north to Archangel in Russia. Instead, the vessels slip into the Baltic and unload at a German port. The seamen, the owners, they're all German agents.'

'Oh, surely not. Not even your father—'

'*Only* my father.' Jack rubbed his brow on his wrists. 'You must know that by now.'

'But someone would have found out! Don't the police watch the ports and harbours?'

'Once a ship's at sea, who knows where it gets to? The ocean's a big place and my father's clever. He doesn't make mistakes.' Jack let his shoulders fall in a long sigh. 'A couple of years ago he was in trouble – financially. No one was supposed to know, but I used to hear things when I went into the factories and I put two and two together: bills not paid, no credit, supplies running low. Building this house just about cleaned him out, though he'd never have admitted it.'

'Max Kassel heard a rumour in London, I remember.'

'He might have done. Anyway, during the first year of the war, everything suddenly changed. It looked as if there was money again, and the bankers kept inviting my father to their dinners. I always wondered how he'd done it. Even in a war, it's impossible to make profits as quickly as that – unless you're selling to both sides.'

When I didn't answer at once, he raised his voice. 'I have the papers here, if you don't believe me. I can prove it to you.'

'There's no need. I believe you. But, oh . . . how *could* he, when all those soldiers are dying!'

'Because he's a Dunstan. Just as I'm a Dunstan. And we don't care who dies, as long as it isn't us. The trouble was, at first, I didn't have any real proof, though I was pretty sure what he was up to.' His voice suddenly rang out fiercely from the tiles. 'How could I look my men in the face, after that? I thought, if only I were killed too, then I'd be no worse than any of the others. I tried to make it happen. If they needed someone for a night patrol, I went. If there was work to be done on the wire, I volunteered. The men used to touch their heads and look at one another. I knew they were wondering why nothing ever seemed to happen to me. Good men – fine men, the heroes – they were killed. But not me. "Dunstan's luck" they called it.' He gave an odd gasp of a laugh. 'More like the luck of the Devil.'

'But when I knew you first, you were so determined to prove you were different—'

'Because all the time, I was afraid I wasn't.' He thrust out an arm. 'What do you think flows through that? Dunstan blood! I warned you once, remember? That day we went off on Noël's motorcycle? If my father had been an artist, I said, you'd have expected me to paint. That's how it goes, handed down, father to son. Why should it be any different, just because my father's a monster?'

He shook his head. 'I poison everything that comes near me. You know it as well as I do. You won't even touch me, I'm so contaminated. That's why I couldn't risk giving you all the pearls. How else could I make you come back here, day after day?'

'Jack – you're wrong. If I try to keep a distance, it's because of *me*, not you, or anything you are . . .' And, quickly, before prudence and respectability could stop me, I slid my hands over his shoulders and rested my cheek against his back. His body was warm and solid; I could hear his heart thudding, just beyond his backbone. When he spoke, his voice seemed to come from somewhere deep inside, like the fatal pronouncement of an oracle.

'I'm my father's son. It's too late to change that.'

'And what about your mother? What about Letty? Did you get nothing from her?'

'Oh, yes, I'd forgotten my mother.' He twisted round, throwing me off and flattening his back against the wall. His eyes were glistening, turned up towards the ceiling. 'What have I inherited from her, I wonder – a woman who seduces a boy younger than her own son and then destroys him when he becomes an inconvenience?'

'That wasn't what happened, Jack! I don't believe Letty ever allowed herself to look ahead, to see what the end might be. She was too lonely and Philip was too much of a miracle. She needed someone so badly – then your father found out, and made her afraid of being old and alone. Can't you understand that – you, of all people?'

Letty's pain rang in my voice, a cry of disillusion and hopelessness. Perhaps her son heard it and recognized its desolate note: his arms rose reluctantly to encircle my shoulders, as if he was afraid of crushing something he didn't quite believe. I laid my cheek against the soft flannel of his shirt and a moment later felt his lips brush my hair. The silence was so profound that the twitter of a bird came to us quite clearly from the roof-gutter above our heads.

As I relaxed against him, longing flew out of me like the sighing of a breeze on the lake. 'If I only knew how to convince you. Whatever your father's done – whatever he *is* – you mustn't make it a prison for yourself.'

I felt a movement above my head. I guessed he was staring up to the ceiling again, not believing. 'Jack, look at me, please. Look at me, here in your arms, of my own free will – because I care about you so much. If Chris could see us, he'd have a fit, because he'd never understand how it is a woman can love two men at the same time. I'm not even sure I understand it myself, except that I know it's true. Doesn't that give me the right to ask you to save yourself, to go back to your regiment and tell them all the things you've told me? If they find you here . . . it could be the end. And yet you're being so pig-headed it's breaking my heart!'

At last he looked down at me. 'I'm breaking *your* heart?'

'Yes, you are – with all this nonsense about Dunstan blood. Of course I can't tell you why you're still alive, but I do know for a fact it has nothing to do with the luck of the Devil. Blame me, if you like, for asking God to keep you safe. I used to pray for you. "God, if you really are there, please don't let anything happen to Jack." Maybe for some reason He listened.'

A damp patch of flannel under my cheek made me realize there were tears running down my face. 'Oh Lord, look at me, I'm getting all emotional. What on earth would Chris say, if he could see me?'

'I hope he'd realize he doesn't deserve you. Neither of us do.' He released me then, gently. 'Did you really pray for me?'

'After Philip died. I couldn't bear the idea of losing you, too.'

A faint furrow appeared between his brows, as if the notion of prayer disturbed him. 'I *will* go back after the twenty-third. I promise you. But I have to stay here until then.'

'Jack—'

'Not before the twenty-third.'

'And what if they find you, and take you away? You know what happens to deserters! What would I do then?'

With a careful finger, he teased back a strand of hair that had become stuck to my brow. 'I dare say if God's looked after me so far, he won't mind doing it for a few more days.'

The next day was Friday, and there was no chance of my getting to Waterside before three o'clock at the earliest. It was Chris's mother's birthday, and I was expected at the Coles' house for lunch.

I'd become conscious, lately, of how hard I was having to practise to fit into my future role as Chris's wife. On this particular day I set off in a tailored suit made of the new Radium poplin, smart boots with heels and canvas uppers and a little straw hat turned up at one side and trimmed with a feather. Though the war had made jackets as plain and military as possible, for some reason it had also brought unaccustomed wide skirts and petticoats.

The widowed Mrs Cole collected porcelain teacups, the decorative kind that perch on special wooden stands with the saucers set up behind. I'd gone to a great deal of trouble to track one down in a bric-a-brac shop in Manchester – apple-green and gilt with piles of fruit – which the owner assured me was Worcester.

'But how nice!' Mrs Cole planted a powdery kiss on my cheek and we sat sedately in the drawing room, sipping sherry, while we waited for Chris to join us after morning surgery.

'Doesn't your fiancée look adorable today?' Mrs Cole sat between us at lunch and kept leaning over to pat my hand, a sure sign that she'd had at least one glass of sherry before I'd arrived. I had a sudden, dismaying vision of myself in twenty years' time as a faded doctor's wife, collecting old teacups in a glass-fronted cabinet and empty sherry bottles in a box in the coal cellar.

Mrs Cole's birthday drink had made her unusually frisky. 'I'm so glad to see you haven't plucked your eyebrows, my dear. So many silly girls seem to wear nothing but pencil these days! Of course, once you're married, you'll have a husband to think of.' My wrist received another playful tap. 'You can hardly expect a man to feel amorous about a wife with no eyebrows!'

She gave a little shriek of a laugh. I noticed Chris sawing determinedly at his chicken.

'Chrissie's far too sensible for that sort of nonsense, I'm pleased to say.' He smiled at me across the table with a kind of brisk fondness. 'Though, speaking personally, I'll be happier once she's forgotten all this technical talk she picked up in France about valve clearances and piston rings. Do you know what she told me last week, as I was driving her home in the Austin?' He laid down his knife and fork to paint the scene. 'The sun was just setting over the lake, and there was hardly a breath of wind . . . She listened for a minute, and then said, "I'd have that big-end bearing looked at, if I were you."' He laughed immoderately, swaying to and fro. 'I ask you – "Have the big-end bearing looked at!"'

'The big-end bearing,' repeated his mother faithfully. 'Well, I never!'

Chris went on chortling for a good deal longer than his story deserved. Then he wiped his mouth on his napkin. 'For a moment, I thought Chrissie was going to insist on stopping at the side of the road and getting under the bonnet there and then!' He smirked at his mother, but I knew the remarks had really been addressed to me.

'You can't actually see the big-end bearing,' I pointed out quietly, 'even with the bonnet open. It's inside the engine. On the connecting rod.'

'The connecting rod . . .'

Chris and his mother were gazing at me with exactly the same expression, a kind of benevolent reproach, as if I were a new puppy they'd acquired, enchanting but not quite house-trained. Mother and son were, in fact, extraordinarily alike, and their joint astonishment began to annoy me. If they'd only known it, my head was utterly empty of plans for my future with Chris, but full of anxiety for Jack Dunstan. I had a desperate desire to go and see if he was any happier, and if he'd got steam up in the *Siren*.

I made an enormous effort to sound like a dizzy fiancée. 'I just thought the white metal in the bearing might need a little scrape, darling, to take off the worn bits – but I wouldn't attempt that myself, of course. I just . . . potter about with plugs and things. You know how I hate to have nothing to do!' Then a malicious little devil compelled me to add, 'Though if I were you, I'd have the bearing seen to before it gets any worse, in case the crankshaft has to be reground.'

I saw Chris and his mother exchange glances. Mrs Cole's flaccid white hand oozed once more across the table and fastened on to mine with surprising tenacity. She crushed her carmine lips into a simper.

'Fingernails are awfully important, dear. I always say you can pick out a lady by the way she looks after her fingernails.'

Chris wanted to take me home in the Austin, but I made him drop me near the gates to Waterside.

'I'd prefer to walk the rest of the way, actually. I could do with a bit of exercise, after so much lunch.'

He leaned across the empty passenger seat as I got out. 'Are you sure, darling? I can easily take you all the way to your door. The Petrol Control Committee have been quite good about fuel this month.'

'I'm quite sure, honestly. The walk will do me good.'

It was almost four o'clock, and I was seething with impatience, dying for Chris to turn the Austin round and disappear back towards the village, so that I could run across the road and slip through the gates of Waterside. Chris, however, appeared reluctant to leave me; he seemed less confident now than he'd been at lunch. I dare say he'd noticed a certain coolness in my manner during the meal. I'd tried not to show it, but I was coming to resent the way my husband-to-be assumed he could make decisions for us both, as if the act of our marriage in just over a month would make us not only one flesh, but one mind as well – his mind. Or his mother's mind, it sometimes seemed to me.

I guessed that in Chris's eyes this made me look petty and 'difficult'. 'Difficult' was another favourite Cole word. 'Difficult' patients demanded more than their share of attention. They refused to get better when instructed to. They (they were usually women) wept in the surgery and begged for help with emotional crises. As often as not, they were sent away with a bottle of blood tonic.

Perhaps now I'd be given one, too. I'd realized long ago that to marry Chris was to marry his family as well; we'd laughed over it between ourselves, but I'd always assumed that if it came to a contest between his wife and a droning uncle or smothering aunt, Chris would automatically take my part. Now, for the first time, I wasn't so sure; and I was beginning to think that if Mrs Cole patted my hand once more, I'd probably bite her.

★

There was no sign of life in the kitchen courtyard at Waterside. There was no one in the kitchen either and no answer when I shouted a couple of times in the hall. Outside again in the sunshine, I took off my boots and my hat, and set about peeling off my stockings. I guessed Jack was in the boathouse, and if I was going to have to clamber about on a steam launch, I could hardly do it in silk hose and high-heeled canvas footwear – and anyway, it seemed to me as I popped my suspenders that I was also popping the Coles for a while. I stuffed my stockings into my hat and left the whole lot just inside the entrance to the larder corridor.

As soon as I opened the boathouse door, I heard the roar of a captive fire. There was a new source of light in the gloom: a fierce crimson glow that coloured the engine-well of the *Siren* and Jack's intent features bending over it.

'That's wonderful!' My bare feet pattered along the wooden pier. 'You're actually going to take her out on the lake?'

'Now that you're here, I am.'

'You waited for me? That was kind.'

'I need you to steer.'

'Oh.' Clearly, Jack was making no further concessions. 'How far are we going?'

'Just far enough to check the valve linkage and make sure the engine's turning smoothly. I'll try and keep inside the point, out of sight of the ferry. Fortunately, it's a bit overcast today.'

I knew him well enough by now to recognize the tightness in his voice. He was trying to make it seem as if this test run hardly mattered, as if endless hours of dismantling and cleaning, grinding and lubricating, were nothing at all, and the *Siren* could steam or not steam as she pleased. Yet his face as he helped me step into the launch told a different story: it was firm and resolute, in the way that young faces can be almost nobly intent before doubt and compromise soften their lines. I wondered if the *Siren* could sense the burden of desperate hope that weighed down her hull.

Jack opened the fire box door and shovelled in some coal, then checked the steam gauge.

'You do know how to steer a boat, I take it?'

He still had his back to me. I laughed aloud – I couldn't help it – the sheer, horrible importance of the occasion was making me hysterical. I was light-headed; I felt like the pirate I'd been when Noël and I had ranged the Spanish Main from the *Siren*'s bow.

'You'll soon find out if I can steer, won't you?'

'It's that, or shovel coal, and you're hardly dressed as a fireman.' Another check of the steam gauge. 'Time to open the main steam line—' A valve twirled under his hand. 'Now, a quick turn of the engine to drive any water out of the system.'

'What'll you do if the propeller doesn't turn?' I was making mischief. I had absolute faith in him.

'It'll run. Either that, or we'll spend the night adrift.'

'It's just as well Mar and Par are away, then, and Mrs Hall's at her daughter's.'

'It'll run, don't you worry. Now – pass me the boat-hook.' Jack went forward, leaned over the launch's bow, and pushed at the black doors leading to the world of water. They swung back uncertainly on their hinges, making whirlpools at their feet.

'Ready?'

'Ready.' I scrambled to my post at the wheel, a pirate in a Radium poplin suit.

'Here goes, then.'

For a moment, the *Siren* seemed reluctant to leave her ancient lair and venture out into the daylight. The black water churned at her stern, flecked with turbulent grey. Her entire hull seemed to give a shudder, like an animal casting off a lingering hibernation, and then, slowly at first, she began to move forward, sliding her long, raked bow out into the busy wavelets of the lake. I could feel the faint vibration of the propeller shaft through my bare toes.

'We're moving! We're moving! Oh, Jack, you've done it!' I couldn't resist clapping my hands.

'Would you mind steering?' Jack's head was turned away from me towards the bow of the launch, but there was no sternness in his voice. It was light, joyful and content – all the things I'd ever hoped to hear. 'You could start swinging her round to the left.' He held out an arm.

'To port, you mean.'

'*This* way, for goodness sake, before they see us from the ferry. Stay in the lee of the point.' He glanced round and grinned. 'None of your fancy seamanship.'

The launch rolled almost imperceptibly as we turned, dipping her bow like a dowager's nod, responding to the homage of the waves. She was regal – stately – in spite of her tattered leather cushions and her grubby brasswork. She moved over the water like a down-and-out duchess, her nobility only heightened by hard times. As Mrs Cole would have said, her circumstances might be reduced, but she'd looked after her fingernails.

Ahead of us, on a spit of land, a heron was treading the shallows like a pair of animated scissors, intent on a ripple. So quiet was the mutter of our engine, even with the housing removed, that the *Siren* was almost upon the bird before it took off with a disdainful flap of its wings and sailed away to a less crowded fishing ground.

Jack leaned over, grinning with pride of ownership, and slapped his hand against a small copper cylinder about the size of a tea urn perched up beside the funnel. He twiddled the brass tap at the bottom. 'Bet you don't know what this is.'

'I do too, it's a Windermere steam kettle. General Milnes told me all about it. You could boil a gallon of water in about ten seconds, he reckoned.'

Jack nodded, delighted. 'Next time we come out, we'll make tea.' He glanced back over the bow to where the dappled water of the lake split cleanly on either side of our stem. 'That's probably far enough for the first day.'

I turned the launch in a wide circle, heading back to the boathouse. The thin trail from our funnel shone silver against a darkening sky; the air was clear and oddly heavy.

'Rain on the way.'

'I think you're right.' Jack rose to his feet beside the funnel. 'Bring her up to the doors where it's shallow, and we'll reverse her in.'

The *Siren* drifted in like a lady, and kissed her pier as if she'd missed it and was content to be back. For several minutes Jack busied himself with raking out the coal box and the ashpit; I couldn't see his face, but I could tell by the briskness of his hands and the set of his shoulders that he was wrapped in some great, deeply personal happiness. I walked softly out of the boathouse and stood by the jetty, looking out across a lake surface pitted with the first heavy drops of rain. After a moment, I heard Jack's step behind me and half-turned. There was a wild, exultant light in his eyes and I realized he'd brought me his triumph to share. He'd awakened the *Siren*. He – Jack – had restored her to life by his own efforts and he wanted my seal upon his victory.

'Who'd have believed it?' His hands described small, inarticulate arcs at his sides.

'I believed it. I always did, right from the start.' There was rain on my face now, but I didn't care. I felt myself grinning like a fool; I couldn't remember ever having felt such pure, unadulterated joy.

Heaven knows which of us took the first step forward. All I know is that our kiss began in the tenderest way imaginable, as if neither of us could quite believe it was happening and didn't dare to destroy so frail an illusion. We came together so slowly, so hesitantly; and then the pulsing blood rushed to swell our lips, splitting them apart like over-ripe fruit, opening one mouth against the other in unimaginable intimacy. If it's possible to be ravished in the mind, in the soul, in the very core of one's being, all without physical penetration, then from that instant my virtue was no more than a word. I had no more resistance. I was utterly thrown open to invasion and capture at Jack Dunstan's pleasure.

'Oh, my God, Chrissie—' Our mouths disengaged suddenly – moved apart, hot and bewildered – cheated of their voluptuous pleasure. Jack held me close against his chest, against the rise and fall of his breathing and the thudding of his heart, and I clung to him like a rock in a savage flood of distress. 'That wasn't any part of the bargain, believe me—'

But it was. I'd known that from the start. Whether Jack realized it or not, there had only ever been one kind of bargain between us; the only one that could be sealed with those pearls, the ancient currency of lust. I suddenly saw the past weeks as Chris would see them. I squirmed out of Jack's arms and fled through the rain, all the way up the lawn towards the terrace, my skirt flying and my bare legs wrenching through the wet grass.

Jack must have gone inside by the conservatory; he could have caught up with me if he'd wanted to. He came out into the courtyard as I was trying to force my wet, dirty feet into my canvas boots, clutching my hat to my chest.

'Wait. Don't go yet.' He was breathless from the run and his arms were wrapped round one of the Sèvres bowls from the drawing room chimneypiece, its vivid green glaze dimmed by grime and fingerprints. 'Hold out your hands.'

The last nine pearls rolled into my palms like huge, heavy tears and their diamond clasp fell on top of them, trailing thread.

'You've got them all now. There's nothing to come back for.' Before I could speak, he added, 'I'll go away from here tomorrow and find somewhere else to hide. I won't try to contact you again.'

I poured the pearls into the crown of my hat, mixed up with my discarded stockings. But my hands shook, sending them clicking against one another with a faint giggling sound.

We didn't risk saying goodbye, just nodded as if too much had been said already. I set off through the puddles towards the archway with my head bowed against the downpour. Just as I reached it, a crashing sound made me glance back in time to see pieces of green Sèvres porcelain dropping out of the creeper that grew over the courtyard wall.

It was the crash that brought me to my senses. There I was, with my hair collapsing round my head in great draggled knots, my suit wet through and my boots cramping my damp and twisted toes, clutching a hat to my bosom full of wet stockings and nine of the world's most priceless pearls. And I didn't know why. What was the point of running away? Did I enjoy being miserable? Did I want to be pinched, and timorous and censorious all my life? Did I want to spend the rest of my days virtuously looking after my fingernails?

I turned round and limped back through the archway. Jack was still at the door, watching me. I walked straight into his arms.

'Come inside.'

We were like a couple of fish, so wet, with rain in our eyes, plastering our hair to our cheeks and making our lips cool like well-springs when they met. In Jack's hands I felt wonderfully contained; they smelt of sweet oil and charred wood. Or perhaps it was his hair I smelt, singed slightly by coal sparks – a whiff of brimstone that made me laugh from deep inside and bend back my head to have my throat kissed.

The range was still hot, and we threw the door wide open so that we could see, making a scarlet world for our love out of a few feet of tiles. There was no doubt, no coyness, over what should happen next. My poplin suit was heavy with water and glittered like fish scales. It slid off easily with its wet, sad, up-to-the-minute petticoat, leaving me standing before him in a damp and clinging chemise and drawers that stuck to my thighs and knees and a proud little brassière. All of a sudden it was so much worse than being naked that I bent my head until a heavy clump of curls tumbled over my face, and pressed against him. And softly, out of honest affection, savouring those last seconds of strangeness, he undressed me with an intense and gentle curiosity.

His hands were work-roughened; they left trails of arousal over my breasts, over my belly, on the inside of my thighs as he drew down my silk drawers. I'd never been gazed at so. I was almost afraid when I saw how the revelation of a pair of narrow hips and the swollen, downy, quickened flesh between them could move him to desire, a desire that hollowed and ravaged his face before he hid it between my thighs. I could feel him breathing there, his hands running up now to the flesh of my buttocks, pulling me towards him as if he wanted to split me, and haul himself into me, and possess me.

I wove my fingers into the soft, dark strength of his hair and he rose to his feet. I spread my naked, fire-coloured body across him to free him from his shirt. He seemed broader than I remembered, or perhaps it was simply the way the firelight played across his shoulders and the dusting of curled hair below his breastbone. I was consumed by a longing to be overwhelmed by his power, engulfed and subjugated by it, and yet I'd no idea how to make it happen and I was ashamed of not knowing. His hand guided mine to the buttons of his trousers and the startling strength inside. It was appalling, exciting and inexplicable. He stopped kissing me as I touched him there, just a feather touch, but enough to make him gasp. And when I slid down as he had done, throwing my arms round his thighs and burying that urgent flesh in my hair, in my fire-dried, flying aureole of curls, he snatched me up with a groan and carried me unceremoniously across the floor.

The mattresses were hard on the tiles, even with blankets pulled under us to cover the knots and the harsh ticking. But the jetty had been hard, and the stony beach, and I'd have given myself to him there, two years earlier, desperate to comfort his need and the rage of his youth. Now there was no rage, but the need was more intense than I could believe. I saw the pain of it in his eyes and the discovery made my breath come unevenly, as if a hand was at my throat and a great boulder of desire filled my chest. My body arched under it, devoured with longing for something cataclysmic and overwhelming; I wanted to be taken, to be consumed, to be opened up shamelessly to my impalement . . .

But Jack was intent on slow, exquisite possession, on kissing each part of me: behind my knees, over my writhing backside, in the hollow of my spine, under my ears, on my breasts, licking and teasing at my nipples, then over my belly and down. There his mouth suddenly began an exploration, a darting, flickering, persistent intrusion, in and around, opening and tormenting, while he held me implacably. I could do nothing to prevent it; and after the first rush of shame and astonishment, I closed my eyes and discovered I wouldn't have stopped him, even if I could. To my surprise, my body had begun to hum like a fiddle string, a strumming that resolved itself into an irresistible rhythm, leaping and shuddering so wildly inside me that I tried again to push him away. But he was merciless, and concentrated the torment until the shuddering finally exploded in spasms of such unbearable sensation, again and again, that I felt myself falling, and cried out. I couldn't breathe. My eyelids were beating involuntarily, allowing me a glimpse of another world. I reached out wildly and fastened my fingers into the flesh of his shoulders.

'I like to see your eyelids flutter like that, as if you can't endure any more.'

'I can't. Oh, heavens . . .'

His face swam before me, fiercely serious. 'I want you to have this, to know this and remember it, in case I hurt you later.'

He didn't hurt me, though I was prepared to be hurt and I was ready for it – would have welcomed it as the price of my exaltation. Instead he led me into a strange and shocking intimacy, a penetration, an invading – a slow, deep, rhythmic assault – that after a while became an unexpectedly pleasurable upheaval, a delightful muffled ache, a fulfilling *rightness* that made me spread my legs to draw him further into me. Then suddenly he left me behind and sped on, hard and tightly swollen inside me, to a place where I couldn't follow, a convulsive place of deep and agonizing

271

satisfaction that bent back his head until it touched his spine, and let it fall forward again.

And yet it was enough afterwards to be held and wondered over, and to stretch out, undefended, against Jack, defenceless, and to surrender to the closeness we had mistrusted for so long.

Chapter Fifteen

JACK MUST have wakened before me and lain for some time with my head against his shoulder and his nose in my hair.

'Why does your hair smell of lemon?'

'I put lemon juice in the last rinse.' I yawned and mumbled, 'It's supposed to give it golden lights.'

'Ah . . .'

My eyelids were still heavy with sleep. I felt sensuous and warm. Jack's skin was darker than mine where the two were fused, and sleep had given it a faintly oily sheen and a woody, autumnal scent. I didn't want to look beyond the curve of his hip to the grey dawn of the tiled kitchen. We'd made our world and I was reluctant to leave it; I nestled against him, rubbing my chin against his shoulder, and he made a place for me in the hollow of his arm.

It was only when he moved that I remembered how young he still was, only two years older than I, still with the supple angularity and too-long wrists of a boy. There'd been nothing of the boy about him the previous night, unless it was the longing that occasionally shone through his desire. But he was older than his years in that, as in so much else. I softly traced the line of his newly-healed wound where it scored the undulating swell of his ribs; he'd had so little time to be young.

He'd been considering me, too. 'What's going on under those curls of yours?'

'Why should anything be going on?'

'Because there always is.'

'Oh, well then, I was thinking of all the other happy women who must have laid their heads on this shoulder and admired what I'm looking at now.'

He gave a gasp of laughter. 'What do you think I am? Hardly out of school—'

I turned over on my stomach and faced him in mock severity. 'Ah, yes, there was a school maid, I seem to remember.'

His eyes were like flashes from a summer sky, clear cobalt blue and guileless. 'How did you know about that?'

'Bea overheard your father lecturing you about it. I think she was quite proud.'

'And what did you think?'

'I was madly jealous for a bit, and then, oh, I suppose it made you wicked and fascinating.'

He glanced away and then back: that look of the boy again. 'You seem destined to know all my secrets.'

'Do you mind that?'

'I've never had anyone to share them with before. It doesn't seem as if I've given anything away, when you know.'

'And now we have another secret.' I leaned over him to be kissed, brushing his chest with my breasts, savouring his quickened breathing.

'There is one thing you ought to know. I mean it, Chrissie.' Gently, he held me off. 'This could be important. Do you remember when I said I had a reason for waiting here until at least the twenty-third, and you didn't believe me?' He was trying to be serious, but there was still heat in his eyes.

'I didn't want to believe you. I was afraid of becoming part of something.'

'And now you are.' He kissed me fleetingly on the lips, as if to confirm it. 'So you might as well know.'

He withdrew his encircling arm, got up off our piled mattresses and went across to the table. I watched him go, enjoying the complimentary rhythm of his shoulders and hips and the pliant channel of his spine. Full of sudden longing to feel that rolling rhythm under my fingers, I slid to the edge of the mattress and followed him.

He opened the table drawer and took out a large brown envelope, its corners softened by handling. 'I want you to look at this, in case anything happens to me.'

Still only half-engaged, I leaned against his shoulder as he spread the table with paper plans, layering them one over the other. They seemed to be designs for a vehicle, though not one I recognized – I'd have called it a boat, if it hadn't been enveloped in belts and turrets and what might have been guns. At the top of each page was a line of print: Landships Committee, War Office, Col. E. D. Swinton, followed by the words TOP SECRET and a serial number. Someone had underlined the 'top secret' in ink, and had written after the number *Mr Alfred Dunstan, Bolton Spring Works*.

'What on earth is it?'

'A landship. Though for secrecy's sake we're supposed to call it a water-carrier or a tank.' His finger moved over the paper, pointing to concentrations of lines. 'It's a development of the armoured car. Thirty tons in weight, it can do about four miles an hour on its tracks, flat out. This one's designed to take two six-pounder guns and Lewis guns – there, you see, and there.' He pointed, and then lifted the page away from the one below. 'The driver sits under this turret with the commander next to him, acting as brakeman. High and low ratio gears, operated by two members of the crew. It's swung round by putting the brake on one track and locking the differential.' He lifted that page in turn. 'No springs in the suspension, but look at the size of the clutch spring and some of these others. That's presumably why my father was involved in the design. It's all to do with getting the right stiffness for each spring, establishing the gauge of metal and the number of coils on the helix.'

'All this – just to carry some guns?'

'No, the guns are only secondary. The beauty of this contraption is that it can crawl over barbed wire as if it didn't exist and cross anything smaller than a ten-foot trench. It can burst its way through for the rest of us coming behind. And it does seem to work; the engineers have been testing one since the start of the year. We had a top secret briefing just before I was wounded. Haig had made up his mind to try them out on the Somme, in our sector.'

'But when?'

'Any time now. That's the point.'

'Then shouldn't you be there, instead of here?'

'Chrissie — these are top secret plans. The idea is to frighten the Germans out of their wits with something no one's ever seen before. But when I went into our drawing office in Bolton while I was back on leave, there they were — these top secret plans — waiting to be copied. Not out in the open, of course. Father's got an old boy who works on special projects and he'd primed him to do the work with some cock-and-bull story about needing more copies. But it doesn't take a genius to know where the copies were going to be sent. Thank God I knew what they were.'

'You really believe your father was going to give the plans to the Germans?'

'*Sell* them to the Germans. Of course he was, and for a damn good pay-out, I should think. But not the originals — just the copies. The originals are numbered and they have to go back to the War Office. That's why I couldn't take them to my colonel, or the police.'

'Your father would have been arrested right away.'

Jack stared at the obscured glass rectangles of the kitchen window. 'I should have turned him in, I know. But I couldn't do it. Not for my father's sake, heaven knows, but for Mother and the girls. What kind of life would they have? "Alfred Dunstan, the well-known traitor."' He let out a long, sighing breath. 'But I still had to stop him. So I took the plans and all the papers I could find dealing with the stuff he's been shipping to Germany and came up here. I thought if I could just stay hidden until the tanks had been used – until the secret was out – then the plans would have no value. I could send them back to Bolton and the War Office need never know they were missing. Then I could go back to the regiment.'

Right away, I spotted an enormous flaw in his plan. 'But if you can't tell your C.O. *why* you didn't go back to France, the Army will still take you for a deserter. You could be shot!'

He continued to fold the sheets of paper, sliding them methodically into the brown envelope. 'I'm banking on the fact they might find that difficult. If I turn up again of my own free will they can hardly say I meant to desert completely. And it wouldn't look very good, shooting an officer who's spent two years in the trenches. And . . .' He pushed the drawer shut. 'To be honest, it didn't matter very much, when I came here first. What happened to me wasn't important.'

I skimmed his chest with my fingers. 'And do you care now?'

'Yes.' He raised his gaze to mine, and slid his arms round my waist. 'I care very much. I want to get out of this mess, quite badly.'

The light behind the window panes was turning to buttermilk. Jack took my hand and turned towards the door. 'Let's go and see the sunrise.'

Our bare feet made a slapping sound on the linoleum of the passage but sank soundlessly into the thick carpet of the dining room. So far, the shadows had clothed our nakedness, but golden morning had already filled the conservatory and its brightness made me falter, instinctively spreading my hands to cover my uncertainty. With a wrench, Jack pulled down one of the long scarlet damask curtains that draped the French windows and wound it round me, toga-fashion, as we walked out on to the terrace.

'You look like a lady in one of those Victorian pictures, with your hair flying out in a mass, trailing your robes among the ivy and the weeds.'

'A Pre-Raphaelite woman. Hosanna Greendew always said I

looked like Jane Morris. It was my straight nose, she used to say, and the big, solemn eyes. Not that they are solemn – not really.'

'That depends on what you're looking at. For instance, now, they're . . . not solemn.'

Whatever he saw inspired him to kiss me, there on the terrace among the leathery straps of the dock leaves, then lead me down the stone steps to the rose garden. After the rain, the shaggy turf beyond the balustrade glowed with a green luminosity; in the rose garden, the growing warmth of the sun was encouraging the blooms to release their night's store of drenching scent. We strolled unhurriedly through the early morning wilderness, hand in hand, to where the roofless summer house sagged under its load of climbing roses, almost black in their velvet redness, each flounce of petals fixed with a fat tassel of golden stamens. The rain had wreaked havoc among the overblown blooms, swelling them like cabbages. Jack pulled off two of the collapsing heads and covered me with a soft blizzard of petals; then we lay down in a pool of scarlet damask and crushed their fragrance between us. And this time I knew what was to come, and welcomed the flooding of the sun on my face and my back, and the urgent ardour of my lover inside me, and relished the pleasure of being a woman, loved.

He was still in my body, lazy, arms outstretched, gazing up at the sky and I was spread over his hips, too indolent to move, when my eye fell on the last petal, clinging like a drop of dark blood over his heart. I no longer accepted his perception of the future; I had developed an acute lover's fear of my own.

'I must go. I don't have your patience. I don't know how you can just – *be* here, waiting for things to happen.'

He cupped my breast with a hand, thoughtfully. 'Because things do happen, in the end.'

'Good things or bad things?'

'Both.' He sat up.

★

He walked with me along the rough ground bordering the road, keeping to the shadow of the trees, and turned back to Waterside when I crossed towards the Fellwood lane. Mrs Hall was back, bustling about in the kitchen.

'You didn't eat the ham I left out. Didn't you care for it, dear?'

'I had an enormous lunch at Chris's. It was Mrs Cole's birthday.'

If Mrs Hall thought it at all odd to see me arrive in a misshapen poplin suit and water-marked canvas boots, crushing a straw hat to my chest, she thought better of saying anything. I tried to pretend I'd gone out early for a walk.

I put the last of the pearls and their diamond clasp safely in the stud box with their sisters. They had such a plump innocence about them now in cheerful daylight that I could hardly believe it. They rolled like piglets in their box, jostling with satisfaction, wearing a look as if to say 'We told you so, didn't we?' They seemed such a spent force, with their miracle achieved – just globes of calcium formed about a grain of irritant matter. They went so meekly into their drawer among my stockings; yet I knew in my heart that pearls do not alter – I was the one who had changed.

I was ashamed too, to realize how I instinctively thought of the pearls now in terms of Jack and me and our own concerns. Hadn't it been for Max Kassel that I'd made my bargain in the first place? And yet, somehow, the pearls that had been intended to secure Max's freedom had brought about mine instead. I owed Max more than he'd ever realize. That evening, I told myself, I'd write to Uncle Hereward at the War Office, explaining that the pearls had been found and that Max Kassel was an innocent man. Uncle Hereward would know how best to proceed after that.

I'd promised Jack I'd go back to Waterside, but I knew I couldn't go back to him as things stood – not as Christopher Cole's fiancée. That surely wouldn't have been right.

279

I was horribly aware that my wedding gown was waiting, virginal under its cotton cover, in the camphor-smelling gentleman's wardrobe in the Chinese bedroom. It was the only garment in there; the room was seldom used and the rest of the wardrobe space was taken up by empty hangers and narrow, fitted drawers marked 'Socks' and 'Handkerchiefs'.

I'd been convinced I truly loved Chris. The odd thing was, I still felt the same quiet, steady, orderly affection for him as before. Only a day earlier, I'd had no fear of a future spent looking after his home, turning up a neat hem, not having dog hairs on my skirt, and making sure he always had the proper tie to go with his suit. And yet now the thought of it was enough to make me draw a deep breath, like a threat of strangulation.

I was absolutely sure that whatever my future might hold – and I hadn't the faintest inkling of that any more – there was no place in it for Chris. I'd discovered how it was possible to love, how I needed to love, in a way I knew I'd never love Chris. And the sooner I went and told him so and begged his pardon for not understanding myself or anything else, the better.

'Will you be in for lunch, Miss Chrissie?'

'No, thank you, Mrs Hall. I have things to do in the village.'

Bathed and changed into a blouse and skirt, I wheeled out my bicycle and set off. Outside the Royal Hotel in Bowness I met Hosanna Greendew, also cycling. She wobbled into my path and put a foot down.

'Just the person!' She regarded me benevolently down her long nose. 'Your parents' invitation arrived this morning – to your wedding – and I shall be delighted to accept, as far as the *service* goes, but, of course, not to the wedding breakfast afterwards. You understand, I simply could not . . . Not so soon.' Her great eyelids drooped and rose again, but she avoided repeating her brother's name.

'But I have written a *work*.' From habit, she reached out a hand to prevent me from interrupting and rummaged in the velvet bag tied to her handlebars. 'I thought, perhaps, since I shan't be there, your father might read it.' A tint of bashful colour warmed the powder on each cheek as she peered into the darkness of her reticule. 'Here it is! The notebook of my heart, I call it. I always carry it with me in case a *thought* occurs. Now, if I may just give you a little flavour—'

Despondently, I climbed off my bicycle. I'd primed myself for a task I was dreading. I'd rehearsed the phrases. I'd planned to deliver them immediately, on the basis that bad news and penitence were best got off my chest straight away before my courage failed me. But Hosanna had already taken up her favourite position – allowing for the bicycle between her legs – with her green Morocco notebook balanced open across one of her large hands and the other sweeping and swooping like a poetical house martin.

'How many families never fathered?' she demanded, 'How many harvests never gathered? – in this part, you see, I include all those killed in the war, on both sides, since so many of the German dead are poor green boys like our own. I really would prefer to exclude the *Turks*, who've been so dreadfully cruel, but if I add "except in Turkey", then it would no longer scan – do you see the problem?'

'Awkward,' I agreed, glancing over her shoulder in the hope of rescue.

'After that, it goes on—

> *How many pictures, songs, inventions*
> *Lost, no more than vague intentions?*
> *As lost – though for one eye or ear*
> *Alone – the words 'I love you, dear.'*
> *How many wisdoms never uttered –*

Now, here I have a line missing. *Uttered* is such a beast of a word, I may have to change it. This section is a summing-up of the *ghostly horde* of wasted youth, you see.' She touched her lower lip in sudden doubt. 'You don't feel there's too much about the war, for a wedding?'

'I think it's a wonderful poem, Hosanna, but just at this moment—' I snatched at the only excuse I thought she might accept. 'I must go and see Chris. You understand.'

'Ah.' She reached out to my sleeve, her eyes moistly wistful, and the notebook disappeared into the depths of her bag. 'My dear, of course you must go. Love's young dream. Another time, another time.'

I could tell from the angle of his half-spectacles that Chris had just finished morning surgery. In fact, he was checking the contents of his black leather bag before going out on calls. His face lit up when he saw me and he held out his arms.

'Well, darling, you're just what I need, I must say! I've seen such a procession of misery this morning, you wouldn't believe. Why – what's the matter?'

I avoided his arms and his eye, to my shame, and heaved an enormous sigh, suddenly overwhelmed by the impossibility of delivering my news. It was only the thought of Jack, waiting for me – needing me – at Waterside, that at last gave me courage.

'Can your calls wait for five minutes? For ten, perhaps?'

'Well, no more than that. I have to drive up to Waterhead.' He inspected me indulgently over his spectacles. 'But I can see I have an emergency on my hands already. What's happened? Has the church been booked for another wedding, or something?'

If only it had been! As I stumbled through my explanation, I watched Chris pass through the various stages of disbelief, indignation and finally anger. By the time I'd said my piece and put my ring down on the table, there was no question of displeasure; he was enraged – controlledly, viciously enraged.

'This man – this unnamed *person* – you tell me you've fallen in love with – he's in a position to marry you, is he?'

'I don't know. We haven't spoken about it. I've no idea if he wants to marry anyone.'

Chris shook his head in perplexity, as if the whole business struck him as insane.

'What on earth is my mother going to say?' He glared at me suddenly. 'What am I supposed to tell Aunt Dora? What about the Rector? How do I explain to him? What about my patients?'

'Chris, I don't know,' I said humbly. 'If you want me to put something in the local newspaper—'

'*No!*' He shouted the word. 'You'll do no such thing! Do you imagine I want the fact that I've been jilted, dropped, *thrown over*, I think the term is, trumpeted all over the Lakes?' He raised a finger to make a point, then lowered it again, remembering something. 'Is that why there was no answer when I called at Fellwood last night?' He was beginning to sound outraged, like a householder who's discovered his home has been robbed. 'I knocked for ages, but nobody came. I couldn't imagine where you'd all gone. You'd insisted on walking home and I thought, perhaps, you were upset. But there was no one there at all.'

'Mar and Par are coming back tonight. Mrs Hall goes to her daughter's on Fridays.'

'And you? Where were you?' He remembered the spectacles and stripped them off. Without them he looked like a belligerent schoolboy. 'It was half past ten at night – if you weren't at home, then where were you? When did you get home? *How* did you get home?' His upper lip formed a hard, aggressive beak. 'Or did you bother to go home at all?'

I felt myself flushing. 'It's none of your business what I do, now that we aren't engaged any longer—'

'We were still engaged last night! Or that's what I thought, at any rate.' By now the scarlet glow of hot blood had suffused his fair skin, absorbing its freckles and making his hair seem oddly light in contrast, like ripe corn against a thundery sky. He regarded me sullenly, with the truculence of the child who cries *Unfair!*

Unfair! 'Well? Where did you spend last night? With this man whose name you can't even tell me? Was that where you were when I was looking for you?'

He'd meant it as a cheap taunt, I think, but there was relief in admitting it. 'Yes. I was with him. All night.'

'God in heaven!' He stepped back as if I'd presented him with something foul and slimy. 'No wonder your mind's been elsewhere for the past few weeks. How long has this *affair* been going on, then? How long have you been making a complete fool out of me?'

'There hasn't been an affair. I've explained to you – I didn't realize until last night that I loved him. And now I've come to tell you, right away. What more can I do?'

'You could have behaved like my fiancée – in the way I had a right to expect.'

'It just happened, Chris. I didn't want it to happen – it just did.'

'I see. And this anonymous lover of yours, this man you're so proud of that you have to hide him away—' He ran out of sarcasm and began to lift himself in little jerks on his toes, searching for inspiration, his mouth open to frame the next word. Then his face altered, as if something he'd said had triggered a memory. 'Sergeant Naylor was fussing around after some fellow. He came here and warned me. Some scoundrel the Army's looking for – a deserter – an officer who didn't go back to his unit in France, after being home on leave. No. Wait. I remember now—' He nodded, and the words came faster. 'It was the Dunstan boy. Alfred Dunstan's son. They thought he might try to hide at Waterside.'

Chris tilted up his nose, a hound on the scent. 'Your mother still has the keys, hasn't she? Sergeant Naylor said he'd checked the place. Cycled round it and said there was no sign of life, not that he'd know—'

'Chris, I don't want to talk about it.'

'The Dunstan boy. Jack Dunstan – that would fit your story.

And you made me drop you at the gates to Waterside yesterday, didn't you, when I wanted to take you all the way home.'

'Chris, please, don't ask me these things.'

'He's there, isn't he? And you've been protecting him, and all the rest! Well, at least *I* know what to do with a rotten coward and a deserter, and that's hand him over to the authorities.' He crossed, stiff-legged, to the desk and picked up the telephone receiver, but I dashed after him and snatched it out of his hand. He leaned against me, grabbing for it, in a ghastly parody of an embrace from which we both recoiled. Yet it left us standing closer than was comfortable; I could smell the ether on his suit and the soapy smell of his hands.

'Chris, I swear to you, Jack has a decent, honourable reason for being at Waterside.'

'Oh, I'm sure he has. Seducing you, for a start!'

'He didn't seduce me. I knew what I was doing.' I made myself look directly into his face. 'You've never really accepted that I can think for myself, have you? You've always wanted to do it for me. Isn't that true?' I touched the lapel of his coat, but he brushed my hand away. 'Chris – I did help him, when he came here first. But I haven't lied to you about loving Jack.' I saw him blink as I spoke the words. 'And I'm not trying to make excuses for him, but he isn't a deserter, I swear it. He's going back to his regiment in a week's time, because he always meant to go back—' I took a deep breath. 'And I want you to promise you won't say a word to the police before then.'

'Well, I must say, you've got a cheek!'

'This is vital, Chris! Jack's risking his life for the sake of this war – his father's probably looking for him as well as the police – and if it all goes wrong he could be shot. I can't tell you exactly what it's all about, but there's nothing dishonourable in helping him stay hidden.'

'The way I feel now, you can both go to the devil before I'd lift a finger. Why should I do anything to save Jack Dunstan's skin?'

'Because you're a fair man. I know I've hurt you and if you hate me for it, it's no more than I deserve, but don't hate Jack, please. I'm begging you. Don't go to the police.'

'I'll think about it, when I've finished thinking about what you've done.'

'I must have your promise, Chris.'

'Then you'll just have to do without it, because I've calls waiting and I'm late already.' He snatched his bag from the table, but I'd placed myself in front of the door, with my arms spread out. 'Now, don't be silly. Get out of my way.'

'Not until you've promised.'

'This is childish! It's bad enough knowing the woman I was going to marry has behaved like a slut. Don't make it any worse.'

The word *slut* hit me like a slap in the face, but it brought home to me how angry he was, and how dangerous he could be to Jack. 'You have to promise.'

We confronted each other, eye to hard, obdurate eye. Without any warning, he capitulated. 'All right, I'll give you my word. I won't tell the police your precious Jack is hiding at Waterside. Now will you get out of my way?'

I stood aside. I'd been holding my breath. 'Thank you, Chris,' I breathed to his retreating back.

All I could think of was getting back to Waterside. I badly needed to be reassured and told I wasn't a slut, but a woman who'd followed her heart, for once, instead of her head.

'Oh, Chrissie! Christabel!'

I pressed my eyes shut in dismay: I could hardly believe it. My route to the main road led me unavoidably past Hosanna Greendew's cottage. When I opened my eyes again, there was Hosanna at her garden gate, holding out a posy of newly cut roses, the secateurs still in her large, capable hand.

'I know you have lots of flowers at Fellwood, but these are rather special. They're an old china rose that Jeremy and I planted before . . . before he went off to France.' She thrust the flowers under my nose. 'If you like them, I thought – perhaps for your wedding bouquet? The stems are a little wet, but I've torn a strip from this morning's *Times*—'

I received the posy as graciously as I could and tucked it into the space between the cycle lamp and my handlebars. An urge to confess, to purge myself of deceit, almost made me tell her there wasn't going to be any wedding. And yet out of loyalty to Chris, I felt bound to wait. She'd find out, no doubt, in due course. In the meantime, she was clearly entranced by the whole idea.

'Your ode is nearly finished. I just have to search for a stanza for the middle. The rough soldiery are already represented, you see.' Hosanna's long, bony fingers drew extravagant curves in the air. 'But now I need something *virginal*, yet hinting at the *wildness* of the female principal, the overpowering urge to *fuse*, to *coalesce*, to bring forth and nurture—'

The knowledge that there would be no coalescing with Chris made me cut her off. 'I'm sure it'll be wonderful, whatever you write.'

'And then it finishes with a valedictory call from the dead soldiers who will never marry and never grow old.' A long finger dashed a suspicion of moisture from her eye. I realized that when her brother died, Hosanna had lost the love of her life, the only man who'd satisfied all her exacting criteria. 'Tell me,' she instructed, 'if you think this is too morbid:

> *If they could speak, they'd surely say*
> *Snatch the moment – live the day!*
> *Sing – laugh – don't wait, for Time grows old,*
> *And freely give, when love takes hold.*

'Hosanna, do you really believe that? Do you honestly think we should risk everything, and just follow our feelings?'

'Well, of course I do!' Hosanna peered at me. 'You don't want to be left like me, do you, spending the rest of your life saying *If only*? What's the point of that? I could never love a man who—'

I leaned over the gate and planted a kiss on her leathery cheek. 'Hosanna – you're a saint.'

As I pedalled off, I heard her calling out behind me,

> *I'd like to think they wish you well,*
> *Christopher and Christabel,*
> *Now pledged, eternal, side by side –*
> *Tomorrow's youth, and hope, and pride!*

Jack was in the scullery, cleaning out a water gauge from the *Siren*. When he saw the look on my face, he opened his dripping arms for me.

'Jack, I've told Chris. I had to. It wouldn't have been fair to let him go on planning our wedding and renting houses. I was right to tell him, wasn't I?'

'I suppose that was honest of you, at least. As long as you didn't say too much.'

'I didn't, not much. But he worked the rest out.' I glanced up. 'He's guessed you're here, I'm afraid.'

'Oh, *hell*.'

'But he's promised not to go to the police. I made him swear.'

'And you trust him? After all we've done? Chrissie, he must hate me! If anyone took you away from me, I'd want to kill him!'

I shook my head. 'Chris isn't like that. Oh, he's angry, but he never does anything extreme. And he will keep his word, once he's given it. He's very serious about promises – that's why I've sinned so badly.'

Jack sighed and leaned on the edge of the sink. He drew the back of his wrist across his forehead. 'I hope you're right. But if my life has to depend on the word of a jilted fiancé—' He turned to glance at me and frowned. 'What's the matter, Chrissie?'

I'd started to unwrap the strip of newspaper from the stems of

Hosanna's roses, when all at once, some words caught my eye. Ordinarily, Par would have read out the principal news reports at breakfast, but Par was away. It was only by the merest chance that I'd noticed it.

Now I stretched out a hand. 'Look at this – Hosanna tore it out of today's *Times*.' Jack moved at once to look over my shoulder, alarmed by the rising excitement in my voice.

'"A new type of heavy armoured car, which has proved of considerable utility." Could that be your tank, do you think? "Little was known of the actual construction of the vehicle. Our inventors have not hesitated boldly to tread unbeaten paths."'

'Where are they getting all this?' Jack's wet thumb and forefinger steadied the wobbling strip of paper. 'A communiqué from Haig? Then the tanks must have been in action yesterday.'

'On the Somme, according to this: "Unearthly monsters, cased in steel, spitting fire and crawling laboriously but ceaselessly over trench, barbed wire and shell crater." That has to be them! Jack – the secret's out! It doesn't matter any more. You don't have to hide, you can go back and give yourself up.' I threw my arms joyfully round his neck; then I remembered that his danger was far from over.

'Promise me—' I leaned back and drew a curl of dark hair from his eyes. 'Promise me that if you have to, if things look really bad – you know what I mean – you'll tell them about your father and his dealings with the Germans and why you had to take the plans.'

'It won't come to that.'

'It might.'

'And what about my mother, and Bea and Ida? What kind of lives do you think they'll have, if my father's dragged into court as a traitor?'

'But Jack, I could *lose* you.' I couldn't bear to give words to the horror that filled my mind.

'I tell you, it won't come to that. It isn't like running away on the battlefield. And I am going back of my own accord, so they can't say I meant to desert.' He turned his back on me, hiding his face, and gathered up the newly cleaned gauge out of the sink. 'Come on, let's put this back where it belongs and then decide how I'm to get back to the regiment without being arrested.'

I'd always known he'd have to go back and take whatever punishment the Army saw fit to impose. I'd just tried not to think about it. Now, however, it was all I could think of. It was uppermost in Jack's mind, too. I could tell as much from his silence as he worked on the *Siren*'s boiler. At last he climbed back on to the wooden pier and gazed regretfully at the launch.

'Well, old girl, I don't suppose I'll see you for a bit. One day, though, if I come through this war.' His hand enveloped mine as we left the boathouse; it saved him from having to say the same thing to me.

We took a detour by the alders at the edge of the lawn, silently conspiring to put off the decisions that awaited us at the top of the slope. Under the trees, the grass was coarse and speckled by fierce white sunlight. Jack tilted my face up to his and began to pull the pins out of my hair. 'I have an idea.'

'You're wicked.'

'For a new kind of valve.'

I could tell from his expression that the subject of desertion and courts martial was closed. Whatever had to happen, would happen. If this was our last day together, so be it. In the meantime, he'd designed a valve.

His hands moved into the warm curve at the back of my neck and slipped into my hair, pulling my lips to his. For a long time, he held me there, as if trying to imprint the sensation on his memory.

'It's a safety valve.' His fingers slid down my throat into the soft cleft between my breasts and began to undo the buttons of my blouse. 'It was the *Siren* that gave me the idea, but it doesn't have to be a steam valve. Anywhere there's pressure.'

I'd begun to undo his shirt. I slid my hand down, across the fastening of his trousers and encountered stiffness.

'Pressure that has to be released.' He slid the straps of my chemise from my shoulders and we slipped down together into the grass. 'It's all to do with the shape of the valve, you see . . .'

His lips were teasing my breast; the murmur of his voice was a buzzing caress that whirred through my belly to flutter between my legs; his hands were under my skirt.

'If the valve lets the pressure fall too low, then—'

I felt him move into me, filling me up, becoming an urgent, living part of me.

'It's inefficient—' The word came out by my ear in a long, rippling sigh of exultation. 'It needs – a spring – not a weight. Oh, my God!'

'Oh, Jack!'

'Because it has to close – hold me, for Christ's sake – when the pressure falls—'

'Go *on*, again, oh, please, like that, *again*—'

'Oh, my *stars*! Below the safety load – I can't – holy *smoke*, when you shudder like that—'

'Oh, yes, oh, yes, oh, *yes*!'

And with a great surge and a convulsion and something like a moan, 'Chrissie Ascham, *I love you* . . .'

I don't know how long we lay there in the warmth of the grass, patterned like snakes with white spots of light that filtered through the trees. Letty and Philip must have been somewhere nearby when I saw them together and ran off, appalled by the carnality of their passion. I wondered if anyone spying on Jack and me would realize that what they saw was the small, glittering pinnacle of a great mountain of love – a love capable of concentrating its whole essence into a tiny, intense, overpowering pinpoint of sensation, of burning its way like the sun through a magnifying glass into the most private and jealously guarded recesses of the soul.

After a long time, I noticed that the leaves of our canopy of trees had turned jewel-green against patches of rosy sky.

'The sun's going down.'

'Cold?' He drew me closer.

'No. Happy. Sleepy. Very much indulged.'

'It might have to last us for a long time.'

The words *for ever* hung in the air, but neither of us dared to say them. Instead, as we strolled through the overgrown rose garden on the way back to the house, I made a great effort to think of the future.

'This safety valve you've invented. Will it really work, do you think?'

'Don't see why it shouldn't. I've thought it out pretty carefully.'

'You'll have to call it something.' We climbed the steps to the terrace and walked towards the kitchen courtyard.

At the same moment we said, 'The Dunstan Patent Safety Valve' and burst out laughing.

We turned the corner and the laughter died. There, just visible through the archway on the other side of the courtyard, was Alfred Dunstan's motor car.

He'd left it at the top of the drive, well away from the house – we walked across to be certain it was his. At that distance I could clearly hear the ticking of over-hot metal; the springmaker had evidently come from somewhere at top speed, not sparing his engine. There was no sign of a chauffeur. He had driven himself.

Jack nodded, as if it was no more than he'd expected. 'He'll be inside the house. You'd better go back to Fellwood. Through the fields would be best.'

'And what about you? I'm not leaving you here.'

'I'm not going to run away from him.'

'Then neither am I. What can he do, except shout? Come on.'

There was no one in the kitchen, though the door to the

scullery stood open and our blankets had been flung on the floor. The pantries beyond were also empty.

'We'll try the hall.'

The heavy door creaked like the devil when Jack pulled it open. I kept telling myself there was nothing to be afraid of, that we'd nothing to fear from one angry middle-aged man. Jack had been capable for years of knocking his father down. Sometimes, I think, it puzzled him that he'd never done it. No, it was the house that unnerved me, with its long, cold, unlit corridors like the tunnels of a mine, and its silence – not a serene, sleeping silence, but the prickling noiselessness of a night stalk.

Jack glanced into the billiard room as we passed. The cue and balls he'd unearthed lay abandoned on the table, but the room was empty of life.

Our initial view of the hall was blocked by the plaster statue of an orange-seller, a nymph with a basket of fruit. The fading light had turned her chalky arms to a lichenous grey; all we could see of the hall was through a gap between her shoulder and the upraised paw of the stuffed bear. We halted, listening, and the hush was broken by the clearing of a throat, an impatient sound, a nervous grating of membranes.

Alfred Dunstan was standing at the first turn of the silver staircase, three steps from the bottom, on the square landing where the family chairs had been set out long ago for Signor Arnoldi's recital. At first sight he didn't seem to have changed at all in the two years since I'd seen him: he was just as belligerently rectangular, and his iron-grey head was thrust forward, chin outstretched, in the taunting attitude I remembered of old. Yet there was something different about his face, as if a slackness had entered it – a bitterness – a habit of disillusion, as if the beliefs which had once tightened its skin and brightened its eye had long since been abandoned.

I wondered if the springmaker was aware of the pastel-coloured ghosts of the past struggling through his furious white-wash, just above his head.

'Well, well, Jack. So you are here, after all.' Alfred Dunstan's smile bared his teeth unpleasantly. 'And Bea's young friend, too.'

His eyes darted from my face to Jack's and back again. I guessed he was wondering how much I knew.

'Fancy you running away from the Army, Jack.' The spring-maker managed a twisted grin. 'The police have been looking all over, you know. They said they'd searched for you here, but not found you. That fellow in the village is an ass. Just as well the local doctor had more sense.'

'The doctor?' The words burst out of me. 'Christopher Cole? But he gave me his word! He promised he wouldn't tell the police.'

'And neither he did.' Alfred Dunstan fixed me with a steady stare, his eyes glassy. 'He telephoned me instead. Boy's father, he said. Ought to know.'

I heard Jack's voice at my elbow, strong and confident. 'You needn't have bothered coming. There's nothing here for you.'

'There's a thief.' The springmaker came down a step, paused, and then descended another. 'I can see a thief here, someone who's stolen something of mine, and made me look a damned fool in front of some very important people. Cost me a lot of money, this has. Money I can't afford.' His stare swept back to me. 'You get out, girl. This has nothing to do with you.'

Jack touched my arm. 'Go home, Chrissie.'

'I will not!' I stood my ground by a plaster Pan, determined to make up for Chris's treachery.

Alfred Dunstan stepped down to the floor. 'Throw her out.'

'There's no point.' Jack put his hands in his pockets. 'I've told her everything.'

'Have you, though?'

His father sauntered over to his favourite spot at the enormous fireplace and contemplated us from there. He wasn't wearing one of his check 'country' suits, but something dark grey, over-supplied with buttons and pockets and his usual heavy watch chain. Chris's telephone call must have caught him in the middle

294

of his business day. And yet there was something else new about him, something I couldn't quite put a finger on. In the poor light his face seemed a dark, earthy red, making his eyes peculiarly light and round. His mouth was pressed shut like a latched carpet-bag and his fleshy nostrils flared to accommodate his heavy breathing. I was just wondering how long he'd stand there, pumping great breaths in and out and staring at us, when he suddenly ducked his head into the inglenook and snatched the brass poker from its elaborate rack.

Slapping the shaft against the palm of his free hand, he glared at Jack.

'Do you know what you've cost me, by taking those plans? Have you any idea?'

'German money – I know that.'

'Money, dammit, that I need! One man's cash is as good as another, if you're in a fix. Did you ever ask who paid for your education, you self-righteous prig? Well, did you? Answer me!'

His hand flashed out, swinging the poker through the air, slicing the shadows where Jack's head had been a moment before and smashing the arm of the plaster fruit-seller. Pieces of arm crashed to the floor; plaster fragments flew everywhere.

'Well?' He was still holding the poker, swishing it in a furious arc. 'You couldn't mind your own business, could you?'

'Chrissie, you'd better go.' Jack indicated the door to the kitchens.

'No.' The springmaker sidled round, blocking my exit. 'She stays.'

'This has nothing to do with her.'

'I said, she stays, damn you!' The poker flashed again, striking the orange-seller's head from her body and sending it spinning across the hall floor. 'And the front door's locked.' His head jerked towards it, a curiously exaggerated movement.

'For heaven's sake—' Jack was watching his father with an expression of disbelief. 'This is stupid. The plans are no use to you any more. The tanks were sent through the wire yesterday.'

'Don't I know it?' Alfred Dunstan was holding the poker two-handed now. 'But I need to cover my tracks. So I need the plans back. And the letters you took, and the bills of lading.'

'You're pathetic! I should have turned you in after all!'

'*Fetch them now!*' The springmaker swung the poker with all the power of his massive shoulders, hitting the plaster Pan amidships and making Jack jump back. Splinters exploded across the room. A huge chunk of torso detached itself and crashed to the floor, leaving a sprouting of bare wires. 'Get me those papers!'

There was an eerie pale light in the springmaker's eyes, like the blue fire of sunlight on ice. His head twisted again in that strange, cramped movement, but his eyes remained fixed on Jack.

'Don't try and take me on, boy! You haven't the grit to carry it through.' He jabbed with the poker. 'You're no Dunstan, that's certain. You're a weakling. A runt.' He leaned forward. '*You disgust me.*'

As he drew back his arm, Jack seized the chance and lunged forward, just as his father launched the poker at his head. By the time the scuffle was over, the springmaker had his back to a marble pillar and once again, I could see the gleam of metal in his hand. It was something smaller than a poker, darker and more deadly.

'Oh, my God.' Jack spoke the words softly, under his breath.

The springmaker bared his teeth once more and twitched the barrel of his pocket pistol.

'Now, let's start again.'

His eyes flitted between us and he began to edge towards me, his feet crunching the shards of plaster. With deliberate precision, he raised the cold muzzle of the weapon and jabbed it under my ear.

'The papers,' he reminded Jack.

'Let Chrissie go free and you can have them.'

Alfred Dunstan let out a bark of harsh laughter. 'Listen to the Oxford man! I may not have much schooling, but I can see through your tricks.' He leaned forward, pushing the pistol unpleasantly into my flesh, and breathed in my ear. 'I invented most of them, after all. Not being raised a gentleman, I'll fight as dirty as you like.'

'You have my word. As soon as Chrissie walks out of this house, I'll give you the plans and the letters.'

'Jack, they're the only way you can prove why you didn't go back to France!'

'Aaah—' The springmaker's hot breath rasped against my cheek. 'She's trembling. Like a little bird.'

'Let her go!'

'I'll need the papers first.'

'And then she goes free.'

'Maybe she will, maybe she won't. But not you, my boy. Not after this.'

Out of the corner of my eye I could see the springmaker's left hand rise up to claw at his ear, and it crossed my mind I might wriggle free. But, as if he'd read my thoughts, he placed that same rough, blunt hand on the far side of my throat, forcing me back against the muzzle of the gun.

'Feel it?' His breath was sour and irregular. 'You will. Don't expect fancy principles from a man like me.'

'Down by the jetty.' I heard Jack's voice, taut with anxiety. 'I buried the papers near the boathouse.'

'Then we'll go and get them. After that, we'll see.'

The sky was streaked with grey and pink as we came out on to the terrace and walked down the steps to the lawn. Jack went ahead as he'd been told and I followed, with the hard nose of the pistol prodding the nape of my neck.

'Jack'll mind his manners while I've got you, Chrissie. He isn't like me. You'd have had to take your chance with me.'

I hated the way his mouth had lingered over the syllables of my name, as if he were chewing it. Now I could hear him breathing noisily through his nose as he negotiated the rough grass behind me.

I kept thinking of the night Bea had challenged us to swim

naked, and we four had walked together down to the lake, angry, half-drunk and dangerously reckless. In sudden panic, I tried to push the memory away. To retrace those steps, to relive the sensation of being so exultantly, blindingly *alive* . . . all the time with a pistol pressing its deadly mouth against my neck; I thought I might be sick with the sheer obscenity of the moment. The springmaker's mood – his casual cruelty – was beyond anything I could have imagined. It was like being in the power of an animal; there was no point of contact, no way of comprehending. I tried to breathe slowly, to keep a clear head, but my heart was thumping in my chest and there were great knots of fear in my stomach.

'Down here.' At the bottom of the lawn, Jack slid down the weedy bank to the little cove. 'Under these stones.'

I tried to guess why he'd brought us there. He was a soldier, after all, his instincts were all for survival. I was the weak link, the one whose vulnerability prevented him from acting. Perhaps he was hoping his father would follow him and stumble, giving us a chance to catch him off-balance.

'Not down there. You and I go this way.' The pistol caressed my neck, propelling me towards the jetty. 'We can watch from up here.'

I saw Jack bend down and make a great business of turning over the largest stones. I stood with the springmaker on the edge of the jetty, my mind racing. As far as I knew, the papers were in the drawer of the kitchen table; what would happen when the springmaker discovered he'd been duped? And if Jack was eventually forced to hand them over – what would happen to us then? Because there was far more at stake now than the papers. I could feel it in the trembling of my captor's hand – a rage, a blood-lust, beyond humanity and beyond reason.

Being too short to see over the top of my head, he'd been forced to step to one side in order to watch Jack at work.

'Hurry up, down there! We don't like waiting – do we, Chrissie?'

The muzzle of the pistol was under my ear again, but his eyes were momentarily on Jack – and that was when everything suddenly started to happen. In an instant I saw Jack crouch down, straighten up and turn, his arms swinging out as he came – and heard his shout of 'Down, Chrissie!' as something heavy flew through the air.

'Run to the boathouse!'

I didn't wait to see what he'd done. All I knew was that the cold metal edge of the pistol had abruptly released its pressure. I slithered down like an eel from the jetty, dropped to the shingle, kicked off my shoes and took off towards the dark bulk of the boathouse as fast as my weakened leg would carry me. My breath was coming in sobs by the time I'd torn my way through the bushes to the path. I wrenched open the door; inside, it was pitch black. I could hear water slopping round the piers and Jack's footsteps skidding down the path behind me, and then, distantly at first but getting louder, the springmaker's voice, shouting oaths. I hesitated, wondering why Jack had chosen the boathouse to hide in; it was dark in there, certainly, but we could easily be cornered.

There was nothing for it now but to go on. I began to feel my way cautiously along the piers, hugging the wall where I remembered the planks were rotten. Jack exploded through the door behind me.

'Quick! He isn't far behind. I didn't catch him squarely with that stone.'

I discovered the rail of the loft steps by barging painfully into it. Jack heard my gasp. 'Into the *Siren*. Hurry up.'

'We can't hide there—'

'Get *in*!'

He'd caught up with me now and pushed me towards the launch. I half-scrambled, half-fell into the passenger well, Jack piled in after me, tearing at the mooring-lines. I heard a boat-hook clang against the funnel as he turned it in his hands.

Twenty feet away across the building, the pale rectangle of the doorway was suddenly filled by a squat, bulky shape. Alfred

Dunstan wasn't used to running. I could hear his rasping breaths as he peered into the gloom, and then his shuffling footsteps as he began to negotiate the piers, trying to get his bearings and work his way round to us.

Jack was lying flat over the stern of the launch; the boat-hook thumped against the pier as he pushed it home and laid his weight against it. Now, at last, I saw what he had in mind.

'Wait!' I leaned over the gunwale, pushing with all my strength at the planks of the pier. Little by little, the launch responded to our efforts. 'She's moving—'

Somewhere in the darkness, the springmaker was edging inexpertly towards us. He'd probably never been inside the boathouse before. He knew we were there, somewhere in the open space between the piers, but he could hear the slopping of water only inches away. Every so often, a rotten plank groaned and split under his feet, trapping an ankle, and I could hear him cursing as he struggled to free himself. But at the sound of my voice, he stopped moving. There was an eerie silence as he tried to focus on the sound, then the darkness was split by a flash of light and the echoing crash of an explosion.

'Jack!' There was no answer to my urgent whisper. 'Jack, are you all right?'

I reached out for him in the darkness, and collided with the warmth of his body and the hard end of the boat-hook.

'I'm all right.' He ran a hand through his hair. 'It was just – the noise.' He shook his head, ridding himself of the memory. 'We'll have to keep quiet, he's shooting towards our voices.'

Silently, I leaned over the gunwale again to push against the pier while Jack leaned on the boat-hook at the stern. But already I had to lean painfully far to reach the wooden baulks; the *Siren* was moving silently forward, putting black water between us and the piers.

'The doors – quick!'

Another shot crashed through the pitch-black. I distinctly heard the whine of its passing.

'Get down!' Jack pushed me down on the boards by main force. He leaned over the side, using the boat-hook as a punt pole, pushing against the bottom to keep the launch gliding on. 'She'll just have to open the doors herself.'

We waited. Then, with a hollow crash and an impact that almost checked her progress, the launch's long, sharp bow met the doors a few inches to the left of their meeting-point. The doors were rotten; the left-hand section shuddered and rocked back, tearing from its hinges at a drunken angle. Jack punted again with the boat-hook, and, serenely, as if breaking out was all in a day's work to her, the launch pressed on, scraping through the gap she'd made, pushing back the ruptured door over the swell of her hull until it fell aside and subsided into the water.

Unfortunately, we were now outlined against the evening sky, a perfect target. As Jack lowered the pole into the shallows once more, there was another explosion behind us and he jerked quickly back into the *Siren*'s well. The launch, however, had smelled freedom. Without any more inducement, she began to drift slowly away from her dark cavern and out on to the evening lake. It was little more than walking pace, but I could tell from the treetops receding beyond the gunwales that the strip of water between us and the shore was widening all the time.

'Keep your head down.' After a few moments Jack began to crawl forward, using the bulk of the boiler as a screen. 'I can't see him. He must still be inside the boathouse. Let's hope this breeze keeps us off the shore until we can get up steam.'

'How long will that take?'

'About half an hour or so. Dash it—' He suddenly ducked down. 'He's come out. He's heading for the jetty.'

Just as he spoke, there was another report from the spring-maker's pistol. This time the bullet pinged against the brass funnel and flew over the side. Two more shots followed, but the bullets splashed harmlessly short.

'That's six. He'll have to reload, won't he?'

I crawled forward to where Jack was crouching and we risked

a glimpse through the valves and pipes that crowded the top of the boiler.

'We must be out of range. Where's he off to now? Back to the house?'

All of a sudden, I felt weak. A surge of nausea rose in my throat and I rested my forehead on the cold iron side of the boiler. Jack put his arm round my shoulders and buried his face in my hair.

'I'd made up my mind. If he'd harmed you I was going to kill him with his own gun.'

I clasped his hand and tried to speak, but all that came out was an inarticulate moan. I was trying to tell him how sorry I was: sorry that the springmaker should be his father, that his father was clearly mad, and that things should ever have come to such a pass.

He squeezed my fingers. 'Better get steam up and decide what to do next.'

Once the fire was lit, there was nothing to do but keep it fed and wait for the boiler to heat. From the lake, Waterside was a slab of dark masonry at the top of its unruly meadow. I wondered what the springmaker was doing in the black halls of his mansion, at the heart of that empty monument to blind ambition.

After a while, a faint light appeared behind one of the blind-shaded windows on the ground floor. He must have found our lamp. And now that it had established itself, the light moved steadily from room to room along the front of the house, raising a brief glow behind each of the terrace windows in turn.

'He's searching the place.'

'Oh, dash it! The plans! They were in the table drawer in the kitchen—'

'Not any more.' Jack was crouching over the fire box. 'They're in the steam kettle now.'

'In here?' I stood up and prised off the copper lid of the cylinder. I could just make out the brown envelope nestling snugly on top of the heating-coil.

'I didn't know who might come sniffing round.'

We watched the progress of the light as the springmaker went on searching. From time to time the facade of the house became dark again as he moved to the back rooms, but the lamp always reappeared, mounting steadily upwards, floor by floor, until it reached the dormer windows on the roof. Then it disappeared, glowed briefly once more from a room on the ground floor, and went out altogether.

There was total blackness for some time afterwards, a blackness like the death of that nomad light. I tried to picture Alfred Dunstan pacing from room to room, tearing open delicate cabinets, ripping the dust sheets from chairs, stuffing his arm into vases, disembowelling cushions and overturning tables without ever finding the papers that proved his guilt. I imagined him in Beatrice's room, frenziedly ripping the upholstery of her red Venetian chairs, in Letty's bedroom, dragging the peacock-blue cover from the bed she'd shared with Philip, in the living hall of that dead house, confronting Letty herself, smiling invitingly down from the mural he'd tried to obliterate, haunting the place with her besotted young Narcissus.

I tried not to think of the shadows closing in on the springmaker as he held his feeble lamp, or the shadows in his mind as he realized the impossibility of finding anything hidden in such an enormous house. Waterside, his creation – his incarnation in bricks and mortar – had turned against him.

As we watched, the glow of the lamp reappeared behind a first-floor window, not steadily this time, but surging and dying as if unsure of its power. After some time a second window lit up alongside the first, weakly to begin with, but growing in strength, and a few moments later, a third window, and a fourth.

'What's he doing? What's happening?'

By now I was clinging so tightly to the gunwale of the launch that my fingers hurt. I hadn't expected an answer. My question had been a cry of dismay, a cry of distress at what was already horribly clear. The light behind the windows of Waterside was nothing like the pale yellow of a lamp; it was an ominous, angry vermilion that flared up behind the window blinds, licking and tasting, until the linen blind itself was suddenly devoured by a tongue of triumphant flame.

Waterside was alight. Whether by accident or design, the springmaker was destroying his creation.

Before long the whole first floor – dry and dusty – was burning, its windows brighter than they'd ever been with their two hundred tungsten-argon electric lamps. The mansion was being consumed by its own magnificence. Faintly at first, but growing louder, the roar of the flames came to us over the water as they made a feast of rosewood and mahogany, of painted canvas and gilt. As we watched, the drawing room ceiling gave way, dragged down by its huge electric chandelier, and the fire tumbled through to ravage the shrouded chairs and the carpets and gorge itself on the window draperies.

Aboard the *Siren* we were helpless. The steam pressure wasn't high enough yet to turn the engine. We could do nothing but wait and drift on the dark water, watching the destruction of the house.

Already in possession of the lower floors, the fire broke through suddenly into the attic and, finding little there to interest it, burst through the roof like the great red claws of some captive beast. Now all the turrets and balustrades were thrown into fantastic black silhouette. The chimneys rose from the centre of the blaze, scarlet towers surrounded by a forest of inky pinnacles and high above, a swelling column of smoke rose, dull black, against a sky of rich medicine-bottle blue. I couldn't tear my eyes away; in death, the springmaker's house had achieved the grandeur that had always escaped it in life.

I heard Jack's voice, slow and steady, behind me. 'That's the main steam line open to drain the system. We'll be under way in a moment.' For a moment his self-control faltered. 'Where should we go? My God – *where*?'

Where? In a world that had suddenly taken leave of its senses, where was there a place for us? I had no answer for him. I was transfixed by the spectacle ashore, fascinated and bewildered.

'Why on earth—'

Jack stared grimly across the water, his face lit by the flames. 'He's destroying the Dunstans – the name, the house, everything. None of it measured up, you see, nothing turned out as he'd planned. He'd have destroyed me, too, if he could.' He moved his head in slow denial. 'He can't live and not succeed.'

I reached out to touch his arm. 'Jack. Look—'

Across the gold-flecked water, high on the edge of the Water-side roof, a small black figure had appeared, steadying itself by one hand on a length of balustrade. I could clearly make out a squat, square silhouette, gazing out over the lake apparently oblivious to the inferno at its feet. Jack's arm had gone rigid under my hand.

Behind me and to the side, I could hear the mutter of the *Siren*'s engine.

'We'll have to go in, Jack. We can't leave him.'

'It's too late. The staircases must have gone by now.'

'Perhaps there's some way – a ladder, if we're quick enough . . .'

Jack's eyes never left the house as our bow swung round. 'There's no way down. He's trapped.'

Flames were spilling out of the windows now, curling up to caress the elaborate stonework. High on the roof, Alfred Dunstan took a few steps along the parapet, and from this new position gazed out again across the lake. I wondered what he was looking at – at us perhaps – at the *Siren* gliding towards the jetty under her own power, just as Jack had always said she would.

Bricks and mortar; that had been the springmaker's claim on the future. Build a house – build a name – then people will step aside for you in the street. Max Kassel had warned of the hollow satisfaction of a house with no heart, but had learned that a heart is not necessarily any protection. Which of them, in the end, had won the argument?

Jack had given up coaling. It was impossible to tell from his face what his feelings might be. He must have seen death many times in the trenches – watched the slow, painful dying of men he admired – and yet, when all was said and done, this was his father. He kept his eyes fixed on that small, unmoving figure as if he felt it his duty to see the thing through to its inevitable end.

By now running figures had begun to appear on the lawn below the terrace. Through the dusk I could hear the frantic ringing of a bell. The figure on the parapet ignored it all. He was still standing calmly, gazing out across the lake, when the roof of the house fell in with a roar, plunging down into its gutted core in a welter of flame, blackened rafters and falling masonry. The fire, set free, thundered towards the sky from the blazing shell. Of the springmaker, there was no sign at all.

We brought the *Siren* alongside the jetty in silence and walked, bound tightly together, up the firelit lawn towards the drive. Knots of onlookers had pressed through the gates. A pump-engine had arrived from somewhere; the firemen were running hoses down towards the lake, more for the look of the thing than for any practical good they might do, since already the house had little left but its walls. A small corps of police were milling around the top of the drive, trying to look as if they were in charge of things, and warning sightseers to stay back.

'Keep back there, sir, miss.' A young constable stretched out his arm. 'Oh, it's Miss Ascham, isn't it? Sergeant Naylor was looking for you, to get the keys to the house.'

'You hardly need them now.'

'No, miss.' The constable peered at Jack. 'And you are?'

'Jack Dunstan.' Jack nodded towards the ruin. 'You may find my father in there somewhere.'

'Ah. Oh, well, just you wait there—' The young constable put his hand up and beckoned. A bulky figure detached itself from the group of police and came across at a trot. 'Sarge, this chap says he's that Dunstan fellow, the deserter.'

'Sergeant Naylor,' I began, 'if you'll let me explain—'

'So it's Mr Dunstan, is it? Mr Jack Dunstan?' The sergeant's face glowed with achievement. 'As it happens, I've been told to keep an eye out for you.'

Jack released my arm. 'It's Captain Dunstan, as a matter of fact.' He looked the policeman in the eye, and added, 'Sergeant. It is *Sergeant*, is it?'

Involuntarily, Sergeant Naylor's feet shuffled together and his hands dropped to his sides. 'It is, yes sir, Station Sergeant.'

Jack nodded coolly. 'Then, Sergeant, I suggest you get these fellows organized to save what they can from the outbuildings. And keep the crowd back. My father has already died in the fire. We don't want any more casualties.'

'Your father, sir? Ah, well, of course, that's unfortunate. Most. But at the same time . . .' Sergeant Naylor hesitated, hopelessly torn between his dual responsibilities. His glance flicked uncertainly between Jack, the crowd, and his men waiting for instructions.

'Come on, man, don't just stand there. Get on with it.'

'You won't – you won't go away anywhere, will you, sir?' For a second longer, Sergeant Naylor dithered. Then, with a moan, he scurried off on his errand.

'He'll be back in a moment,' I said.

'I know.'

The crowd of policemen began to disperse in the direction of the garages and the powerhouse and, there, behind them, untouched by the fire, stood the springmaker's motor car. Jack followed my gaze.

'Well?' I said.

'There's bound to be some fuel in it. It would get me part of the way.'

'You'd have to go at once, while the police are busy.'

'And leave you? No, I won't do it.'

'I'll be all right. Look – there's Mar and Par. They're back.' I'd spotted my parents' anxious faces among the crowd by the drive. 'Come over to the car while no one's looking.'

Mar and Par fluttered round me like pigeons. 'When we got back—'

'And found you weren't there—'

'And we heard about the fire—'

'We came along at once.'

Mar peered at Jack. 'Aren't you—'

'Jack Dunstan.'

'Ah, what a tragedy – to see such a house destroyed!' Par hooked up his spectacles. Now that Waterside was a ruin, he'd forgotten his contempt for it. 'Electrical fault, no doubt. This is what comes of clever inventions, I always say. Nothing the matter with oil lamps. No wires, with lamps. Much, much safer.'

'Par,' I said. 'Do you see Sergeant Naylor over there? Now, I think he'd be very grateful, if you went across and explained to him all about electrical faults. Very grateful indeed.'

'Benedict—' called my mother, but it was too late. 'What on earth was all that about?'

'Go on.' I pushed Jack gently towards the motor car. 'You can't let them arrest you. Not after all this.' I indicated the brown envelope under his arm. 'You will tell them the whole story now, won't you?'

'I don't suppose it matters any longer, if I do. They can hardly haul my father into court now.' To my mother's astonishment, he put his arms round me and held me tightly. 'Will you still be here, when it's all over? The war, and everything else?'

'Will you come and find me?'

'The instant they let me go.'

'Then I'll still be here.'

The lights of the motor cut a curving channel through the dusk of the drive, and he was gone.

9th May, 1919

Report from British Embassy, Rome, to MI5 and MI2 (a) Italian Section, Directorate of Military Intelligence, War Office, London:

I am informed by our Consulate in Venice that a Mr Maximilian Kassel, travelling on a German passport but resident in Chester Square, London (in whom the Section maintains an interest), arrived in Venice on the 1st of this month – allegedly to attend the marriage of Miss Christabel Maud Ascham and Major Jack Dunstan (son of the late Alfred Dunstan of the Dunstan Patent Coil Spring, whose German connections during the War are well-documented).

This ceremony was held on Friday, 2nd May in the English Church in Venice, and, thereafter, the company proceeded by water to the Danieli Hotel. Our agents inform me that the register at the Danieli lists Major Dunstan's sisters Beatrice and Ida, his mother, Mrs Letitia Dunstan, and his bride's parents, Dr and Mrs Benedict Ascham, on whom I have no intelligence beyond the fact that Dr Ascham enjoys a considerable reputation in Renaissance art circles, and appears to be quite genuine. There is also, however, a Miss Hosanna Greendew, who describes herself as a poetess . . .

THE END